TERRORS OF DARKNESS STALK THE LIGHT—

He was about to discover that sometimes when the phone rings you just shouldn't answer. . . .

There wasn't anything dangerous about picnicking outside a graveyard—or was there?

Invited to a performance of an ancient Greek play, he never thought he might be cast as one of the players. . . .

There was something about the bag lady that made him want to paint her portrait, but when art began to become life even a masterpiece might be better left unfinished. . . .

Enter the realm where reality takes a sudden twist and the everyday is shadowed by sudden, overwhelming fear—

THE YEAR'S BEST HORROR STORIES: XX

ACKNOWLEDGMENTS

Ma Qui by Alan Brennert. Copyright © 1990 by Alan Brennert for *The Magazine of Fantasy and Science Fiction,* February 1991. Reprinted by permission of the author.

The Same in Any Language by Ramsey Campbell. Copyright © 1991 by Ramsey Campbell for *Weird Tales,* Summer 1991. Reprinted by permission of the author.

Call Home by Dennis Etchison. Copyright © 1991 by Dennis Etchison for *Psycho-Paths.* Reprinted by permission of the author.

A Scent of Roses by Jeffrey Goddin. Copyright © 1991 by Jeffrey Goddin for *Dark Infinity*, Spring 1991. Reprinted by permission of the author.

Root Cellar by Nancy Kilpatrick. Copyright © 1991 by Nancy Kilpatrick for *The Vampire's Crypt #4*. Reprinted by permission of the author.

An Eye for an Eye by Michael A. Arnzen. Copyright © 1991 by Michael A. Arnzen for *Outlaw Bikers' Tattoo Revue* #16. Reprinted by permission of the author.

The Picnickers by Brian Lumley. Copyright © 1991 by Brian Lumley for *Final Shadows.* Reprinted by permission of the author and of the author's agent, the Dorian Literary Agency.

With the Wound Still Wet by Wayne Allen Sallee. Copyright © 1990 by Richard T. Chizmar for *Cemetery Dance*, Summer 1991. Reprinted by permission of the author.

My Giddy Aunt by D.F. Lewis. Copyright © 1991 by D.F. Lewis for *Chills*, Spring 1991. Reprinted by permission of the author.

The Lodestone by Sheila Hodgson. Copyright © 1991 by

Sheila Hodgson for *Ghosts & Scholars 13*. Reprinted by permission of the author.

Baseball Memories by Edo van Belkom. Copyright © 1989 by East Tennessee State University and Sport Literature Association for *Aethlon*, Fall 1989. Reprinted by permission of the author.

The Bacchae by Elizabeth Hand. Copyright © 1991 by Elizabeth Hand for *Interzone*, July 1991. Reprinted by permission of the author.

Common Land by Joel Lane. Copyright © 1991 by Joel Lane for *Darklands*. Reprinted by permission of the author.

An Invasion of Angels by Nina Kiriki Hoffman. Copyright © 1991 by Nina Kiriki Hoffman for *Pulphouse*, Winter 1991. Reprinted by permission of the author.

The Sharps and Flats Guarantee by C.S. Fuqua. Copyright © 1991 by C.S. Fuqua for *Atopos* #1. Reprinted by permission of the author.

Medusa's Child by Kim Antieau. Copyright © 1991 by Kim Antieau for *Final Shadows*. Reprinted by permission of the author.

Wall of Masks by t. Winter-Damon. Copyright © 1990 by Hell's Kitchen Productions, Inc. for *Grue*, Winter 1991. Reprinted by permission of the author.

Moving Out by Nicholas Royle. Copyright © 1990 by Nicholas Royle for *Skeleton Crew*, January 1991. Reprinted by permission of the author.

Better Ways in a Wet Alley by Barb Hendee. Copyright © 1991 by Not One of Us for *Not One of Us* #7. Reprinted by permission of the author.

Close to the Earth by Gregory Nicoll. Copyright © 1991 by Gregory Nicoll for *Cold Shocks*. Reprinted by permission of the author.

Churches of Desire by Philip Nutman. Copyright © 1991 by Philip Nutman for *Borderlands 2*. Reprinted by permission of the author.

Carven of Onyx by Ron Weighell. Copyright © 1991 by Ron Weighell for *Tales of Witchcraft*. Reprinted by permission of the author.

DEDICATION

To My Lady Louise
Who helped me make it through the night

CONTENTS

Introduction: Garage Band Fiction
by Karl Edward Wagner 15

MA QUI
by Alan Brennert 19

THE SAME IN ANY LANGUAGE
by Ramsey Campbell 42

CALL HOME
by Dennis Etchison 58

A SCENT OF ROSES
by Jeffrey Goddin 68

ROOT CELLAR
by Nancy Kilpatrick 84

AN EYE FOR AN EYE
by Michael A. Arnzen 91

THE PICNICKERS
by Brian Lumley 99

WITH THE WOUND STILL WET
by Wayne Allen Sallee 124

MY GIDDY AUNT
by D.F. Lewis 130

THE LODESTONE
by Sheila Hodgson 136

BASEBALL MEMORIES
by Edo van Belkom 161

THE BACCHAE
by Elizabeth Hand 174

COMMON LAND
by Joel Lane 193

AN INVASION OF ANGELS
by Nina Kiriki Hoffman 208

THE SHARPS AND FLATS GUARANTEE
by C.S. Fuqua 224

MEDUSA'S CHILD
by Kim Antieau 232

WALL OF MASKS
by t. Winter-Damon 245

MOVING OUT
by Nicholas Royle 264

BETTER WAYS IN A WET ALLEY
by Barb Hendee 271

CLOSE TO THE EARTH
by Gregory Nicoll 283

CHURCHES OF DESIRE
by Philip Nutman 298

CARVEN OF ONYX
by Ron Weighell 323

Introduction: Garage Band Fiction

I hear that the market for horror novels is dwindling, with most of the major publishers cutting back their lists. This doesn't appear to be the case for horror short fiction, however, if the monstrous pile of anthologies and magazines I've read this past year is any indication. Maybe this, my thirteenth excursion as editor of *The Year's Best Horror Stories*, is just a lucky year. Not really. Each year since I began as editor here has seen an ever increasing output of horror stories—ranging from anthologies from major publishers to small press magazines handwritten in blood on parchment of dubious origin. At the end of each year's reading I've had to stack them all into boxes and carry them to my rental storage area. Who knows what they plot together there in the darkness?

Unfortunately, there's a downside. Most of those short stories are hopelessly awful. Sorting out the good from the bad and the ugly gets to be more of a task each year. While I have made this complaint in the past, each new year as the output increases, I find myself wondering: *Why* are these people writing the same bad stories over and over and over?

Here are your latest basic ingredients: A serial killer. Teenagers having sex. A vampire/werewolf. Sharp objects. A maniac. Child abuse. Contents of a human body. Bits of a human body.

Combine any or all of the above: A serial killer stalks teenagers who have sex and removes their naughty bits, until he encounters a vampire. A victim of child abuse grows up to become a maniac who slices and dices small children until he encounters a werewolf cub. A vampire serial killer stalks teenagers and impales them in inventive places. An aborted fetus zombie seeks revenge on his teenaged parents by sucking out their brains through their eyesockets.

It's important to go into careful detail as to bodily fluids: A victim should bleed, shit, piss, come, and vomit while being eviscerated. A total disregard of anatomical feasibility is necessary also: A victim should be flayed scalp to toes with a rusty nailfile in a matter of seconds, allowing her time to thrash about screaming and leaking fluids.

I will not tell you how many stories about serial killers I have read this past year, but I know that I will be reading lots and lots more this year. Many body parts will be excised. Many body fluids will run across the page. Many writers will believe that the only horror plot in the whole bloody world concerns a maniac, a sharp object, a stalked victim, and an orgy of chopped bits and gushing fluids.

The *really* depressing part is that each new writer steams into this slough of clichés with the buoyant enthusiasm of one who believes that no one has ever written such a terrifying concept before.

Garage band fiction.

You know about garage bands. A bunch of the kids in the neighborhood are, like, really into rock music, and they get some instruments and equipment, and one of them has a detached garage where they can practice. So they listen to tapes of all their favorite groups, and they watch all their favorite videos, and they learn how to dress like their idols, and they learn how to prance and posture and swing microphone stands. Now they're ready to play. So they write a bunch of their own material, cloned from whatever they can grasp of their favorite groups—only they're going to play it louder, and they're not going to pull any punches.

What results is a lot of derivative, strident noise—sounding much like all the other garage bands around town—and the fact that their models are mostly derivative and strident clones of *their* favorite groups doesn't help matters. Well, it's all in good fun, and there's no harm done. Most garage bands disband for one good reason or another: The lead guitar goes to law school, the bass gets a job as produce manager, the drummer explodes on stage, the usual.

It's a similar situation in horror fiction. New writers read a few books by favorite authors, watch a lot of really bad films, then sit down to write something just like it all—only louder, stronger, no punches pulled. The result is a lot of derivative, strident noise.

Trends change. When *The Year's Best Horror Stories* began twenty years ago, the thing to do was to try to write like H.P. Lovecraft. Just now serial killers are the rage—explicit gore having replaced polysyllabic adjectives, splatter videos the thesaurus.

Again, it's all good clean fun. The main difference is that there are far more outlets for garage band horror fiction today than there were twenty years ago. Tough on your editor, who has to sort through all this. Good for you, because it means the genre is both flourishing and changing.

And new blood is essential.

The hard truth is that good writers can't really afford to write short fiction. They can't pay for groceries and a mortgage at five-to-ten cents a word. They write short fiction when they can spare time from earning a living, and they do it because they want to. It would be really cool if a writer could be paid as much for a short story as for a novel. Until that happens, writing short fiction remains a labor of love—both for the award-winning veteran and for the enthusiastic novice.

No one joins a garage band who doesn't want to do what he's doing. A few of the garage bands make the big time, a few wanna-be rockers become megastars.

Most of us started out as garage band writers. For the record, my first stories were published in my high school newspaper, beginning in my freshman year. Boy, did *I* show Poe and Lovecraft a thing or two! My first *good* story, written in 1960 for the Halloween issue, was about a demonic car, resembling a 1958 Packard Hawk, that preyed on teenagers (they were playing hooky—as bad as you could be in a 1960 high school paper). I popped a zit and smeared blood and pus across the bottom of the last page—thus becoming the first splatterpunk. Miss Phelps, our faculty advisor/censor, pulled the story as being too long. Well, others have done better with the idea since then.

The essential thing for new writers is to persevere until you find your own voice, and then write what you want to write. Maybe someone will be influenced by you in a few years.

And that's what makes editing *The Year's Best Horror Stories* still fun after thirteen years at the helm. Sure, I know I'm going to read another hundred or so stories about serial killers next year, but I know I'll also find gems by established names, rising stars, and raw talent.

And that's what *The Year's Best Horror Stories* is all about. No taboos. No invitation-only. No quotas. No politically correct guidelines. No restrictions. Stephen King or first-story writer, traditional ghost story or punker outrage, subtle terror or extreme horror. You're all welcome here. You just have to be the *best*.

And here are the best of 1991.

— Karl Edward Wagner

Chapel Hill, North Carolina

MA QUI

by Alan Brennert

Born in Englewood, New Jersey in 1954, Alan Brennert has lived in California since 1973—which may explain why most of his work has been as scriptwriter, although he is also author of two novels. Time and Chance *and* Kindred Spirits, *and two short story collections,* Her Pilgrim Soul and Other Stories *and* Ma Qui and Other Phantoms. *Currently supervising producer on* L.A. Law, *Brennert has written about fifty television scripts for series like* China Beach, L.A. Law, *and* The Twilight Zone. *"Ma Qui" is an outgrowth of one of his* China Beach *scripts, "The Unquiet Earth," which was the third-season premiere for the series. Brennert credits series writer/researcher Toni Graphia for unearthing the Vietnamese folklore that, while he was unable to incorporate it into his* China Beach *teleplay, Brennert subsequently made use of in "Ma Qui."*

As for his latest projects, other than teleplays and prose, Brennert says: "In my copious free time I'm finishing the libretto for a musical, Weird Romance, *debuting at the WPA Theatre in New York in May. It's an anthology of sf/fantasy love stories, adapting James Tiptree/Alice Sheldon's 'The Girl Who Was Plugged In' and my own story 'Her Pilgrim Soul,' with music by Alan Menken (*Little Shop of Horrors, Beauty and the Beast*) and lyrics by David Spencer."*

At night the choppers buzz the bamboo roof of the

jungle, dumping from three thousand feet to little more than a hundred, circling, climbing, circling again, no LZ to land in, no casualties to pick up. Above the roar of the rotorwash come the shrieks of the damned: wails, moans, plaintive cries of Vietnamese. It's real William Castle stuff, weird sounds and screaming meemies, but even knowing it's coming from a tape recorder, even hearing the static hiss of the loudspeakers mounted on the Hueys, it still spooks the shit out of the VC. "The Wandering Soul," it's called—the sounds of dead Cong, their bodies not given a proper burial, their spirits helplessly wandering the earth. Psychological warfare. Inner Sanctum meets Vietnam. Down in the tunnels Charlie hears it, knows it's a con, tries to sleep but can't, the damn stuff goes on half the night. The wails grow louder the lower the choppers fly, then trail off, to suitably eerie effect, as they climb away. Until the next chopper comes with its cargo of souls in a box.

What horseshit.

It's not like that at all.

I watch the last of the choppers bank and veer south, and for a while, the jungle is quiet again. Around me the ground is a scorched blister, a crater forged by mortar fire, a dusty halo of burnt ground surrounding it, grasses and trees incinerated in the firefight. The crater is my bed, my bunk, my home. I sleep there—if you can call it sleep—and when I've grown tired of wandering the trails, looking for my way back to Da Nang, or Cam Ne, or Than Quit, I always wind up back here. Because this seared piece of earth is the only goddamned thing for miles that isn't Nam. It's not jungle, it's not muddy water, it's not punji sticks smeared with shit. It's ugly, and it's barren, and it looks like the surface of the fucking moon, but it was made by my people, the only signature they can write on this steaming rotten country, and I sleep in it, and I feel at home.

I was killed not far from here, in a clearing on the banks of the Song Cai River. My unit was pinned down, our back-up never arrived, we were racing for the LZ where the dust-off choppers were to pick us up. Some of us got careless. Martinez never saw the tripwire in the grass and caught a Bouncing Betty in the groin; he died before we could get him to the LZ. Dunbar hit a punji beartrap, the two spiked boards snapping up like the jaws of a wooden crocodile, chewing through his left leg. I thought Prosser and DePaul had pried him loose, but when I looked back I saw their bodies not far from the trap, cut down by sniper fire as they'd tried to rescue him. The bastards had let Dunbar live, and he was still caught in the trap, screaming for help, the blood pouring out between the two punji boards. I started back, firing my M16 indiscriminately into the treeline, hoping to give the snipers pause enough so that I could free Dunbar—

They took me out a few yards from Dunbar, half a dozen rounds that blew apart most of my chest. I fell, screaming, but I also watched myself fall; I saw the sharp blades of elephant grass slice into my face like razors as I struck the ground; I watched the blood spatter upward on impact, a red cloud that seemed to briefly cloak my body, then dissipate, spattering across the grass, giving the appearance, for a moment, of a false spring—a red dew.

Dunbar died a few minutes later. To the west, the distant thunder of choppers rolled across the treetops. I stood there, staring at the body at my feet, thinking somehow that it must be someone else's body, someone else's blood, and I turned and ran for the choppers, not noticing that my feet weren't quite touching the ground as I ran, not seeing myself pass through the tripwires like a stray wind.

Up ahead, dust-off medics dragged wounded aboard a pair of Hueys. Most of my unit made it. I watched Silverman get yanked aboard; I saw Esteban claw at a medic with a bloody stump he still believed was his hand. I ran to join them, but the big Chinooks started to climb, fast, once everyone was on. "Wait for me!" I yelled, but they couldn't seem to hear me over the whipping of the blades; "Son of a bitch, wait for *me*!"

They didn't slow. They didn't stop. They kept on rising, ignoring me, abandoning me. Goddamn them, what were they *doing*? Motherfucking bastards, come *back*, come—

It wasn't until I saw the thick, moist wind of the rotorwash fanning the grass—saw it bending the trees as the steel dragonflies ascended—that I realized I felt no wind on my face; that I had no trouble standing in the small hurricane at the center of the clearing. I turned around. Past the treeline, in the thick of the jungle, mortars were being lobbed from afar. Some hit their intended targets, in the bush; others strayed, and blasted our own position, unintentionally. I could hear the screams of VC before and after each hit; I saw Cong rushing out of the trees, some aflame, some limbless, only to be knocked off their feet by another incoming round. By now I knew the truth. I wandered, in a daze, back toward the treeline. I walked through sheets of flame without feeling so much as a sunburn. I saw the ground rock below me, but my steps never wavered, like the old joke about the drunken man during an earthquake.

At length the mortars stopped. The clearing was seared, desolate; bodies—Vietnamese, American—lay strewn and charred in all directions. I walked among them, rising smoke passing through me like dust through a cloud . . . and now I saw other wraiths, other figures standing above the remains of their own bodies; they looked thin, gaseous, the winds from the chopper passing overhead threatening their very solidity.

Prosser looked down at his shattered corpse and said, "Shit."

Dunbar agreed. "This sucks."

"Man, I *knew* this was gonna happen," Martinez insisted. "I just got laid in Da Nang. Is this fuckin' karma, or what?"

I made a mental note never to discuss metaphysics with Martinez. Not a useful overview.

"So what happens now?" I asked.

"Heaven, I guess." Dunbar shrugged.

"Or hell." Martinez. Ever the optimist.

"Yeah, but when?"

"Gotta be any time now," Prosser said, as though waiting for the 11:00 bus. He looked down at our bodies and grimaced. "I mean, we're dead, right?"

I looked at Dunbar's mangled leg. At Martinez's truncated torso. At . . .

"Hey. Collins. Where the hell are *you*?"

I should have been just a few feet away from Dunbar's body, but I wasn't. At first I thought the half dozen rounds that had dropped me had propelled my body away, but as we fanned out we saw no trace of it, not anywhere within a dozen yards. And when I came back to where Dunbar's body lay, I recognized the matted elephant grass where I had fallen—recognized too the tears of blood, now dried, coloring the tips of the grass. I squatted down, noticing for the first time that the grass was matted, in a zigzag pattern, for several feet beyond where my body fell.

"Son of a bitch," I said. "They took me."

"What?" said Martinez. "The VC?"

"They dragged me a few feet, then"—I pointed to where the matted grass ended—"two of them must've picked me up, and taken me away."

"I didn't see anyone," Dunbar said.

"Maybe you were preoccupied," I suggested.

Prosser scanned the area, his brow furrowing. "DePaul's gone, too. He went down right next to me—we were near the river, I remember hearing the sound of the water—but he's gone."

"Maybe he was just wounded," I said. At least I hoped so. DePaul had pulled me back, months before, from stepping on what had seemed like a plot of dry grass on a trail, but what revealed itself—once we'd tossed a large boulder on top of it—as a swinging man trap: kind of a see-saw with teeth. If not for DePaul, I would've been the one swinging from it, impaled on a dozen or more rusty spikes studding its surface. DePaul had bought me an extra few months of life; maybe, when I'd run forward, firing into the treeline,

I'd done the same for him, distracting the snipers long enough for him to get away.

"Hey, listen," said Dunbar. "Choppers."

The mop-up crew swooped in, quick and dirty, to recover what bodies it could. The area was secured, at least for the moment, and two grunts pried loose Dunbar's mangled leg from the punji beartrap and hefted him into a bodybag. The zipper caught on his lip, and the grunt had to unsnare it. Dunbar was furious.

"Watch what you're doing, assholes!" he roared at them. He turned to me. "Do you believe these guys?"

Two other grunts gingerly disconnected an unexploded cartridge trap not far from Martinez's body, then scooped up what remained of the poor bastard—torso in one bodybag, legs in another—and zipped the bags shut. Martinez watched as they loaded them onto the chopper, then turned to me.

"Collins. You think I should—"

I turned, but by the time I was facing him he was no longer there.

"Martinez?"

Dunbar's body was hefted onto the Huey, it hit the floor like a sack of dry cement, and I could almost feel the air rushing in to fill the sudden vacuum beside me.

I whirled around. Dunbar, too, was gone.

"Dunbar!"

The Huey lifted off, the branches of surrounding trees shuddering around it, like angry lovers waving away a violent suitor, and I was alone.

Believe it or not, I enlisted. It seemed like a good idea at the time: lower-middle-class families from Detroit could barely afford to send one kid to college, let alone two, and with my older sister at Ann Arbor I figured a student deferment wasn't coming my way anytime soon. So I let myself swallow the line they feed you at the recruiter's office, about how our *real* job over here was building bridges and thatching huts and helping the Vietnamese people; they made it sound kind of like the Peace Corps, only more humid.

My dad was a construction foreman; I'd been around buildings going up all my life—liked the sound of it, the feel of it, the smell of lumber and fresh cement and the way the frame looked before you laid on the plasterboard. . . . I'd stand there staring at the girders and crossbeams, the wood and steel armatures that looked to my eight-year-old mind like dinosaur skeletons, and I thought: The people who'll live here will never see, never know what their house *really* looks like, underneath; but *I* know.

So the idea of building houses for homeless people and bridges for oxen to cross sounded okay. Except after eight months in Nam, most of the bridges I'd seen had been blown away by American air strikes, and the closest I'd come to thatching huts was helping repair the roof of a bar in Da Nang I happened to be trapped in during a monsoon.

All things considered, enlisting did not seem like the kind of blue-chip investment in the future it once had, just now.

For the first few days I stuck close to the crater, wandering only as far as I could travel and return in a day, searching for a way back—but the way back, I knew, was farther than could ever be measured in miles, and the road was far from clearly marked. I tried not to dwell on that. If I had, I would never have mustered the nerve to move from my little corner of hell. I wasn't sure where the nearest U.S. base was in relation to here, but I remembered a small village we'd passed the previous day, and I seemed to recall a Red Cross Jeep parked near a hut, a French doctor from Catholic Relief Services administering to the villagers. Maybe he would show up again, and I could hitch a ride back to—the question kept presenting itself—*where*? What the hell did I do, ask directions to the Hereafter? With my luck, the Army was probably running *it*, too.

(Now that was a frightening thought; frighteningly plausible. This whole thing was just fucked up enough to be an Army operation. Had I forgotten to fill out a form somewhere down the line?)

I headed back down the trail we'd followed to our deaths, but this time, along with the usual sounds of the jungle—the rustling in the bush that you hoped was *only* a bamboo viper, or a tiger—I heard the jungle's other voice. I heard the sounds the choppers, with their souls-in-a-box, only played at.

I heard weeping.

Not moaning; not wailing; none of that Roger Corman, Vincent Price shit. Just the sound of grown men weeping, uncontrollably and unconsolably—coming, it seemed, from everywhere at once. And slowly, I began to see them: VC, blood spattered over their black silk pajamas, crouched in the bush in that funny way the VN sit—squatting, not sitting, on the ground—and crying. I stopped, dumbfounded. I'd never seen a VN cry before. I'd seen them scared, hell, I'd seen them fucking terrified, but I never saw them cry. All that crap you heard about how the VN are different from us, how they don't *feel* the way we do, I knew that was bullshit. They felt; they just didn't show it the way we did. But goddamned if these guys weren't giving our guys a run for their money. Maybe, if you're a VC and you're dead, it's okay to cry. Maybe it's expected. I moved on.

And somewhere along the trail, as I followed the Song Cai in its winding path south, I began to consider that I might not, in fact, be among the dead; that I might just be alive, after all.

Maybe, I thought, the rounds that had dropped me had just wounded me; maybe the VC took my body so they could get information out of me, later. The more I thought about it, the more reasonable it sounded. They take me, nurse me back to health, so they can torture me later. (That sounded as logical as anything else in this screwy country.) And somewhere along the way, I split off from my body. Got left behind, like a shadow shaken loose from its owner. I listened to the weeping all around me—Christ, I almost wished they *were* wailing and moaning; I could've borne that a lot easier—and I decided that I wasn't, couldn't be dead.

Up ahead, the trail widened briefly into a clearing, in the middle of which stood what looked like a giant birdhouse: a bamboo hut, little more than a box really, perched on the stump of a large tree trunk. There were spirit houses like this scattered all over Nam, small homes erected for the happiness of departed relatives, or for embittered spirits who might otherwise prey on hapless villagers. The Army briefed us on the local customs and superstitions before we even arrived over here—things like, you never pat a VN on the head 'cause the head, to the Vietnamese, is the seat of the soul; and *whatever* you do, don't sit with your legs crossed so that your foot is pointing toward the other person's head, because that's the grossest kind of insult. Shit like that. Some dinks would even name their male babies after women's sexual organs to try and fool evil spirits into thinking the kid was a girl, because boys were more valuable and needed to be protected. Jesus.

So I knew about spirit houses, and when we passed this one the other day I remember thinking, hey, that's kind of neat, even better than the treehouse I built in my grandparents' yard when I was twelve, and went on walking.

Today, I stopped. Stared at it.

Today, there were people inside the birdhouse.

One was an elderly papa-san, the other a young woman, maybe twenty-eight, twenty-nine. They were burning Joss sticks, the sweet fragrance carried back on the thick wind, and around them I saw candles, tiny hand-made furniture, and a few books. I started walking again, more slowly now, and as I got within a couple yards of the birdhouse, the papa-san looked up at me, blinked once in mild surprise, then smiled and held his hand over his chest in a gassho—a traditional form of greeting and respect. His other arm, I now noticed, was askew beneath its silk sleeve, as though it had been broken, or worse.

"Welcome, traveler," he said. He was speaking in Vietnamese, but I understood, somehow, despite it.

"Uh . . . hello," I said, not sure if this worked both ways, but apparently it did; he smiled again, gesturing to his woman companion.

"I am Phan Van Duc. My daughter, Chau."

The woman turned and glared at me. She was pretty, in the abstract, but it was hard to get past the sneer on her face. So fixed, so unwavering, it looked like it'd been tattooed on. And since I wasn't sure if her anger was directed at me or not, I decided to ignore it, turned to the old man.

"My name is William Anthony Collins," I said. I wasn't sure if having three names was requisite over here, but I figured it couldn't hurt.

"May we offer you shelter?" Phan asked cordially. His daughter glowered.

There was barely enough room in the birdhouse for two, and I had no desire to be at close quarters with Chau. I declined, but thanked him for the offer.

"Have you been dead long?" the papa-san asked suddenly. I flinched.

"I'm not dead," I said, stubbornly.

The old man looked at me as though I were crazy. His daughter laughed a brassy, mocking laugh.

I explained what had happened to me, what I *thought* had happened to me, and how I was heading for the village downriver to see if the Viet Cong had taken my body there. Phan looked at me with sad, wise eyes as I spoke, then, when I'd finished, nodded once—more out of politeness, I suspected, than out of any credence he put in my theory.

"What you say may be true," he mused, "though I have never heard of such a thing. I would imagine, however, that rather than take a prisoner to a village, where he might easily be discovered, they would take him to one of their tunnel bases."

The VC had hundreds of tunnels running beneath most of I-Corps: a spiderweb of barracks and underground command posts and subterranean hospitals so vast, so labyrinthine, that we were only just beginning to understand the full scope of them. If I had been taken prisoner in one of them, the odds of finding myself were about equal to winning bets on the Triple Crown, the World Series, and the Super Bowl, all in one year.

"In that case," I said, not really wanting to think about it, "I'll just wait for my—body—to die, and when it does, I'm gone."

Papa-san looked at me with a half-pitying, half-perplexed look, as though I had just told him the sky was green and the moon was made of rice. Hell, come to think of it, maybe the dinks *did* think the moon was made of rice.

"What about you?" I said, anxious to shift the topic. "Why are you—here?"

Phan showed no trace of pain, or grief, as he replied.

"I was mauled by a tiger and left to bleed to death," he said simply, as though that should explain everything. Then, at my blank look, he explained patiently, "Having died a violent death, I was denied entry to the next world."

I blinked. I didn't see the connection.

"Getting mauled by a tiger, that's not your fault," I said, baffled.

He looked as baffled by my words as I was by his. "What difference does fault make? What is, is." He shrugged.

I opted not to pursue the subject. Phan and Martinez would've gotten along just fine. "And your daughter?"

He looked askance at her, she threw me a nasty look, then she scrambled forward into the birdhouse, hands gripping the lip of the floor, spitting the words at me: the hard edges of the Vietnamese consonants as sharp as the bitterness in her words.

"I died childless," she snapped at me. "Is that what you wanted to hear? Are you happy? I died childless, worthless, and I am condemned because of it."

"That's crazy," I said, despite myself.

She laughed a brittle laugh. "You are the crazy

one," she said, "a *ma qui*, thinking he is alive. I pity you."

"No," the papa-san said gently, "you pity no one but yourself."

She glared at him, her nostrils flaring, then laughed again, shortly. "You are right," she said. "I pity no one. I don't know why I let you keep me here. I can do anything I want. I can bring disease back to the village, kill the children of my former friends. Yes. I think I would like that." She grinned maliciously, as though taking relish in the wickedness of her thought.

"You will not," Phan warned. "I am your father, and I forbid it."

She muttered a curse under her breath and retreated to the rear of the birdhouse. The papa-san turned and looked at me sadly.

"Do not judge my daughter by what she is now," he said softly. "Death makes of us what it wishes."

Jesus Christ; these people actually believed that. And so, I guess, that's just what they got. Well, not me. No fucking way, man. Not me.

I backed away. "I have to go."

"Wait," Phan said. I halted, I'm not sure why; he leaned forward, as though to share something important with me. "If you go into the village . . . you must be careful. Do not walk in the front door of a house, because the living keep mirrors by the doorway, to reflect the image of those who enter. If a spirit sees himself in the mirror, he will be frightened off. Also, if red paper lines the entrance, stay away, for you will anger the God of the Doorway. Do you understand?"

I nodded, numbly, thanked him for his advice, and got the hell out of there, fast.

I hurried down the trail, past the weeping guerrillas in black silk, feeling a sudden, black longing for something as violent and mundane as a mortar strike; yearning for the sound of gunships, the bright spark of tracer fire, the crackling of small arms fire or the din of big Chinook choppers circling in for the kill. God *damn*. This was the dinks' Hell, not mine; I wasn't going to be a part of it, I would *not* buy into their stupid, superstitious horseshit. The weeping around me grew louder. I started running now, phantom limbs passing harmlessly through tripwires and across punji traps, even the elephant grass not so much as tickling my calves as I ran along the banks of the Song Cai—

The weeping changed. Became different: deeper. I knew instantly that it was not the cries of a Vietnamese; knew, suddenly and sickeningly, that it was an American's cries I was hearing.

I stopped; looked around. I saw no one lying wounded in the bush, but heard, now, too, a voice:

"—Jesus, Mary, and Joseph, *help me*—"

Oh, Christ, I thought.

DePaul.

I looked up. He was floating about five feet above the muddy waters of the river, like a tethered balloon, his big, six-foot frame looking almost gaseous, his black skin seeming somehow pale. His hands covered his face as he wept, prayed, swore, and wept again. At first I thought he was moving upstream, but I soon realized that it was the water flowing under him that gave the illusion of movement; he swayed back and forth slightly, but was utterly motionless, completely stationary.

It took me a moment to recover my wits. I shouted his name over the roar of the rapids.

He looked up, startled.

When he saw me—saw me looking at *him*—his face lit up with a kind of absolution. "Oh, Jesus," he said, so softly I almost couldn't hear it. "*Collins*? Are you real?"

"I sure as shit hope so."

"Are you alive?"

I dodged the question. "What the hell happened to you, man? Prosser said you went down right next to him, but your body—"

"Charlie hit me in the back." I could see the hole torn in his skin at the nape of his neck, and the matching one in front, just below his collarbone, where the bullet had exited. "I couldn't breathe. Couldn't think. Got up, somehow, ran—but in the wrong direction. Dumped into the river. Christ, Bill, it was awful. I was choking *and* drowning, and the next thing I knew—" His hand had gone, reflexively, to his throat, covering the ragged hole there. "—my body had floated downriver, then got snagged on some rock. Over there."

I followed his gaze. His body was pinned between two rocks, the waters flowing around it, flanking it in white foam. I turned back to DePaul, floating in place above the river, and I took a step forward.

"Christ, De," I said softly. "How—I mean, what—"

"I *can't get down*, man," he said, and for the first time I heard the pain in his voice; "I been here two, three days, and it *hurts*. Oh Christ, it hurts! It's not like floating, Jesus, it's like treading water, every muscle in my body aches—I'm so *tired*, man, I'm so—" He broke off into sobs; something I'd never seen him do. He looked away, let the tears come, then looked back at me, his eyes wide. "Help me, Collins," he said, softly. *"Help me."*

"Just tell me how," I said, feeling helpless, horrified. "Why—why are you *like* this, man? You have any idea?"

"Yeah. Yeah, I know," he said, taking a ragged gulp of air. "It's—it's 'cause I died in water, see? You die in water, your spirit's tied to the water till you can find another one to—"

"*What*? Jesus Christ, De, where'd you *get* that shit from?"

"Another spook. VC, half his head blown away, wanderin' up and down the river. He told me."

"You bought *into* this crap?" I yelled at him. "These dinks believe this shit, man, *you* don't have to—you're an *American*, for Chrissake!"

"Collins—"

"You believe it, it happens. You stop believing, it stops happening. Just—"

His eyes were sunken, desperate. "Please, man. Help me?"

No matter what I thought of this shit, there was

only one thing that mattered: he'd saved my life, once; and even if there was no more life in him to save, I could, at least, try to ease his pain. I *had* to try.

"All right," I said. "What can I do?"

He hesitated.

"Bring me a kid," he said, quietly.

"Why?"

He hesitated again; then, working up his nerve, he said, "To release me. A life for a life."

My eyes went wide. *"What?"*

"It's the only way," he said quickly. "You die in water, the only way to be set free is to—drown—a kid, as an offering." His eyes clouded over, his gaze became hooded and ashamed even as he said it. For a long minute the only sound was the rushing of water past the dam of DePaul's corpse, and the distant sounds of weeping carried on the wind.

Finally I said, "I can't do that, man."

"Bill—"

"Even if I believed it'd work—*especially* if I believed it'd work—I couldn't—"

"Not a healthy kid," DePaul interrupted, desperation and pleading creeping into his tone, "a sick one. One that's gonna die anyway. Shit, half the gook kids over here die before they're—"

"Are you crazy, man?" I snapped. "Gook or not, I can't—"

I stopped. Listened to what I was saying.

DePaul's face was ashen; in torment. "Collins . . . please. I hurt so bad—"

I was buying into this crap. Just like him. Someone'd filled his head with dink superstition, and now he was living—or dying—by it. That was it, wasn't it? You die, you get pretty much what you expect: Catholics, heaven or hell; atheist, maybe nothing, nonexistence, loss of consciousness; dinks—this. And we'd been over here so long, wading knee deep in their fucking country, that we were starting to believe what they believed.

But the DePaul I knew would never kill a kid. Not

even to save himself. Maybe the only way to shake him loose from this bullshit was to show him that.

I waited a long minute, thinking, devising a plan, and then finally I spoke up.

"A sick kid?" I asked, carefully, as though I actually believed all this.

He looked up, hopefully. "One that's gonna die anyway. You've seen 'em, you know what they look like, you can see it in their eyes—"

"I won't bring one that's gonna live."

"No no, man, you don't have to. A sick kid. A real sick kid." God, he sounded pathetic.

I told him I didn't know how long it would take, but that I would head into the village we passed through a few days ago and see what I could do. I told him I'd be back as soon as I could.

"Hurry, man. Hurry." It was the last thing I heard before I headed back into the bush once again. He'd bought the line. Now all I had to do was show him he'd bought another—and, more important, that he could buy out of it.

The village was about two hours up the road. There was no Red Cross Jeep in sight, no Catholic Relief doctor handing out aspirin and antibiotics; just the squalid little huts, the half-naked kids running through muddy puddles probably rife with typhoid, tired-looking women doing laundry in a small stream tributary to the Song Cai. There was a huge crater at the edge of town—the mortar strike that was too late to save me and Dunbar and DePaul. Nearby roofs were scorched, at least two huts had been burned to the ground. Friendly fire. Any more friendly and half the village would be greeting me personally. I walked up the main road, peeking in windows. If I was going to make it look genuine I'd have to bring back a genuinely sickly kid: though exactly how, I still wasn't sure.

Outside one hut I heard the sound of a mother comforting a squalling baby, and decided to go in and take a look. Sure enough, just as the old Papa-san had predicted, the doorway was lined with red paper to ward off evil spirits. I stepped across the threshold. Big fucking deal. Up yours, God of the Doorway. I turned—

I screamed.

In the mirror positioned just inside, I saw a man with a foot-wide hole blasted in his chest: the torn edges of the wound charred to a crisp, the cavity within raw and red as steak tartar. A pair of lungs dangled uselessly from the slimmest of folds of flesh, swaying as I jumped back, reflexively; beside them, a heart riddled with a half dozen jagged frag wounds throbbed in a stubborn counterfeit of life.

And behind me in the mirror, a glimpse of something else: a shadow, a *red* shadow, red as the paper above the doorway . . . moving not as I moved but looming up, and quickly, behind me.

I ran.

Out of the house, down the street, away from the huts, finally collapsing on a patch of elephant grass. At first I was afraid to look down at myself, but when I did, I saw nothing—saw exactly what I'd seen up till now, the drab green camouflage fatigues stained with blood. All this time, I realized, I had seen everyone else's wounds but mine. Not till now.

I sat there, gathering my wits and my courage, trying to work up the nerve to enter another hut. I didn't think about the mirror, didn't dwell on what I'd seen. Better just to think of myself this way, the way some part of me *wanted* to see myself. When I finally got up and started round to the huts again, I steered well clear of the doors.

There was the usual assortment of sickly kids—malaria, mostly, but from the look of them, a few typhoid, influenza, and parasitic dysentery cases as well. I felt gruesome as hell, trying to choose which one to take, even knowing this was only a ruse, something to shock DePaul back to normalcy. *Just get it over with.* I looked in one window and saw what appeared to be a two-year-old girl—in a dress made of old parachute nylon, an earring dangling too large from one tiny lobe—being washed by her mother. It was only when the mother turned the child over and I saw the small brown penis that I remembered: the mother was trying to deceive the evil spirits into thinking their sickly boy-child was really a girl, and thus not worth the taking.

Jesus, I thought. Said a lot about the place of women over here. But it did mean the kid was probably seriously ill, and after I'd used her—him—to get DePaul back to normal, I could take the poor kid to the nearest Evac . . . leave it on the doorstep of the civilian ward with a note giving the name of his village.

Assuming I could *write* a note.

Assuming I could even *take* the kid in the first place.

I took a deep breath and, once the mother had left the room, walked through the wall of the hut. I didn't feel the bamboo any more than I'd felt the tripwires I'd run through. I stood over the infant, now worried that my hands would pass through him, too . . . then slowly reached down to try and pick him up.

I touched him. I didn't know how, or why, but I could touch him.

I scooped the boy up in my arms and held him to my chest. He looked up at me with old, sad eyes. All the kids here had the same kind of eyes: tired, cheerless, and somehow knowing. As though all the misery around them, all the civil wars and foreign invaders—from the French to the Japanese to the Americans—as though all that were known to them, before they'd even been born. Rocked in a cradle of war, they woke, with no surprise, to a lullaby of thunder.

I walked through the wall of the hut, the child held aloft and carried through the window. When we were clear of the building, I hefted the boy up, held him in my arms, and headed into the bush before anyone could see.

I wanted to stay off the main road, for fear that someone might see me: not me, I guess, since I *couldn't* be seen, but the kid, the boy. (What, I wondered, would someone see, if they did see? A child carried aloft on the wind? Or an infant wrapped in the arms of a shadow, a smudge on the air? I didn't know. I didn't want to find out.) Every once in a while I'd see a dead VC look up from where he was squatting, on the banks of the river or in the shade of a rubber tree, and look at me, sometimes with curiosity, sometimes resentment, sometimes fear. They never said anything. Just stared, and at length went back to their mourning, their weeping. I hurried past.

About half a mile from DePaul I caught a glimpse of a squad of still-living VC, about a dozen yards into the jungle, carrying what looked like an unconscious American GI, probably an LRRP. I immediately squatted down in the bush, hiding the kid from view as best I could, dropping a fold of blanket over his face to protect him from the prickly blades of grass. I watched as one of the VC bent down, reaching for what looked like a patch of dry dirt, his fingers finding a catch, a handle of some sort, and then the earth lifted and I saw it was actually a trapdoor in the ground itself—a piece of wood covered with a thin, but deceptive, layer of dirt. One by one the VC crawled headfirst into the tunnel, until only two were left—the two carrying the unconscious GI. I debated what to do—was there anything I *could* do?—but before I could make a decision, I saw the GI's head tilt at an unnatural angle as he was lowered into the ground . . . and I knew, then, that I'd been mistaken. He wasn't unconscious; he was dead. And, very quickly, lost from sight.

Psychological warfare. Drove Americans crazy when we couldn't recover our dead, and Charlie knew it. Just like we played on their fears with the Wandering Soul, they played on ours, in their own way. I got up and moved on.

Less than half an hour later I was back at the river. DePaul still floated helplessly above the rapids. He looked up at my approach, the torment in his face quickly replaced by astonishment and—fear?

I brought the kid to the edge of the river, looked

up at DePaul, made my voice hard, resolute—all that Sergeant York shit.

"He's got malaria," I said, tonelessly. "You can tell when you pull down his lower eyelid, it's all pink; he's anemic, can't weigh more than twenty pounds. They could save him, at the 510 Evac. Or you can take him, to save yourself." I stared him straight in the eye. "Which is it, DePaul?"

I'd known DePaul since boot camp. Faced with the reality of it, I knew what he'd answer.

And as I waited, smugly, for him to say it, his gaseous, wraithlike form spun round in midair, rocketed downward like a guided missile, and slammed into me with vicious velocity, sending me sprawling, knocking the kid out of my arms.

Stunned, I screamed at him, but by the time I'd scrambled to my feet he had the kid in a vise grip and was holding the poor sonofabitch under the water. I ran, slammed into De with all my strength, but he shrugged me off with an elbow in my face. I toppled backward.

"I'm sorry, man," he kept saying, over and over; "I'm sorry . . ."

I lunged at him again, this time knocking him off-balance; he lost his grip on the kid, and I dove into the water after the boy. It felt weird; the water passed *through* me, I didn't feel wet, or cold, nothing at all; and the waters were so muddy I could barely see a foot in front of me. Finally, after what seemed like forever, I saw a small object in front of me and instinctively I reached out and grabbed. My fingers closed around the infant's arms. I made for the surface, the kid in my arms; I staggered out of the water, up the embankment—

I put the boy down on the ground. His face was blue, his body very still. I tried to administer mouth-to-mouth, but nothing happened; and then I laughed suddenly, a manic, rueful laugh, at the thought of me, of all people, trying to give the breath of life.

I looked up, thinking to see DePaul towering above me . . . but he was nowhere to be seen. And when I looked up at the spot above the river where he had been tethered, helplessly, for so long—

I saw the spirit-form of the little boy, floating, hovering, crying out in pain and confusion.

I screamed. I screamed for a long time.

And knew, now, why I'd been able to touch the child, when I hadn't been able to touch anything else: I was the *ma qui*, I was the evil spirit come to bear the sickly child away, and I had done my job, followed my role, without even realizing I'd been doing it. I thought of Phan, of his daughter Chau, of DePaul and of myself.

Death makes of us what it wishes.

I wept, then, for the first time, as freely and as helplessly as the VC I'd seen and heard; wept like the Wandering Soul I knew, at last, I had to be.

I must've stayed there, on the banks of the river, for at least a day, trying to find some way to atone, some way to save the soul of the child I'd led to perdition. But I couldn't. I would've traded places with him willingly, but didn't know how. And when I went back to the spirit house where Phan and his daughter dwelled, when I told him of what I'd done, he showed no horror, expressed no rage; just puzzlement that it had taken me so long to realize my place in the world.

His daughter, on the other hand, gleefully congratulated me on my deed. *"Ma qui,"* she said, and this time, hearing the word, I understood it not just as ghost, but as devil, for it meant both. "Did it not feel good?"

A terrible gladness burst open, someplace inside me—a black, cold poison that felt at once horrifying and invigorating. It was relief, expiation of guilt by embracing, not renouncing, the evil I'd done. Chau, as though sensing this, laughed throatily. She leaned forward, her spiteful smile now seductive as well. *"Yêu dâu,"* she said, *"yêu quái."*

Beloved demon.

"Together we could do many things," she said, twisting a lock of long black hair in her fingers. Her eyes glittered malevolently. "Many things." She laughed again. Cruel eyes, a cold-blooded smile. I felt betrayed by my own erection. I wanted her, I didn't want her. I loathed her, and in my loathing wanted her all the more, because perverse desire was, at least, desire; I wanted my cock, dead limb that it was, inside her, to make me feel alive.

When I realized how badly I wanted it, I ran.

She only laughed all the louder.

"Beloved demon!" she called after me. "You shall be back!"

But I haven't been back. Not yet. Nor back to the crater, the place of my death, not for many months. I still search for my body, but I know that the odds of finding it, in the hundreds of miles of tunnels that honeycomb this land, are virtually nil. I search during the days, and at night I come back to my new home to sleep.

I have a birdhouse of my own, you see, just outside the village; a treehouse perched on a bamboo stump, filled with Joss sticks and candles and little toy furniture. I come back here, and I fight to remind myself who I am, what I am; I struggle against becoming the *yêu quái*, the demon Chau wishes me to be. Except, that is, when the bloodsong sings to me in my voice, and I know that I already *am* the demon—and that the only thing that stops me from acting like one is my will, my conscience, the last vestiges of the living man I once was. I don't know how long I can keep the demon at bay. I don't know how long I want to. But all I can do is keep trying, and not think of Chau, or of how wonderfully bitter her lips must taste, bitter as salt, bitter as blood.

Damn it.

Above me, the Wandering Soul cries out from its box, wailing and moaning in a ridiculous burlesque of damnation, and I think about all the things we were told about this place, and the things we weren't. Back in Da Nang, when anyone would talk about the Army's "pacification" program—about winning the "hearts and minds" of the Vietnamese—the joke used to be: Grab 'em by the balls, and their hearts and minds will follow. Except no one told us that while we were working on their hearts and minds, they were winning over our souls. The Army trained us in jungle warfare, drilled us in the local customs, told us we'd have to fight Charlie on his own terms—but never let on that we'd have to die on his terms, too. Because for all the technology, all the ordnance, all the planning that went into this war, they forgot the most important thing.

They never told us the rules of engagement.

THE SAME IN ANY LANGUAGE

by Ramsey Campbell

Ramsey Campbell is one of two authors in this, the twentieth volume of The Year's Best Horror Stories, *who was also on board for the first volume. Since then Campbell has gone from Rising Young Star to Grand Master—perhaps to be expected of a kid who sold his first book when he was sixteen. Born in Liverpool on January 4, 1946, Campbell has now ferried cross to Merseyside—probably to escape all the nasty creatures that haunt his vision of Liverpool. His recent books include a novel,* The Count of Eleven, *and a short story collection,* Waking Nightmares. *He is presently completing a new novel,* The Long Lost, *awaiting publication of* Alone with the Horrors, *a thirty-years' retrospective collection from Arkham House, and has edited an anthology of horror stories,* Uncanny Banquet.

Writers often find inspiration for stories while on holiday (making their vacation tax-deductible), and so has Campbell with "The Same in Any Language"—as he explains: "When we visited Spinalonga I was already playing with the notion of a tourist who falls in with a tour party whose guide proves to be speaking not so much a foreign language as, shall we say, a dead language. The island itself pretty well did the rest—that and my observations of some English abroad. (They were even worse in our hotel in Turkey, bemoaning the lack of roast beef and Yorkshire pud and Wat-

ney's Red Barrel.)" I think there's a Monty Python skit on that.

The day my father is to take me where the lepers used to live is hotter than ever. Even the old women with black scarves wrapped around their heads sit inside the bus station instead of on the chairs outside the tavernas. Kate fans herself with her straw hat like a basket someone's sat on and gives my father one of those smiles they've made up between them. She's leaning forward to see if that's our bus when he says, "Why do you think they call them lepers, Hugh?"

I can hear what he's going to say, but I have to humor him. "I don't know."

"Because they never stop leaping up and down."

It takes him much longer to say the first four words than the rest of it. I groan because he expects me to, and Kate lets off one of her giggles I keep hearing whenever they stay in my father's and my room at the hotel and send me down for a swim. "If you can't give a grin, give a groan," my father says for about the millionth time, and Kate pokes him with her freckly elbow as if he's too funny for words. She annoys me so much that I say, "Lepers don't rhyme with creepers, dad."

"I never thought they did, son. I was just having a laugh. If we can't laugh we might as well be dead, ain't that straight, Kate?" He winks at her thigh and slaps his own instead, and says to me, "Since you're so clever, why don't you find out when our bus is coming."

"That's it now."

"And I'm Hercules." He lifts up his fists to make his muscles bulge for Kate and says "You're telling us that tripe spells A Flounder?"

"Elounda, dad. It does. The letter like a Y upside down is how they write an L."

"About time they learned how to write properly, then," he says, staring around to show he doesn't care who hears. "Well, there it is if you really want to trudge round another old ruin instead of having a swim."

"I expect he'll be able to do both once we get to the village," Kate says, but I can tell she's hoping I'll just swim. "Will you two gentlemen see me across the road?"

My mother used to link arms with me and my father when he was living with us. "I'd better make sure it's the right bus," I say, and run out so fast I can pretend I didn't hear my father calling me back.

A man with skin like a boot is walking backward in the dust behind the bus, shouting "Elounda" and waving his arms as if he's pulling the bus into the space in line. I sit on a seat opposite two Germans who block the aisle until they've taken off their rucksacks, but my father finds three seats together at the rear. "Aren't you with us, Hugh?" he shouts, and everyone on the bus looks at him.

When I see him getting ready to shout again I walk down the aisle. I'm hoping nobody notices me, but Kate says loudly, "It's a pity you ran off like that, Hugh. I was going to ask if you'd like an ice cream."

"No thank you," I say, trying to sound like my mother when she was only just speaking to my father, and step over Kate's legs. As the bus rumbles uphill I turn as much of my back on her as I can, and watch the streets.

Aghios Nikolaos looks as if they haven't finished building it. Some of the tavernas are on the bottom floors of blocks with no roofs, and sometimes there are more tables on the pavements outside than in. The bus goes downhill again as if it's hiccuping, and when it reaches the bottomless pool where young people with no children stay in the hotels with discos, it follows the edge of the bay. I watch the white boats on the blue water, but really I'm seeing the conductor coming down the aisle and feeling as if a lump's growing in my stomach from me wondering what my father will say to him.

The bus is climbing beside the sea when he reaches us. "Three for leper land," my father says.

The conductor stares at him and shrugs. "As far as you go," Kate says, and rubs herself against my father. "All the way."

When the conductor pushes his lips forward out of his mustache and beard my father begins to get angry, unless he's pretending. "Where you kept your lepers. Spiny Lobster or whatever you call the damned place."

"It's Spinalonga, dad, and it's off the coast from where we're going."

"I know that, and he should." My father is really angry now. "Did you get that?" he says to the conductor. "My ten-year-old can speak your lingo, so don't tell me you can't speak ours."

The conductor looks at me, and I'm afraid he wants me to talk Greek. My mother gave me a little computer that translates words into Greek when you type them, but I've left it at the hotel because my father said it sounded like a bird which only knew one note. "We're going to Elounda, please," I stammer.

"Elounda, boss," the conductor says to me. He takes the money from my father without looking at him and gives me the tickets and change. "Fish is good by the harbor in the evening," he says, and goes to sit next to the driver while the bus swings round the zigzags of the hill road.

My father laughs for the whole bus to hear. "They think you're so important, Hugh, you won't be wanting to go home to your mother."

Kate strokes his head as if he's her pet, then she turns to me. "What do you like most about Greece?"

She's trying to make friends with me like when she kept saying I could call her Kate, only now I see it's for my father's sake. All she's done is make me think how the magic places seemed to have lost their magic because my mother wasn't there with me, even Knossos where Theseus killed the Minotaur. There were just a few corridors left that might have been the maze he was supposed to find his way out of, and my father let me stay in them for a while, but then he lost his temper because all the guided tours were in foreign languages and nobody could tell him how to get back to the coach. We nearly got stuck overnight in Heraklion, when he'd promised to take Kate for dinner that night by the bottomless pool. "I don't know," I mumble, and gaze out the window.

"I like the sun, don't you? And the people when they're being nice, and the lovely clear sea."

It sounds to me as if she's getting ready to send me off swimming again. They met while I was, our second morning at the hotel. When I came out of the sea my father had moved his towel next to hers and she was giggling. I watch Spinalonga Island float over the horizon like a ship made of rock and gray towers, and hope she'll think I'm agreeing with her if that means she'll leave me alone. But she says "I suppose most boys are morbid at your age. Let's hope you'll grow up to be like your father."

She's making it sound as if the leper colony is the only place I've wanted to visit, but it's just another old place I can tell my mother I've been. Kate doesn't want to go there because she doesn't like old places—she said if Knossos was a palace she was glad she's not a queen. I don't speak to her again until the bus has stopped by the harbor.

There aren't many tourists, even in the shops and tavernas lined up along the winding pavement. Greek people who look as if they were born in the sun sit drinking at tables under awnings like stalls in a market. Some priests who I think at first are wearing black hatboxes on their heads march by, and fishermen come up from their boats with octopuses on sticks like big kebabs. The bus turns round in a cloud of dust and petrol fumes while Kate hangs onto my father with one hand and flaps the front of her flowery dress with the other. A boatman stares at the tops of her boobs which make me think of spotted fish and shouts "Spinalonga" with both hands round his mouth.

"We've hours yet," Kate says. "Let's have a drink. Hugh may even get that ice cream if he's good."

If she's going to talk about me as though I'm not there I'll do my best not to be. She and my father sit under an awning and I kick dust on the pavement outside until she says "Come under, Hugh. We don't want you with sunstroke."

I don't want her pretending she's my mother, but if I say so I'll only spoil the day more than she already has. I shuffle to the table next to the one she's sharing with my father and throw myself on a chair. "Well, Hugh," she says, "do you want one?"

"No thank you," I say, even though the thought of an ice cream or a drink starts my mouth trying to drool.

"You can have some of my lager if it ever arrives," my father says at the top of his voice, and stares hard at some Greeks sitting at a table. "Anyone here a waiter?" he says, lifting his hand to his mouth as if he's holding a glass.

When all the people at the table smile and raise their glasses and shout cheerily at him, Kate says "I'll find someone and then I'm going to the little girls' room while you men have a talk."

My father watches her crossing the road and gazes at the doorway of the taverna once she's gone in. He's quiet for a while, then he says, "Are you going to be able to say you had a good time?"

I know he wants me to enjoy myself when I'm with him, but I also think what my mother stopped herself from saying to me is true—that he booked the holiday in Greece as a way of scoring off her by taking me somewhere she'd always wanted to go. He stares at the taverna as if he can't move until I let him, and I say "I expect so, if we go to the island."

"That's my boy. Never give in too easily." He smiles at me with one side of his face. "You don't mind if I have some fun as well, do you?"

He's making it sound as though he wouldn't have had much fun if it had just been the two of us, and I think that was how he'd started to feel before he met Kate. "It's your holiday," I say.

He's opening his mouth after another long silence when Kate comes out of the taverna with a man carrying two lagers and a lemonade on a tray. "See that you thank her," my father tells me.

I didn't ask for lemonade. He said I could have some lager. I say "Thank you very much" and feel my throat tightening as I gulp the lemonade, because her eyes are saying that she's won.

"That must have been welcome," she says when I put down the empty glass. "Another? Then I should find yourself something to do. Your father and I may be here for a while."

"Have a swim," my father suggests.

"I haven't brought my cossy."

"Neither have those boys," Kate says, pointing at the harbor. "Don't worry, I've seen boys wearing less."

My father smirks behind his hand, and I can't bear it. I run to the jetty the boys are diving off, and drop my T-shirt and shorts on it and my sandals on top of them, and dive in.

The water's cold, but not for long. It's full of little fish that nibble you if you only float, and it's clearer than tap water, so you can see down to the pebbles and the fish pretending to be them. I chase fish and swim underwater and almost catch an octopus before it squirms out to sea. Then three Greek boys about my age swim over, and we're pointing at ourselves and saying our names when I see Kate and my father kissing.

I know their tongues are in each other's mouths—getting some tongue, the kids at my school call it. I feel like swimming away as far as I can go and never coming back. But Stavros and Stathis and Costas are using their hands to tell me we should see who can swim fastest, so I do that instead. Soon I've forgotten my father and Kate, even when we sit on the jetty for a rest before we have more races. It must be hours later when I realise Kate is calling "Come here a minute."

The sun isn't so hot now. It's reaching under the awning, but she and my father haven't moved back into the shadow. A boatman shouts "Spinalonga" and points at how low the sun is. I don't mind swimming with my new friends instead of going to the island, and I'm about to tell my father so when Kate says "I've been telling your dad he should be proud of you. Come and see what I've got for you."

They've both had a lot to drink. She almost falls across the table as I go to her. Just as I get there I see what she's going to give me, but it's too late. She grabs my head with both hands and sticks a kiss on my mouth.

She tastes of old lager. Her mouth is wet and bigger than mine, and when it squirms it makes me think of an octopus. "Mmm-*mwa*," it says, and then I manage to duck out of her hands, leaving her blinking at me as if her eyes won't quite work. "Nothing wrong with a bit of loving," she says. "You'll find that out when you grow up."

My father knows I don't like to be kissed, but he's frowning at me as if I should have let her. Suddenly I want to get my own back on them in the only way I can think of. "We need to go to the island now."

"Better go to the loo first," my father says. "They wouldn't have one on the island when all their willies had dropped off."

Kate hoots at that while I'm getting dressed, and I feel as if she's laughing at the way my ribs show through my skin however much I eat. I stop myself from shivering in case she or my father makes out that's a reason for us to go back to the hotel. I'm heading for the toilet when my father says, "Watch out you don't catch anything in there or we'll have to leave you on the island."

I know there are all sorts of reasons why my parents split up, but just now this is the only one I can think of—my mother not being able to stand his jokes and how the more she told him to finish the more he would do it, as if he couldn't stop himself. I run into the toilet, trying not to look at the pedal bin where you have to drop the used paper, and close my eyes once I've taken aim.

Is today going to be what I remember about

Greece? My mother brought me up to believe that even the sunlight here had magic in it, and I expected to feel the ghosts of legends in all the old places. If there isn't any magic in the sunlight, I want there to be some in the dark. The thought seems to make the insides of my eyelids darker, and I can smell the drains. I pull the chain and zip myself up, and then I wonder if my father sent me in here so we'll miss the boat. I nearly break the hook on the door, I'm so desperate to be outside.

The boat is still tied to the harbor, but I can't see the boatman. Kate and my father are holding hands across the table, and my father's looking around as though he means to order another drink. I squeeze my eyes shut so hard that when I open them everything's gone black. The blackness fades along with whatever I wished, and I see the boatman kneeling on the jetty, talking to Stavros. "Spinalonga," I shout.

He looks at me, and I'm afraid he'll say it's too late. I feel tears building up behind my eyes. Then he stands up and holds out a hand toward my father and Kate. "One hour," he says.

Kate's gazing after a bus that has just begun to climb the hill. "We may as well go over as wait for the next bus," my father says, "and then it'll be back to the hotel for dinner."

Kate looks sideways at me. "And after all that he'll be ready for bed," she says like a question she isn't quite admitting to.

"Out like a light, I reckon."

"Fair enough," she says, and uses his arm to get herself up.

The boatman's name is Iannis, and he doesn't speak much English. My father seems to think he's charging too much for the trip until he realizes it's that much for all three of us, and then he grins as if he thinks Iannis has cheated himself. "Heave ho then, Janice," he says with a wink at me and Kate.

The boat is about the size of a big rowing-boat. It has a cabin at the front and benches along the sides and a long box in the middle that shakes and smells of petrol. I watch the point of the boat sliding through the water like a knife and feel as if we're on our way to the Greece I've been dreaming of. The white buildings of Elounda shrink until they look like teeth in the mouth of the hills, and then Spinalonga floats up ahead.

It makes me think of an abandoned ship bigger than a liner, a ship so dead that it's standing still in the water without having to be anchored. The evening light seems to shine out of the steep rusty sides and the bony towers and walls high above the sea. I know it was a fort to begin with, but I think it might as well have been built for the lepers. I can imagine them trying to swim to Elounda and drowning because there wasn't enough left of them to swim with, if they didn't just throw themselves off the walls because they couldn't bear what they'd turned into. If I say these things to Kate I bet more than her mouth will squirm—but my father gets in first. "Look, there's the welcoming committee."

Kate gives a shiver that reminds me I'm trying not to feel cold. "Don't say things like that. They're just people like us, probably wishing they hadn't come."

I don't think she can see them any more clearly than I can. Their heads are poking over the wall at the top of the cliff above the little pebbly beach which is the only place a boat can land. There are five or six of them, only I'm not sure they're heads; they might be stones someone has balanced on the wall—they're almost the same color. I'm wishing I had some binoculars when Kate grabs my father so hard the boat rocks and Iannis waves a finger at her, which doesn't please my father. "You keep your eye on your steering, Janice," he says.

Iannis is already taking the boat toward the beach. He didn't seem to notice the heads on the wall, and when I look again they aren't there. Maybe they belonged to some of the people who are coming down to a boat bigger than Iannis's. That boat chugs away as Iannis's bumps into the jetty. "One hour," he says. "Back here."

He helps Kate onto the jetty while my father glowers at him, then he lifts me out of the boat. As soon as my father steps onto the jetty Iannis pushes the boat out again. "Aren't you staying?" Kate pleads.

He shakes his head and points hard at the beach. "Back here, one hour."

She looks as if she wants to run into the water and climb aboard the boat, but my father shoves his arm round her waist. "Don't worry, you've got two fellers to keep you safe, and neither of them with a girl's name."

The only way up to the fort is through a tunnel that bends in the middle so you can't see the end until you're nearly halfway in. I wonder how long it will take for the rest of the island to be as dark as the middle of the tunnel. When Kate sees the end she runs until she's in the open and stares at the sunlight, which is perched on top of the towers now. "Fancying a climb?" my father says.

She makes a face at him as I walk past her. We're in a kind of street of stone sheds that have mostly caved in. They must be where the lepers lived, but there are only shadows in them now, not even birds. "Don't go too far, Hugh," Kate says.

"I want to go all the way round, otherwise it wasn't worth coming."

"I don't, and I'm sure your father expects you to consider me."

"Now, now, children," my father says. "Hugh can do as he likes as long as he's careful and the same goes for us, eh, Kate?"

I can tell he's surprised when she doesn't laugh. He looks unsure of himself and angry about it, the way he did when he and my mother were getting ready to tell me they were splitting up. I run along the line of huts and think of hiding in one so I can jump out at Kate. Maybe they aren't empty after all; something rattles in one as if bones are crawling about in the dark. It could be a snake under part of the roof that's fallen. I keep running until I come to steps leading up from the street to the top of the island, where most of the light is, and I've started jogging up them when Kate shouts "Stay where we can see you. We don't want you hurting yourself."

"It's all right, Kate, leave him be," my father says. "He's sensible."

"If I'm not allowed to speak to him I don't know why you invited me at all."

I can't help grinning as I sprint to the top of the steps and duck out of sight behind a grassy mound that makes me think of a grave. From up here I can see the whole island, and we aren't alone on it. The path I've run up from leads all round the island, past more huts and towers and a few bigger buildings, and then it goes down to the tunnel. Just before it does it passes the wall above the beach, and between the path and the wall there's a stone yard full of slabs. Some of the slabs have been moved away from holes like long boxes full of soil or darkness. They're by the wall where I thought I saw heads looking over at us. They aren't there now, but I can see heads bobbing down toward the tunnel. Before long they'll be behind Kate and my father.

Iannis is well on his way back to Elounda. His boat is passing one that's heading for the island. Soon the sun will touch the sea. If I went down to the huts I'd see it sink with me and drown. Instead I lie on the mound and look over the island, and see more of the boxy holes hiding behind some of the huts. If I went closer I could see how deep they are, but I quite like not knowing—if I was Greek I expect I'd think they lead to the underworld where all the dead live. Besides, I like being able to look down on my father and Kate and see them trying to see me.

I stay there until Iannis's boat is back at Elounda and the other one has almost reached Spinalonga, and the sun looks as if it's gone down to the sea for a drink. Kate and my father are having an argument. I expect it's about me, though I can't hear what they're saying; the darker it gets between the huts the more Kate waves her arms. I'm getting ready to let my father see me when she screams.

She's jumped back from a hut which has a hole behind it. "Come out, Hugh. I know it's you," she cries.

I can tell what my father's going to say, and I cringe. "Is that you, Hugh? Yoo-hoo," he shouts.

I won't show myself for a joke like that. He leans into the hut through the spiky stone window, then he turns to Kate. "It wasn't Hugh. There's nobody."

I can only just hear him, but I don't have to strain to hear Kate. "Don't tell me that," she cries. "You're both too fond of jokes."

She screams again, because someone's come running up the tunnel. "Everything all right?" this man shouts. "There's a boat about to leave if you've had enough."

"I don't know what you two are doing," Kate says like a duchess to my father, "but I'm going with this gentleman."

My father calls me twice. If I go to him I'll be letting Kate win. "I don't think our man will wait," the new one says.

"It doesn't matter," my father says, so fiercely that I know it does. "We've our own boat coming."

"If there's a bus before you get back I won't be hanging around," Kate warns him.

"Please yourself," my father says, so loud that his voice goes into the tunnel. He stares after her as she marches away; he must be hoping she'll change her mind. But I see her step off the jetty into the boat, and it moves out to sea as if the ripples are pushing it to Elounda.

My father puts a hand to his ear as the sound of the engine fades. "So every bugger's left me now, have they?" he says in a kind of shout at himself. "Well, good riddance."

He's waving his fists as if he wants to punch something, and he sounds as if he's suddenly got drunk. He must have been holding it back while Kate was there. I've never seen him like this. It frightens me, so I stay where I am.

It isn't only my father that frightens me. There's

only a little bump of the sun left above the water now, and I'm afraid how dark the island may be once that goes. Bits of sunlight shiver on the water all the way to the island, and I think I see some heads above the wall of the yard full of slabs, against the light. Which side of the wall are they on? The light's too dazzling, it seems to pinch the sides of the heads so they look thinner than any heads I've ever seen. Then I notice a boat setting out from Elounda, and I squint at it until I'm sure it's Iannis's boat.

He's coming early to fetch us. Even that frightens me, because I wonder why he is. Doesn't he want us to be on the island now he realises how dark it's getting? I look at the wall, and the heads have gone. Then the sea puts the sun out, and it feels as if the island is buried in darkness.

I can still see my way down—the steps are paler than the dark—and I don't like being alone now I've started shivering. I back off from the mound, because I don't like to touch it, and almost back into a shape with bits of its head poking out and arms that look as if they've dropped off at the elbows. It's a cactus. I'm just standing up when my father says "There you are, Hugh."

He can't see me yet. He must have heard me gasp. I go to the top of the steps, but I can't see him for the dark. Then his voice moves away. "Don't start hiding again. Looks like we've seen the last of Kate, but we've got each other, haven't we?"

He's still drunk. He sounds as if he's talking to somebody nearer to him than I am. "All right, we'll wait on the beach," he says, and his voice echoes. He's gone into the tunnel, and he thinks he's following me. "I'm here, dad," I shout so loud that I squeak.

"I heard you, Hugh. Wait there. I'm coming." He's walking deeper into the tunnel. While he's in there my voice must seem to be coming from beyond the far end. I'm sucking in a breath that tastes dusty, so I can tell him where I am, when he says "Who's that?" with a laugh that almost shakes his words to pieces.

He's met whoever he thought was me when he was

heading for the tunnel. I'm holding my breath—I can't breathe or swallow, and I don't know if I feel hot or frozen. "Let me past," he says as if he's trying to make his voice as big as the tunnel. "My son's waiting for me on the beach."

There are so many echoes in the tunnel I'm not sure what I'm hearing besides him. I think there's a lot of shuffling, and the other noise must be voices, because my father says "What kind of language do you call that? You sound drunker than I am. I said my son's waiting."

He's talking even louder as if that'll make him understood. I'm embarrassed, but I'm more afraid for him. "Dad," I nearly scream, and run down the steps as fast as I can without falling.

"See, I told you. That's my son," he says as if he's talking to a crowd of idiots. The shuffling starts moving like a slow march, and he says "All right, we'll all go to the beach together. What's the matter with your friends, too drunk to walk?"

I reach the bottom of the steps, hurting my ankles, and run along the ruined street because I can't stop myself. The shuffling sounds as though it's growing thinner, as if the people with my father are leaving bits of themselves behind, and the voices are changing too—they're looser. Maybe the mouths are getting bigger somehow. But my father's laughing, so loud that he might be trying to think of a joke. "That's what I call a hug. No harder, love, or I won't have any puff left," he says to someone. "Come on then, give us a kiss. They're the same in any language."

All the voices stop, but the shuffling doesn't. I hear it go out of the tunnel and onto the pebbles, and then my father tries to scream as if he's swallowed something that won't let him. I scream for him and dash into the tunnel, slipping on things that weren't on the floor when we first came through, and fall out onto the beach.

My father's in the sea. He's already so far out that the water is up to his neck. About six people who look stuck together and to him are walking him away as if they don't need to breathe when their heads start to sink. Bits of them float away on the waves my father makes as he throws his arms about and gurgles. I try to run after him, but I've got nowhere when his head goes underwater. The sea pushes me back on the beach, and I run crying up and down it until Iannis comes.

It doesn't take him long to find my father once he understands what I'm saying. Iannis wraps me in a blanket and hugs me all the way to Elounda, and the police take me back to the hotel. Kate gets my mother's number and calls her, saying she's someone at the hotel who's looking after me because my father's drowned, and I don't care what she says, I just feel numb. I don't start screaming until I'm on the plane back to England, because then I dream that my father has come back to tell a joke. "That's what I call getting some tongue," he says, leaning his face close to mine and showing me what's in his mouth.

CALL HOME

by Dennis Etchison

Dennis Etchison returns to The Year's Best Horror Stories *after a few years' absence—primarily due to the fact that he has been too busy on other projects to write short stories in recent years. Since last seen here, Etchison has edited the three-volume* Masters of Darkness *anthology series for Tor (this has been collected into one mammoth hardcover omnibus by Underwood-Miller), and he has edited an anthology of original horror stories,* MetaHorror, *for Dell (also to be published in hardcover by Grant). This last is "a kind of unofficial follow-up to* Cutting Edge,*" Etchison's much-heralded anthology of modern horror fiction. Just now he is struggling to finish a new horror novel for Dell (and in hardcover from Lord John Press), tentatively titled* The Shadow Man.

Born in Stockton, California on March 30, 1943, Etchison currently resides in Los Angeles with his wife, Kristina. His short fiction tends to focus upon unexpected paranoid fears of people caught up in urban life—a vision that transforms the commonplace into the sinister. Makes me wonder what Woody Allen might do if he traded humor for horror.

When he walked in, the red light on the answering machine was blinking.

He dropped the mail on the coffee table and sat

down. He ran a hand through his hair and leaned into the sofa, his ears still ringing from the rush-hour traffic.

He was in no hurry to replay his messages. It was easy to guess what they wanted: time, money, answers. He had none to spare. He reached out and stirred the pile of letters.

More of the same.

He got up, went to the bedroom and changed his clothes. Then he came back and sank deeper into the cushions. He propped his feet up and closed his eyes.

When the phone rang again, he let the machine take over.

"I'm not home right now," he heard his own recorded voice say, *"but if you care to leave a message, please begin speaking when you hear the tone. Thank you for calling. . . ."*

Beep.

A pause, and the incoming tape started rolling.

He waited to monitor the call.

Static. A rush of white noise. Like traffic.

No one there. Or someone who did not like talking to a machine.

A few more seconds and it would hang up automatically.

"Daddy? Is t-that you?"

He opened his eyes.

"Please, c-can you come get me? I don't know how to get home . . . and I'm scared!"

What?

"It's getting cold . . . and dark . . ."

He sat forward.

"There's a man here . . . and he's bothering me! I think he's crazy! And it's going to rain and . . . and . . . Daddy, tell me what to do!"

He got to his feet.

"I don't like this place! There's a rooster . . . it's burning . . . and a gas station . . . and a sign. It says, um, it starts with a p. P-I-C-O . . ."

He crossed the living room.

"Daddy, please come quick . . . !"

He snatched up the receiver.

"Hello?" he said.

The child's voice began to sing brokenly.

"Ladybird, ladybird, fly away home . . . your house is on fire . . . and your children will burn. . . ."

Her voice trailed off as she started to cry.

"Hello? Hello?"

Click.

He stood there holding the phone, wondering what to do.

He was sure of only one thing.

He had no daughter.

So what if it was a wrong number? She was in trouble. A child, a little girl. What if something happened to her?

He couldn't let it go.

She had spelled out a word. P-I-C-O. The sign. A rooster, a gas station . . . yes, it sounded familiar.

The chicken restaurant. Next to the 76 station. On Pico Boulevard.

It wasn't far.

The traffic was still gridlocked. He crossed Wilshire in low gear, then Santa Monica, and turned west. A stream of cars growled past him, ragged music and demanding voices leaking from beneath shimmering hoods. He made a left on Westwood and kept to the right as he passed Olympic, slowing to a crawl as he came to the next corner.

She was huddled in the doorway of El Pollo Muerto, a school book bag at her feet. Her legs were dirty and her hair was in her eyes. A few yards away, at the gas station, was the phone booth. She did not look up as he braked by a loading zone.

He leaned over and rolled down the window.

"Hey!"

The people at the bus stop glanced his way blankly, then stared past him down the street.

She lowered her head, resting her forehead on her arms.

He cleared his throat and shouted above the din. "Hey, little girl!"

She raised her head.

A woman eyed him suspiciously.

"Hi!" he called. "Hello, there! Do you need any help?"

The woman glared at him.

He ignored her and spoke to the girl.

"Are you the one who—?" Suddenly he felt foolish. "Did you call me?"

The little girl's face brightened.

"Daddy?"

The crowd moved closer. Then there was a rumbling and a pumping of brakes. He saw in his rearview mirror that an RTD bus had pulled up behind him.

"Come on," he said. "And your books—"

He opened the door for her as the bus sounded its horn.

"Daddy, it *is* you!"

The crowd surged past. The woman took notice of his license plate. The bus tapped his bumper.

"Get in."

He slipped into gear and got away from the curb. The pressure of traffic carried him across the intersection.

"Where do you want to go?" he asked. He passed another corner before it was possible to turn. "What's the address?"

"I don't know," said the little girl.

"You don't remember?"

She did not answer.

"Well, you'll have to tell me. Which way?"

"Want to go home," she said. She was now sitting straight in her seat, watching the lights with wide eyes.

"Are you all right?"

"I guess so."

At least it hasn't started to rain, he thought. "Did anyone hurt you?"

"I'm kind of hungry," she said.

He idled at a red light and got a good look at her. Seven, maybe eight years old and skinny as a rail.

The bones in her wrists showed like white knuckles through the thin skin.

"When was the last time you had anything to eat?"

"I don't know."

She crossed her legs, angling a bruised ankle on a knobby knee, and he saw that her legs were streaked and smudged all the way up. My God, he thought, how long since she's had a bath? Has she been living on the streets?

"Well then," he said, "the first thing we'll do is get you some food." And then he would figure out what to do with her. "Okay?"

He took her to a deli. She gulped down a hot dog, leaving the bun on the plate, and watched him as he chewed his sandwich. He started to order her another, and realized something. He touched his hip pocket. Empty. He had forgotten his wallet when he changed his clothes.

"Take half of mine," he told her, trying to think.

"I don't like that kind."

She continued to watch him.

Finally he said, "Do you want another hot dog?"

"Yes, please!"

He ordered one more and saw to it that she drank her milk.

Afterward, while the waitress was in another part of the restaurant, he said abruptly, "Let's go."

They drove away as the waitress came out onto the sidewalk.

"That was good," said the little girl.

"Glad you liked it. Now—"

"The way you did that. You didn't even leave a tip. You did it for me, didn't you?"

"Yes." What was I supposed to do? he thought. I'll come back tomorrow and take care of it. "Now where are we going?"

"Home," she said. "Oh, Daddy, you're so silly! Where did you think?"

"You've got to tell me," he said in the driveway.

"Tell you what?"

She got out and skipped to the front door, dragging her book bag. She waited for him on the porch.

He shook his head.

"Well," he said once they were inside, "are you going to tell me?"

"Um, where's the bathroom?"

"In there." He went to the phone. "But first—"

He heard water running.

He stood outside the bathroom door and listened. The shower was hissing, and presently she began to sing a song.

In the living room, the phone rang.

"I'm not home right now—"

"Jack, would you pick it up, please? I know you're there. . . ."

"Hello, Chrissie. Sorry. I just got in."

"So late? Poor baby . . ."

"Listen, Chrissie, can I call you back? There's something I have to—"

"Are Ruth and Will there yet?"

"What?"

"Don't tell me you forgot! Well, I guess I can pick up something on the way over. You know, maybe we can get rid of them early. Would you like that?"

"Yeah, sure. But—"

"See you in a few minutes, love. And Jack? I've missed you . . . !"

Click.

"Daddy," called the little girl, "can you come here?"

He entered the darkened bedroom.

The bathroom door was open and steaming. She wrapped herself in a big towel and jumped up on the bed. She opened the towel.

"Dry me?"

"Listen," he said, "who told you to do this? I don't think it's such a good idea to—"

" 'S okay. I can do it myself." She made a few swipes with the towel and dropped it on the bed. Even in the faint light he could see how pink, how clean she was. And how small, and how vulnerable. She lay down and wriggled under the sheet.

"Sleepy," she said.

He sat next to her, on the edge of the mattress.

"Kiss me good-night," she said. Her pale arms stretched out. He started to push her away, but she clung to him with all her might. He felt her tears as sobs wracked her body.

"There," he told her, patting her between sharp shoulder blades. "Shh, now . . ."

"Don't go," she said.

"I'm not going anywhere."

"Promise?"

"I promise."

He lay down next to her till her breathing became slow and regular. After a while he covered her with the blanket, and planted a kiss on her cool forehead before he left the room.

Ruth and Will parked behind Chrissie. He watched from the porch as they helped her carry the take-out food into the house.

He cleared his throat. "There's something I have to tell you."

"We already know," said Ruth.

"How?"

"They didn't hear it from me, I swear," said Chrissie.

"A little bird told me," Ruth said. "And all I can say is, it's about time."

Will plopped down on the sofa. "Well, I think it's great. No point in paying rent on two places."

"*This* place sure isn't big enough," said Ruth. She stopped on the way to the kitchen and scanned the dining room. "Even if you got rid of these bookcases, it wouldn't work. You need more space."

"You know, Jack," said Will, "I have a friend in the real estate business. If you need any advice. Where's the Scotch?"

"Hold on . . ."

Chrissie winked at him as she passed. "They want

to know if we've set the date. What do you think? Should we tell them everything?"

"Yes," he said.

"Wait a minute," said Will, rising and navigating for the bedroom door. "I want to hear this."

His stomach clenched. "Where are you going?"

Will grinned. "To take a leak. That all right with you?"

"Uh, would you mind using the other bathroom? This one's—stopped up."

Chrissie said, "It is? You didn't tell me that."

"I was going to. I was going to tell you all."

"Tell us what?" asked Ruth, coming out of the kitchen.

They looked at him expectantly. There was a long pause. His hands were shaking.

"I don't know where to start," he said. He tried a laugh but it came out wrong.

"Take your time," said Ruth. "We've got all evening."

Chrissie squeezed his arm. "Who needs a drink?" she said.

"Yes," he said. "Maybe we could have a drink first."

"What's this?" said Chrissie. She kicked the book bag on the floor, where the little girl had left it.

"Nothing," he said. "Here. Let me give you a hand."

He walked her to the kitchen.

"I can explain," he said.

"Explain what? You look tired, Jack. Was it an awful week?"

He took a deep breath. "Just this. I know it sounds crazy, but—"

On his way out of the small bathroom, Will stuck his head in the kitchen.

"Am I interrupting anything?"

"Of course not," said Chrissie.

"If this is a bad night for you two—"

There was a piercing scream from another part of the house.

He knew what it was before he got there.

The little girl was in the bedroom doorway, rubbing her eyes. She had on one of his shirts.

"Daddy?"

Ruth and Will looked at her. So did Chrissie. Then they looked at him.

"Oh, Daddy, there you are! I had a nightmare. There were people. Are they going now?"

"Daddy?" Chrissie stared at him as though she had never seen him before.

He focused on the little girl as his stomach clenched tighter.

"Tell them," he said.

"What?"

"Everything."

"I don't know what you mean, Daddy."

"All right," he said, "that's it. You're leaving—right now. I'll tell them the whole story myself. Come on. Let's go."

"No! I'll tell. How you picked me up at the bus stop and got me in the car in front of all those people? Or how you cheated and stole for me? Or the part where you gave me a bath and dried me and kissed me and we took a nap together?"

"I think we'd better be leaving," Ruth said.

"Yes," said Chrissie. "That might be a good idea. A very, very good idea."

"Wait." He followed her out. "Chris, I—"

"Don't," she said. "I have to think. And don't call me."

He watched numbly as the cars drove off. It started to rain softly, a misting drizzle in the trees above the mercury-vapor lamps. He watched until their red taillights turned the corner, like the reflection of a fire passing and moving on, leaving the street darker than ever.

"No," he said, hunching his shoulders. "No. No. No . . ."

He went back into the house.

"Where are you?" he shouted.

She was in the kitchen, helping herself to the food.

"Hi, Daddy," she said. "You got dinner for us. Just you and me. Thank you!"

"Who the hell do you think you are?"

He shook her violently.

"Daddy, you're hurting me!"

"I'm not your daddy and you know it, you little wretch."

"You're scaring me!"

"Don't bother to turn on the tears this time," he said. "It won't work."

She broke free and ran.

He braced himself against the table to stop shaking while he reached for the bottle of Scotch and poured a double shot.

Then he walked slowly, deliberately to the living room.

"Out," he said. "I don't care if it's raining. You've done enough. Get your things and—"

She had the phone in her hand.

"Daddy?" she said into the mouthpiece. "C-can you come get me? I don't know how to get home . . . and I'm scared!"

He tried to take the phone away, but she dodged him and kept on talking.

"It's cold . . . and dark . . . and there's a man here . . . I think he's crazy! Daddy, tell me what to do! I don't like this place!"

She gave a description of his street.

"Daddy, please come quick!"

Then she began to sing sweetly, a high, plaintive keening like the wind outside, and the rain that blew with it, settling so coldly over the house.

"Ladybird, ladybird, fly away home . . . your house is on fire . . . and your children will burn. . . ."

Her voice trailed off as she started to cry.

She hung up. She stopped crying. Then she went about her business, collecting her clothing and her book bag as though he no longer existed.

He stood there, wondering what it was that was supposed to happen next.

A SCENT OF ROSES

by Jeffrey Goddin

Jeffrey Goddin first appeared in The Year's Best Horror Stories *with his story, "The Smell of Cherries." Nine years later he offers us "A Scent of Roses." The man has a commitment to olfactory horror. In between he has published two horror novels,* The Living Dead *and* Blood of the Wolf, *and a variety of short stories, mainly horror.*

Born in a small town in Indiana on July 7, 1950, Goddin now resides in Bloomington, Indiana. There he teaches business communications and occasionally lectures middle school classes on creative writing. In common with other writers, Goddin gets all or part of some of his stories from dreams, explaining: "Particularly when our main source of income is rather boring, our psyches sometimes compensate by giving us a wild and crazy dream life, complete with plot, image, subtlety of scene—it's the best! This story derives from a visit with a mala Czeska devka to a very real and very strange place on the Ohio River, a weird dream, and various intoxicants."

She had not known that there was a part of the city like this. It looked almost like the fishing village under the Pontchartrain overpasses, north of her native New Orleans—rows of tin-roofed shacks, with beat-up brown, red, primer-colored pickups in front, and here and there boats up on blocks. But she was far from New Orleans, in an old decaying factory city along the

Ohio River. She couldn't decide whether this view was picturesque or just plain depressing.

The heat on this July day was definitely depressing. It had to be near a hundred in the humid river valley, and the air conditioning in Sergeant Gray's four-door Chevy just wasn't quite keeping up. She tried rolling down a window, but the gust of steamy breeze that came through was tainted with pollution. She rolled the window back up.

They'd stopped and talked with perhaps half a dozen people. None of them had seen a blonde eight-year-old girl, maybe still wearing the cutoffs and Bon Jovi t-shirt she'd had on when she disappeared.

The blacktop ended at the old floodwall. Gray took the Chevy through one of the permanently open flood-gates, onto a packed dirt road that seemed to head more directly toward the water. From this elevation Cindy could see a couple of speedboats shooting along the far, Kentucky side of the river, graceful roost-ertails of water crossing behind them. Closer in she saw a couple of small boats with tanned figures fish-ing. Maybe there's a breeze out there, she thought.

"Got any ideas?" she asked finally, turning to the narrow-faced patrolman. When he turned to look at her, his pale eyes crinkled, setting up smile wrinkles around his eyes. He seemed too good-humored for the kind of job they were on, and it irritated her a little bit. "Maybe. Ever heard of the New Vision Church?"

She frowned. It sounded vaguely familiar, but then, all the names of these new evangelical sects sounded alike to her.

"Nope, can't say that I have."

"There's a place they've taken over down at the end of the road. We've had a few complaints about them, off and on. Some weird stories, too. They have young people, orphans, in the church. Sanctioned by the Board of Health and all, but . . ." He shook his head. He had abruptly stopped smiling. "I had to go out there once or twice. Think they're all a little brain-washed, if you ask me. Run by a woman minister named Cambridge, tough lady, and boy do they do what she says!

"Anyway, long shot they might have heard something. They sell plants, and get quite a bit of trade."

"Plants?"

"For yards and landscape. Like in a nursery."

She nodded, looking back out at the water. She was worried about this girl. The flesh merchants cropped up now and then in the rural Midwest and just made young girls—and boys—disappear. She had met the girl's parents. Her father worked in a foundry, and was about to be laid off. Her mom was a substitute teacher in grade school. Very nice, simple people, and very worried. They probably wouldn't let their second daughter out of the house for months. And maybe they shouldn't.

Cindy had felt helpless, talking with them, trying to reassure them. Something awful had stepped into their safe, middle class world and they were in shock. She probably hadn't helped much at all.

The road snaked around by the river and, oddly enough, turned into blacktop again. Now, straight ahead, Cindy saw something that made her gasp.

"What the Hell is that?"

The building was huge and white, with a circular center, as if to house a rotunda, or a dome, flanked by two rectangular Bauhaus wings. The only visible windows were on ground level. It looked vaguely like some 1950s comic book rendition of alien architecture.

Gray chuckled.

"That's what the visitors used to say. It used to be a cultural tourist center for the old Malthus settlement, the communal living group that settled in the river valley near here. But nobody came, and it couldn't pay for itself, so it went broke and sat empty for years until the New Vision people took it over."

They got out of the car. She took a deep breath and was nearly overwhelmed by the river valley heat and humidity. The air smelled a little like a city down here, an edge of sulfur pollution.

She looked beyond the outlandish building and saw

a small greenhouse, multipaned slanted windows glinting in the sun like a fly's eyes, and military rows of flowers and shrubs in neat plots extending toward a group of trees perhaps fifty yards away, making an impressionistic setting of green and dark shadows on the river bank.

Some wooden picnic tables were set up under the trees, and Cindy saw what appeared to be a couple of dozen children and three or four adults, sitting at the tables. At this distance she couldn't see if they were eating, or having some kind of a service, or what.

She really felt kind of out of it. God, she hoped they'd get a lead on that girl soon! She found a handkerchief in her purse and mopped her forehead. Her shirt was formed to her sides with sweat like she'd been poured into it.

"Looks like some of them down there," she said, nodding at the trees.

Sergeant Gray smiled down at her. He was one of those people who made her very conscious of being short.

"You look about to wilt," he said. "Why don't you go inside and talk to whoever's official, and I'll go down and question the outdoor group."

She felt a wave of irrational irritation at being told what to do. Just the heat, she said to herself, just the heat.

"Suits me," she said sweetly. "Let's meet in the lobby, or whatever's by the front door of that monolith."

"Great." He started off purposefully across the grass toward the group under the trees. She walked up the path of hex-shaped steps toward the broad double doors of the weird white building.

The door opened smoothly, and a rush of cool dry air swept over her. This is a real breath of heaven, she thought. Heaven must have air conditioning!

She wandered into the building, and faced a smoothly convex inner wall. No reception desk, nothing but that gently swelling wall. It was odd, all this white. Bare interior furnishings, these white white walls that curved into aisles at regular intervals indeed made the place seem alien. A curve to her left, a curve to her right; and no indication of anything like a directory to help her find somebody to talk to.

A boy appeared suddenly, at one of the points where the walls curved together. He was running toward her. He was eight or nine, slender, with tousled blonde hair, wearing jeans and a white t-shirt. She had a sudden brush of fear, the way he ran right at her, his face expressionless. It was weird, almost like an animal charging he ran past her, pushed open the front door. She felt the brief touch of hot air that entered the building as he left, and had a sudden urge to be out there again in the natural sun. But no, she was going to explore this place.

She turned resolutely and walked into the incurved entrance to the passage the boy had run out of. The passage opened into a broad curving terrace that ran around more rooms in the center, a balustraded staircase rising gracefully just ahead of her, and another perhaps fifty yards to her right. The building was built like a Chinese box: a central core within an outer core.

She was bemused. She hadn't seen anyone in here except for the boy, and there were no signs or markers on any of the doors she'd passed. As if for something familiar, she tried to smell the river scent, and failed. No, this place was well-sealed. She began to walk to the right, around the central core.

Suddenly she realized what had seemed odd to her about the light. It was very even, oddly fluctuating. She looked up, and up, to see that there were skylight panes set in the distant ceiling. The odd occasional variation in the light must have to do with passing clouds. She suddenly realized that she was breathing shallowly, her body tense. She'd come in here to explore, to see if anyone could have heard of the missing girl—and while she was at it, to see if there was anything out of the ordinary about this "minister's" operation. Instead she'd fallen into a kind of dreamland.

I should have questioned that boy, she thought, but

he seemed to be in such a hurry. I should have gotten directions to an administrative office, but I didn't think of it.

She searched the slightly convex central walls for an elevator. She was still on the ground floor, and she'd seen no definite sign of an office, nor did she see any sign of an elevator. The few doors she came to were all alike, and unmarked. She tried all of them, and found them locked.

Out of patience, she walked on to the staircase and began to climb. It was one of those staircases that always made her a little nervous—it had openings between the stairs, through which you could see the empty air below. Looking into those openings brought back her childhood fear of heights full force. She held onto the banister, focussed her eyes straight ahead, and climbed. I'm closer to thirty than twenty, she thought, but I'm still not about to look down.

It seemed a long way between floors. She just kept going up those weird stairs. Up. Looking up was okay. She saw the next floor, not far away on the spiral. She almost jumped away from the stairs onto that smooth white floor set with greenish traction strips.

Nerves. For some reason I've got 'em bad today. She recalled why she was here. It was odd that she still hadn't seen anybody but that one boy. She wondered how Sergeant Gray was doing outside.

She went through the same routine as before on the second floor, looking for doors. She indeed found doors, all locked. No names, or even numbers above them to give any orientation. And she passed three more spiral stairwells that went both up and down.

It seemed that she walked for miles.

She looked at her watch. She had been exploring this place for half an hour, and had encountered nobody but one skittish boy. She was beginning to think the damned place was deserted.

Just how was this building laid out, anyway? If it was a place where church members lived, worked and worshiped, there had to be living areas, and areas for other activities. The second floor was definitely not very active.

Well, maybe one more try. She walked around the circular walls, past the closed doors of more unknown, unmarked rooms until, once again, she saw one of the spiral stairwells. She knew now that they couldn't be all in the center of the building. She had passed four stairwells altogether. Maybe they were each in a quarter of the building?

Yet she'd only seen one on the ground floor.

It was confusing. She climbed the stairwell, careful not to look down, and quickly reached another floor.

This floor was much like the others, but as she stood on the landing, she saw that there was an unusual effect to the walls. Near her, they were off-white, as was most of the building, but as they receded into that gentle curvature that characterized the place, so the off-white faded into an ivory, then into a very pale blue, that seemed to darken into distance. It was pretty, but it was an effect she'd never seen in any functional building. She was beginning to get weirded out.

Then she heard the chanting: somewhere above her, voices raised in some kind of chant that seemed to be Latin, but not a Latin of any sort she'd ever heard in church. The chant rumbled on, seeming to flow down the stairwell, mostly male voices picking up a rhythm and counterpoint that seemed somehow menacing, as do those medieval crusader songs of going off to war.

She felt the vibration in the landing, then. Whoever was chanting was coming down the stairwell.

Her feelings were mixed. It seemed she'd been searching for someone to talk with in this weird building for ages. But was this something she'd want to interrupt?

As the chanting drew closer, the faint vibration in the metal at her feet more noticeable, so the tone became increasingly strange. She wished she knew Latin, for what these voices were chanting of was definitely something more emotional than anything she'd heard in parish services—darkly emotional, something of night, and blood, and death . . .

She shivered, seemed to see the smoke of burning cities under a cerulean sky, to hear the screams of people slashed by the sword, and left to die beneath an unforgiving sun—and cries of rape, of the anguish of children stolen from their parents' arms.

She blinked. What the Hell was happening to her? The chanting was very loud now, and she wondered what would happen when those descending found her wandering, unescorted, in the upper reaches of their building. That rhythm! She almost heard the sound of tabors and sackbuts mingled with the medieval cadence, now utterly menacing, promising death and destruction, and the vengeance of an unforgiving God.

They had to be just above her. In a few moments they'd come into view. What the Hell would they look like?

Her nerve broke. She began to skip back down the stairwell, trying not to look between the stairs, trying to remember which floor had the stairs that led to the ground level. She'd had enough of this. She'd get back with Gray and see what he'd found out, and then maybe together they could turn up someone who might know something.

She descended one level, two, three, four. She realized that she'd missed the floor she sought, but at least she could no longer hear that menacing cadence.

Then the stairs stopped going down. I've gone below ground level, she thought. What the Hell? It was another place to explore. She walked down the pale white corridor that seemed dimmer than those above, as if lights were out, or the indirect lighting here were not so strong. Also, this corridor seemed somehow older, and the walls had a look more of polished stone than the hardshell plaster she'd seen above.

The corridor ended abruptly at a doorway, just in front of her. Through the doorway was a wall-sized picture of an outdoor scene: grass, low bush plants, a path of some sort under a pale overcast, like a heat-haze sky.

She blinked. The scene had depth, three dimensions. It wasn't a picture.

Something was wrong here—wrong with a wrongness that defied description. She looked through the doorway at that mimicry of verdure, and saw the scene as oddly misty. It was warmer down here, she could feel it. It was almost as if, in descending, she'd come upon some inversion of the natural order of things.

Somewhere to her rear was the way back up and out of this place. Yet her sense of mission combined with her feeling of unwholesome mystery to propel her forward, through that misty doorway.

She was in a room, a very odd room, with green things growing from a ground that seemed half earth, half moldy carpets of mismatched greens, blues, muted browns. Above her was a kind of broad pale translucent ceiling that had a faint violet hue about it, as if it were some huge growlite. The air was heavy with water vapor, like the air in a greenhouse. Her lungs felt full when she inhaled, and the soil/carpet mix was slightly yielding as she walked.

Some of the plants were tall, a lovely blue-green. She thought she recognized a stand of bamboo—and a cluster of tall marijuana plants reaching well above her height, though the shapes of the notched leaves were somehow not quite right. If they were growing marijuana here, that would perhaps account for some of the mystery. Still . . .

She walked on across the room, and saw another doorway, very roughly oval, leading off into distance. She passed through, and was in what seemed a blue-white misty tunnel, with brightness that promised another room at the end.

She passed through the tunnel into another circular room, with the same carpet strewn earth. This room was smaller, and she could see a number of doorways opening off of it, ahead, and to her left and right.

Now she became more aware of the smell of the place, a smell of rancid organic decay oddly mingled with a sickly sweet scent. Roses, it was like roses, but not the real flower, more like the artificial scent of roses. A faint breeze moved in the room, coming from her right, and the scent seemed to be borne on this breeze.

She actually cried out when a woman appeared in one of the doorways to her left. The woman was about thirty, her dark hair on top of her head, wearing the kind of pale summer suit that someone who worked in a visitor's center might wear. She stopped dead when she saw Cindy, and seemed to have trouble not shouting.

"You shouldn't be here!" Her voice was almost panicked. "Get out of here at once!"

Cindy started to reply, but the look on this woman's face silenced her. She seemed to be having a fit of some kind. The woman's mouth gaped wide, showing pink gums around her teeth in something like a snarl, and her eyes were open so widely as to make her face look like the mask of a demon.

"You . . ." Saliva drooled down her chin and spotted her pristine summer suit. She took a step forward, hands half clenched into claws.

Cindy ran. She ran through the first doorway she came to, on her right.

"No! Not in there!" The woman screamed. Cindy ran all the harder.

This corridor was narrower, and was actually filled with mist, and with that white glow that seemed to emanate from walls and ceiling. That sickly smell of artificial roses was even stronger here, as was the decay smell. She ran and ran and came out into another oval room.

She was startled into motionlessness, her eyes trying to take in what she saw, her brain refusing to process the information.

In the center of the room was something like a pool, with a blue-tiled coping, though somehow it reminded her more of a well. From the pool swelled blue-white clouds of smoky mist. Just to the right of the pool stood a strange tableau: a tall, white-haired man in a dark suit, a tall blonde woman in jeans and white man's shirt, a stocky, round-faced woman in a dark suit who had a definite air of authority, and two early teenaged boys who held another, smaller boy between them on a kind of inclined white couch.

Cindy saw with a shock that this captive boy's feet were bound to the base of the couch by a thin silvery chain hooked through metal rings that seemed to be there for this express purpose, though the grasp of the two older boys was all that held his shoulders down. And she recognized the boy—it was the same boy she'd seen running through the building when she'd first arrived.

She stood very still, uncertain how to take this scene. The sickly sweet air seemed to be draining all her initiative. As she watched, two things happened almost simultaneously. The young boy saw her, and his doe brown eyes widened, his mouth stretching into a soundless scream for help.

And a thick black vapor that was like the supple column of a tree, or a serpent swollen to impossible thickness, arched from the pool amidst the white vapors and poured obscenely over the boy's body. The boy began to thrash frantically, trying to free himself from the hands that gripped his shoulders, kicking at the chain that bound his feet.

The black vapor closed over the boy's writhing form, and Cindy thought she heard his scream, suddenly choked off. She gagged as she smelled a scent like boiled pork. A strong hand jerked her around. Cindy looked into the eyes of the woman she'd left in the other room. The woman held her gaze like a cruel lover, and there was something so perversely self-satisfied in that look that it sent Cindy's nerves over the edge.

She lashed out, felt her fist come up hard under the woman's jaw. She plunged by the staggering woman into the corridor, but the dense air made it impossible to breathe, and the soft ground was slowing her steps, and her lungs strained for oxygen, and she found her legs collapsing under her. It seemed she fell slowly, as if easing herself into a soft seat. Wavy fronds of green were moving languidly in front of her face, and the heavy scented air was drugging her, slowing her breathing. It was so hard to think! She reached out to touch delicate green leaves, but her eyes closed before she completed the motion.

She heard voices. She lay on something soft, but firm, and she was somewhere much cooler than before. She knew that she had been asleep, or passed out. She had a splitting headache. She wanted to be up, get some water, aspirin. But some instinct made her stay motionless, her eyes closed. The first voice she heard was Sergeant Gray's:

"Is she going to be all right?"

A woman's voice, mature, cultured:

"Certainly. She breathed too much methane and carbon monoxide when she was running down there. The plants love the carbon monoxide, so we keep the pumps on most of the time. The effects will wear off soon."

"Good. I'd rather nothing happened to her."

"What happens to her remains to be seen." The woman's voice changed, went hard. "Why did you bring an investigator here?"

"I brought her here because she'd have found the place on her own sooner or later. I never thought that she'd stumble into your sanctuary. What did she see, exactly?"

"She saw the God taking the last one you sent us."

"Oh Christ. What'll we do?"

"It depends on what she remembers. She may think it was all a dream."

"Maybe, but she's a sharp one. I don't want to jeopardize our relationship, though. You've definitely put a dent in our street people problem. For those who know, your work is appreciated."

"We're pleased to be of service. And the old God is happy," said the woman. "Long years he waited, for those with the sense to worship him again. But he only takes what he needs of them. The rest of their bodies, the dross, nourish our plants well." Cindy wished that she could wake up from this awful dream. Yet she knew that what she heard was no dream at all. It was too strange to fully take in yet, but she'd heard the statement about street people very clearly. The woman Gray was talking with must be the minister, Cambridge. Gray and Cambridge had worked something out together, involving street people, and an old God . . .

She had a sudden awful insight into that scent of roses that pervaded the lower corridors. If not for that scent, she'd have recognized the sharp edge of decay in the air—what fed the plants, their unholy nourishment of lost children. Even now, in this closed room, she could faintly smell it, that sickly rose fragrance, with the acid edge of underlying decomposition.

Some weird cult was in operation here, a cult that involved murder and kidnapping. She had to get out, get the information to a cop who wasn't crooked. She'd really have to calculate how to play this one. Pretend to wake up, pretend she'd forgotten what happened.

The policeman's voice cut in on her thoughts.

"Is it possible she'll just forget what she saw?" asked Gray.

The minister's tone was ironic:

"She's been listening to us for several minutes now. Why don't we ask her?"

The woman knew, had known all along that Cindy was feigning sleep. Time to get moving. Cindy tried to roll off of the low couch as she opened her eyes and rapidly assessed the plain white room, the stocky woman in a gray business suit, Sergeant Gray. But strong hands immediately gripped her shoulders, and another hand covered her forehead, skillfully holding her in position. She thrashed her legs, and someone else, a tall, teenaged boy with a thatch of wild black hair, moved quickly to grab her ankles. He blushed as her skirt rose up her thighs, but he didn't loosen his grip.

Cindy began to talk fast.

"You can't get away with this. You can't just make

me disappear. This is all going to come out anyway . . ." Sergeant Gray wasn't even looking at her. The Cambridge woman left the room and returned quickly with a white plastic bottle and a cloth. She upended the bottle over the cloth, then walked to Cindy's side.

"Simple chloroform," said the minister. "Painless."

Cindy began to scream, but there was no one anywhere near who might help her. The cloth, with its sweet, sweet fumes, was pressed over her mouth, and she couldn't help but inhale. A menthol numbness moved down her throat into her chest. Soon she couldn't move at all.

But she didn't pass out entirely. She was lifted from the couch and carried for several minutes, and when she was put down on another smooth couch, she opened her eyes and stared, half-comprehending, at the blue-tiled coping around the pool in the floor. Part of her tried to be frightened, but her nerves were numb, her body cool, floating, and even fear had little reality. She breathed the sickly scent of artificial roses, and a dense form of black vapor coiled from the pool and enveloped her body.

She had been cool. Now she was warm, growing warmer in darkness moist like the underbelly of the earth after rain, where things are decaying with minute phosphorescence to feed the roots of green growing things. She knew she wasn't dreaming, but she could put no familiar feeling to the soft tingling darkness that began to enter her at her nose, her lips, her ears, her vagina and anus. Its invasion of her was erotic, in the sense that death is erotic; the touch was minutely thorough, caressing every nerve of her body with a fierce possessiveness, and then plunging into her mind and touching every thought. In her mind, she was growth and decay at once. She felt her nerves extend like tendrils. She felt her cells die and begin the slow process of being flushed from her body. And she felt this presence as it fingered her oldest and most private memories like a pile of photographs, pausing here, shuffling there, discarding what it had no interest in. It was rape, of a sort, a rape of the mind. The God barely sniffed her sex, an idle reflex in passing.

It was so fast, so thorough, that she hardly felt the sense of violation—that is, until it came to her most recent memories, her entrance into the strange white building, her search, her discovery in the lower levels, her flight. Here the entity ripped and tore like a scraping abortion and she screamed inside as portions of her mind were left raw and bloody, the electrical matrix of her memories blasted and erased. She screamed in her mind with the incredible agony of it, and she screamed out loud at this true embrace of the God.

And when the God was finished, it left her body abruptly, receding, she knew, down the well with the blue tiled coping, leaving her body limp, barely breathing, on a smooth white couch. She awoke sitting in the patrol car, and automatically ran a hand over her sweaty face. Through the window she saw the oily river carrying its invisible burden, leaves, sticks, fish, bits of human flotsam and jetsam, ever southward toward the Gulf. She stretched, looked at her watch. She couldn't believe her eyes. She must have slept for hours.

She jumped as Sergeant Gray opened the door and slid into the car.

"Any luck?" he asked.

She shook her head.

"Couldn't find anybody at all in the building. It's like an empty museum. Guess I just came back and went to sleep in the car—but I don't even remember coming back here." Gray smiled at her.

"You're a little spacey," he said. "Me too. Hot as Hell in this Goddamned valley." He started the car and turned on the air conditioning. "I didn't do any good either. They haven't seen or heard of the girl. But it was worth a try."

"Sure," she said, feeling a twinge of pain in the back of her head, and reaching around to find a small lump there. And how the Hell had she done that?

Maybe this arrogant cop is right, and I am getting spacey, she thought.

"I'm out of it," she said. "Let's call it a day."

"Suits me." Gray smiled that boyish smile of his. "Let's get the Hell out of here!"

Cindy never did get any leads on the girl. She finally had to give it up, and she was backlogged with basic counseling stuff anyway, and there were plenty of other missing kids when she had the time to run investigations. After a while the girl in the Bon Jovi t-shirt just became a name in a file.

A year passed, and Cindy moved to Chicago, and went back to college to get the next degree. Soon that summer in the old river city began to seem a lot like a weird dream.

There was only really one change in her psyche dating from that summer. She developed a near hatred for roses. But then, she'd never much liked roses anyway. They always made her think of hospitals, and funerals. Just the smell of them made her want to throw up.

ROOT CELLAR

by Nancy Kilpatrick

Nancy Kilpatrick is a newcomer to The Year's Best Horror Stories *and, indeed, to horror fiction. She has placed stories recently in various small press magazines, as well as in three anthologies just published:* Freak Show, Book of Shadows, *and* Northern Frights. *At the moment her agent is trying to market a horror novel and a horror trilogy. No elves, one assumes.*

Born in Philadelphia, Pennsylvania, Kilpatrick now lives in Toronto with her Canadian husband. She confesses to be "fascinated with the psychological and mythological and generally the shadowy side of life (why else would I write horror?), with a penchant for the archetypal vampire." Just when I'd sworn never to read another vampire story . . .

As Vadim struggled to get out of the Toyota, rain slammed him back. Nearby maple branches, bereft of leaves, clung to one another. The mid-winter sky was dead-gray but he noticed black storm clouds rush to squelch even that little light.

Five strides and Vadim hit the porch of the farmhouse, just as thunder broke. Lightning cracked a willow across the road, severing a branch. An omen, he thought, shivering, hating himself for even thinking that way. The way *she* had taught him to think. He hurried indoors.

The "new" part of his grandmother's house, built

seventy-five years ago, looked the same. Too-tall ceilings. Cavernous rooms. Sparsely-patterned wallpaper. Under the dust covers, like stern guardians, lay furniture Vadim had no intention of exposing. His memories were olfactory and reeked of blood and decay. He would not be here now if Lola had not gone out of the country. Lola, his younger sister, was still a baby at twenty. Lola desperately pleaded for specific memorabilia before he boarded up the property forever.

Vadim had no such desires. His memories of years spent in this house were of dead space, the weighted stillness as heavy as his grandmother's hand. He had distanced himself mentally and eventually physically from her insidiousness. And soon the disconnection would be permanent.

He glanced into the kitchen. The electricity had been shut off three months ago, but lightning flashed; it was frightening how nothing had changed. Except the corner. No willow switch stood ready for duty. Still, he would not have been surprised to see his grandmother's severe face in the doorway or hear her diseased rantings echo through the rooms.

Vadim went to the cupboard above and to the left of the sink. Second shelf at the back. He retrieved the empty sugar bowl with the butterfly on the lid that Lola wanted. He felt no sentimental feelings, just a sense of claustrophobia, as if the past were crushed against the present, intent on devouring the boundaries, desperate to consume it. He hurried upstairs.

The master bedroom his grandparents had shared until sixteen years ago when Grandpa Bentz died was as silent as ever. The lifeless blue duvet had been flung across the foot of the bed. His grandmother ended her existence wrapped in that comforter, alone in a pool of foul-smelling excrement. Alone until her rotting flesh had been discovered. "Death only comforts the living," she had said with authority often enough. The clock in the corner no longer ticked and he was grateful.

He crossed the short hallway and took the attic

stairs to the cramped and airless rooms to which he and Lola had once been banished. In his: wall cracks, as familiar and permanent as the creases of disapproval in his grandmother's face. A small dresser, its mirror wavy with age, unable to offer a true reflection. Vadim's single bed—springs that creaked so easily he had been afraid to breathe. That had creaked too often in rhythm to willow switches imprinting the family's ancient beliefs beyond his bare skin and deep into his cells.

In Lola's room he found the glass unicorn music box and carried it and the sugar bowl down the narrower back stairs leading to the old part. He entered a shabby room that dated back two hundred years. Back to the fierce great-great-grandparents whom he had heard so much about. The ancestors who had immigrated from the old country where they had been persecuted. He had never felt safe in this part of the house.

Vadim paused. Outside black clouds smothered all light. He trembled as he reached into his raincoat pocket to pull out the flashlight. The sugar bowl slipped from his fingers. It hit the sloped hardwood and, even before he dropped the beam into the pieces, Vadim knew it had shattered. Fear gripped him, the old, suffocating terror. But no ghost bent on punishment materialized. He exhaled; his nerves were on edge.

A flicker of blue lightning showed him something peculiar and Vadim ran the flashlight beam over the sills of the three large windows. "Mother of . . ." he whispered. Each sill was littered with fly carcasses, an inch thick. And the floor below the windows. And by the door. Thousands. No, tens of thousands. Black and iridescent green. Crisp hollowed shells that crunched beneath his soles. They clustered near the routes of egress but for them there had been no escape from this place.

Vadim no longer worried about the sugar bowl, he just wanted out before this tomb-of-the-dead sealed him in. But Lola had only asked for one thing more.

Another object to cement her fantasy of happy memories and relegate the reality to insubstantial phantoms. The two of them were all that was left now. He needed her to ground him in the present, a world cleansed of superstition. Take it easy, he thought. Grandma Bentz is gone. I'll be out of here in five minutes.

The door to the root cellar was locked, as it always had been, but he broke the rusted padlock easily. The hinges squeaked as the door, warped from age and the moisture imbedded in this part of the house, scraped the floor.

Moldy air wafted out. Vadim aimed his light like a weapon into the appalling darkness. Ashamed, he watched his hand shake and heard ragged breath.

I can't do it, he thought. Memories of nights spent in the root cellar, crouched beneath the stairs, the smell of earth and vegetation and rot clogging his nostrils. And the sounds. Like nothing he had heard since, except in dreams. Over time he had learned to hum softly, loud enough to cover the noise, low enough not to bring down Grandma Bentz.

The doll Lola needed had been buried in a storage trunk for a decade and a half. The trunk in the cellar. Now that he'd broken the sugar bowl, there was no way to avoid getting it.

He stepped down into the dark pit. Cobwebs attacked his face and he gasped. "Weakling!" he admonished, repeating the word hurled so often at him. A word that must have traveled through generations.

Along the left of the stairs was a wall of shelves stocked with pickles and preserves. He read the aging labels from the lowest shelf up: chili sauce; corn relish; pickled cauliflower; carrots and dills dating back to 1790. A jar of murky contents, the yellowed label smudged. Beets, maybe. These had been here when he was a child, since before his grandmother was a girl. Every generation added to the store and Grandma Bentz contributed the row second from the top. She had not allowed any of the jars to be touched, calling them, "Memories." Food uneaten. Life preserved forever.

The steps creaked in familiar spots as Vadim made his way to the dirt floor. He waved the light into each corner. The steamer trunk sat furthest from the stairs. In front of the metal door.

He placed the unicorn securely in his coat pocket and tucked the flashlight under one arm, ready to tackle this lock. But the latch was open, as if someone had expected him to come this way. Vadim glanced at the door and listened. Nothing.

He lifted the lid of the trunk. On the left, as if unaware of her surroundings, Lola's porcelain doll grinned up at him.

Only two other objects competed for his attention. A piece of barn board with post cards nailed to it. A small black coffin.

At the sight of the coffin, Vadim shook with fear and rage. Tears threatened to swell over his eyelids and he could not stop himself from yelling "Bitch!" She knew him so well. She had tricked him. Again.

He was startled by a noise behind the door. A rat. Or his imagination. He did not believe either.

Vadim wanted to grab the doll and bolt but decades of anger solidified. And he was curious. He lifted the board and ran the light from left to right along both rows. Each Victorian card was a pastel sketch. Together the eight pictures told a story:

WOMAN ALONE, HAPPILY SWINGING ON PORCH SWING.
MAN IN CLOAK APPROACHES.
MAN KISSES WOMAN ON NECK.
WOMAN DEAD IN COFFIN.
WOMAN RISES TO JOIN MAN.
MAN AND WOMAN KISS BOY ON NECK.
BOY DEAD IN COFFIN.
BOY RISES TO JOIN WOMAN AND MAN.

A quaint gothic record of family madness, he thought. To be handed down from generation to generation with the silver. But he had no intention of passing it further.

Vadim placed the board carefully back into the trunk. He snatched up the doll and stuffed it in his other pocket, ready to abandon this prison forever. Yet he felt compelled to look inside the coffin. She must have known he would. "You'll die of curiosity," Grandma Bentz had always predicted. He had believed she intended to fulfill that prophesy.

He picked up the crude wooden box and shook it but had no sense of what lay within. Less than a foot long, three inches at the widest part, shaped like an old-fashioned casket. A morbid miniature in flat black. The dead crawled from his memory: A nighthawk he had buried in a box he made, much like this one. His mother and father, killed in a barn fire. Grandpa Bentz—who knows how he died. It was only his grandmother's corpse he had not viewed. Neither he nor Lola attended the service. Nor went to the cemetery. "If you don't witness the dead, how do you know they are?" Grandma Bentz had repeated at every demise, and the words haunted him now.

Vadim used his car key to pry between the lid and the box. The birch was hard and he was careful to wedge the metal in and lift the nails without damaging the wood. Images formed in his mind, gruesome pictures, parts severed from the living, stolen away from the light, drained of vitality, suspended in darkness forever to shrivel and emaciate slowly.

The lid was a quarter inch above the box and he was sweating. Suddenly time and space expanded. Endless. Hopeless. The eternity he had always feared clawed at the edges of his consciousness.

There was no point in hesitating and Vadim no longer considered it. Instead he struggled to defend himself from his most recent ancestor's bequest. A gift that he would leave to rot in the belly of this house. That would end with him and Lola, the last of a tortured line.

He yanked the lid away. The root cellar became a frozen grave. "What did you expect?" he chided, his voice unfamiliar and cold in the hollowness.

A sharp wooden stake lay inside the casket. Who

had she intended it for? She had forced him to this point just as she had meticulously nurtured every dark and savage impulse in him. He threw his head back and laughed until tears flowed and then he began to howl like the doomed animal he felt himself to be. Scratching behind the door brought him to his senses.

Vadim took the stake out and dropped the coffin back into the trunk then slammed the lid. The sound was heavy and final in the stillness. But he was not sure what to do. Every possibility seemed annihilating. And he had no idea which act would be giving in to her iron will and which constituted resisting.

While he waited, thinking, listening, Vadim spun the stake in his fingers, the tip pointing toward him and then away. Him. Away. But he did not wait for long. All too soon the metal door opened inward.

AN EYE FOR AN EYE

by Michael A. Arnzen

Michael A. Arnzen is not only a newcomer to The Year's Best Horror Stories, *but one of the younger writers to appear as well. Born in Amityville, New York (good start for a horror writer) on May 17, 1967, Arnzen now lives in Pueblo, Colorado, where he has problems finding newsstands that stock the magazines he writes for—at least, in the case of this story, from* Outlaw Biker's Tattoo Revue. *Tough to find around here, too.*

Arnzen served in Germany in the Army Signal Corps, where, he explains: "I used to write horror stories to pass around the platoon to kill the boredom at night while in the field." After the Army, he earned a B.A. in English from the University of Southern Colorado, and is currently pursuing graduate work. He has been writing and selling horror stories and poetry for about four years, and has about a hundred published works in everything from slick magazines to small press publications. He is now editing a chapbook of psychological horror verse, entitled Psychos. *The following story is also an excerpt from his novel,* Grave Markings, *forthcoming from Dell in 1993. Tattoos not included.*

The homeless biker walked his rusty ol' Harley up to my doorstep, leaned it up against the brick wall outside, and trotted into my tattoo shop like he owned the place. He always showed up on Thursday afternoons, when business was deader than Ted Bundy. I never could tell if Thursdays sucked because that's just the way Thursdays were, or if people avoided the place like the plague because that's when *he* was there, all scraggly and stinking like a urinal.

I know, I should have kicked the piss-stained fucker out the door the first day he walked in. But I'd taken to the poor beggar, and I pitied his poverty-stricken life. The only thing that made his life worth living was his dilapidated frame of a scooter, and I had to give him credit for that.

He called himself One-Eyed Jack, and I figured that was because he wore a black patch on his eye . . . whether it was for show or not I couldn't tell, but because of the grime on it, the patch looked legit. His clothes were in tatters: the beer-stained long underwear shirt he wore was frayed at the bottom, where his lint-filled belly button peeked out over ratty and stringy denim jeans. He didn't have any tats of his own, and looked naked to me without them. If he didn't drag his broken-down bike along with him wherever he went, you wouldn't have known he was once a biker . . . you'd just think he was some weird-looking bum with a silly patch on his right eye.

Anyway, he came in that Thursday and plopped his ass down in the seat where my patrons either sit to read mags when I'm busy or to bullshit when I'm not. For two months going, Jack always came in to bullshit, since he couldn't afford my rates, meager as they were.

"Hey, Mick, how's biz?" He always asked the same thing when he came inside, and I always ignored it. His voice grumbled like tires spinning in gravel when he spoke, and there was something buried inside the sound that said "I'm hungry," though he was too proud to actually say the words.

He picked up one of my art books, and started flipping through the laminated pages. From the way he "oohed" and "ahhed" you'd think he was my Number One Fan. I guess he really was, though I had my regulars, who paid good money for my work. But he seemed to *really* appreciate my skill. Maybe that was why I took such a liking to him, when no one else in their right mind would.

After a half hour of going through his routine, he tossed the book down on the coffee table, and looked me square in the eye. "I got a proposition for ya, Mick. Wanna hear it?"

"What?" My reply was flat, though I was a bit thrown off by the way the hungry sound of his voice changed from wheels rumbling in gravel to new tires gracing a smooth blacktop. He sounded sure of himself, like the asshole salesmen I sometimes get at the shop.

"If you'll break down and give me a tattoo, I'll give you my Harley."

His bike was shit, but I couldn't believe he was offering his most prized possession to me. Still, I said, "No," folding my heavily-inked forearms across my chest for emphasis.

"I'll work for you, then. I can sweep up the place, and I know a little bit about . . ."

"No."

"Aw, c'mon, Mick. You know I'm good for it."

"No," I said again. Did he really think I'd waste my precious time and colors on him?

"Wait, wait," he said, lifting his cheeks to dig into the back pocket of his jeans. "Before you make a decision, I got somethin' I want you to check out." He dug harder into his back pocket, looking like he was scratching hemorrhoids. After awhile he withdrew a crumpled piece of paper, unfolded it, and handed it to me, smiling his gap-toothed pirate's grin at me.

I looked at the paper. It was a glossy page ripped out of a magazine, with a slick close-up photo of some Yuppie-looking faggot on one side. The Yuppie—probably one of those male fashion models—smiled up from the page at me, turning my stomach. I flipped the paper over, looking for something significant. "What the hell is this?"

"The guy, Mick, look at the guy."

I stared at the faggot gawking up from the page. "What about him? You go for queers?"

"I want his eye."

"What?"

I looked up at One-Eyed Jack. He had a pistol pointed at my face. It looked loaded, and he cocked it for emphasis. "I want his eye, Mick. And I want it today."

Fucking Thursdays.

Since he'd been hanging around my shop so much, he knew where I kept my .44, and helped himself to it. Next he drew the blinds and locked the door.

Then, when the room was nice and shadowy, he ripped off his patch, and tossed it on the floor, revealing his disfigured face. The right side of his face was smooth and pale, as if both his eyeball and eyebrow had been erased clean off. Unlike the other side of his face, there was no sunken-in socket . . . it was just a flat surface of white virgin flesh.

"What are you starin' at?" he asked, wiggling the gun at me.

"Nothin', Jack. Nothing at all."

"Hey, don't get cocky with me, man. I gave you a chance at doin' this the easy way. I thought you were different, Mick. But you're not—you're as stingy as the rest of the bastards that spit on me when they walk by the homeless hangout every day."

I didn't say anything. He was obviously teetering on the edge, and I wasn't gonna be the one to push him over it—not with a gun in each of his shaking hands.

His one good eye rolled around in its socket, as he considered his options. Then he sighed. "Now," he said, waltzing over to my barber's chair and falling into it. "I want you to give me an eye, just like the ones the guy in that picture has." He used the tip of my .44 as a pointer, tapping it against the ugly side of his face: "I want you to ink it in, right here." I hoped the gun would go off while he had it near his temple, but nothing happened.

There was nothing I could do, except to humor him

and do what he said. Being twice his size, I really felt like an asshole following his orders, but I knew he was crazed enough to shoot. So I got my needles prepped for the job.

With hummer in hand, I sat down on my stool and tried to decide where to begin. The spot he wanted me to ink looked like it would pop like a boil if I touched it. It wasn't leathery like real skin—it was smooth and alien. I admit I was a little too spooked to go near it.

I felt a barrel nudge into my ribs. "And you better do a good job, too. I've seen your other stuff—and it really is good art—but I want your best. It has to look *real.*" He poked harder with the pistol. "Get it?"

I nodded. He wasn't making my job any easier.

I went to work, laying down the outline, using the magazine photo for reference. The Yuppie's eye color was different than Jack's, but I wasn't gonna question his word. I inked it in, line for line, and gave him a matching eyebrow to make up for it. All the while I could have sworn I felt something moving beneath Jack's skin, as if the eyeball was still there beneath the flesh, trying to watch every move I made, checking every dot I laid down for accuracy. It was fucking eerie.

Jack didn't do too much fidgeting like most first-timers. He just kept the gun trained on me, with his muscles locked. His good eye watered, but he didn't mind the small tears that dribbled out when he blinked. I think he kinda liked the pain.

After about an hour of inking his weird flesh, the hum of the needle began to get on my nerves. It was spooking me bad, so I tried to make conversation, which I would have done anyway under normal circumstances. My first words sounded forced: "What's the story, Jack?"

"No story."

I tried to keep my voice steady. "Where'd you get the gun?"

"It's mine, Mick." His voice sounded like it was softening. I hoped he was calming down. "I've had it for a long time. Other than my bike, it's all I've really got left."

"Uh-huh." The tone of his voice proved to me that he had something to get off his chest. I waited.

"I guess I should level with you. Can't hurt none, since after you finish you'll never see me again, and I don't think you're the sort to call the cops." He lifted a cigarette from the pack I keep for customers on a nearby table, and fired it up. His gun was still in hand, but he had unloaded my .44 and set it on the table.

"I'm on the run. This homeless look is just a cover. I'm filthy rich, actually, but my money is stashed, and I can't touch the stuff till I know the time is right, when no one can finger me. That's part of the reason I want the eye, Mick."

"Uh-huh," I said, egging him on. I wasn't sure if he was telling the truth or if he was one brick short, but I didn't really give a damn with that gun pointed at my chest.

"See, they had an A.P.B. out on me. I saw a wanted poster at the fucking post office . . . can you believe that shit? It even had a picture of me and my patch on it. Probably got it from one of those security cameras in the bank I did. Anyway, there I was, my face hanging in the post office for the world to see: WANTED. I got the fuck out of that post office, but I'll never forget the line on that wanted poster, in bold print: 'DISTINGUISHING MARKS/FEATURES: Missing right eye. Perpetrator wears black patch to cover scar.' " His face flushed red, and I could feel the heat of anger boiling in his skin. "How the hell could I beat that rap? Anyone could identify me! I'm a walking freak show."

His hand was twitching—the one holding the gun. "So you decided to hide out with the bums at the park, eh?"

He paused a minute, then chuckled. He was glad to see someone could appreciate the logic of his cover. "Yeah! I figured everyone ignores them. Hell, no one wants to make eye contact with a bum. And if they do . . . well, they're all freaks there anyway, so I fit right in. It's the perfect hideout, a foolproof cover!" He laughed again. "I even fooled you, Mick!"

I began shading in the green iris of the eye I had drawn. I was almost done, and—hopefully—Jack was almost out of my life. Something about the way he was so proud of himself made my stomach turn. He was no better than the people who he said spit on the homeless: he was using them, and that's even worse. I pitied Jack more than I had before. But I had to ask: "So what's the deal? Why do you want this tattoo?"

"You just don't get it, do ya?" He was still smiling his pirate's grin, but it looked pathetic without his patch on. "I've been casing you, and the city, too. But I've had it with this bum routine. I'm coming out of hiding, so I can get my money and get the fuck out of here." His voice was stressed, and raised in pitch. "And I wanna look *normal*, so no one will see my fucking 'distinguishing feature.' I'm sick of being old *One-Eyed* Jack. This tattoo is the perfect solution to all my troubles."

Pathetic. Who the hell did he think he was gonna fool?

I quickly detailed the finishing touches, and leaned back to look at my work. It was the most realistic piece of art I had ever seen . . . more lifelike than the photo I had cribbed it from. The whites were off-white and slightly veined, the pupil had a shining wet gleam on it, the brow was a tad disheveled so as not to look as if every hair had been airbrushed. It appeared as natural on his face as the other one, despite their opposing colors of blue and green. It *was* my best. Grace under pressure, I guess.

I handed him a mirror, and the minute he saw it he howled, amazed at its perfection: "You did it! I can't believe you fucking did it!" Then he *really* lost his marbles.

It was a sick sight: Jack's one eye rolling around on his face like a loose ball bearing as he gawked at his new image. His real eye looked inhuman compared to the tat as he oggled the mirror. In opposition, the tattoo looked peacefully forward in the steady look of a sane man. The tattoo was so good, so *real*, that it was obvious an eye like that didn't belong on Jack's twisted, psychotic face. He looked like that TV detective—Columbo—on acid.

He was so soaked-up in himself, that he had forgotten the gun was in his hand. It lolled side-to-side on his lap, begging for me to reach out and disarm the lunatic.

I did. He didn't even notice. He just sat there, still staring at his ugly mug in the mirror.

I pointed the gun at him. He might as well have been in another world, a world that only he could see.

He was whispering to himself, uttering what sounded like baby talk. I leaned an ear in closer. Over and over, he spoke with the disjointed and maniacal voice of a madman: "I can see, I can see . . . my God, I CAN SEE WITH BOTH EYES!"

I didn't even bother trying to intimidate him with the gun. Still, I kept it trained on him while I picked up the phone and dialed. All the while he was telling himself that he could see, describing the psychedelic visions he saw. It was pathetic.

No, I didn't call the cops. He was right; I'm not the sort to go narcing on a man who's down on his luck. I called the asylum, and they came and jacketed him. He screamed when they took the mirror out of his hands, but they injected him with some sort of drug to knock him out so he could be carted away without a struggle. As they dragged him by the shoulders out the door of my shop, his left eyelid was closed and fluttering. His other one—the new one—was looking directly at me . . . *inside* of me. It was as if Jack was somehow winking at me, the tattoo giving me that beaming look on the side that says, "We know what's what."

I haven't seen him since then, but every Thursday afternoon when this place is dead I wonder just what that look meant when they carted him away. And I wonder if the asylum is just like the pen—where you can tattoo teardrops down your cheek for every year you do time.

THE PICNICKERS

by Brian Lumley

Born in Horden, Durham on December 2, 1937, Brian Lumley now lives with his wife, literary agent Dorothy Lumley, in Torquay, Devon. Fans of the British television comedy series, Fawlty Towers, *will recall Torquay (rhymes with "door key"). However, Brian Lumley is more interested in scaring readers to death, rather than splitting their sides with laughter.*

Lumley is the second writer in this anthology who also was present in the first volume. Also in common with friend and fellow countryman Ramsey Campbell, Lumley started his writing career in the 1960s with stories and books based on the Cthulhu Mythos of H.P. Lovecraft. Both writers have long since gone on to develop their own special visions of horror, and Lumley is better known today for his best-selling Psychomech and Necroscope series of novels. However, he has not completely abandoned short fiction, and here, once again, Lumley is directly on target with a tale set in the well-remembered environs of his youth.

This story comes from a long time ago. I was a boy, so that shows how long ago it was. Part of it is from memory, and the rest is a reconstruction built up over the years through times when I've given it a lot of thought, filling in the gaps; for I wasn't privy to everything that happened that time, which is perhaps as well. But I do know that I'm prone to nightmares, and I believe that this is where they have their roots, so maybe getting it down on paper is my rite of exorcism. I hope so.

The summers were good and hot in those days, and no use anyone telling me that that's just an old man speaking, who only remembers the good things; they *were* better summers! I could, and did, go down to the beach at Harden every day. I'd get burned black by the time school came around again at the end of the holidays. The only black you'd get on that beach these days would be from the coal dust. In fact there isn't a beach anymore, just a sloping moonscape of slag from the pits, scarred by deep gulleys where polluted water gurgles down to a scummy, foaming black sea.

But at that time . . . men used to crab on the rocks when the tide was out, and cast for cod right off the sandbar where the small waves broke. And the receding sea would leave blue pools where we could swim in safety. Well, there's probably still sand down there, but it's ten foot deep under the strewn black guts of the mines, and the only pools now are pools of slurry.

It was summer when the gypsies came, the days were long and hot, and the beach was still a great drift of aching white sand.

Gypsies. They've changed, too, over the years. Now they travel in packs, motorized, in vehicles that shouldn't even be on the roads: furtive and scruffy, long-haired thieves who nobody wants and who don't much try to be wanted. Or perhaps I'm prejudiced. Anyway, they're not the real thing anymore. But in those days they were. Most of them, anyway . . .

Usually they'd come in packets of three or four families, small communities plodding the roads in their intricately painted, hand-carved horse-drawn caravans, some with canvas roofs and some wooden; all brass and black leather, varnished wood and lacquered chimney stacks, wrinkled brown faces and shiny brown eyes; with clothespegs and various gewgaws, hammered trinkets and rings that would turn your fingers green, strange songs sung for halfpennies and fortunes told from the lines in your hand. And occasionally a curse if someone was bad to them and theirs.

My uncle was the local doctor. He'd lost his wife in the Great War and had never remarried. She'd been a nurse and died somewhere on a battlefield in France. After the war he'd traveled a lot in Europe and beyond, spent years on the move, not wanting to settle. And when she was out of his system (not that she ever was, not really; her photographs were all over the house), then he had come home again to England, to the northeast where he'd been born. In the summers my parents would go down from Edinburgh to see him, and leave me there with him for company through the holidays.

This summer in question would be one of the last—of that sort, anyway—for the next war was already looming; of course, we didn't know that then.

"Gypsies, Sandy!" he said that day, just home from the mine where there'd been an accident. He was smudged with coal dust, which turned his sweat black where it dripped off him, with a pale band across his eyes and a white dome to his balding head from the protection of a miner's helmet.

"Gypsies?" I said, all eager. "Where?"

"Over in Slater's Copse. Seen 'em as I came over the viaduct. One caravan at least. Maybe there'll be more later."

That was it: I was supposed to run now, over the fields to the copse, to see the gypsies. That way I wouldn't ask questions about the accident in the mine. Uncle Zachary didn't much like to talk about his work, especially if the details were unpleasant or the resolution an unhappy one. But I wanted to know anyway. "Was it bad, down the mine?"

He nodded, the smile slipping from his grimy face as he saw that I'd seen through his ruse. "A bad one, aye," he said. "A man's lost his legs and probably his life. I did what I could." Following which he hadn't wanted to say any more. And so I went off to see the gypsies.

Before I actually left the house, though, I ran upstairs to my attic room. From there, through the binoculars Uncle Zachary had given me for my birthday, I could see a long, long way. And I could even see if he'd been telling the truth about the gypsies, or just pulling my leg as he sometimes did, a simple way of distracting my attention from the accident. I used to sit for hours up there, using those binoculars through my dormer window, scanning the land all about.

To the south lay the colliery: "Harden Pit," as the locals called it. Its chimneys were like long, thin guns aimed at the sky; its skeletal towers with their huge spoked wheels turning, lifting or lowering the cages; and at night its angry red coke ovens roaring, discharging their yellow- and white-blazing tonnage to be hosed down into mounds of foul-steaming coke.

Harden Pit lay beyond the viaduct with its twin lines of tracks glinting in the sunlight, shimmering in a heat haze. From here, on the knoll where Uncle Zachary's house stood—especially from my attic window—I could actually look down on the viaduct a little, see the shining tracks receding toward the colliery. The massive brick structure that supported them had been built when the collieries first opened up, to provide transport for the black gold, one viaduct out of many spanning the becks and streams of the northeast where they ran to the sea. "Black gold," they'd called coal even then, when it cost only a few shillings per hundredweight!

This side of the viaduct and toward the sea cliffs, there stood Slater's Copse, a close-grown stand of oaks, rowans, hawthorns and hazelnuts. Old Slater was a farmer who had sold up to the coal industry, but he'd kept back small pockets of land for his and his family's enjoyment, and for the enjoyment of everyone else in the colliery communities. Long after this whole area was laid to waste, Slater's patches of green would still be here, shady oases in the gray and black desert.

And in the trees of Slater's Copse . . . Uncle Zachary hadn't been telling stories after all! I could glimpse the varnished wood, the young shire horse between his shafts, the curve of a spoked wheel behind a fence.

And so I left the house, ran down the shrub-grown slope of the knoll and along the front of the cemetery wall, then straight through the graveyard itself and the gate on the far side, and so into the fields with their paths leading to the new coast road on the one side and the viaduct on the other. Forsaking the paths, I forged through long grasses laden with pollen, leaving a smoky trail in my wake as I made for Slater's Copse and the gypsies.

Now, you might wonder why I was so taken with gypsies and gypsy urchins. The truth is that even old Zachary in his rambling house wasn't nearly so lonely as me. He had his work, calls to make every day, and his surgery in Essingham five nights a week. But I had no one. With my "posh" Edinburgh accent, I didn't hit it off with the colliery boys. Them with their hard, swaggering ways, and their harsh northeastern twang. They called themselves "Geordies," though they weren't from Newcastle at all; and me, I was an outsider. Oh, I could look after myself. But why fight them when I could avoid them? And so the gypsies and I had something in common: we didn't belong here. I'd played with the gypsies before.

But not with this lot.

Approaching the copse, I saw a boy my own age and a woman, probably his mother, taking water from a spring. They heard me coming, even though the slight summer breeze off the sea favored me, and looked up. I waved . . . but their faces were pale under their dark cloth hats, where their eyes were like blots on old parchment. They didn't seem like my kind of gypsies at all. Or maybe they'd had trouble recently, or were perhaps expecting trouble. There was only one caravan and so they were one family on its own.

Then, out of the trees at the edge of the copse, the head of the family appeared. He was tall and thin, wore the same wide-brimmed cloth hat, looked out at me from its shade with eyes like golden triangular lamps. It could only have been a sunbeam, catching him where he stood with the top half of his body shaded; paradoxically, at the same time the sun had seemed to fade a little in the sky. But it was strange and I stopped moving forward, and he stood motionless, just looking. Behind him stood a girl, a shadow in the trees; and in the dappled gloom her eyes, too, were like candlelit turnip eyes in October.

"Hello!" I called from only fifty yards away. But they made no answer, turned their backs on me and melted back into the copse. So much for "playing" with the gypsies! With this bunch, anyway. But . . . I could always try again later. When they'd settled in down here.

I went to the viaduct instead.

The viaduct both fascinated and frightened me at one and the same time. Originally constructed solely to accommodate the railway, with the addition of a wooden walkway it also provided miners who lived in one village but worked in the other with a shortcut to their respective collieries. On this side, a mile to the north, stood Essingham; on the other, lying beyond the colliery itself and inland a half mile or so toward the metaled so-called coast road, Harden. The viaduct fascinated me because of the trains, shuddering and rumbling over its three towering arches, and scared me because of its vertiginous walkway.

The walkway had been built on the ocean-facing side of the viaduct, level with the railway tracks but separated from them by the viaduct's wall. It was of wooden planks protected on the otherwise open side by a fence of staves five feet high. Upward-curving iron arms fixed in brackets underneath held the walkway aloft, alone sustaining it against gravity's unending exertions. But they always looked dreadfully thin and rusty to me, those metal supports, and the vertical distance between them and the valley's floor seemed a terribly great one. In fact it was about one hundred and fifty feet. Not a *terrific* height, really, but it only takes a fifth of that to kill or maim a man if he falls.

I had an ambition: to walk across it from one end

to the other. So far my best attempt had taken me a quarter-way across before being forced back. The trouble was the trains. The whistle of a distant train was always sufficient to send me flying, heart hammering, racing to get off the walkway before the train got onto the viaduct! But this time I didn't even make it that far. A miner, hurrying toward me from the other side, recognized me and called, "Here, lad! Are you the young 'un stayin' with Zach Gardner?"

"Yes, sir," I answered as he stamped closer. He was in his "pit black," streaked with sweat, his boots clattering on the wooden boards.

"Here," he said again, groping in a grimy pocket. "A threepenny bit!" He pressed the coin into my hand. "Now *run*! God knows you can go faster than me! Tell your uncle he's to come at once to Joe Anderson's. The ambulance men won't move him. Joe won't let them! He's delirious but he's hangin' on. We diven't think for long, though."

"The accident man?"

"Aye, that's him. Joe's at home. He says he can feel his legs but not the rest of his body. It'd be reet funny, that, if it wasn't so tragic. Bloody cages! He'll not be the last they trap! Now scramble, lad, d'you hear?"

I scrambled, glad of any excuse to turn away yet again from the challenge of the walkway.

Nowadays . . . a simple telephone call. And in those days, too, we had the phone; some of us. But Zachary Gardner hated them. Likewise cars, though he did keep a motorcycle and sidecar for making his rounds. Across the fields and by the copse I sped, aware of faces in the trees but not wasting time looking at them, and through the graveyard and up the cobbled track to the flat crest of the knoll, to where my uncle stood in the doorway in his shirtsleeves, all scrubbed clean again. And I gasped out my message.

Without a word, nodding, he went to the lean-to and started up the bike, and I climbed slowly and dizzily to my attic room, panting my lungs out. I took up my binoculars and watched the shining ribbon of road to the west, until Uncle Zachary's bike and sidecar came spurting into view, the banging of its pistons unheard at this distance; and I continued to watch him until he disappeared out of sight toward Harden, where a lone spire stood up, half hidden by a low hill. He came home again at dusk, very quiet, and we heard the next day how Joe Anderson had died that night.

The funeral was five days later at two in the afternoon; I watched for a while, but the bowed heads and the slim, sagging frame of the miner's widow distressed me and made me feel like a voyeur. So I watched the gypsies picnicking instead.

They were in the field next to the graveyard, but separated from it by a high stone wall. The field had lain fallow for several years and was deep in grasses, thick with clover and wildflowers. And up in my attic room, I was the only one who knew the gypsies were there at all. They had arrived as the ceremony was finishing and the first handful of dirt went into the new grave. They sat on their colored blanket in the bright sunlight, faces shaded by their huge hats, and I thought: *how odd*! For while they had picnic baskets with them, they didn't appear to be eating. Maybe they were saying some sort of gypsy grace first. Long, silent prayers for the provision of their food. Their bowed heads told me that must be it. Anyway, their inactivity was such that I quickly grew bored and turned my attention elsewhere . . .

The shock came (not to me, you understand, for I was only on the periphery of the thing, a child, to be seen and not heard) only three days later. The first shock of several, it came first to Harden village, but like a pebble dropped in a still pond its ripples began spreading almost at once.

It was this: the recently widowed Muriel Anderson had committed suicide, drowning herself in the beck under the viaduct. Unable to bear the emptiness, still stunned by her husband's absence, she had thought to follow him. But she'd retained sufficient of her senses to leave a note: a simple plea that they lay her coffin next to his, in a single grave. There were no children, no relatives; the funeral should be simple, with as few people as possible. The sooner she could be with Joe again the better, and she didn't want their reunion complicated by crowds of mourners. Well, things were easier in those days. Her grief quickly became the grief of the entire village, which almost as quickly dispersed, but her wishes were respected.

From my attic room I watched the gravediggers at work on Joe Anderson's plot, shifting soil which hadn't quite settled yet, widening the hole to accommodate two coffins. And later that afternoon I watched them climb out of the hole, and saw the way they scratched their heads. Then they separated and went off, one toward Harden on a bicycle, heading for the viaduct shortcut, and the other coming my way, toward the knoll, coming no doubt to speak with my Uncle Zachary. Idly, I looked for the gypsies then, but they weren't picnicking that day and I couldn't find them around their caravan. And so, having heard the gravedigger's cautious knock at the door of the house, and my uncle letting him in, I went downstairs to the study.

As I reached the study door I heard voices: my uncle's soft tones and the harsher, local dialect of the gravedigger, but both used so low that the conversation was little more than a series of whispers. I've worked out what was said since then, as indeed I've worked most things out, and so am able to reconstruct it here:

"*Holes,* you say?" That was my uncle.

"Aye!" said the other, with conviction. "In the side of the box. Drilled there, like. Fower of them."

"Wormholes?"

"Bloody big warms, gaffer!" "Big as half crowns, man, those holes! And anyhow, he's only been doon a fortneet."

There was a pause. Then: "And Billy's gone for the undertaker, you say?"

"Gone for Mr. Forster, aye. I told him, be as quick as you can."

"Well, John"—my uncle sighed—"while we're waiting, I suppose I'd better come and see what it is that's so worried you . . ."

I ducked back then, into the shadows of the stairwell. It wasn't that I was a snoop, and I certainly didn't feel like one, but it was as well to be discreet. They left the house and I followed on, at a respectful distance, to the graveyard. And I sat on the wall at the entrance, dangling my long skinny legs and waiting for them, sunbathing in the early evening glow. By the time they were finished in there, Mr. Forster had arrived in his big, shiny hearse.

"Come and see this," said my uncle quietly, his face quite pale, as Mr. Forster and Billy got out of the car. Mr. Forster was a thin man, which perhaps befitted his calling, but he was sweating anyway, and complaining that the car was like a furnace.

"That coffin"—his words were stiff, indignant—"is of the finest oak. Holes? Ridiculous! I never heard anything like it! Damage, more like," and he glowered at Billy and John. "Spade damage!" They all trooped back into the graveyard, and I went to follow them. But my uncle spotted me and waved me back.

"You'll be all right where you are, Sandy my lad," he said. So I shrugged and went back to the house. But as I turned away I did hear him say to Mr. Forster: "Sam, it's not spade damage. And these lads are quite right. Holes they said, and holes they are—four of them—all very neat and tidy, drilled right through the side of the box and the chips still lying there in the soil. Well, you screwed the lid down, and though I'll admit I don't like it, still I reckon we'd be wise to have it open again. Just to see what's what. Joe wouldn't mind, I'm sure, and there's only the handful of us to know about it. I reckon it was clever of these two lads to think to come for you and me."

"You because you're the doctor, and because you were closest," said Forster grudgingly, "and me because they've damaged my coffin!"

"No," John Lane spoke up, "because you built it—your cousin, anyhow—and it's got holes in it!"

And off they went, beyond my range of hearing. But not beyond viewing. I ran as quickly as I could.

Back in my attic room I was in time to see Mr. Forster climb out of the hole and scratch his head as the others had done before him. Then he went back to his car and returned with a tool kit. Back down into the hole he went, my uncle with him. The two gravediggers stood at the side, looking down, hands stuffed in their trouser pockets. From the way they crowded close, jostling for a better position, I assumed that the men in the hole were opening the box. But then Billy and John seemed to stiffen a little. Their heads craned forward and down, and their hands slowly came out of their pockets.

They backed away from the open grave, well away until they came up against a row of leaning headstones, then stopped and looked at each other. My uncle and Mr. Forster came out of the grave, hurriedly and a little undignified, I thought. They, too, backed away; and both of them were brushing the dirt from their clothes, sort of crouched down into themselves.

In a little while they straightened up, and then my uncle gave himself a shake. He moved forward again, got down once more into the grave. He left Mr. Forster standing there ringing his hands, in company with Billy and John. My binoculars were good ones and I could actually see the sweat shining on Mr. Forster's thin face. None of the three took a pace forward until my uncle stood up and beckoned for assistance.

Then the two gravediggers went to him and hauled him out. And silent, they all piled into Mr. Forster's car, which he started up and headed toward the house. And of course I would have liked to know what this was all about, though I guessed I wouldn't be told. Which meant I'd have to eavesdrop again.

This time in the study the voices weren't so hushed; agitated, fearful, even outraged, but not hushed. There were four of them and they knew each other well, and it was broad daylight. If you see what I mean.

"Creatures? Creatures?" Mr. Forster was saying as I crept to the door. "Something in the ground, you say?"

"Like rats, d'you mean?" (John, the senior gravedigger.)

"I really don't know," said my uncle, but there was that in his voice which told me that he had his suspicions. "No, not rats," he finally said; and now he sounded determined, firm, as if he'd come to a decision. "Now look, you two, you've done your job and done it well, but this thing mustn't go any further. There's a guinea for each of you—from me, my promise—but you can't say anything about what you've seen today. Do you hear?"

"Whatever you say, gaffer," said John, gratefully. "But what'll you do about arl this? I mean—"

"Leave it to me." My uncle cut him off. "And mum's the word, hear?"

I heard the scraping of chairs and ducked back out of sight. Uncle Zachary ushered the gravediggers out of the house and quickly returned to his study. "Sam," he said, his voice coming to me very clear now, for he'd left the door ajar, "I don't think it's rats. I'm sure it isn't. Neither is it worms of any sort, nor anything else of that nature."

"Well, it's certainly nothing to do with me!" The other was still indignant, but more shocked than outraged, I thought.

"It's something to do with all of us, Sam," said my uncle. "I mean, how long do you think your business will last if this gets out, eh? No, it has nothing to do with you or the quality of workmanship," he continued, very quickly. "There's nothing personal in it at all. Oh, people will still die here, of course they will—but you can bet your boots they'll not want to be *buried* here!"

"But what on earth *is* it?" Forster's indignation or shock had evaporated; his voice was now very quiet and awed.

"I was in Bulgaria once," said my uncle. "I was staying at a small village, very tranquil if a little backward, on the border. Which is to say, the Danube. There was a flood and the riverbank got washed away, and part of the local graveyard with it. Something like this came to light, and the local people went very quiet and sullen. At the place I was staying, they told me there must be an 'obour' in the village. What's more, they knew how to find it."

"An obour?" said Forster. "Some kind of animal?"

My uncle's voice contained a shudder when he answered: "The worst possible sort of animal, yes." Then his chair scraped and he began pacing, and for a moment I lost track of his low-uttered words. But obviously Mr. Forster heard them clearly enough.

"*What?* Man, that's madness! And you a doctor!"

My uncle was ever slow to take offense. But I suspected that by now he'd be simmering. "They went looking for the obour with lanterns in the dark—woke up everyone in the village, in the dead of night, to see what they looked like by lantern light. For the eyes of the obour are yellow—and triangular!"

"Madness!" Forster gasped again.

And now my uncle *was* angry. "Oh, and do you have a better suggestion? So you tell me, Sam Forster, what *you* think can tunnel through packed earth and do . . . that?"

"But I—"

"Look at this book," my uncle snapped. And I heard him go to a bookshelf, then his footsteps crossing the room to his guest.

After a while Forster said, "Russian?"

"Romanian—but don't concern yourself with the text, look at the pictures!"

Again a pause. "But . . . this is too . . ."

"Yes, I know it is," said my uncle, before Forster could find the words he sought. "And I certainly hope I'm wrong, and that it is something ordinary. But tell me, can *anything* of this sort be ordinary?"

"What will we do?" Forster was quieter now. "The police?"

"What?" my uncle snorted. "Sergeant Bert Coggins and his three flat-foot constables? A more down-to-earth lot you couldn't ask for! Good Lord, no! The point is, if this really is something of the sort I've mentioned, it mustn't be frightened off. I mean, we don't know how long it's been here, and we certainly can't allow it to go somewhere else. No, it must be dealt with here and now."

"How?"

"I've an idea. It may be feasible, and it may not. But it certainly couldn't be considered outside the law, and it has to be worth a try. We have to work fast, though, for Muriel Anderson goes down the day after tomorrow, and it will have to be ready by then. Come on, let's go and speak to your cousin."

Mr. Forster's cousin, Jack Boulter, made his coffins for him; so I later discovered.

"Wait," said Forster, as I once more began backing away from the door. "Did they find this . . . this *creature,* these Bulgarian peasants of yours?"

"Oh, yes," my uncle answered. "They tied him in a net and drowned him in the river. And they burned his house down to the ground."

When they left the house and drove away I went into the study. On my uncle's desk lay the book he'd shown to Mr. Forster. It was open, lying facedown. Curiosity isn't confined to cats: small girls and boys also suffer from it. Or if they don't, then there's something wrong with them. I turned the book over and looked at the pictures. They were woodcuts, going from top to bottom of the two pages in long, narrow panels two to a page. Four pictures in all, with accompanying legends printed underneath. The book was old, the ink faded and the pictures poorly impressed; the text, of course, was completely alien to me.

The first picture showed a man, naked, with his arms raised to form a cross. He had what looked to be a thick rope coiled about his waist. His eyes were three-cornered, with radiating lines simulating a shining effect. The second picture showed the man with the rope uncoiled, dangling down loosely from his waist and looped around his feet. The end of the rope seemed frayed and there was some detail, but obscured by age and poor reproduction. I studied this picture carefully but was unable to understand it; the rope appeared to be fastened to the man's body just above his left hip. The third picture showed the man in an attitude of prayer, hands steepled before him, with the rope dangling as before, but crossing over at knee height into the fourth frame. There it coiled upward and was connected to the loosely clad body of a skeletally thin woman, whose flesh was mostly sloughed away to show the bones sticking through.

Now, if I tell my reader that these pictures made little or no sense to me, I know that he will be at pains to understand my ignorance. Well, let me say that it was not ignorance but innocence. I was a boy. None of these things which I have described made any great impression on me *at that time*. They were all incidents—mainly unconnected in my mind, or only loosely connected—occurring during the days I spent at my uncle's house; and as such they were very small pieces in the much larger jigsaw of my world, which was far more occupied with beaches, rock pools, crabs and eels, bathing in the sea, the simple but satisfying meals my uncle prepared for us, and so on. It is only in the years passed in between, and in certain dreams I have dreamed, that I have made the connections. In short, I was not investigative but merely curious.

Curious enough, at least, to scribble on a scrap of my uncle's notepaper the following words:

> Uncle Zachary,
> Is the man in these pictures a gypsy?

For the one connection I *had* made was the thing about the eyes. And I inserted the note into the book and closed it, and left it where I had found it—and then promptly forgot all about it, for there were other, more important things to do.

It would be, I think, a little before seven in the

evening when I left the house. There would be another two hours of daylight, then an hour when the dusk turned to darkness, but I would need only a third of that total time to complete my projected walk. For it was my intention to cross the fields to the viaduct, then to cross the viaduct itself (!) and so proceed into Harden. I would return by the coast road, and back down the half-metaled dene path to the knoll and so home.

I took my binoculars with me, and as I passed midway between Slater's Copse and the viaduct, trained them upon the trees and the gleams of varnished woodwork and black, tarred roof hidden in them. I could see no movement about the caravan, but even as I stared so a figure rose up into view and came into focus. It was the head of the family, and he was looking back at me. He must have been sitting in the grass by the fence, or perhaps upon a tree stump, and had stood up as I focused my glasses. But it was curious that he should be looking at me as I was looking at him.

His face was in the shade of his hat, but I remember thinking, I wonder what is going on behind those queer, three-cornered eyes of his? And the thought also crossed my mind, I wonder what he must think of me, spying on him so rudely like this!

I immediately turned and ran, not out of any sort of fear but more from shame, and soon came to the viaduct. Out onto its walkway I proceeded, but at a slow walk now, not looking down through the stave fence on my left but straight ahead, and yet still aware that the side of the valley was now descending steeply underfoot, and that my physical height above solid ground was increasing with each pace I took. Almost to the middle I went, before thinking to hear in the still, warm evening air the haunting, as yet distant whistle of a train. A train! And I pictured the clattering, shuddering, rumbling agitation it would impart to the viaduct and its walkway!

I turned, made to fly back the way I had come . . . and there was the gypsy. He stood motionless, at the far end of the walkway, a tall, thin figure with his face in the shade of his hat, looking in my direction—looking, I knew, at me. Well, I wasn't going back *that* way! And now there *was* something of fear in my flight, but mainly I suspect fear of the approaching train. Whichever, the gypsy had supplied all the inspiration I needed to see the job through to the end, to answer the viaduct's challenge. And again I ran.

I reached the far side well in advance of the train, and looked back to see if the gypsy was still there. But he wasn't. Then, safe where the walkway met the rising slope once more, I waited until the train had passed, and thrilled to the thought that I had actually done it, crossed the viaduct's walkway! It would never frighten me again. As to the gypsy: I didn't give him another thought. It wasn't him I'd been afraid of but the viaduct, obviously . . .

The next morning I was up early, knocked awake by my uncle's banging at my door. "Sandy?" he called. "Are you up? I'm off into Harden, to see Mr. Boulter the joiner. Can you see to your own breakfast?"

"Yes," I called back, "and I'll make some sandwiches to take to the beach."

"Good! Then I'll see you when I see you. Mind how you go. You know where the key is." And off he went.

I spent the entire day on the beach. I swam in the tidal pools, caught small crabs for the fishermen to use as bait, fell asleep on the white sand and woke up itchy, with my sunburn already peeling. But it was only one more layer of skin to join many gone the same way, and I wasn't much concerned. It was late afternoon by then, my sandwiches eaten long ago and the sun beginning to slip; I felt small pangs of hunger starting up, changed out of my bathing costume and headed for home again.

My uncle had left a note for me pinned to the door of his study where it stood ajar:

Sandy,

I'm going back to the village, to Mr. Boulter's yard and then to the Vicarage. I'll be in about 9:00 p.m.—maybe. See you then, or if you're tired just tumble straight into bed.

—Zach

P.S. There are fresh sandwiches in the kitchen!

I went to the kitchen and returned munching on a beef sandwich, then ventured into the study. My uncle had drawn the curtains (something I had never before known him to do during daylight hours) and had left his reading lamp on. Upon his desk stood a funny contraption that caught my eye immediately. It was a small frame of rough, half-inch timber off-cuts, nailed together to form an oblong shape maybe eight inches long, five wide and three deep—like a box without top or bottom. It was fitted where the top would go with four small bolts at the corners; these held in position twin cutter blades (from some woodworking machine, I imagined), each seven inches long, which were slotted into grooves that ran down the corners from top edge to bottom edge. Small magnets were set central of the ends of the box, level with the top, and connected up to wires which passed through an entirely separate piece of electrical apparatus and then to a square three-pin plug. An extension cable lay on the study floor beside the desk, but it had been disconnected from the mains supply. My last observation was this: that a three-quarters-inch hole had been drilled through the wooden frame on one side.

Well, I looked at the whole setup from various angles but could make neither head nor tail of it. It did strike me, however, that if a cigar were to be inserted through the hole in the side of the box, and the bolts on that side released, the cigar's end would be neatly severed! But my uncle didn't smoke . . .

I experimented anyway, and when I drew back two of the tiny bolts toward the magnets, the cutter on that side at once slid down its grooves like a toy guillotine, thumping onto the top of the desk! For a moment I was alarmed that I had damaged the desk's finish . . . until I saw that it was already badly scored by a good many scratches and gouges, where apparently my uncle had amused himself doing much the same thing—except that he had probably drawn the bolts mechanically, by means of the electrical apparatus.

Anyway, I knew I shouldn't be in his study fooling about, and so I put the contraption back the way I had found it and returned to the kitchen for the rest of the sandwiches. I took them upstairs and ate them, then listened to my wireless until about nine o'clock—and still Uncle Zachary wasn't home. So I washed and got into my pajamas, which was when he chose to return—with Harden's vicar (the Reverend Fawcett) and Mr. Forster, and Forster's cousin, the joiner Jack Boulter, all in tow. As they entered the house I hurried to show myself on the landing.

"Sandy," my uncle called up to me, looking a little flustered. "Look, I'm sorry, nephew, but I've been very, *very* busy today. It's not fair, I know, but—"

"It's all right," I said. "I had a smashing day! And I'm tired." Which was the truth. "I'm going to read for a while before I sleep."

Then the conversation faded a little, or perhaps I was falling asleep. But I do remember Jack Boulter's voice saying, "Me, ah'll wark at it arl neet, if necessary. An' divven worry, it'll look no different from any other coffin. Just be sure you get them wires set up, that's arl, before two o'clock."

And my uncle answering him, "It will be done, Jack, no fear about that . . ."

The rest won't take long to tell.

I was up late, brought blindingly awake by the sun, already high in the sky, striking slantingly in through my window. Brushing the sleep from my eyes, I went and looked out. Down in the cemetery the gravediggers John and Billy were already at work, tidying the edges of the great hole and decorating it with flowers, but also filling in a small trench only inches deep, that led out of the graveyard and into the bracken at the foot of the knoll. John was mainly responsible for the latter, and I focused my glasses on him. There was something furtive about him: the way he kept looking this way and that, as if to be sure he wasn't observed, and whistling cheerily to himself as he filled in the small trench and disguised his work with chippings. It seemed to me that he was burying a cable of some sort.

I aimed my glasses at Slater's Copse next, but the curtains were drawn in the caravan's window and it seemed the gypsies weren't up and about yet. Well, no doubt they'd come picnicking later.

I washed and dressed, went downstairs and breakfasted on cereal with milk, then sought out my uncle—or would have, except that for the first time in my life I found his study door locked. I could hear voices from inside, however, and so I knocked.

"That'll be Sandy," came my uncle's voice, and a moment later the key turned in the lock. But instead of letting me in, he merely held the door open a crack. I could see Jack Boulter in there, working busily at some sort of apparatus on my uncle's desk—a device with a switch, and a small colored light bulb—but that was all.

"Sandy, Sandy!" my uncle sighed, throwing up his hands in despair.

"I know," I said with a smile. "You're busy. It's all right, uncle, for I only came down to tell you I'll be staying up in my room."

That caused him to smile the first smile I'd seen on his face for some time. "Well, there's a bit of Irish for you," he said. But then he quickly sobered. "I'm sorry, nephew," he told me, "but what I'm about really is most important." He opened the door a little more. "You see how busy we are?"

I looked in and Jack Boulter nodded at me, then continued to screw down his apparatus onto my uncle's desk. Wires led from it through the curtains and out of the window, where they were trapped and prevented from slipping or being disturbed by the lowered sash. I looked at my uncle to see if there was any explanation.

"The, er—the wiring!" he finally blurted. "We're testing the wiring in the house, that's all. We shouldn't want the old place to burn down through faulty wiring, now should we?"

"No, indeed not," I answered, and went back upstairs.

I read, listened to the wireless, observed the land all about through my binoculars. In fact I had intended to go to the beach again, but there was something in the air: a hidden excitement, a muted air of expectancy, a sort of quiet tension. And so I stayed in my room, just waiting for something to happen. Which eventually it did.

And it was summoned by the bells, Harden's old church bells, pealing out their slow, doleful toll for Muriel Anderson.

But those bells changed everything. I can hear them even now, see and *feel* the changes that occurred. Before, there had been couples out walking: just odd pairs here and there, on the old dene lane, in the fields and on the paths. And yet by the time those bells were only halfway done the people had gone, disappeared, don't ask me where. Down in the graveyard, John and Billy had been putting the finishing touches to their handiwork, preparing the place, as it were, for this latest increase in the Great Majority; but now they speeded up, ran to the tiled lean-to in one tree-shaded corner of the graveyard and changed into clothes a little more fitting, before hurrying to the gate and waiting there for Mr. Forster's hearse. For the bells had told everyone that the ceremony at Harden church was over, and that the smallest possible cortege was now on its way. One and a half miles at fifteen miles per hour, which meant a journey of just six minutes.

Who else had been advised by the bells, I wondered?

I aimed my binoculars at Slater's Copse, and . . .

they were there, all four, pale figures in the trees, their shaded faces turned toward the near-distant spire across the valley, half hidden by the low hill. And as they left the cover of the trees and headed for the field adjacent to the cemetery, I saw that indeed they had their picnic baskets with them: a large one which the man and woman carried between them, and a smaller one shared by their children. As usual.

The hearse arrived, containing only the coffin and its occupant, a great many wreaths and garlands, and of course the Reverend Fawcett and Mr. Forster, who with John and Billy formed the team of pallbearers. Precise and practiced, they carried Muriel Anderson to her grave where the only additional mourner was Jack Boulter, who had gone down from the house to join them. He got down into the flower-decked hole (to assist in the lowering of the coffin, of course) and after the casket had gone down in its loops of silken rope finally climbed out again, assisted by John and Billy. There followed the final service, and the first handful of soil went into the grave.

Through all of this activity my attention had been riveted on the graveyard; now that things were proceeding toward an end, however, I once again turned my glasses on the picnickers. And there they sat cross-legged on their blanket in the long grass outside the cemetery wall, with their picnic baskets between them. But *motionless* as always, with their heads bowed in a sort of grace. They sat there—as they had sat for Joe Anderson, and Mrs. Jones the greengrocer lady, and old George Carter the retired miner, whose soot-clogged lungs had finally collapsed on him—offering up their silent prayers or doing whatever they did.

Meanwhile, in the graveyard the ceremony was over at last, and John and Billy set to with their spades while the Reverend Fawcett, Jack Boulter, and Mr. Forster climbed the knoll to the house, where my uncle met them at the door. I heard him greet them, and the vicar's high-pitched, measured answer:

"Zach, Sam here tells me you have a certain book—with pictures? I should like to see it, if you don't mind. And then of course there's the matter of a roster. For now that we've initiated this thing I suppose we must see it through, and certainly I can see a good many long, lonely nights stretching ahead."

"Come in, come in," my uncle answered. "The book? It's in my study. By all means come through."

I *heard* this conversation, as I say, but nothing registered—not for a minute or two, anyway. Until—

There came a gasping and a frantic clattering as my uncle, with the Reverend Fawcett hot on his heels, came flying up the stairs to the landing, then up the short stairs to my room. They burst in, quite literally hurling the door wide, and my uncle was upon me in three great strides.

"Sandy," he gasped then, "what's all this about gypsies?" I put my glasses aside and looked at him, and saw that he was holding the sheet of notepaper with my scribbled query. He gripped my shoulder. "Why do you ask if the man in these pictures is a gypsy?"

Finally I knew what he was talking about. "Why, because of their eyes!" I answered. "Their three-cornered eyes." And as I picked up my binoculars and again trained them on the picnickers, I added: "But you can't see their faces from up here, because of their great hats . . ."

My uncle glanced out of the window and his jaw dropped. "Good Lord!" he whispered, eyes bulging in his suddenly white face. He almost snatched the glasses from me, and his huge hands shook as he put them to his eyes. After a moment he said, "My God, my God!" Simply that; and then he thrust the glasses at the Reverend Fawcett.

The Reverend was no less affected; he said, "Dear Jesus! Oh, my dear sweet Jesus! In broad daylight! Good heavens, Zach—*in broad daylight*!"

Then my uncle straightened up, towered huge, and his voice was steady again as he said, "Their shirts—look at their shirts!"

The vicar looked, and grimly nodded. "Their shirts, yes."

From the foot of the stairs came Jack Boulter's sudden query: "Zach, Reverend, are you up there? Zach, why man ar'm sorry, but there must be a fault. Damn the thing, but ar'm getna red light!"

"Fault?" cried my uncle, charging for the door and the stairs, with the vicar right behind him. "There's no fault, Jack! Press the button, man—*press the button*!"

Left alone again and not a little astonished, I looked at the gypsies in the field. Their shirts? But they had simply pulled them out of their trousers, so that they fell like small, personal tents to the grass where they sat. Which I imagined must keep them quite cool in the heat of the afternoon. And anyway, they always wore their shirts like that, when they picnicked.

But what was this? To complement the sudden uproar in the house, now there came this additional confusion outside! What could have startled the gypsies like this? What on earth was wrong with them? I threw open the window and leaned out, and without knowing why found my tongue cleaving to the roof of my mouth as once more, for the last time, I trained my glasses on the picnickers. And how to explain what I saw then? I saw it, but only briefly, in the moments before my uncle was there behind me, clapping his hand over my eyes, snatching the window and curtains shut, prizing the glasses from my half-frozen fingers. Saw *and* heard it!

The gypsies straining to their feet and trying to run, overturning their picnic baskets in their sudden frenzy, seeming anchored to the ground by fat white ropes which lengthened behind them as they stumbled outward from their blanket. The agony of their dance there in the long grass, and the way they dragged on their ropes to haul them out of the ground, like strangely hopping blackbirds teasing worms; their terrified faces and shrieking mouths as their hats went flying; their shirts and dresses billowing, and their unbelievable screams. All four of them, screaming as one, but shrill as a keening wind, hissing like steam from a nest of kettles, or lobsters dropped live into boiling water, and yet cold and alien as the sweat on a dead fish!

And then the man's rope, incredibly long and taut as a bowstring, suddenly coming free of the ground—and likewise, one after another, the ropes of his family—and all of them *living things* that writhed like snakes and sprayed crimson from their raw red ends!

But all glimpsed so briefly, before my uncle intervened, and so little of it registering upon a mind which really couldn't accept it—not then. I had been aware, though, of the villagers advancing inexorably across the field, armed with the picks and shovels of their trade. (What? Ask John and Billy to keep mum about such as this? Even for a guinea?) And of the gypsies spinning like dervishes, coiling up those awful appendages about their waists, then wheeling more slowly and gradually crumpling exhausted to the earth; and of their picnic baskets scattered on the grass, all tumbled and . . . empty.

I've since discovered that in certain foreign parts "obour" means "night demon" or "ghost" or "vampire," while in others it means simply "ghoul." As for the gypsies: I know their caravan was burned out that same night, and that their bones were discovered in the ashes. It hardly worried me then and it doesn't now, and I'm glad that you don't see nearly so many of them around these days; but of course I'm prejudiced.

As they say in the northeast, a burden shared is a burden halved. But really, my dreams have been a terrible burden, and I can't see why I should continue to bear it alone.

This then has been my rite of exorcism. At least I hope so. . . .

WITH THE WOUND STILL WET

by Wayne Allen Sallee

Born in Chicago, Illinois on September 19, 1959, Wayne Allen Sallee has made frequent use of his native city for grim settings in his downbeat fiction. As he has published more than 800 stories and poems, it's little wonder that he was run over one night, probably by someone from the Chicago Tourist Bureau. Undaunted, Sallee continues to haunt Chicago, amusing himself by including odd insane bits with his manuscript submissions. While virtually all of Sallee's writing has been for the small press, recently he has begun to sell stories to major anthologies. His first novel, The Holy Terror, *has just been published by Ziesing, along with a collection of his short stories,* Running Inside My Skin. *His novel-in-progress is* Cult of Freaks.

In this city, you get used to the word *unseasonable*. It's always one or the other, too cold or too warm for the norm. On Tuesday, 16 January 1990, it was 53 degrees at ten in the morning, and by that time, I had already heard the "U" word on a half-dozen weather reports over the radio. With the temperature, balmy for Chicago, being what it was, fog had fallen over the streets like a coffin lid. The rain would come soon enough.

When Louden called me just before noon, I had already turned on the kitchen lights. Clay Louden was a staff reporter for the *NorthSide Herald*, and he had tossed the idea of doing a story on me to the city room a few weeks back. He got the go-ahead, and had called to say that the fog outside would make for some great photo shots to accompany the piece. Graceland Cemetery was just across the elevated tracks from my apartment on Belle Plaine.

The horror of the day would come later, with the rain. But, there in the fog that was thick as a brain fugue, the two of us had some serious thoughts on death while we wandered past the rows of tombstones. The subject matter was right there in front of us, but Clay was first to make mention of the gravesites. Many housed the remains of Chicago's last century of movers and shakers, and we both scanned inscriptions to find a stone with CASSADY or NESS, hoping to find a "prop" for me to stand against.

Clay noticed how so many of the interred had been dead more than seventy years, and that many of the stones had most likely gone unvisited in years, all the family members dead or incapacitated now.

It has always been my belief that more gravesites are recognized by complete strangers than by family members, over the course of years. Who hasn't looked at other stones when paying respect to their own dead? Who hasn't touched another concrete cross in hopes of leaving behind some of their own private griefs? The dead don't care.

We shot through a roll of b & w, with a couple of wide-angle shots near the Gorshin Needle for effect, and it certainly was eerie enough. The trees with their bare branches were like minimalist sketches, the ground itself stretching back into a thin-lipped, bloodless grin. When we left the cemetery, the dew on the grass had soaked my jeans past the ankles.

Driving down Petitt Boulevard, Clay mentioned that he would pop for a hot chocolate at the White Castle on Belmont, and ask me a few questions over the sliders, instead of doing a phone interview later.

The interview wasn't going to happen that easily, though, because as we turned onto Broadway, we found ourselves at the scene of an accident. Though it hadn't begun raining yet, the streets were slick, and you could see the skid marks where the Ford Econoline van had smashed into the rear of a Liquid Carbonics truck.

The fire engines and ambulance could be heard in the distance, from opposite directions. Clay looked at me and reached for his camera case in the back seat, telling me to flip the visor down over the passenger seat. Pinned to it was a green and white PRESS card, identifying Clay as working for Virlik Publications, the State of Illinois emblem affixed to the lower right corner.

"It's my job," Clay said to me, almost apologetically. We parked in the lot of a Dunkin Donuts. I followed him to the twisted mess.

My job, too, I thought. With my horror writings, there are all kinds of ways to get away with being ghoulish. As I'm writing this, I don't know if the guy Clay photographed will live. His head completely shattered the windshield. Black hairs were stuck to webbed glass by streaks of blood.

I looked down at his ruined face, the left side sliced away as cleanly as in any passage I could ever hope to write. I was transfixed in wondering how it was his eye did not fall free of its socket.

Louden snapped an additional role of film, it took so long to cut the guy out of his seat. He knew the men from the Wellington Street firehouse, so they let him click away from all angles, as long as their work wasn't impeded. I helped a bit by taking down names and descriptions. This, to justify my standing there close enough to see the steam coming away from the blood in the guy's chest, instead of back with the other gaping monsters in the lot across Broadway.

The rain started coming down as we trotted back to the car. I wasn't beyond shivering as we drove on to White Castle.

"Sometimes you get lucky," Clay said, grinning at me.

"Right place at the right time." Hey, it sells papers. No one bought the *Herald* for its articles on neighborhood bake sales and church bingo extravaganzas. Those "news" items were simply a bonus to the carnage.

We were even more soaked by the time we crossed the lot into the restaurant. Clay sprung for the hot chocolate and we ended up making a pass on the sliders when we saw what the grill looked like. The styrofoam cups still read HAPPY HOLIDAYS.

"How's this look so far?" Clay let me read as he went back to the counter for a plastic stirrer. I read the opening line to his article from the tiny note pad he carried: *Hunched over his journal on the elevated trains or buses like a pained cadaver, he grips his pen like a lunatic playing she-loves-me-she-loves-me-not with the limbs of a dead rodent . . .*

"I like it," I said. And I did. An unusual beginning for an article in the *Herald,* but it rang true. Every time I write a story, I tear out another piece of my heart.

We were sitting near the front windows; in the distance, because the fog had let up when the rain came, we could both see the flashing cherries of the fire engines, still at the scene even after the body was removed.

Clay took down all the basics for the article—they were doing the article because I was a neighborhood resident for a quarter-century—and then asked me, apologizing for it ahead of time, where I came up with my story ideas.

I told him that much of what I write is based on fact, that if a certain thing occurs to me at just the right time, well, the subject matter, or possibly the emotion it creates in me, is enough to get me going. In many cases, I told him, I write something to answer a question in my mind. Louden grinned again, his teeth big and white against his full, black beard.

It was funny—I didn't mention it aloud—but, there we were, talking about terror and, sitting across the aisle, were a young woman with three young children, playing with french fries. Straight out of a television commercial.

And beyond them, still visible, the carnage on Broadway. Yet they were unaware of it. Maybe that was why the mother was playing with the fries, so that the children not see the accident scene.

Clay was still conscious of it, though. Agreeing with what I said about subject matter in my stories, he said how a lot of the photos he took stayed with him. He was still thinking about the crash.

We tied things up quick, Clay wanting to get back to the darkroom with his rolls of film—I couldn't help but think of how one roll was staged, the other mercilessly not—and I had to get back to a story I was working on about my days doing PR work for an Elvis impersonator, "Only The Dead Know Graceland."

As we walked back to Louden's Sentra, I saw the woman and her children following close behind. Clay was just starting the defogger and wipers when a van pulled into the lot. A flash of lightning illuminated a sky as dark as night now. I thought of lungs filled with cancer, just to avoid a bad feeling. The driver of the van stopped alongside the woman and spoke to her.

Somehow I knew what was going down. Maybe Clay did, too, though I never asked him. He had gotten it all down in the paper for the 18 January edition. The neighbor knowing where to find the wife of the maimed man, how she took the kids out for burgers every Tuesday after Morgan the Pirate Pre-School had let out its classes. How the neighbor had been one of the gapers back at the scene, not knowing at first who the victim was because he was driving a different company van that day, and then how she learned that it was her friend's husband after one of the firemen mentioned his name to the responding beat cop.

Loudon didn't care that the downpour was soaking his camera. We both had our jobs to do. The lightning flashed again and the rain battered my face. The wind came in from the lake and already the simple act of opening my mouth to breathe made it feel like my face was rictusing.

There was a low rumble of thunder, but the next flash came from Clay Louden's Konica. When I shut my eyes, the image remained. The horrified woman, her mouth sliced open by scream, her children staring up at her . . .

As clean and neat as any passage I could ever hope to write in my career.

MY GIDDY AUNT

by D.F. Lewis

When obtaining permission from the authors to reprint their stories in The Year's Best Horror Stories, *I ask for some information to use in these introductions, assuming that readers might want to learn a bit about the person who is about to mess with their brains. Someday I'll write a book about these responses. Thus far unique, however, is that of D.F. Lewis, who this time out sent me four closely typed pages quoting reviews and comments on his stories that variously call for knighthood or a lynching. Talk about giving equal time!*

A writer who has published over 300 stories in the small press since 1987 (even if they are very *short stories) can be expected to draw attention, of all sorts. Lewis got an early start in 1968, when August Derleth at Arkham House rejected his stories as being "pretty much pure grue." Evidently Lewis spent the next twenty years developing his own disturbingly strange style, displaying a command of language and a genuine weirdness that defy categorization. Born in 1948, Lewis resides in Coulsdon, Surrey, where he works for an insurance company. Seems safe enough.*

The woman's corpse (if a corpse *can* be described as belonging to anybody) lay on the dining-room table. The men acted simple-mindedly as they fussed over her cleaning, one moment thinking they had been hired by the local undertaker and the next realising they were the woman's co-lodgers who had not even informed the Authorities about her death let alone her illness. The needle was beached upon a cracked run-off groove, punctuating the silence until the spring wound down.

One of the men called himself Hubert and the other Bill. Today was a dithering sort of day. The death had come as a bit of a shock. The woman had moved into the bedsit on the top floor only two months ago, struggling with her battered luggage. Hubert was the only one in that day and he had traipsed after with the key that had been left in his safekeeping by the landlady pending the new lodger's arrival.

"These stairs are going to be too steep for me," she gasped on reaching the dark narrow landing at the topmost newel post.

"You'll get used to them," mumbled Hubert, never wondering how he knew.

He handed her the rusty key. These flats had once borne the brunt of the '53 storms. The whole place stunk of Essex salt, even now, to the very rafters.

"Thank you, I'll be all right now."

"Mrs Phipps said make yourself at home. She'll be getting a shade next week." He pointed at the bare bulb hanging from its rose.

"I'm sure I'll be comfy here. Not sure about all the stairs, though. I didn't really notice them the first time. We share amenities, don't we?"

"Yes, I think so. There's another one called Bill. You'll meet him tonight when he comes home from work."

She stared meaninglessly at Hubert. Perhaps she wondered how you could call a place like this "home" or what he was doing there all during the small hours of the afternoon.

"What shall we call you?"

Everything had to have a name.

"Rachel. Yes, that'll do."

"Yes, that'll do fine. Can I do any shopping for you? There's a nice bread shop on the front near the pier. You must be feeling tired." Hubert never questioned why he said such things. Anybody would think he was thoughtful.

"No, thank you. I've got a few Typhoo teabags and some Marie biscuits. They'll do nicely till tomorrow."

"But tomorrow's Sunday . . . isn't it?" But so what?

Hubert tried in vain to recall the rest of that first conversation. He was now in what he called the kitchen, his nose an inch from the blow-top shaving-mirror, busy busy with the nail scissors at his nasal hair. It steamed up. He was still in pajamas, the tassel of the cord in a compromising position. Bill was in the parlor dressing the body. They had rifled through her clothes and with a selection of underwear, frocks, stockings and other items they had returned as quietly as possible down the stairs, dropping bits and pieces in their wake.

Earlier on, when Bill had been introduced to Rachel, he was short of breath from cycling from Frinton, where he worked as a shelf-filler.

"Blow it, the dynamo's busted!"

"Never mind that. Bill . . . this is Rachel. Rachel . . . this is Bill."

Hubert was a sucker for niceties. He beamed as the other two shook hands.

"Nice to meet you. Taken the top room, eh? You'll be all right up there—the old floods could never reach that far." She reminded Bill of his mother's sister in her younger days before she turned demented.

"Yes . . . for a while. Just a short holiday, really."

"Oh, you're not here permanent, like, then?" chimed in Hubert.

She shook her head, but both men wondered whether that meant yes or no . . . or neither. As it turned out, in the fullness of time her residence there was not permanent by a long chalk, but equally she herself never decided to move on elsewhere. The universe has mysteries deeper and far worthier of concern than such considerations, in any event.

Bill's dungarees were hanging like an anorexic ghost in the backyard. The outside toilet door swung to and fro in the wind. Rachel gazed across the landscape of chimneystacks, barely managing a glimpse of the gray swell of the sea beyond the smoky curtain of Autumn. The two men she could hear in the distance shuffling crockery in the kitchenette. They had nuisance value, if nothing else. They took her mind off the sadness and the revenge . . . and the encroaching illness. She felt her own bones seizing up. Waking nausea regularly stretched to dinnertime when she would prepare herself sausages, onions and a heap of mash within a moat of grease.

She was a widow, following her husband's ghost trail nearly as far as the Naze. In his drunken furors he had often threatened to haunt her, when he was dead . . . in retribution for a life of bitter misery. Having never allowed *any* man to get the better of her, Rachel had decided to beat the ghost at its own game. Haunt it. Hound it to the limits of the land. Till it was cornered between her and the deep blue sea. Ghosts haunted by the living, that's the direction fear should go. She smirked. She had reached her goal at last. The sand swirls she watched from the prom were little more than the dervishes of her fancy. The *real* ghost clung, in the hope of concealment, to the underpillars of the pier, coils of curdled salt spume. *She* saw it cowering there—waiting for a fate beyond fate itself—as it listened shivering to the trundle of dodgem cars shaking the struts of the superstructure—and the joyless screams of those mortals on the ghost train—the lurching battens of the Big Wheel as it leant imperceptibly out of true.

Only just in time. She herself had defeated both death and fate to get this far. Bitterness is the only great healer. Salt in the wounds is a great reinvigorator. Revenge: the only way to prolong life beyond the natural span. She'd leave her husband's ultimate nemesis until the very last moment. Let it suffer, let his ghost pine in unassuageable pain, let that ectoplasmic remnant of the one she had loved really suffer. The longer the better. The licking of the Winter waves into the open sores of white pus, she felt even in her own flesh. Ghosts feel pain more exquisitely than mortals—she was sure. Rachel had convinced herself. If it were only not for those steep stairs . . .

Bill stirred the stew, discovering tiny succubic faces staring up at him from the configurations of the mince. Hubert lounged in the deckchair pilfered from the front.

"Rachel's ill, you know. I've been timing her climb up the stairs. They've doubled since she first got here." Hubert's words were clear enough in his head, but they did not sound right to Bill. Blurred minds link better without the intervention of over precise words. Knowing looks are easier to interpret, even if wrongly.

"I don't know. Maybe she needs a doctor to give her the once over."

"That stew smells awful."

Bill nodded. His honesty would not allow him to pilfer anything before the sell-by date.

In the distance, the Salvation Army band struck up a chord. Even on blowy out-of-season days, they encouraged a number of hymnsters to gather at the top of the beach. Headscarves flickering. Mouths gaping. Hands plunged deep in pockets, the words of the songs having been learnt by rote. Bill and Hubert often went themselves on fine days to participate. But their spirituality fell short of submitting their only bodies to the cruel elements of God's nature.

"I wonder if Rachel has gone."

"I didn't hear her come down the stairs."

The roar of raised voices. Or was it the sea understraining the gulls? They could not pick out Rachel's piping. Then, the creaking of floorboards told them the answer to their queries. She was at home, pottering about her room, trying to keep the bones from further binding.

Of late, she'd seemed literally desperate to escape the boarding-house. But the illness, whatever it was, took gradual hold of her. The pitifully wide eyesockets spoke pining volumes. She wanted merely *one* last look at the sea. That'd be sure to make her better. But the legs gave up the ghost—became clear jelly, with all the blue veins of coral showing,

They offered to buy a wheel chair and take her for an airing along the prom . . . when the weather turned finer, that is.

"Yes, yes, please. Don't mind about the weather, on my account. I must get out there. To the pier." Her face lit up with eager childlike anticipation, a magic lantern show of emotions. She had not left it too late, after all. She bit her lip, in self-infliction. She now felt the deepest love possible for those two dull men for whom she'd hardly had the time of day previously. They would be her saviours. She'd have done anything for them. Brinkmanship was no longer a foolhardy game she played with herself.

"Where will you get the wheelchair?"

"Should be easy. People are dying all the time. Even as we speak. There must be millions of empty wheelchairs." Hubert knew he made sense. Bill nodded in agreement, rubbing his hands together over the flaring gas fire.

That evening, she died . . . in Hubert's arms. She had allowed him to undo her winceyette blouse to the navel, to make the breathing easier. He had sunk his head into the cushion of lacy fabric within.

When they were sure she would not be able to complain, they undressed her body and cleaned it meticulously. They dressed her up again in the freshly laundered garments they had discovered in her room but never seen her wear before. She looked good as new. At peace with the world. She had died with a kind of smile upon her lips which stayed put throughout the whole process.

The wind roared in the chimney.

Bill and Hubert crouched over the hissing fire, mumbling unheard things. Rachel was propped up in the wing armchair, head resting on the cambric antimacassar, hands delicately posed in the lap. The gas flames gave a healthy flush to the face. The bones had ceased grinding long since. The smile still very much in place, even smilier. Hubert spooned stew to her lips, as if he were feeding a baby.

Abruptly, Bill stood up and with a shuddering hand placed a heavy black record on the wind-up. He grabbed Rachel in his arms and twirled her round the parlor in frantic waltz.

It was good to be indoors on a night like this, as the wailing storm off the sea violently splattered streaks of rain and spores of salt across the uncurtained window-panes. (Mrs Phipps had promised to put some curtains up in the Spring.)

THE LODESTONE

by Sheila Hodgson

*London-born Sheila Hodgson began her career in the theater before joining the BBC in 1960 as a staff writer. Six years later she turned free lance, writing for both commercial television and the BBC in addition to working extensively for radio. Several of her radio plays have been based upon story suggestions given by M.R. James in his essay, "Stories I Have Tried To Write," and some, as with "The Lodestone," have used James himself as a lead character. This story is adapted by Sheila Hodgson from her play of the same title, which was broadcast on BBC Radio 4 on April 19, 1989. For the curious, James did write a book on English abbeys (*Abbeys*, published by The Great Western Railway in 1925), but with a different illustrator than the one you'll read about here.*

As to Sheila Hodgson's recent adventures, she writes: "I'm working on a new BBC series called Spooky Tales. *In the studio next month with one set in Scandinavia. Also busy on a new crime novel, which hopefully should be finished by Easter. Otherwise living peacefully in much-haunted Wiltshire: to the usual collection of Roman soldiers, ghostly nuns and knights who frequent the Salisbury Plain I can add my own modern apparition. I was driving down a long straight road across the Plain, which had—pay attention at the back—*no side turnings. *Ploughed fields and trees* *on either side. In the mirror I saw a maroon car coming up fast behind me, I saw it pull out to overtake— And then it vanished. I don't mean it shot off down the road. I mean it disappeared. One moment it was there and the next moment it wasn't. Explanations gratefully received!"*

Amongst the most exciting, the most exhilarating of pleasures is that moment when—against all reasonable odds—you find yourself face to face with genius. Not mere talent, not some minor facility, but genuine original genius. I had been invigilating on a hot summer's day, the college hall stood bathed in dusty sunshine, I remember a fly which bumped irritatingly along the ceiling. I walked down the aisle and caught Master Francis Lippiat in the act: no, no, he was not cheating. Neither was he doing his Latin paper. He was making a sketch of me and the picture was so lively, so accurate, I burst out laughing; then of course I ordered him from the room and expressed myself in terms of suitable indignation. Francis Lippiat. I discovered later he could draw landscapes and buildings with equal skill and a marvelous attention to detail; a feeling for the shape, the flow, the essence of a scene. Francis Lippiat. Oh dear me.

At the time I could only admire his gift, but a few years on, my publisher George Masterman asked if I would suggest an artist to illustrate my book on English Abbeys. I told him "No"—and then "Yes", yes indeed, if he could find a young man called Lippiat. He could and he did. He did more; he commissioned the boy, and I must say it felt most gratifying, to please Masterman and get from Francis Lippiat a letter positively incoherent with gratitude. When the publishing firm invited me to view the first sketches, I traveled to London in a mood of the happiest anticipation.

"Dr. James. How very good of you to come. Delighted."

He did not look delighted. He looked, to be honest, like a man who has inadvertently swallowed a piece of lemon and is trying in the interests of good manners to keep his mouth shut. He had a portfolio in front of him, and for some reason he avoided my eyes.

"You've got the sketches?"

"Yes." His hands tightened on the file; he now looked like a man who has swallowed a lemon whole and is in imminent danger of choking. "Dr James. Dr James. Have you seen these things?"

"Well, no." A foolish question as they had obviously been sent direct to the publishers. "If I may . . . ?"

He pushed them across the desk. I opened the folder; the top drawing showed an excellent view of Romsey, a good clear angle on the tower, clever detail. Masterman sounded curt.

"I have shown them to our board of directors. Their unanimous decision is that we reject the lot."

"Good heavens. But—why?" I studied the draft; and then I saw the problem.

"You have found it?" asked Masterman dryly.

Extraordinary. I stared. In the left hand corner Lippiat had drawn a Gothic tombstone, inscribed "Let The Waters Rise Up."

"Is there any such tombstone at Romsey?"

I had to admit there wasn't.

"Thank you. We wrote to Mr Lippiat pointing out his mistake. He wrote back apologizing. Several weeks later we received this!"

Masterman flicked over the pages and jabbed at another sketch; a clever impression of the Benedictine cloister at Winchcombe. A fine piece of work. Only—rather larger, rather more prominent, was a tombstone with the words "Let The Waters Rise Up."

"He's drawn it again," I said weakly. The publisher sniffed; it was, I suppose, a statement of the obvious.

"We thought it must be a childish piece of artistic licence. We wrote once more, explaining that this would mislead the public; it was also totally unacceptable to us."

"Oh, quite. Oh, yes. Oh, dear me."

"The tombstone reappears in all his drawings, getting closer and larger every time! We wrote on

Wednesday, demanding an explanation and a fresh set of sketches. Yesterday *that* arrived by the mid-morning post!" He tugged angrily at the bottom sheet. It showed Reading Abbey and in the foreground—enormous, out of all proportion—a tombstone blackly lettered "Let The Waters Rise Up."

"I have no wish to criticize you," said Masterman bleakly. "You recommended the man, no doubt you acted in good faith. But are you certain this protégé of yours is entirely sane?"

I felt most horribly embarrassed. It was so odd. So inexplicable. George Masterman was understandably in a rage and babbling of publication dates and printers. I made a stupid attempt to calm him.

"I can only regret—my dear fellow—I am at a loss . . ."

"So are we," said Masterman nastily, "unless we can find another artist rather quickly."

In the end I persuaded him to give Lippiat one last chance. I promised to see the boy myself; perhaps he had fallen ill. I would call at the house and personally check his work.

I left Masterman studying the wall calendar in a pessimistic silence.

The address for Francis Lippiat proved to be a terraced house in Saffron Walden. I was shown into a room full of army souvenirs and found myself talking to an elderly person in tweeds.

"It concerns your son, Mr. Lippiat . . ."

"My name is Colonel Lippiat and he is not my son."

"I beg your pardon. I was given to understand . . ."

"Nephew. Damn nuisance. And who the hell are you?"

I gave him my card, which had the curious effect of making his withered face turn scarlet.

"Oh, God!" said Colonel Lippiat. "I know who *you* are!"

I blinked. I really did not expect a retired military man to have heard of me; perhaps my books were more popular amongst the armed forces than I had any right to suppose.

"You're that clown who wrecked Frankie's life!"

He glared at me. The situation was absurd, incomprehensible. Presently I discovered he blamed me for the fact that his nephew had taken up an artistic career instead of following the path of every right-minded Englishman and going into the Army. Or Navy. Or Church, if all else failed. I pointed out that Francis Lippiat had a remarkable talent: it would be terrible to waste such a gift; he might in time become a major artist.

"Art!" said Colonel Lippiat bleakly. "And I paid for his education."

After some minutes of this exhausting conversation, I discovered that the boy was not even in Saffron Walden; he had left several weeks ago and gone to Cornwall. It took another ten minutes to winkle the address out of the Colonel, who still regarded me with ill-concealed suspicion. He had given me a scrap of paper with the name Tregarth on it. I foresaw a long and wearisome train journey, but what I did not foresee was the fact that I should have to change three times in places with unsheltered platforms and no waiting room. By the time I got to Tregarth it had grown dark; I picked my way through grubby alleyways and arrived in a singularly bad temper outside a kind of lodging house.

"Why, Dr. James! My goodness, this is an honor. You're wet, sir—come in, come in—I'll make you a cup of tea."

If he thought I had traveled over three hundred miles to indulge in some mad social occasion he was very much mistaken. As we trudged up the stairs I expressed myself in no uncertain terms: I was seriously displeased, what on earth did he think he was doing, how dare he ignore explicit orders from the Masterman Press; he had probably lost his commission and he had bitterly disappointed me.

"Shall I take your coat?"

I looked at him. Francis had red hair, the faintly blotched complexion that sometimes goes with that coloring, his eyes were small and blue and apparently had difficulty in focusing on distant objects. He might not have heard what I said.

"Francis! This is a very urgent matter!"

"Yes."

He heard me now; he dropped my coat on a chair, of which there were only two visible. A fire of sorts burnt sluggishly in the grate. Lippiat fell on his knees and prodded at the coal, whereupon the room instantly filled with smoke.

"We have a publication date! You have not produced a single acceptable drawing! What are you going to do?"

"I don't know, sir."

"For heaven's sake! What's wrong with you, boy? Why do you keep sketching in some wretched gravestone?"

"I don't know!" whispered Lippiat. "I don't know, Dr. James, I think I'm going mad." The poker fell clattering to the floor and he covered his face with his hands.

A nervous breakdown? A mental collapse, brought on by overwork? Fever, perhaps? There was a lot of illness about this season.

"Come, come," I said gently. "We will talk later. Meanwhile, if you can find your kettle I really should appreciate a cup of tea."

The tea tasted disgusting. I had the prudence to refuse a carraway biscuit. After a while he began to speak, stumbling at first and then with mounting urgency. I gathered the compulsion had seized him overnight, he could not stop drawing that monstrous object: a tombstone with the words "Let The Waters Rise Up".

"It's as if my hand had a life of its own."

His hand kept shaking, the teacup rattled uncontrollably. He began, he said, to fear for his sanity and, hunting for some genetic flaw, had studied the past history of his family. It appeared that in 1691 one of his ancestors, suspected of being a witch, had been burnt alive by hysterical villagers.

"I believe it was here! In Tregarth!"

"Mr. Lippiat," I said wearily. "The fact that some

misguided country folk had a witch hunt in 1691 has nothing to do with sketches which have not been delivered to the Masterman Press in 1892."

"But that's the stone I keep drawing! I found a record of it—it's in a History of Judge Jeffreys—it was put up in memory of the Lippiat Witch."

"Very well," I said. "Very well, or rather, very ill, particularly for the witch. But now you have solved the matter and now you can forget it."

"Do you believe there's a curse on me?"

"No."

"But my ancestor, she . . ."

"Was burnt at the stake, yes, yes, yes. We all have family skeletons, though in your case I fear it would be a pile of ashes. My dear boy, surely you realize this is absurd? I suggest you come back with me to Cambridge and together we can still get the sketches finished in time."

"I'm sorry."

"Never mind. I believe there is another train tonight."

"I'm sorry, I can't come."

"Francis . . ."

"I have to find the stone!"

He stared mulishly at the fire. No amount of arguing would shift him. He could not rest until he had seen the memorial, erected—I felt rather ill-advisedly—by the victim's family. More to the point, he could not work. It ended with my agreeing to spend the night in the local inn and go with him to the vicarage in the morning. He was having trouble with the vicar, said Lippiat. That cleric kept pretending the stone wasn't there.

Matthew Bodmin, vicar of Tregarth, proved to be a great bony man with a prominent nose and the air of a brooding vulture. He regarded Lippiat with ill-concealed dislike and asked him to be so good as to close the garden gate or sheep would certainly find their way into the churchyard. Then he turned to me and hissed, *"Take him away!"*

"I beg your pardon?"

"Your friend! Or relation! Or whoever he is! I really cannot have it. The fellow is a trouble maker, a nuisance . . ."

I could not imagine what the luckless Francis had done to arouse such violent resentment. From Bodmin's agitated hisses I gathered the main offence was bribery; he had gone from cottage to cottage offering money to anyone who could help him find the Lippiat stone.

"A waste of time and an open invitation to fraud! He is upsetting the whole village. And this—this bizarre memorial is not here, sir! It has never been here! Do I make myself plain?"

"Perfectly," I said.

The Reverend Matthew gave an exasperated sigh. He had, he declared, looked at the parish register. Unfortunately the records only went back to 1693, for in 1692 Tregarth had been devastated by a great flood and all the papers lost. Still, he himself was reasonably expert in such matters and prepared to swear . . .

At which point Lippiat rejoined us.

I began to understand the vicar's irritation; Francis kept on and on, he would not leave the subject alone though faced with a blank denial. The headstone was in Tregarth! It must be in Tregarth!

"You are mistaken!" snapped Bodmin, and then—clearly goaded too far—"In heaven's name! You are the second person to arrive here in one week asking ridiculous questions about a witch."

"The second?"

"Yes, sir, the second! And now I will bid you good day."

We had, I fear, strained the reverend gentleman's Christian charity to breaking point. I thanked him and made for the door. With a modicum of luck we should be able to get a train back to Cambridge. Lippiat protested all the way to the station: lies, everybody was lying to him, there must be a sinister purpose behind their lies.

"My dear boy. Do consider it possible that you have made a mistake."

"Ha!"

There is really no answer to "Ha." Rain began to fall in a steady drizzle; we arrived at Tregarth Halt just as a train was pulling out. As Lippiat seemed sunk in impenetrable gloom, I went to the booking office myself and ascertained that there was indeed another train. In four hours time. Fortunately Tregarth possessed a waiting room of sorts; I had no intention of trailing round the village in the wet. We sat in what was, I must admit, a slightly hostile silence, water dripping from my umbrella to the floor and forming a small misshapen puddle. Suddenly Lippiat, who had been thumbing through a pile of notes, looked up and exclaimed, "You're right!"

"Indeed."

"Dr. James, I apologize, I beg your pardon, how could I have been so stupid! I'm wasting my time here!"

"Yes."

"Please forgive me, what was I thinking about? It's obvious! I've got the wrong village!" He waved his notebook triumphantly in my face. "There was another place where the villagers took the law into their own hands and burnt a witch—Of course! I ought to be in Horden!"

"You ought to be in Cambridge," I said unpleasantly. "Honoring your commitments to the Masterman Press and to me."

"Oh, I will, don't worry, later, later—Oh, now I understand!"

He rushed from the waiting room, and skipped along the platform like an excited school boy. Presently he came back wreathed in smiles.

"We can get to Horden from here! We only have to change at Barnstaple, Taunton, Langport and Yeovil."

I could scarcely believe my ears; surely even Lippiat could not be lunatic enough to propose . . .

"Where is Horden?"

"In Dorset." He sat, beaming at me; then—possibly noticing my expression—added, "Of course, you don't have to come, sir. If you don't want to."

Now you will ask me why in the name of reason and common sense I did it. I can give you only one answer: my book. I clung to the hope that somehow in spite of the time element and the odds against it, Francis Lippiat would regain his sanity and illustrate my book. It could be done by another artist, it could be done with no illustrations—yet I knew that those pictures, given the strange quality of Lippiat's work, would make the difference between a major production and just another text book for scholars.

We spent the night at the railway hotel in Barnstaple and arrived in Horden some time after lunch. It became immediately apparent to me that we should not have arrived at all. Horden was even smaller than Tregarth; a dismal cluster of farm cottages and one Norman church of absolutely no merit. Oh, well, at least it had stopped raining. The vicar was responsible for three or four churches and we had great difficulty in finding him; his name it seemed was Simeon Mullins and his hobby the making of dandelion wine. After one glass I feared for his parishioners, after two glasses I ceased to care. The Reverend Mullins could not have been more of a contrast to the Reverend Bodmin. He was a little gnome of a man whose wrinkled trousers were held tight to his ankles with bicycle clips.

"God be gracious, I have the care of three parishes—St Cuthman's, St Peter's, and St Agnes in the Field. Work, work, work!" He twinkled at us. "And what can I do for you?"

"We are looking for a large Gothic headstone," began Lippiat. "It bears the words . . ."

" 'Let The Waters Rise Up'; yes, I know; so sorry to disappoint you."

We stared at him. A curious feeling of unease spread through me, a conviction that something was about to go wrong. Yet if he knew the stone . . .

"Oh, God be gracious, I've been asked before. Yes, there was somebody here only a day or two back, asking exactly the same question. What a coincidence!"

I did not believe it to be a coincidence. In both

villages someone had been ahead of us, searching for the same memorial. Why? And who?

"I have no idea. I'm afraid I couldn't help them either. 'Let The Waters Rise Up'; a most peculiar inscription. I remember it well."

"Then you've seen it?" Lippiat started forward. Mr. Mullins pursed his lips.

"Seen it? No, of course not; it isn't here. No, no, no, but the words lodged in my mind; so odd, don't you think? And a monument to a witch, in memory of a witch. I ask myself, is that entirely Christian? One should most certainly forgive one's enemies but not, I feel, in the churchyard. No matter, no matter, it isn't in my churchyard. Your very good health, sir!"

"Are you positive?"

"The parish records . . ."

"Oh, those." He sipped delicately at his glass. "I consulted those when the other visitor came. So sad; we have no records before 1793. You see, Horden was destroyed by a most catastrophic flood in 1792 and the earlier papers have utterly vanished. What a loss to posterity! So sad, so sad!"

We left him sighing over his dandelion wine. In spite of the very definite denial, Francis insisted on searching through all three graveyards—St Cuthman's, St Peter's and St Agnes', which was indeed in the fields and ploughed fields at that. As we went down the muddy lane, I heard a voice shouting behind us and saw to my surprise the Reverend Simeon in hot pursuit on his bicycle.

"Winterset!" he shouted.

"I beg your pardon?"

He skidded to a halt, splashing mud in all directions. "It occurs to me. One does so like to help the stranger in one's midst. I had a thought—God be gracious—Winterset?"

"What do you mean?" snapped Lippiat. The dirt had coated his shoes, and he attempted to wipe them on the grass verge.

"We were talking of witches, young man. After my last visitor had left I did a little minor research work on the subject; not perhaps the most suitable occupation for a man of the cloth but never mind, never mind. I believe they burnt a witch at Winterset. It's a village in Wiltshire," he added kindly.

"Thank you," I said, with horrid foreboding. Wiltshire! First Cornwall and then Dorset and now Wiltshire. Lippiat had already turned his face in the direction of the railway station. There would be no trains for several hours. We gained what passed for the main road as the Reverend Mr Mullins overtook us, bicycling merrily.

"Do let me know how you get on! I should be most interested!"

He twisted round in an excess of cordiality, waved his arm and shot headfirst into a ditch.

It might have been very much worse. We got to Salisbury before midnight. We found a perfectly acceptable hotel from where I managed the next morning to send a message to Masterman—exaggerating, I fear, if not actually lying—assuring him that all would be well. We had woken to dismal weather; a high wind sent clouds swirling across the plain and my one comfort lay in the discovery that Winterset was only a few miles to the north. If his search failed there then surely, surely Lippiat must abandon the whole idea and come back to London! I smiled across at him. The boy's hand seemed to be moving. He was sketching a headstone on the tablecloth, and as I watched he inked in the letters "Let The Waters Rise Up."

I fled before the hotel manager could discover the ruin of his table linen. He was a perfectly respectable man and deserved better. I felt exceedingly depressed.

My depression lasted all the way to Winterset. Trailing after Francis Lippiat, I must have been quite twenty yards behind as he rushed toward the church and hurried between the tombs, and I was entirely unprepared for his sudden yell of triumph.

"Dr. James! Dr. James! I've found it!"

I rounded a corner in the path and came upon him; he had fallen on his knees in the wet grass, and touched the monument with little gasps of pleasure.

It was the same, it was identical; exactly as he had drawn it. A great block carved with strange interwoven lines and—etched blackly across the bottom—"Let The Waters Rise Up."

Extraordinary. Well, well. No doubt there would be some rational explanation; a childhood memory, a picture once seen and forgotten. Meanwhile he had found the wretched thing and might now consent to get on with his work.

"My dear boy. I congratulate you. Splendid. Do you want to see the vicar before we leave?"

I glanced toward the vicarage and, rather to my embarrassment, saw a figure I took to be the vicar approaching; no doubt about to ask us what we were doing in the churchyard. I murmured to Francis, "get up, get up." As the person drew nearer I realised suddenly that it was a woman wearing a long cloak and hood; a tall slim creature with her eyes fixed on the boy.

"Oh, my dear!" she said. "I thought you would never come."

He stumbled to his feet and stared at her—as indeed I did. She threw back the hood and laughed; she had black hair piled high in shining coils, her face held a curious, a remarkable beauty, and her voice sounded low and melodious.

"I have been waiting so long!"

"Eleanor?" whispered Lippiat, and in one amazed moment I realized he knew the girl.

The scene became absurdly formal. He introduced me to his friend: her name was Eleanor Howard, she had partnered him at the May Day ball in Cambridge where they had discovered a distant relationship via a mutual great-grandfather. I gathered they had talked of ghosts and witches, and he had mentioned the strange obsession which even then was beginning to grip hold of him. I found her to be one of the new breed of ladies who contrive to get themselves to Cambridge University; a trend I must confess I deplore.

"You object to female students, Dr. James?"

"Madam," I said, "I might as well object to the incoming tide."

It had grown exceedingly cold. The appearance of Miss Eleanor Howard at least solved the enigma, for she was that mysterious character who had been ahead of us throughout our enquiries in Cornwall and Dorset, apparently conducting her own research into the Lippiat Stone.

"I hope to write an article on the subject."

Oh, dear me. A lady journalist. She and Lippiat were talking happily together, comparing notes, describing their various adventures and misadventures with the clergy.

"Where are you staying, Eleanor?"

"At the Harrier. It's a local inn."

"Could they put us up?"

"The question is academic," I told them, "as we are not staying there. Please excuse us, Miss Howard, we have to get back to Cambridge."

"No!"

In retrospect I am ashamed of the scene that followed, but I had wasted several days accompanying Lippiat on his mad search. I was wet, tired, and the publication date was approaching very fast indeed.

"Francis! I have treated you with patience and courtesy. I have indulged this bizarre fantasy of yours on the clear understanding that, once the tombstone was found, you would return to your work and deliver eight line drawings to the Masterman Press!"

"Oh, I'll start work again soon, sir, but just for the moment . . ."

"I regret," I said curtly, "there are no more moments available. I shall return to Cambridge and tell Mr. Masterman to cancel the contract. You will, I trust, have the common decency to refund the advance money."

I turned my back on them and walked away across the cemetery. I glanced round once, but they were not even looking at me. As I watched, I saw the girl put out her hand and touch Francis Lippiat on the cheek.

It was really too bad. I wept inwardly for my book.

I wept outwardly when I got to the station and discovered I had missed the only train that day, which left me with no alternative but to return to Winterset village and ask the Harrier if they had a bed for the night. The prospect of meeting either Lippiat or Miss Howard again seemed altogether too embarrassing. I told the landlady to send a tray of food up to the bedroom and retired to bed in an exceedingly bad temper.

I slid into an uneasy sleep; a horrid dream in which I found myself pursuing Francis Lippiat on a bicycle down a railway track. From time to time he turned his head to see me and, grinning over the handle bars, cried "No trains! No trains!" I woke with a start. There was a most unpleasant taste in my mouth and I could actually hear voices. Dragging my mind clear of sleep, I realized two people were quarrelling in the passage.

". . . you must leave at once!"

"Oh, no. Oh, no."

"But you have found the stone! There is no reason to stay!"

This was monstrous. I peered at my watch; it lacked ten minutes to seven o'clock. Who were these wretched people disturbing the household in the early hours of the morning?

"You ask me to *go,* Eleanor?"

Oh, dear me. Lippiat and his lady companion. I had absolutely no desire to eavesdrop on them; I did not wish to hear their conversation, but they were outside in the corridor. I was in my night clothes, I could not even get to the bathroom. Presently there came a silence and I opened my door a crack. To my horror they were still there, locked in some incomprehensible argument.

"Francis, you are in serious danger."

"From what? From whom? From you, Eleanor?"

I had thought them lovers. I had evidently been mistaken. Their voices rose now, the girl's in shrill entreaty, the boy's shaken by a kind of hidden rage.

"Please, please believe me!"

"And go? And let you triumph? Oh, you followed me, didn't you, Eleanor, you tracked me down."

"I was frightened for your sake!"

Silence again.

"Who are you?"

He must have stepped forward or seized her arm. I heard the woman gasp and then whisper, "This is absurd."

"Who are you? Do you come back, generation after generation, full of ancient malice?"

"Let me pass! Or I shall scream!"

"I know who you are!"

She screamed then; a piercing sound which echoed down the stair well. I threw the door open and hurried out in great alarm. Lippiat had his hands round the girl's neck; both of them turned and froze on seeing me, and for a full minute we all seemed locked in a weird tableau resembling some Gothic print. The girl moved first, breaking away to run panic-stricken across the landing and headlong toward the stairs. Francis leant against the banisters, staring at me and breathing hard, sucking in air in harsh gulps. I really could not control my horror.

"Good God, sir! Are you out of your mind?"

I could see the perspiration trickling along his forehead, saliva leaking from one corner of his mouth.

"Dr. James!" he said. "Ill met by moonlight. Or sunlight. What devil brought you here?" He gave the most extraordinary laugh, flung himself down the stairway and vanished.

I was left to explain the uproar to the landlady who presently emerged from the basement and who had understandably come to the conclusion that, despite the time of day, we were all drunk. She took particular exception to my night wear, turning her back on me with the one word, "Londoners." I could see no virtue in protesting that we came from Cambridge, as she very well knew.

Over a solitary breakfast—both the young people having prudently disappeared—I learnt that Miss Howard had paid her bill and left, Lippiat was nowhere to be found, and if I hurried I could catch a bus at the crossroads.

"I don't suppose you'll want to stay."

In a sense she was right; the bed had been lumpy and her food virtually inedible; yet curiosity prompted me to search the grounds. I walked across the village green and came upon Lippiat standing beside a small brackish river. He seemed pale and ill; his manner disconcerted me, verging as it did on hysterical levity.

"That was comical, sir! You bursting out of your bedroom in your dressing gown when I thought you were miles away in Cambridge!"

I told him coldly I could see nothing amusing in the situation. Quite frankly, I considered it the mercy of God I had been there to prevent violence and worse.

"What in the name of heaven possessed you? You were about to attack that poor girl."

He shook his head as if trying to rid the brain of some tormenting memory; he ran one hand over his hair and said astonishingly, "Dr. James. Do you believe in reincarnation?"

It was neither the time nor the place to discuss abstract philosophy. As I informed him.

"That woman is a witch! I have evidence! I can prove she is a witch."

He ranted on in this vein for several minutes while the rooks called above us and the conversation grew steadily more preposterous. Miss Howard had shown an unholy interest in the Lippiat stone, she had deliberately followed him to Winterset (here I felt compelled to interrupt: Miss Howard had not followed him, she had been in front of him. Mostly, I regret to say, because her research was rather better than his). She pretended friendship and then tried to force him to go back to Cambridge and abandon his search! I confess I found myself in total agreement with the lady.

"She has put a curse on me! You have seen what has happened to me—to my work—to my mind. She is a witch, *the* witch!"

"Bless my soul. I have no particular liking for female undergraduates but even I should hesitate to call them witches."

The boy laughed at that. Gradually he grew calmer, more rational. He apologized for his deplorable, his violent behavior; it was unforgivable.

"Dr. James. I have been extremely foolish. I am so very sorry."

"Yes," I said. "You are well-favored. You met her at a dance. Quite frankly, I consider the young lady's objective more likely to be marriage than black magic."

"You think she's in love with me?"

"I have no opinion on the subject. I merely state my hypothesis."

I led him back to the inn and there all would have been well, we might even have caught a train back to Cambridge, had not that wretched landlady waylaid us in the hall. She held a letter. Somebody had written to Mr. Lippiat, somebody had sent a message care of the Winterset vicarage. It was from the Reverend Mullins. He babbled at great length in purple ink: he had no address save Winterset but wanted Mr Lippiat to know—he felt the gentleman ought to know—God be gracious, he had news of the headstone!

"Oh, dear," I said. Oh, dear indeed. Oh, dear, dear, dear. The whole idiotic business began again. According to the Reverend Mullins the stone had stood in Horden until 1791; it vanished in the great flood of 1792 together with various church documents and a chalice worth forty-two shillings.

"Flood?" murmured Lippiat, staring at the note. "Flood? Why, Dr. James, do you realize what this means?"

It meant we should miss the bus to the station; it also meant I should almost certainly never get my beautiful illustrations. I expressed myself with some force. I might as well have talked to the row of beer pumps which lined the stained bar counter.

"Tregarth was destroyed by flood water in 1692. Horden was destroyed by flood water in 1792. And now the stone has appeared at Winterset! In 1892!"

At this point, mercifully, logic came to my aid. I suddenly realized how I might put an end to this nonsense once and for all. Lippiat, as far as I could make out, was arguing that a curse descended every hundred years on any place where the mob had rampaged out of control and burnt a suspected witch. Remarkable, I agreed; truly remarkable. And the date of the outrage at Tregarth had been November 2nd.

"You see?"

"I do indeed. I also see that today is November 14th."

"What?"

"I am sorry to have to wreck your splendidly melodramatic theory, Francis, but the Ides of March have not only come, my dear boy, they have gone. Without, as I remember, even a drop of rain."

He had the grace to look abashed and the common sense to admit I was right. Presently he admitted his obsession had got altogether out of hand. Which made the attack on poor Miss Howard appear for what it was—inexcusable barbarity. The sky faded to a dull gray pulsating with cloud, fallen leaves whispered against the window pane. I judged him in no condition to travel and with some reluctance arranged for us to spend another night at the Harrier Inn.

Toward midnight I woke in wriggling discomfort; the bed was quite abominably hard and some elusive thought kept twitching at my mind—something to do with calendars, something to do with dates. Oh, yes! Oh, dear! I sat up, for now I remembered.

Tregarth had been flooded in 1692. In 1692 they would have been using the Julian calendar, not our modern Gregorian one. As I recall, England fell in line with the continent of Europe in the middle of the eighteenth century. To do so they had to lose twelve days from the year 1751 and they did it by the simple expedient of cutting out . . . But in that case, bless my soul, November 2nd in 1692 would be November 14th in 1892.

Well, well. I was certainly not going to pass that

piece of information on to Francis Lippiat; he would read heaven knows what into it! In any case the fatal date had nearly gone; in ten minutes it would be November 15th.

As I drifted back towards sleep, I became aware of a faint noise, rather like a dripping tap; it must have been raining. No doubt some broken bit of guttering was splashing onto the ground. I rose and crossed to the window, I drew back the curtain and to my astonishment I saw him—Francis Lippiat—standing outside the inn, fully dressed. I leant over the window sill and called "Francis! Francis!" He paid no attention. I pulled an overcoat over my night wear, found a pair of shoes and hurried downstairs. I struggled with the bolts on the worn oak front door and ran across the path—"Francis, Francis!"

He might have been sleepwalking. His eyes when I came face to face with him were blank, he seemed not to know me, and made no attempt to answer my questions: what was wrong, what was he doing there, did he feel ill?

Perhaps the boy had had a stroke. I tried to take his arm but he shook me off and turned and raised both hands to shoulder height.

"Let the waters rise up!" whispered Francis Lippiat.

He must be dreaming, his subconscious mind still preoccupied with the Lippiat stone, the tragedies of the past, his absurd conviction that Eleanor Howard had been a witch. A nervous breakdown? I determined to send for a doctor first thing in the morning; the boy needed help and proper medical attention. For the moment all I could hope to do was get him back into the house, out of the cold night air and safely in bed.

"Come with me, my dear fellow! Come along!"

He turned then, stumbling a little. I glanced at the ground and saw a tiny thread of water snaking across the grass. I could hear a hissing noise; difficult to identify, sibilant, gaslike. How absurd—they had no gas in the village, we had gone to bed by candle-light. The next moment the earth heaved and rippled and a great spurt of water shot up from the graveyard.

"Run!" I cried. "Raise the alarm, it's a flood!"

I fled back into the inn shouting, "Wake the village, get help, get the people out". Even as I spoke there came a loud crash behind me as the cob walls of the cemetery fell and a surging wave of water swept towards the Harrier, sweeping mud and chalk in front of it.

By now the landlady had appeared, screaming; a man—who I took to be the vicar—put his head out of the vicarage window, muttered "Dear God" and vanished. Presently the church bells began to ring in clamorous warning. Water swirled along the main street. Most of the villagers had been asleep and came to their doors in various stages of undress and bewilderment; somebody—who might have been the local squire—rode on horseback through the rising tide attempting to give orders and rally the crowd.

"Upstairs! Don't stop to collect your possessions— Get upstairs or onto the roof— Make sure everyone in your family is accounted for."

Then, seeing me and deciding I seemed relatively calm, he said, "You, sir! Assemble anybody you find wandering and lead them up onto the high ground."

I cried that I was a stranger. He pointed to a small hill beyond the village and rode on, his mare splashing through the torrent which was rapidly gaining in strength and height.

My memories of that appalling night are confused and disconnected. I remember a girl who called out that her father was a cripple and she couldn't move him; beer barrels which floated out of the Harrier Inn and bobbed across the courtyard; a man who sat astride the roof holding a sheep on his lap; the whinny of terrified horses as their owners tried to lead them to safety; improvised rafts and ropes and ladders; a woman clutching my coat and saying, "Where's Jennie, have you seen Jennie, where's my

Jennie"; and everywhere the roar, the rumble of shattered walls and splintering timber and steadily advancing water.

By early dawn I had gathered together a group of some fifteen people, too frightened and confused to help themselves. I led them to the lee of a hill where we huddled together and waited for the morning. In all this I had lost sight of—no, I had totally forgotten—Francis Lippiat.

Daylight revealed a scene of quite ghastly devastation. The river had drained back into the earth leaving thick mud and broken trees and smashed masonry right across the village; two cottages had been completely swept away; dead animals lay in the fields; furniture and bits of carpet and pots and pans were strewn over half a mile. When the final count was made and a report presented to the authorities, it emerged that four buildings had been destroyed, eight rendered uninhabitable, numerous cows and sheep had been killed and eleven people were dead. Of Francis Lippiat there was no sign, and his name appeared on a list pinned to the church door—"Missing. Believed drowned."

I carried the dismal news to his uncle in Saffron Walden. Colonel Lippiat asked only that the body should be brought home for burial in the family plot, but this, unfortunately, proved impossible as the body could never be found. "So that's the end of it," said the Colonel bleakly. "Bloody waste."

It was not, as it turned out, entirely the end. Two years later I chanced to be in the Reading Room of the British Museum and found myself face to face with a young woman who stared at me across the catalogues and then said, "Dr. James."

It was Eleanor Howard. We retreated to the entrance hall where I discovered she knew of the death of Francis and the tragedy at Winterset. There was another matter I really felt should be made clear to her.

"In justice to the dead, Miss Howard, I think I

should tell you he bitterly regretted that extraordinary attack on your person."

"It hardly matters now."

"Ah, but I would very much prefer to set the record straight. The poor boy was suffering from delusions, brought on, I fear, by overwork. He saw you as some kind of witch!"

A school party hustled past us, clutching notebooks, shepherded by an anxious teacher and gazing in wonder at a huge Pharoah. Eleanor Howard blinked.

"Francis? Francis thought *I* was a witch?"

"Oh, and more," I told her lightly. "He believed you were the reincarnation of the Tregarth witch!"

The school party straggled through the main doors, their guide chivvying behind and uttering yelps of command.

"Yes. I see." She sighed. "The trouble with reincarnation, Dr. James, or so it seems to me, is that if you do not know you are reincarnated the whole thing becomes pointless."

I agreed. She was a most logical young lady of no mean intelligence. She went on to tell me how she had traced the Lippiat stone; that curious memorial put up by a woman in memory of her son.

"Her son?" I said.

"Oh, yes. The Tregarth witch was a man. Didn't you know?"

I did not. Neither, it seemed, did Lippiat. He really had no talent for research. In common with most people he had merely assumed a witch to be female, though I believe in ancient Scotland they were more usually male. I would have liked to question Eleanor Howard further but the doorman was calling "Closing time, please! Closing time in half an hour. All books to the counter."

So she left me to return her books.

During the Long Vacation, curiosity took me back to Winterset: I thought I might re-examine that strange monument to past folly. It wasn't there. I searched the entire cemetery. It must have been destroyed by the flood, only . . . It was a great slab of marble, heavily rooted in iron work. And it wasn't there.

You do see what really worries me?

Mmmm?

Where has *he* gone?

BASEBALL MEMORIES

by Edo van Belkom

Born in Toronto in 1962, Edo van Belkom obtained a B.A. in Creative Writing from York University in Toronto. He has been a newspaper reporter for almost seven years, working for weekly and daily newspapers in and around Toronto on both the sports and police beats. Primarily a writer of horror, he also writes science fiction and fantasy and has published about twenty stories since his first sale in 1989.

As editor, I get a lot of strange submissions, many of them from stranger sources, but "Baseball Memories" takes this year's prize. This one was first published in something called Aethlon: The Journal of Sport Literature. *It gets weirder, as van Belkom explains: "While the publication date on the issue is Fall, 1989 it was just published in January 1991. The lag-time was caused by the magazine going through a name change (formerly* Arrete*) and a transfer from San Diego State University to East Tennessee State University." No doubt E.T.S.U. had to throw in a first-round draft choice.*

Samuel Goldman had a memory like most of us when it came to regular things. He forgot the odd birthday or anniversary now and then but no one ever thought him forgetful.

He was no more absent-minded than his neighbor, who still hadn't returned Sam's lawn-mower even though Sam's lawn was rapidly becoming a neighborhood eyesore.

Sam remembered what he wanted. His wife Bea could tell him a hundred times to take out the garbage but he never took notice of her if he was doing something important—like watching a baseball game.

Sam had a talent for the sport which relied so heavily on numbers and statistics as a measure of a player's worth. He could ramble off records for all of the Toronto Blue Jays' pitchers from opening day, 1977. He knew, by heart, the averages of the top hitters of every major league team in baseball as well as records for stolen bases, home runs, RBI's and ERA's for just about anybody who was anything in the sport.

It was a hobby of course, something he liked to do with a cup of coffee and a book late at night after his family had gone to bed.

His seemingly boundless knowledge of baseball was always good for a few laughs among his friends. All of them were baseball fanatics; the only difference being, they didn't have his talent.

He was a great conversationalist at parties too, as long as talk centered around his favorite subject. Once he got his hands on somebody who was willing to drill him or be drilled about baseball history, he never let them out of his sight. The only way to get rid of Sam was to ask him how much he knew about hockey—which was nothing at all.

Some of Sam's friends began calling him "Pschyclo" because he was a walking, talking encyclopedia of baseball. They would sit around the picnic table shooting the breeze over a few beers and suddenly the discussion's decibel level would turn up a few notches. A finer point of the game would come under question and it was up to Sam to turn the volume down and restore order.

"Sammy, what did George Bell hit on the road in 1986?"

".293," Sam would say without hesitation.

"And how many homers?"

"Sixteen of his thirty-one were hit on the road."

"Thanks, Sam. See, I told you," one pal would say to another before the talk moved on to another trivial statistic that might ultimately change the world.

Sam considered himself gifted. He thought that what he had was a natural talent for numbers; something that might one day get him on the cover of a magazine or on some television talk show where he might finally be recognized for his achievement.

Sam's wife Bea wasn't so crazy about baseball.

She put up with it though, as most wives do with their husband's vices. She thought it was better for him and their marriage if he spent late nights with his nose buried in a baseball book instead of some bar flirting with a woman with an "x" in her first name.

"As long as he sticks to baseball it's pretty harmless," she always said—half telling someone, half telling herself.

And then one day she began to wonder.

The two were sitting at the breakfast table one Saturday morning when Sam said something that put a doubt in her mind about the mental well-being of her husband.

"Why don't we take a drive up north today and visit your cousin Ralph?" he said.

Bea was shocked. She looked at Sam for several seconds as if trying to find some visible proof that he was losing his mind.

"Ralph died last winter, don't you remember? We went to the funeral, there was six inches of snow on the ground and you bumped into my mother's car in the parking lot. She still hasn't forgiven you for it."

Sam was shocked too. He could remember how many triples Dave Winfield hit the last three seasons but the death of his wife's cousin had somehow slipped his mind.

"Oh yeah, that's right. What the hell am I thinking about?" he said and added, "I better go out and wash the car."

Things were fairly normal for the next few weeks and Sam was able to wow them with his lightning-fast answers and astounding memory. As long as baseball was in season, Sam was one of the most popular guys around.

A co-worker of Sam's even figured out a way to make some money with it and the two were making a few hundred dollars a week—tax free. After work they'd go out to some bar where nobody knew about Sam. Armed with the *Sports Encyclopedia of Baseball*, they'd bet some sucker he couldn't stump Sam with a question.

"Who led the Cleveland Indians in on-base-percentage in 1952?" the sucker would ask, placing a $10 bill on the bar.

"Larry Doby, .541, good enough to lead the American League," answered Sam and after a quick check in the encyclopedia for verification, the two had some pocket change for the week.

Sam was astonished at the financial benefit of his talent. He always thought of himself as an oddball, but if he could make some money at it—tax free to boot—then why the hell not. Money made him study the stats even harder, looking to increasingly older baseball publications to make sure he knew even the most trivial statistic.

Late at night he would thumb through the rabbit-eared encyclopedia and discover a new figure he hadn't known about.

"Well, would you look at that," he said as his eyes bore down on the page and his brain went through the machine-like process of absorption, processing and filing. It took less than ten seconds for him to remember forever that a guy by the name of Noodles Hahn led the Cincinnati Reds pitching staff in 1901 with a 22-19 record. Hahn pitched 41 complete games and had 239 strikeouts, leading the league in both categories. No mean feat considering the Reds finished last with a 52-87 record.

The information was stored in a little cubby-hole in his brain and could be recalled at any time like a book shelved in a library, picked up for the first time in fifty years. The book, a little dusty, would always be there and its story would always be the same.

* * *

Bea went to see Doctor Manny Doubleday, the family physician, after Sam did another all-nighter with his books. She was concerned about him.

It was true Sam had brought her some very nice things since he'd been making money in bars but she felt the items were tainted. The fur coat had been in the hall closet since the day he bought it for her, not only because it was summer, but because she was ashamed of it. She wouldn't show it to guests, even the ones who might have thought Bea the luckiest girl in the world—and Sam the greatest husband.

She sat quietly in the office waiting for the good doctor. Dr. Doubleday had been the Goldman's family physician for what seemed like forever. He delivered both Sam and Bea into the world and always looked upon the couple as a match made by his own hands. He was also a former minor league pitcher and big baseball fan. He had gone to several ball games with Sam over the years, he liked Sam and thought it wonderful that he knew so much about the sport.

The office was decorated like a tiny corner of Cooperstown. On the walls hung various team photos and framed newspaper clippings about Manny Doubleday in his heyday. On the desk were baseballs signed by Mickey Mantle and Hank Aaron, even one signed by Babe Ruth, although no one really believed it because the "Bambino" had allegedly signed his name in crayon.

From down the hall the doctor's melodic whistle pierced through a crack in the door and into the room. Moments later the door burst open and in strode the portly doctor.

"What seems to be the problem, Bea?" he asked, picking up a dormant baseball and wrapping his fingers around it as if to throw a split-fingered fastball right over the plate.

"It's Sam, I think he's—"

"How is the old dodger?" the doctor interrupted as he took a batter's stance and imagined swinging through on a tape-measure home run. "You know I've never seen anyone with a memory like his, it's uncanny the way he can tell you anything you want to know at the drop of a hat."

"Yes that's what I mean, I think he's overdoing it a bit," said Bea sitting up on the edge of her chair anxious to hear some words of support.

"Nonsense," replied the doctor. Bea slumped back in her chair.

"What your husband has is a gift. He has a photographic memory that he's chosen to use for recording baseball statistics. It's harmless."

"It used to be harmless, he used to do it in his spare time but now he let's other things slide just so he can cram his head with more numbers. He's beginning to forget things."

"Bea," the doctor said putting down his invisible bat, forgetting about baseball. "Forget for a minute that I'm your doctor and consider this a discussion between two friends."

"Most people are able to use about ten percent of the brain's full capacity. Your husband has somehow been able to tap in and exceed that ten percent. Maybe he's using twelve or thirteen percent, I don't know, but it happens. He could be making millions at the black jack tables in Atlantic City but he chose to use it for baseball. Just be happy it's occupying him instead of something more dangerous. I'll talk to him the next time he's in. How are the kids?"

Bea was brought sharply out of her lull and answered in knee-jerk fashion. "Fine, and yours."

She was satisfied, but marginally. It was one thing for the doctor to talk about Sam's mind in the comfort of the office, it was another thing entirely to sit at the dinner table and watch him try to eat his soup with a fork.

"Honey," she'd say. "Why don't you try using your spoon? You'll finish the soup before it gets cold."

"Yeah, I guess you're right *handed batters versus lefties*," Sam would reply and then sit silently for a few moments. "Did I say that? Sorry, Bea, I don't know where my head is."

Sam knew he was spending a little too much time with his baseball books. He was weary of the numbers and after a couple hours' study some nights the inside of his skull pounded incessantly and felt as if it might explode under the growing pressure. But he loved the game too much to give it up.

Anyway, the money he earned on the bar circuit was good. It was so good in fact that he could probably put the kids through college with his winnings; something he could never do working at his regular job.

Sam worked as an airplane mechanic in the machine shop at the local airport. He was good at his job and always took the time to make sure it was done right.

One day he was drilling holes in a piece of aluminum to cover a wing section they had been working on. The work was monotonous so Sam occupied his time thinking about the previous night's study.

"Pete Rose hit .273 his rookie year, .269 his second, .312 his third . . ."

The drill bit broke and Sam was brought back into the machine shop. He stopped the press, replaced the bit, tightening it with the key.

"Lou Gehrig hit .423 in 13 games for New York in 1923, .500 in 10 games in 1924, .312 in his first full season in 1925 . . ."

Sam started the drill press and the key broke free of its chain, flew across the shop and hit another mechanic squarely on the back of his head.

He was once again brought back into reality, shut the drill off and rushed over to see if his fellow worker was still alive. A crowd gathered around the prone man and all eyes were on Sam as he neared the scene.

"What the hell were you thinking of?"

"You gotta be more careful."

"That was pretty stupid."

The mechanics crowed in unison and Sam felt like a baseball that had been used too long after its prime. His insides felt chopped up and unravelled as he looked at the man lying on the floor.

A groan escaped the downed man's lips, "What the

hell was that?" he asked and the group around him breathed easier. Sam felt better too, but just a little. The shop foreman walked up to him, placed a comforting hand on his shoulder and told him to go home.

"Why don't you take the rest of the day off, before he gets off the floor and these guys turn into a lynch mob."

"Sure, boss. I'll go home *run leaders for the past twenty years*."

"What?"

"Nothing, nothing. I don't know what I was thinking of."

On the way home Sam stopped by "The Last Resort", a local sports bar with a big-screen T.V. and $2 draughts. He needed a drink.

After what happened at the shop, Sam thought he was going crazy. Baseball trivia was fun but if it turned him into an accident waiting to happen, he might as well forget all about his baseball memory.

He sat on a stool in front of the bartender and eased his feet onto the brass foot-rail. Comfortable, he ordered the biggest draught they had.

As he sipped the foam off the top of the frosted glass, he overheard a conversation going on down at the other end of the bar.

"Willie Mays was the best player ever to play the game, and believe me I know . . . I know everything there is to know about the greatest game ever invented."

Sam watched the man speak for a long time. He stared at him—trying to see right through his skull and into the folds of his brain. Sam wanted to know just how much this blow-hard really knew.

"Go ahead, ask me anything about baseball, anything at all. I'll tell you the answer. Heck I'll even put $10 on the bar here—if you stump me it's yours."

"How many home runs did Hank Aaron hit in his first major league season?" asked Sam as he carried his beer down the bar toward the man.

"Aw that's easy, thirteen, Milwaukee, 1954. I want some kind of challenge."

"All right then, in what year did Nolan Ryan pitch two no-hitters and who did he pitch them against?"

"Another easy one. Nolan Ryan was pitching for the California Angels and beat Kansas City 3–0, May 15, and Detroit 6–0, July 15, 1973."

Sam was startled. No-hitters were something he studied just the night before. This guy was talking about them like they were old news.

"Okay, now it's my turn," the man said massaging his cheeks between his thumb and forefinger. "But first would you care to put a little money on the table?"

"Take your best shot," answered Sam slamming a $50 bill on the bartop.

"Well, a $50 bill," the man was impressed. "That deserves a $50 question!"

The man looked into Sam's eyes. A little sweat began to bead on Sam's forehead but he was still confident the bozo had nothing on him.

"Okay, then. Who was the Toronto Blue Jays' winning pitcher in their opening game 1977 and what was the score?"

Sam smiled, he knew that one. But suddenly something about the way the other man looked into his eyes made his mind draw a blank. It was as if the man reached inside and pulled the information out of Sam's head before Sam had gotten to it. The beads of sweat on Sam's forehead grew bigger.

"I'm waiting," said the man, enjoying the tension. "Aw, c'mon, you know that one. I only asked it so you'd give me a chance to win my money back."

Sam closed his eyes and concentrated. Inside his brain, pulses of electricity scrambled through the files searching for the information, but all pulses came back with the same answer.

"I don't know," said Sam.

"Too bad. It was Bill Singer, April 7, 1977, 9-5 over Chicago. $50 riding on it too. Better luck next time, pal."

The man picked up the money and walked out of the bar. Sam stood in silence. He'd never missed a question like that—never! He finished his draught and ordered another.

Sam said nothing about the incident to Bea over dinner. He ate in silence, helped his wife with the dishes and told her to enjoy herself bowling with the girls.

When she was safely out of the driveway, Sam dove into his books. He vowed never to be made a fool of again and intensified his study. He looked up Bill Singer and put the information about him back on file in his head. He studied hundreds of pitchers and after a few hours their names became a blur.

Noodles Hahn, Cy Young, Ambrose Putman, Three Finger Brown, Brickyard Kennedy, Kaiser Wilhelm, Smokey Joe Wood, Wild Bill Donovan, Twink Twining, Mule Watson, Homer Blankenship, Chief Youngblood, Clyde Barfoot, Buckshot May, Dazzy Vance, Garland Buckeye, Bullet Joe Bush, Boom Boom Beck, Bots Nickola, Jumbo Jim Elliot, George Pipgrass, Schoolboy Rowe, Pretzels Puzzullo, General Crowder, Marshall Bridges, Van Lingle Mungo, Boots Poffenberger, Johnny Gee, Dizzy Dean, Prince Oana, Cookie Cuccurullo, Blackie Schwamb, Stubby Overmire, Webbo Clarke, Lynn Lovenguth, Hal Woodeshick, Whammy Douglas, Vinegar Bend Mizell, Riverboat Smith, Mudcat Grant, John Boozer, Tug McGraw, Blue Moon Odom, Rollie Fingers, Billy McCook, Woody Fryman, Catfish Hunter, Vida Blue, Goose Gossage, Rich Folkers, Gary Wheelock.

Sam closed the book shut. His head was spinning.

He felt like he couldn't remember another thing, not even if the survival of baseball depended on it.

But then a strange thing happened. Sam swore he heard a clicking sound inside his head. His brain felt as if it buzzed and whirred and was suddenly lighter.

He reopened the book and looked at a few more numbers. He took them in, closed the book once more and recited what he had learned.

"We're back in business," Sam said out loud and

returned, strangely refreshed, to the world of statistical baseball.

Bea came home around eleven o'clock and found Sam in the den asleep with his face resting on a stack of books.

Doesn't he ever get enough? she thought and poked a finger into his shoulder trying to wake him.

"Huh, what . . . *Phil Niekro, Atlanta Braves 1979, 21-20 at the age of 40. Gaylord Perry, San Diego Padres 1979, also 40, 12-11 . . .*"

"Sam, wake up. Isn't it time you gave it a rest and went to bed?" Bea said pulling on his sleeve hoping to get him out of his chair.

"Who are you?" asked Sam looking at Bea as if they were meeting in a long narrow alleyway somewhere late at night.

"Well, I'll say one thing for you Sam, you still have your sense of humor. C'mon, time for bed."

"Which way is the bedroom?" Sam thought his surroundings familiar, but he wasn't too clear about their details.

"Into the dugout with you. Eight innings is more than we can ask from a man your age!" said Bea, caught up in the spirit of the moment.

After the two were finally under the covers, Sam lay awake for a few minutes looking the bedroom over. The pictures on the wall looked familiar to him and he thought he might be in some of them himself. Comfortable and exhausted he finally dozed off.

Sam's brain was hard at work while the rest of his body rested in sleep.

It had started with a faint click but now his brain hummed and buzzed with activity. After being bombarded with information over the past months, every available cubby-hole in Sam's brain had been filled. There wasn't room for one more ERA, one more home run, not even one more measly single.

But like an animal that has been adapted to its environment over the course of generations, Sam's brain was evolving too, and decided it was time to clean house.

The torrent of information it had been receiving must be essential to the survival of the species, the brain reasoned. Why else would so many names and numbers be needed to be filed away? So the brain began a systematic search of every piece of information previously stored, from birth to present, and if it did not resemble the bits of information the brain was receiving on a daily basis, out the window it would go.

Sam's brain decided it wasn't essential that he remember how to use the blow-torch at work so it was erased to open up new space for those supremely important numbers.

By the time Sam awoke, a billion cubby-holes had been swept clean.

Sam walked sleepily toward the kitchen where Bea already had breakfast on the table.

"What's that?" asked Sam pointing to a yellow semi-sphere sitting on a perfect white disk.

"Are you still goofing around?" Bea answered. "Hurry up and eat your grapefruit or you'll be late for work."

Sam watched Bea closely, copying her movements exactly. He decided he liked the yellow semi-sphere called grapefruit and every bite provided a brand new taste sensation on his tongue. Sam's brain couldn't be bothered to remember what grapefruit tasted like, not even for a second.

Bea helped Sam get dressed for work because he said he couldn't remember which items on the bed were the ones called pants and which were the ones called shirts.

Bea decided she'd see Dr. Doubleday the moment she got Sam out of the house and insist he come by and give Sam a check-up. She nearly threw Sam out of the door in her rush to see the doctor.

As the door of the house closed behind him, Sam tried to remember just exactly where he worked and what it was he did for a living.

He also wanted to go back to "The Last Resort" and show that joker at the bar that Samuel Goldman was no fool.

If only he could remember how to get there.

THE BACCHAE

by Elizabeth Hand

Elizabeth Hand first appeared in The Year's Best Horror Stories *three years ago with her strange tale, "Prince of Flowers." She's back this year with another strange outing, "The Bacchae." Look for more strangeness from her in future, as she has quickly established herself as one of the genre's foremost stylists.*

Born in California in 1957, Hand grew up in Pound Ridge, New York, received her degree and worked for several years in Washington, D.C., and then moved to the Maine coast, where she has worked as a full-time writer these past few years. She has sold short fiction to numerous magazines and anthologies, and she has published two novels, Winterlong *and* Aestival Tide. *Hand also writes book reviews and criticism for the* Washington Post Book World, Detroit Metro Times, Science Fiction Eye, *and* Penthouse.

She got into the elevator with him, the young woman from down the hall, the one he'd last seen at the annual Coop Meeting a week before. Around her shoulders hung something soft that brushed his cheek as Gordon moved aside to let her in: a fur cape, or pelt, or no, something else. The flayed skin of an animal, an animal that when she shouldered past him to the corner of the elevator proved to be her Rottweiler, Leopold. He could smell it now: the honeyed stench of uncured flesh, a pink and scarlet veil still clinging to the pelt's ragged fringe of coarse black hair. It had left a crimson streak down the back of her skirt, and stippled her legs with pink rosettes.

Gordon got off at the next floor and ran all the way down the hall. When he got into his own apartment he locked and chained the door behind him. For several minutes he stood there panting, squinting out the peephole until he saw her turn the corner and head for her door. It still clung to her shoulders, stiff front legs jouncing against the breast of her boiled-wool suit jacket. After the door closed behind her Gordon walked into the kitchen, poured himself a shot of Jameson's, and stood there until the trembling stopped.

Later, after he had changed and poured himself several more glasses of whisky, he saw on the news that the notorious Debbie DeLucia had been found not guilty of the murder of the young man she claimed had assaulted her in a parking garage one evening that summer. The young man had been beaten severely about the face and chest with one of Ms. DeLucia's high-heeled shoes. When he was found by the parking lot attendant most of his hair was missing. Gordon switched off the television when it displayed photographs of these unpleasantries followed by shots of a throng of cheering women outside the courthouse. That evening he had difficulty falling asleep.

He woke in the middle of the night. Moonlight flooded the room, so brilliant it showed up the tiny pointed feathers poking through his down comforter. Rubbing his eyes Gordon sat up, tugged the comforter around his shoulders against the room's chill. He peered out at a full moon, not silver nor even the sallow gold he had seen on summer nights but a color he had never glimpsed in the sky before, a fiery bronze tinged with red.

"Jeez," Gordon said to himself, awed. He wondered if this had something to do with the solar shields tearing, the immense satellite-borne sails of mylar and solex that had been set adrift in the atmosphere to protect the cities and farmlands from ultraviolet radiation. But you weren't supposed to be able to see the shields. Certainly Gordon had never noticed any difference in the sky, although his friend Olivia claimed she could tell they were there. Women were more sensitive to these things than men, she had told him with an accusing look. There was a luminous quality to city light that had formerly been sooty and gray at best, and the air now had a russet tinge. Wonderful for outdoor setups—Olivia was a noted food photographer—or would be save for the odd bleeding of colors that appeared during developing, winesap apples touched with violet, a glass of Semillon shot with sparks of emerald, the parchment crust of an aged camembert taking on an unappetizing salmon glow.

It would be the same change in the light that made the moon bleed, Gordon decided. And now he had noticed it, even though he wasn't supposed to be sensitive to these things. What did that mean, he wondered? Maybe it was better not to notice, or to pretend he had seen nothing, no sanguine moon, no spectral colours in a photograph of a basket of eggs. Strange and sometimes awful things happened to men these days. Gordon had heard of some of these on television, but other tales came from friends, male friends. Near escapes recounted in low voices at the gym or club, random acts of violence spurred by innocent offers of help in carrying groceries, the act of holding a door open suddenly seen as threatening. Women friends, even relatives, sisters and daughters refusing to accompany family on trips to the city. An exodus of wives and children to the suburbs, from the suburbs to the shrinking belts of countryside ringing the megalopolis. And then, husbands and fathers disappearing during weekend visits with the family in exile. Impassive accounts by the next of kin of mislaid directions, trees where there had never been trees before. Evidence of wild animals, wildcats or coyotes perhaps, where nothing larger than a squirrel had been sighted in fifty years.

Gordon laughed at these tales at first. Until now. He pulled a feather from the bed-ticking and stroked his chin thoughtfully before tossing it away. It floated down, a breath of tawny mist. Gordon determinedly pulled the covers over his head and went back to sleep.

He was reading the paper in the kitchen next morning, a detailed account of Ms. DeLucia's trial and a new atrocity. Three women returning late from a nightclub had been harassed by a group of teenage boys, some of them very young. It was one of the young ones the women had killed, turning on the boys with a ferocity the newspaper described as "demonic." Gordon turned to the section that promised full photographic coverage and shuddered. Hastily he put aside the paper and crossed the room to get a second cup of coffee. How could a woman, even three women, be strong enough to do that? He recalled his neighbor down the hall. Christ. He'd take the fire stairs from now on, rather than risk seeing her again. He let his breath out in a low whistle and stirred another spoonful of white powder into his cup.

As he turned to go back to the table he noticed the MESSAGE light blinking on his answering machine. Odd. He hadn't heard the phone ring during the night. He sipped his coffee and played back the tape.

At first he thought there was nothing there. Dead silence, a wrong number. Then he heard faint sounds, a shrill creaking that he recognized as crickets, a katydid's resolute twang, and then the piercing, distant wail of a whippoorwill. It went on for several minutes, all the way to the end of the message tape. Nothing but night sounds, insects and a whippoorwill, once a sharp yapping that, faint as it was, Gordon knew was not a dog but a fox. Then abrupt silence as the tape ended. Gordon started, spilling coffee on his cuff, and swearing rewound the tape while he went to change shirts.

Afterward he played it back. He could hear wind in the trees, leaves pattering as though struck by a soft rain. Had Olivia spent the night in the country? No: they had plans for tonight, and there was no country within a day's drive in any direction from here.

She wouldn't have left town on a major shoot without letting him know. He puzzled over it for a long while, playing back the gentle pavane of wind and tiny chiming voices, trying to discern something else there, breathing or muted laughter or a screen door banging shut, anything that might hint at a caller. But there was nothing, nothing but crickets and whippoorwills and a solitary vixen barking at the moon. Finally he left for work.

It was the sort of radiant autumn day when even financial analysts wax rapturous over the color of the sky—in this case a startling electric blue, so deep and glowing Gordon fancied it might leave his fingers damp if he reached to touch it, like wet canvas. He skipped his lunchtime heave at the gym. Instead he walked down to Lafayette Park, filling his pockets with the polished fruit of horse-chestnuts and wondering why it was the leaves no longer turned colors in the fall, only darkened to sear crisps and then clogged the sewers when they fell, a dirty brown porridge.

In the park he sat on a bench. There he ate a stale ersatz croissant and shied chestnuts at the fearless squirrels. A young woman with two small children stood in the middle of a circle of dun-colored grass, sowing crusts of bread among a throng of bobbing pigeons. One of the children pensively chewed a white crescent. She squealed when a dappled white bird flew up at her face, dropped the bread as her mother laughed and took the children's hands, leading them back to the bench across from Gordon's. He smiled, conspiratorially tossed the remains of his lunch onto the grass and watched it disappear beneath a mass of iridescent feathers.

A shadow sped across the ground. For an instant it blotted out the sun and Gordon looked up, startled. He had an impression of something immense, immense and dark and moving very quickly through the bright clear air. He recalled his night-time thoughts, had a delirious flash of insight: it was one of the shields torn loose, a ragged gonfalon of Science's floundering army. The little girl shrieked, not in fear but pure excitement. Gordon stood, ready to run for help; saw the woman, the children's mother, standing opposite him pointing at the grass and shouting something. Beside her the two children watched motionless, the little girl clutching a heel of bread.

In the midst of the feeding pigeons a great bird had landed, mahogany wings beating the air as its brazen feathers flashed and it stabbed, snakelike, at the smaller fowl. Its head was perfectly white, the beak curved and as long as Gordon's hand. Again and again that beak gleamed as it struck ferociously, sending up a cloud of feathers gray and pink and brown as the other birds scattered, wings beating feebly as they tried to escape. As Gordon watched blood pied the snowy feathers of the eagle's neck and breast until it was dappled white and red, then a deeper russet. Finally it glowed deep crimson. Still it would not stop its killing. And it seemed the pigeons could not flee, only fill the air with more urgent twittering and, gradually, silence. No matter how their wings flailed it was as though they were stuck in bird-lime, or one of those fine nets used to protect winter shrubs.

Suddenly the eagle halted, raised its wings protectively over the limp and thrashing forms about its feet. Gordon felt his throat constrict. He had jammed his hands in his pockets and now closed them about the chestnuts there, as though to use them as weapons. Across the grass the woman stood very still. The wind lifted her hair across her face like a banner. She did not brush it away, only stared through it to where the eagle waited, not eating, not moving, its baleful golden eye gazing down at the fluttering ruin of feather and bone.

As her mother stared the little girl broke away, ran to the edge of the ruddy circle where the eagle stood. It had lifted one clawed foot, thick with feathers, and shook it. The girl stopped and gazed at the sanguine bird. Carelessly she tossed away her heel of bread, wiped her hand and bent to pluck a bloodied feather from the ground. She stared at it, marveling, then pensively touched it to her face and hand. It left a rosy smear across one cheek and wrist and she laughed in delight. She glanced around, first at her mother and brother, then at Gordon.

The eyes she turned to him were ice-blue, wondering but fearless; and absolutely, ruthlessly indifferent.

He told Olivia about it that evening.

"I don't see what's so weird," she said, annoyed. It was intermission of the play they had come to see: Euripides' "The Bacchae" in a new translation. Gordon was unpleasantly conscious of how few men there were at the performance, the audience mostly composed of women in couples or small groups, even a few mothers with children, boys and girls who surely were much too young for this sort of thing. He and Olivia stood outside on the theater balcony overlooking the river. "Eagles kill things, that's what they're made for."

"But here? In the middle of the city? I mean, where did it come from? I thought they were extinct."

All about them people strolled beneath the sulfurous crimelights, smoking cigarettes, pulling coats tight against the wind, exclaiming at the full moon. Olivia leaned against the railing and stared up at the sky, smiling slightly. She wore ostrich cowboy boots with steel toes and tapped them rhythmically against the cement balcony. "I think you just don't like it when things don't go as you expect them to. Even if it's the way things really are supposed to be. Like an eagle killing pigeons."

He snorted but said nothing. Beside him Olivia tossed her hair back. Thick and lustrous dark-brown hair, like a caracal's pelt, hair that for years had been unfashionably long. Though lately it seemed that more women wore it the way she did, loose and long and artlessly tangled. As she pulled a lock away from her throat he saw something there, a mark upon her shoulder like a bruise or scrape.

"What's that?" he wondered, moving the collar of her jacket so he could see better.

She smiled, arching her neck. "Do you like it?"

He touched her shoulder, wincing. "Jesus, what the hell did you do? Doesn't it hurt?"

"A little." She shrugged, turned so that the jaundiced spotlight struck her shoulder and he could see better. A pattern of small incisions had been sliced into her skin, forming the shape of a crescent, or perhaps a grin. Blood still oozed from a few of the cuts. In the others ink or colored powder had been rubbed so that the little moon, if that's what it was, took on the livid shading of a bruise or orchid: violet, verdigris, citron yellow. From each crescent tip hung a gold ring smaller than a teardrop.

"But why?" He suddenly wanted to tear off her jacket and blouse, search the rest of her to see what other scarifications might be hiding there. "Why?"

Olivia smiled, stared out at the river moving in slow streaks of black and orange beneath the sullen moon. "A melted tiger," she said softly.

"What?" The electronlc ping of bells signalled the end of intermission. Gordon grasped her elbow, overwhelmed by an abrupt and unfathomable fear. He recalled the moon last night, not crescent but swollen and blood-tinged as the scar on her shoulder. "What did you say?"

A woman passing them turned to stare in disapproval at his shrill voice. Olivia slipped from him as though he were a stranger crowding a subway door. "Come on," she said gently, brushing her hair from her face. She flashed him a smile as she adjusted her blouse to hide the scar. "We'll miss the second act." He followed her without another word.

After the show they walked down by the river. Gordon couldn't shake a burgeoning uneasiness, a feeling he might have called terror were it not that the word seemed one he couldn't apply to his own life, this measured round of clocks and stocks and evenings on the town. But he didn't want to say anything to Olivia, didn't want to upset her; more than anything he didn't want to upset her.

She was flushed with excitement, smoking cigarette after cigarette and tossing each little brand into the moonlit water snaking sluggishly beside them.

"Wonderful, just wonderful! The Post really did it justice, for a change." She stooped to pluck something from the mucky shadows and grimaced in distaste. "Christ. Their fucking beer cans—"

She glared at Gordon as though he had tossed it there. Smiling wanly he took it from her hand and carried it in apology. "I don't know," he began, and stopped. They had almost reached the Memorial Bridge. A path curved up through the tangled grasses toward the roadway, a path choked with dying goldenrod and stunted asters and Queen Anne's Lace that he suspected should not be such a luminous white, almost greenish in the moonlight. Shreds of something silver clung to the stunted limbs of lowgrowing shrubs. The way they fluttered in the cold wind made him think again of the atmospheric shields giving way, leaving the embarrened earth beneath them vulnerable and soft as the inner skin of some smooth green fruit. He squinted, trying to see exactly what it was that trembled from the branches. His companion sighed loudly and pointedly where she waited on the path ahead of him. Gordon turned from the shrubs and walked more quickly to join her.

"We should probably get up on the street," he said a little defensively.

Olivia made a small sound showing annoyance. "I'm tired of goddam streets. It's so peaceful here . . ."

He nodded and walked on beside her. A little ways ahead of them the bridge reared overhead, the ancient iron fretwork shedding green and russet flakes like old bark. Its crumbling concrete piers were lost in the blackness beneath the great struts and supports. The river disappeared and then materialized on the other side, black and gold and crimson, the moon's reflection a shimmering arrow across its surface. Gordon shivered a little. It reminded him of the stage set they had just left, all stark blacks and browns and greens. Following a new fashion for realism in the theater there had been a great deal of stage blood that had fairly swallowed the monolithic pillars and bound the proscenium with bright ribbons.

"I thought it was sort of gruesome," he said at last. He walked slowly now, reluctant to reach the bridge. In his hand the beer can felt gritty and cold, and he thought of tossing it away. "I mean the way the king's own mother killed him. Ugh." The scene had been very explicit. Even though warned by the *Post* critic Gordon had been taken aback. He had to close his eyes once. And then he couldn't block out their voices, the sound of knife ripping flesh (and how had they done that so convincingly?), the women chanting *Evohe! Evohe!*, which afterward Olivia explained as roughly meaning "O ecstacy" or words to that effect. When he asked her how she knew that she gave him a cross look and lit another cigarette.

No wonder the play was so seldom revived. "Don't you think we should go back? I mean, it's not very safe here at night."

"Huh." Olivia had stopped a few feet back. He turned and saw that she didn't seem to have heard him. She squatted at the river's edge, staring intently at something in the water.

"What is it?" He stood behind her, trying to see. The water smelled rank, not the brackish reek of rotting weeds and rich mud but a chemical smell that made his nostrils burn. The ruddy light glinted off Olivia's hair, touched her steel boot-tips with bronze. In the water in front of her a fish swam lethargically on its side, sides striped with scales of brown and yellow. Its mouth gaped open and closed and its gills showed an alarming color, bright pink like the inside of a wound.

"Ah," Olivia was murmuring. She put her hand into the water and lifted the fish upon it. It curled delicately within her palm, its fins stretching open like a butterfly warming to the sun as the water dripped heavily from her fingers. It took him a moment to realize it had no eyes.

"Poor thing," he said; then added, "I don't think

you should touch it, Olivia. I mean, there's something wrong with it—"

"Of course there's something wrong with it!" Olivia spat, so vehemently that he stepped backward. The mud smelled of ammonia where his heels slipped through it. "It's dying, poisoned, everything's been poisoned—"

"Well then for Christ's sake drop it, Olivia, what's the sense in *playing* with it—"

Hissing angrily she slid her hand back through the water. The fish vanished beneath the surface and floated up again a foot away, fins fluttering pathetically. Olivia wiped her hand on her trousers, heedless of the dark stain left upon the silk.

"I wasn't playing with it," she announced coldly, shaking her head so that her jacket slipped to one side and he glimpsed the gold rings glinting from her shoulder. "You don't care, do you, you don't even notice anymore what's happened. There'd be nothing left at all if it was up to people like you—"

He swore in aggravation as she stormed off in the direction of the bridge, then hurried after her. Muck covered his shoes and he stumbled upon another cache of beer cans. When he looked up again he saw Olivia standing at the edge of the bridge's shadow, hands clenched at her sides as she confronted two tall figures.

"Oh, fuck," Gordon breathed. He felt sick with apprehension but hurried on, finally ran to stand beside her. "Hey!" he said loudly, pulling at Olivia's arm.

She stood motionless. One of the men held something small and dark at his side, a gun, the other wore a tan trenchcoat and looked calmly back and forth, as though preparing to cross a busy street. Before Gordon could take another breath the second man was shoving at his chest. Gordon shouted and struck at him, his hand flailing harmlessly against the man's coat. His other hand tightened around the beer can and he felt a sudden warm rush of pain as the metal sliced through his palm. He glanced down at his hand, saw blood streaming down his wrist and staining the white cuffs of his shirt. He stared in disbelief, heard a thudding sound and then a moan. Then running, stones rattling down the grassy slope.

The man in the trenchcoat was gone. The other, the man with the gun, lay on the ground at river's edge. Olivia was kicking him in the head, over and over, her boots scraping through the mud and gravel when they missed him and sending up a spume of gritty water. The gun was nowhere to be seen. Olivia paused for an instant. Gordon could hear her breathing heavily, saw her wipe her hands upon her trousers as she had when she freed the dying perch. "Olivia," he whispered. She grunted to herself, not hearing him, not looking; and suddenly he was terrified that she *would* look and see him there watching her. He stepped backward, and as he did so she glanced up. For an instant she was silhouetted against the glimmering water, her white face spattered with mud, hair a coppery nimbus about her shoulders. Behind her the moon shone brilliantly, and on the opposite shore he could see the glittering lights of the distant airfield. It did not seem that she saw him at all. After a moment she looked down and began to kick again, more powerfully, and this time she would bring her heel back down across the man's back until Gordon could hear a crackling sound. He looked on paralyzed, his good hand squeezing tighter and tighter about the wrist of his bleeding hand as she went on and on and on. One of her steel boot-tips tore through his shoulder and the man screamed. Gordon could see one side of his face caved in like a broken gourd, dark and shining as though water pooled in its ragged hollows. Olivia bent and lifted something dark and heavy from the shallow water. Gordon made a whining noise in his throat and ran away, up the hill to where the crimelights cast wavering shadows through the weeds. Behind him he heard a dull crash and then silence.

A crowd had gathered in front of his apartment building when he finally got there. He shoved a bill at the cab driver and stumbled from the car. "Oh, no," he said out loud as the cab drove off, certain the crowd had something to do with Olivia and the man by the river: policemen, reporters, ambulances.

But it didn't have anything to do with that after all. There was music, cheerful music pouring from a player set inside one of the ground floor windows. Suddenly Gordon remembered talk of this at the Coop meeting last week: a party, an opportunity for the tenants to get to know one another. It had been his neighbor's idea, the one with the dog. Someone had strung Christmas lights from another window, and several people had set up barbecues on the gray front lawn. Flames leaped from the grills, making the shadows dance so it was impossible to determine how many people were actually milling about. Quite a few, Gordon thought. He smelled roasting meat, bitter woodsmoke with the unpleasant reek of paint in it—were they burning *furniture?*—and a strange sweetish scent, herbs or perhaps marijuana. The pain in his hand had dulled to a steady throbbing. When he looked down he closed his eyes for a few seconds and grit his teeth. There was so much blood.

"Hi!" a voice cried. He opened his eyes to see the woman from down the hall. She was no longer wearing her Rottweiler, nor the expensively tailored suits she usually favored. Instead she wore faded jeans and the kind of extravagantly beaded and embroidered tunic Gordon associated with his parents' youth. These and the many jingling chains and jewels that hung from her ears and about her wrists and ankles (she was barefoot, in spite of the cool evening) gave her a gypsy air. In the firelight he could see that her face *sans* makeup was childishly freckled. She looked very young and very happy.

"Mm, hi," Gordon mumbled, moving his blood-soaked arm from her sight. "A block party." He tried to keep his tone polite but uninterested as he pushed through the crowd of laughing people, but the young woman followed him, grinning.

"Isn't it great? You should come down, bring something to throw on the grill or something to drink, we're running out of hooch—"

She laughed, raising a heavy crystal wineglass and gulping from it something that was a deep purplish color and slightly viscous, certainly not wine. When she lowered the goblet he saw there was a small crack along its rim. This had cut the girl's upper lip which spun a slender filament of blood down across her chin. She didn't notice and threw her arm around his shoulders. "Promise you'll come back, mmm? We need more guys so we can *dance* and stuff, there's just never enough guys anymore—"

She whirled away drunkenly, swinging her arms out like a giddy spinning child. Whether purposely or not the goblet flew from her hand and shattered on the broken concrete sidewalk. A cheer went up from the crowd. Someone turned the music up louder. A number of people by the glowing braziers seemed to be dancing as the girl was, drunkenly, merrily, arms outstretched and hair flying. Gordon heard the tinkling report of another glass breaking, then another; then the sharper crash of what might have been a window. He put his face down and fairly ran through the swarm to the front door, which had been propped open with an old stump overgrown with curling ivy. The neatly lettered sign warning against strangers and open doors had been yanked from the doorframe and lay in a twisted mass on the steps inside. Gordon kicked it aside and fled down the hall to the firestairs.

There were people in the stairwell, sitting or lying on the steps in drunken twos and threes. One couple had shed their clothes and stood grunting and heaving in the darkened corner near the fire extinguisher. Gordon averted his eyes, stepping carefully among the others. A small pile of twigs had been ignited on the floor and sweet-smelling smoke trailed upward through the dimness. And other things were scattered upon the steps: branches of fir-trees scenting the air with balsam, sheaves of goldenrod, empty wine bottles. One of these clattered underfoot, nearly tripping him. Gordon looked over his shoulder to see it roll downstairs, bumping the head of a woman passed out near the bottom and then spinning across the floor, finally coming to rest beside the couple in the corner. No one noticed it; no one noticed Gordon as he flung open the door to the fifth floor and ran to his apartment.

He walked numbly through the kitchen. The answering machine blinked. Mechanically he reset it as he passed, paused between the kitchen and living room as the tape began. A sound of wind filled the room, wind and the rustle of many feet in dead leaves. Gordon swallowed, pressed his shaking hands together as the tape played on behind him. The wind grew louder, then softer, swelled and whispered. And all the while he heard beneath the faint staticky recording the ceaseless passage of many feet, and sometimes voices, murmurous and laughing, eerie and wild as the wind itself. The tape ended. The apartment was silent save for the dull insistent clicking of the answering machine begging to be switched off, that and the muffled sound of laughter from outside.

Gordon stepped warily into the next room. He had forgotten to leave a light on. But it was not dark: moonlight flooded the space, glimmering across the dark wooden floor, making the shadowed bulk of armchairs and sofa and electronic equipment seem black and strange and ominous. On the sill of the picture window that covered an entire wall the moonlight gleamed upon one of his treasures, a fish of handblown Venetian glass, hundreds of years old. Its mauve and violet swirls glowed in the milky light, its gaping mouth and crystalline eyes reminding him of the perch he had seen earlier, eyeless, dying. He stepped across the living room and stood there at the window staring down at the glass fish. And suddenly his head hurt, his chest felt heavy and cold. Looking at the glass fish he was filled with a dull puzzling ache, as though he were trying to remember a dream. He pondered how he had come to have such a thing, why it was that this marvel of spun glass and pastel coloring had ever meant more to him than a blind perch struggling through the poisonous river. His hand traced the delicate filigree of its spines. They felt cold, burning cold in the cloudy light spilling through the window.

There was a knock at the door. Gordon started, as though he had been asleep, then crossed the darkened room. Through the peephole he saw Olivia, her hair atangle, a streak of black across one cheek. Her expression was oddly calm and untroubled in the carmine glare of the EXIT light. He tightened his hand about the doorknob, biting his lip against the pain that shot up through his arm as he did so. He wondered dully how she had gotten into the building, then remembered the chaos outside. Anyone could come in; even a woman who had seemingly just kicked a man to death by the polluted river. Perhaps it was like this all across the city, perhaps doors that had been locked since the riots had this evening suddenly sprung open.

"Gordon," Olivia commanded, her voice muffled by the heavy door that separated them. He was not surprised to feel the knob twist beneath his throbbing palm, or see the door swing inward to bump against his toe. Olivia slipped in, and with her a breath of incense-smelling smoke, the muted clamour of voices and laughter and pulsing music.

"Where'd you go?" she asked, smiling. He noticed that behind her the door had not quite closed. He reached to pull it shut but before he could grasp it she took him by the hand, the one that hurt. Grunting softly with pain he turned from the door to follow her into the living room.

"What's happening?" he whispered. "Olivia, what is it?" Without speaking she pulled him to the floor beside her, still smiling. She pulled his jacket from him, then his shoes and trousers and finally his blood-stained shirt. He reached to remove her blouse but Olivia pushed him away ungently, so that he cried out. As she moved above him his hand began to bleed again, leaving dark petals across her blouse and arms. The pain was so intense that he moaned, tried in vain to slow her but she only tightened her grip about his upper arm, tossing her hair back so that it formed a dark haze against the window's milky light. The blouse slipped from her shoulder and he could see the scars there, the little golden rings against her skin, drops of blood like rain flashing across her throat. Behind her the moon shone, bloated and sanguine. He could hear voices chanting counterpoint to the blood thudding in his temples. It took him a long time to catch his breath afterward. Olivia had bitten him on the shoulder, hard enough to bruise him. The pain coupled with that from his cut hand had suddenly made everything very intense, made him cry out loudly and then fall back hard against the cold floor as Olivia slipped from him. Now only the pain was left. He rubbed his shoulder ruefully. "Olivia? Are you angry?" he asked. She stood impassively in front of the window. The torn blouse had slipped from her shoulder. She had kicked her silk trousers beneath the sofa but pulled her boots back on, and moonlight glinted off the two wicked metal points. She seemed not to have heard him, so he repeated her name softly.

"Mmmm?" she said, distracted. She stared up at the sky, then leaned forward and opened the casement. Cold air flooded the room, and a brighter, colder light as well, as though the glass had ceased to filter out the lunar brilliance. Gordon shivered and groped for his shirt.

"Look at them," whispered Olivia. He got unsteadily to his feet and stood beside her, staring down at the sidewalk. Small figures capered across the broken tarmac, forms made threatening by the lurid glow of myriad bonfires that had sprung up across the dead gray lawn. He heard music too, not music from the radio or stereo but a crude raw sound, thrumming and beating as of metal drums, voices howling and forming words he could not quite make out, an unknown name or phrase—

"Evohe," whispered Olivia. The face she turned to him was white and merciless, her eyes inflamed. *"Evohe."*

"What?" said Gordon. He stepped backward and stumbled on one of his shoes. When he righted himself and looked up he saw that there were other people in the room, other women, three four six of them, even more it seemed, slipping silently through the door that Olivia had left open behind her. They filled the small apartment with a cloying smell of smoke and burning hair, some of them carrying smoking sticks, others leather pocketbooks or scorched briefcases. He recognized many of them: though their hair was matted and wild, their clothes torn: dresses or suits ripped so that their breasts were exposed and he could see where the flesh had been raked by their own fingernails, leaving long wavering scars like signatures scratched in blood. Two of them were quite young and naked and caressed each other laughing, turning to watch him with sly feral eyes. Several of the older women had golden rings piercing their breasts or the frail web of flesh between their fingers. One traced a cut that ran down her thigh, then lifted her bloodied finger to her lips as though imploring Gordon to keep a secret. He saw another gray-haired woman whom he had greeted often at the newstand where they both purchased the *Wall Street Journal*. She seemingly wore only a fur-trimmed camel's-hair coat. Beneath its soft folds Gordon glimpsed an undulating pattern of green and gray and gold. As she approached him she let the coat fall away and he saw a snake encircling her throat, writhing free to slide down between her breasts and then to the floor at Gordon's feet. He shouted and turned to flee.

Olivia was there, Olivia caught him and held him so tightly that for a moment he imagined she was embracing him, imagined the word she repeated was his name, spoken more and more loudly as she held him until he felt the breath being crushed from within his chest. But it was not his name, it was another name, a word like a sigh, like the whisper of a thought coming louder and louder as the others took it up and they were chanting now:

"*Evohe, evohe . . .*"

As he struggled with Olivia they fell upon him, the woman from the newstand, the girl from down the hall now naked and laughing in a sort of grunting chuckle, the two young girls encircling him with their slender cool arms and giggling as they kissed his cheeks and nipped his ears. Fighting wildly he thrashed until his head was free and he could see beyond them, see the open window behind the writhing web of hair and arms and breasts, the moon blazing now like a mad watchful eye above the burning canyons. He could see shreds of darkness falling from the sky, clouds or rain or wings, and he heard faintly beneath the shrieks and moans and panting voices the wail of sirens all across the city. Then he fell back once more beneath them.

There was a tinkling crash. He had a fleeting glimpse of something mauve and lavender skidding across the floor, then cried out as he rolled to one side and felt the glass shatter beneath him, the slivers of breath-spun fins and gills and tail slicing through his side. He saw Olivia, her face serene, her liquid eyes full of ardor as she turned to the girl beside her and took from her something that gleamed like silver in the moonlight, like pure and icy water, like a spar of broken glass. Gordon started to scream when she knelt between his thighs. Before he fainted he saw against the sky the bloodied fingers of eagle's wings, blotting out the face of a vast triumphant moon.

COMMON LAND

by Joel Lane

Joel Lane returns to The Year's Best Horror Stories *with one of his infrequent stories—all too infrequent, as he is a master at creating a mood of disturbing and disorienting strangeness set against backgrounds of urban decay. It's as if Walter de la Mare sat down to write about urban blight and disintegrating relationships one afternoon while he was feeling depressed.*

Born in Exeter in 1963, Lane grew up in Birmingham, studied at Cambridge, and currently lives in Birmingham, where he is working for an educational publisher. Recently he has had stories published in Skeleton Crew, Ambit, Critical Quarterly, *and* Exuberance, *as well as critical articles on Lovecraft and Dr. Seuss (separate articles, although the connection could be mind-boggling). "Common Land" is from Nicholas Royle's excellent small press anthology,* Darklands. *Keep reading, and you'll find one of Royle's own stories here in a bit.*

She went to New Street Station to meet him. Stephen's letter had been forwarded from her old address, and he wouldn't know where to look for her. Rosalind waited outside the ticket barrier, in a brightly lit underground hall that, late at night, was filled with silent people. Some were waiting for trains, others for people walking through from the street; and others would stand until they were moved on. In his letter, Stephen had said he was homeless now. Rosalind wondered just what that meant. But the letter had a local postmark; why had he made her come here, when he could have met her in town during the day? She supposed it was one of his gestures, intended to make her feel something. Just after eleven, Rosalind thought she saw Stephen waving goodbye to someone on the far side of the ticket barrier. He came through alone, carrying a weekend bag and wearing a green overcoat that she'd not seen before, though it looked old.

He was pleased to see her. "I didn't know if you'd be free. I've got a lot to tell you." They walked up through the shopping arcades to the New Street ramp. Stephen was visibly tired, though he seemed inwardly worked up about something. His eyes flickered briefly at everyone who passed by. Rosalind didn't know what to ask him. Besides, she realized, the silence that had brought them face to face again might be broken by discussion. They were in time for the last bus to Northfield. The city center seemed full of young couples, embracing in the bus shelters and shop doorways. The rain whitewashed the pavements.

Rosalind's flat—strictly speaking, a bedsit with its own sink and electric cooker—was part of one of the large houses on the main road. There was no light on the staircase. Stephen followed her up to the second floor. Inside, he stared around him as though displaced. The room was fairly chaotic; half of it was taken up by the table, on which she'd placed a large square of hardboard. This was now covered with newspaper and twisted hulks of red clay, parts of which glistened like poor special effects. Stephen sat on the couch and wrapped his arms across his chest. The stubble on his cheeks only showed up how pale his skin was. Rosalind lit the gas fire, though it was only September and she didn't feel cold herself.

"Do you remember our first year?" he said. He meant the first year at art college, when the two of them had lived in a house with three other students. They hadn't been going out together then. "I'm trying to get another group together, like that. A commune, really. I'd like you to meet them." He hesitated, and glanced across at the table. "What are you doing now? Selling your work?"

"Trying to. I'm on an enterprise allowance." They both laughed at that. Among the rough figures drying on the hardboard were a child's head with pale blue marbles for eyes and a human foot with wings growing from either side of the Achilles tendon. "From now until next June, I'll be trying to make and sell things like these."

"That's good. I've not done anything like that since leaving college. Actually I've been traveling around. Meeting different kinds of people." He talked slowly, letting gaps form between his words and what he meant to say. Rosalind was just glad that he was back. Behind where he was sitting, though he hadn't noticed it, there was a painting which he'd done of her the year before last. It caught her in a rather stiff posture, closed in by an abstract gray background. She was half turned away, her features sharply defined and detailed, eyes shut. Rosalind had used to think the painting proof of Stephen's feelings for her.

"I'm not working," he went on. "Not officially, anyway. There's a group of us, we're moving into an empty house in Deritend, this week. It's not easy. You'll have to see for yourself, the way we live. And what the point of it is. We use whatever we can find. Like gypsies. Self-help, I suppose you could call it. That's the way I was brought up." Stephen had come from a deprived region, one of the enclosed towns of the Black Country that had a city's landscape and a village's culture. Rosalind had a comfortable suburban background, and the differences had always stuck between them. He fell into silence. The room was warm now, the steady firelight stamping a grid on Rosalind's eyes.

"We can talk in the morning," she said. It was ridiculous for them to have said so little to each other; but she needed to sleep, not to think. They sat on the bed under the window at the far end of the room. Stephen muttered something, thanked her for going to meet him. She unbuttoned his shirt. He was thinner than she remembered. Her hand stopped just below his rib-cage, on the left side. There was something there that felt solid and cold under the skin, though the surface was unmarked. "Does that hurt?" He shook his head. She pressed it, and thought of touching the half-frozen snow on a hedge. Her hands began to shake.

"Don't worry," he said. "There's nothing the matter." He took her hands and pressed them together, then drew her head forward and kissed her, breathing into her throat. They made love very slowly and tenderly, hardly moving, as though it hurt them to draw apart. The night seemed to dissolve the building, pulling them down into each other. Rosalind felt lost; she was never at home in passion. At a rational level, she didn't believe that she had missed him this much. Stephen held her without forcing, almost childlike in his need. The thread of joy stretched tighter in the darkness, then broke, letting them slip apart from each other and into sleep.

When Rosalind awoke, her first thought was that it had somehow become winter. Stephen's breath was misted above his face, like scratches on a window. He was lying on his side, facing her; his dark hair was stuck to his forehead. His eyelids were twitching, as though his dreams were struggling toward the light. As she watched, a series of white threads drifted from his mouth and joined the cloud that was forming there. It seemed about to assume some definite shape. Stephen's mouth opened wider, and a continuous stream of fibers linked it to the slowly hardening veil that now covered his face, becoming nearly opaque.

Shocked at herself, Rosalind reached up and touched the caul. It was soft as cotton, with harder fragments like seeds or crystals. The material did not tear, but the warmth of her hand dissolved it; soon there was nothing left. Stephen's face tensed, losing the gentleness of sleep; his eyes opened. They looked at each other. "We need your help," he said.

"We? You mean—"

"Me and the others." He smiled. "Or me and . . . whatever's inside. What did it look like? I mean, *who* did it look like?"

Rosalind hadn't asked herself that. "I don't know. Not like anyone in particular. Have you seen . . ."

"It seems to take different shapes. From me, from other people. There are five of us. In the house." He sat up, and began to dress. Rosalind held back; she was afraid to touch him, for various reasons. Stephen made no move toward her. "There's nothing to explain," he said. "What we really need is some way to form. It's no good trying on your own. We need someone who can bring it together for us. Then we'll know what's going on." He was very nervous; Rosalind knew that he was afraid she'd reject him. She knew what he was like. Stephen broke the deadlock by putting on his coat. He took a notebook from the inside pocket, wrote something down and tore out the page. "That's where we're going to live," he said. "Come and visit us, if you want to. Soon." He kissed her goodbye; his mouth tasted quite ordinary.

Over the next fortnight, Rosalind found a craft shop in Hagley and another in Evesham that would take her clay sculptures. She began working on a series of rather delicate masks, using paler clay and a brittle varnish that made her feel light-headed and sickly. The week after that, she went to find Stephen's house. Deritend wasn't an area where a great many people lived—or at least, not one where many people had homes. It was a district in transition between the city center and the suburbs. Nothing old there had remained intact, but nothing had been removed either. Parts of various buildings had been taken over by wholesalers or manufacturers, who had put new signboards over the ground-floor windows; while the upper stories were left to decay, their elaborately carved roofs and window-frames stripped naked by the weather. Just off the High Street, a church had been turned into a warehouse for general works equipment; its roof now consisted of reinforced glass set in a lattice of wooden beams.

Even the A-Z map was an unreliable guide to the maze of backstreets, overlaid with railway bridges and new expressways. Series of identical terraced houses were juxtaposed with minor factories, car parks, derelict buildings, canals. Near where Stephen lived, the windows of a pub had been boarded over; someone had chalked WELCOME across one of the boards. Next to that, a scrap yard was full of cars piled three or four high and rusting steadily, like toys in the back of a cupboard. Rosalind walked under a bridge that crossed the main road, in the dip of a little valley. The sudden darkness and smell of rot made her pause and struggle to remember something. She felt displaced. The roof of the bridge was furred with black crystals. What looked like nails driven through it from above were in fact hollow pipes of lime sediment, formed by gradual seepage of water. A few of their tips glittered with an unexpected brightness, dripping.

Beyond the bridge, a line of houses faced the brick embankment of the railway. This was where the commune, Stephen and his friends, were staying. The house was thin and crusted with the same pollution as the bridge; but the windows and their net curtains were clean. There was a small front yard, where rose bushes and brambles were tangled together, obstructing the path. Rosalind knocked on the door. A middle-aged woman in a baggy green sweater opened it. "Are you Rosalind?" she asked. Rosalind nodded, taken aback. "Well then, come inside." The interior of the house smelled of cooking and damp. Stephen and two younger men, who looked very like one another, were sitting in the kitchen. Stephen looked worse than he had the last time; he embraced her before speaking. Then he introduced her to the others. The woman's name was Sandra; she came from Leeds, and had been an actress. The two youths, Lee and Mike, were non-identical twins; they came from Glasgow. There was another tenant, a bearded silent man called Alan, whom Rosalind met later.

To begin with, Stephen was the only one that Rosalind had any real contact with. She came over to the house every few days, and slept with him; or sometimes he stayed over at her flat in Northfield. For Rosalind, it seemed like a chance to relive the early weeks of their relationship, now three years in the past. His illness, or whatever it was, had the effect of making him gentler and more dependent. She enjoyed taking care of him, and using the therapy to ease her own tensions and fears at the same time. He was a mirror for her, as she secretly knew and had always known. She assumed it would end, either when he recovered himself and got bored with her (as had happened before), or when she found a permanent job and moved away from the area.

If Rosalind got used to the strange material, it was only because she didn't allow anything to do with Stephen to be quite real. That was her way of not getting too involved. The sight and touch of it fascinated her. She remembered having seen photographs of séances from the nineteenth century where the same effect was produced. Stephen needed to be asleep for it to happen. She watched him in the night, until something formed out of his throat and diffused above him. It was colder than flesh, and didn't respond to air currents. Once the tissue spread across the upper half of Stephen's body, like fresh bark on a silver birch tree. It cocooned him for hours. Rosalind thought he was dying; she lay there unable to move, until his skin was clear again.

Sometimes Rosalind thought of it as a living thing, a homeless being that had taken possession of Stephen and made him alien to her. Then she'd draw away from him, make him come to her and prove that she was needed. When they were close once more, she thought of the emissions as inert: a waste product, the traces of some unrecognizable industry. By day, she and Stephen worked together on her sculptures and pottery. They ate together, went for walks, saw films, sometimes made love. Stephen watched her all the time, obsessed as before with her image. In early December, when the frost and the shrunken daylight made traveling difficult, and she couldn't afford the heating costs of her flat, Rosalind moved in with the commune.

The others accepted her, without particularly trying to make her feel at home. Rosalind and Stephen shared one room; Lee and Mike shared another; while Sandra and Alan had their own rooms. It took Sandra more than a week to start talking to Rosalind, but after that she seemed to take to the newcomer in a maternal kind of way, proving an unexpected source of advice. Her conversation was a mixture of practicality and folklore. She told Rosalind a lot about her past: traveling, the theater, cities and lovers. Much of it was inconsistent and probably made up. But Rosalind found it strangely reassuring to think that she, too, would eventually have a past. Something else that Sandra told her stuck in her mind: that you could get a man by making a clay effigy of one and wrapping it in coils of your own hair.

One evening, when Sandra had a cold and stayed in her room, Rosalind took her up a bowl of soup. She knocked on the door and heard the answer: "Come in." When she opened the door, she thought Sandra was lying under a sheet. At once, her mind registered the presence of the dead. "It's all right," Sandra said clearly; a whitish skein lifted from her and hung between the two women, losing itself as Rosalind's eyes focused in the half-light. She felt as though her own reflection had glanced off a window or a basin of water. She knelt beside Sandra's bed, feeling giddy, and put the bowl down. The smell of boiled onions twisted in her head. The older woman reached down and took her hands, saying, "It's all right. You're just not ready yet. Give it time."

It wasn't until Rosalind had moved in that she realized one of the area's deficiencies. There were almost no telephone boxes. She had to walk nearly a mile toward the city center to make a phone call. What the area did have was many public toilets, at least the small kind built into the alcoves of walls: uniform metal boxes with ornate designs on the panels. They were useless to women. By night, it was anybody's guess which buildings were derelict and which in use. Local business was a testament to the idea of self-help. That could mean opening bed and breakfast accommodation on the ground floor of an abandoned building, leaving the upper stories empty and blackened with half a century's dirt. Or cutting the shell of a factory down to head level, making it an enclosed scrap yard. Or using a terraced house with barred windows as a small warehouse for building materials or the like. Houses and churches were just more kinds of wall.

The dead tissue that Stephen and the others breathed limited the commune. That was how Rosalind came to see it, without being able to explain the effect. The simplicity of their lives was partly chosen and partly involuntary. They were poor, but that wasn't it. They were like patients; life had closed in on them. They worked, on and off, in the local trades. Alan was a factory's night watchman. Sandra cooked and served in an all-night café. The twins helped to load and unload trucks for the salvage department. Stephen was probably the most idle of the group; his main occupation was being the leader of their peculiar rituals. The house wasn't very fit to live in. They kept the kitchen hygienic, but the damp and grime elsewhere couldn't be dealt with. A lot of their furniture came from local rubbish tips or empty houses. They had electricity, but expense and dangerously faulty wiring deterred them from using the power points. For warmth, they depended on paraffin heaters and clothing. Rosalind tried to believe that the end would justify the means.

If only so much weren't hidden from her. One night, when she went to the bathroom to relieve herself, the washbasin was furred up with strands of ectoplasm. She tore a piece of it away; it had the feel of numbness. She could just make out her hand behind it in the dark. Another time, Rosalind tried to call Stephen's bluff. "Why do you want me here?" she said. "I don't belong. Nothing happens when I'm around . . . What does it mean? It's that different I can't talk about it or think about it. I don't know how you can live here." Stephen faced the window, staring at the blackened wall of the embankment, the arches bricked up. "Speak to me. Tell me something."

He turned round and looked at her, without changing his expression. Rosalind walked out of their bedroom and down the stairs to the front door. Stephen leaned over the banister in the hallway and appeared to blow her a kiss. Clouds trailed from his hand. She spent that night in the café, wrapped in her depression as though it were alcohol, watching all the homeless people come, stay and eventually go. They could make a cup of coffee or a cigarette last an hour and occupy them completely. They talked in rituals, giving bits of themselves that they were used to giving, holding onto familiar phrases. *Nearly morning. Where you been? Just one more.* If you said something unexpected, they wouldn't hear you.

Over Christmas, Rosalind went to stay with her father and stepmother in Stafford. They'd been living there for five years, and were gradually redecorating and refurnishing the house, so that every time she went back it was like somewhere different. She felt like a child again. What she couldn't mention seemed to get into every word she said and take away its impulse. Rather than sit in the living-room and watch TV, she walked around the town, which looked unreal in its coating of frost and sodium light. For some reason, the sound of carol-singers frightened her; not the songs, but the chorus of voices. On Christmas Eve they attended midnight mass at the cathedral. Rosalind kept thinking: *You haven't got me fooled, you two. Pretending to belong.* Her childhood hadn't been this peaceful, or this normal. It wasn't reality either.

I could tell you a few things about communion. Her last night with Stephen, she'd taken some of the plasma and tried to eat it. She'd stopped almost at once, because of the images it brought to mind. It tasted of nothing at all. She'd thought of cancer, the body eating itself. Or of primitive magic, someone eating nerves to make herself better able to feel.

Rosalind went back to the house near the end of December. In the thin daylight the countryside seemed pure and featureless, like a face that hid its age in sleep. Trees and hedges were sketched in charcoal. As the train came into Birmingham, the environment darkened. It was slightly warmer here; the veneer of frost gave way to a matte vapor. Factory chimneys bruised the clouds gray and yellow. She was thinking of Stephen. Perhaps she'd get him away from the others, soon, and the two of them could go to live somewhere in the country, say in Evesham. She wanted to hide in the privacy of their bedroom. Sculpt figures and make love with Stephen, and sleep through the long vacant nights. Everything seemed possible again.

She had to try several times before her key would turn in the lock. Evidently the cold had warped the doorframe. None of the windows were lit. As she stood cursing at the front door, a goods train shuddered along the embankment behind her. Eventually Rosalind got the door open; the hall was dark. She flicked the light switch. *Fucking hell.* Either the antique wiring had given out or they'd been disconnected. Or else it was a power cut. Some light came through the windows in the kitchen. All the commune were standing in there. Just standing together, quite close, facing inward. They must have heard her struggling with the door. But even now, they ignored her. She was so angry that at first she didn't notice what they were looking at.

It was rather like the stream of ashes in the heat-haze over a bonfire. But as Rosalind watched, it took on form, becoming a kind of effigy. This time, she knew it was using her eyes to define itself. Each member of the group standing round it was connected to it at the mouth, by a glistening thread of vapor. The plasma only shone where it caught the light. Rosalind couldn't identify the figure, no matter how intently she looked at it. It had a thin body, with arms folded over its breasts, and a wreath of long hair around its face. But the face itself was somehow impersonal. The features were empty. Rosalind had the impression that they were reversed, the eyes and mouth opening inward; though that was not what she saw. It made her think of an identikit face in a newspaper; though she had never seen a female one, and found it very hard to accept this image as a woman. She pressed herself against the wall, feeling powerless, and wrapped her arms around herself in an unconscious mimicry of the creature.

The others drew back, apparently sensing that they had done what they could. For the first time, Rosalind could see how tired they were, as if they had not slept since her departure. Sandra sat down at the kitchen table and covered her face with her hands. Lee and Mike caught hold of each other and stood motionless by the window. Alan walked slowly through the doorway and up the stairs. Stephen turned toward Rosalind, reached out and touched her arm. "Look after her," he said. That was all he said. It was Rosalind he was speaking to. The gray-white figure settled itself on the floor, its arms around its knees; its head dropped forward. It grew fainter and lost some of its outline, but did not go away. It would not move for several hours.

More out of fear than concern for the others, Rosalind made herself do some housework. The sink was heaped with plates and cups, none of which appeared to have been used recently. She scrubbed a few clean and piled the rest on the sideboard, not knowing when they'd have some hot water. Probably the others needed a meal; she certainly did, after the journey. The only food in the larder was dried, and months old: rice, lentils, pasta shells. There weren't even any tins. She went out to buy some fresh food and milk. When she came back, nothing had happened. She took the shirts and underclothes from the clotheshorse at the foot of the stairs, folded them and piled them up on a chair. They had dried hard, though the air had touched them with damp. She cooked some soup on the paraffin stove, though its fumes nearly made her pass out.

Rosalind and Stephen ate, leaving a half-full pot on

the stove for the others. The cold thing of breath and threads watched them from the floor, passively. When it grew dark outside, since they had no light, they went up to bed. Stephen fucked her twice, hard; her release was like shedding a skin. They slept huddled under the blankets. The next day they awoke after dawn; they clung together, kissing and whispering, until it was dark once more. The day after that, they got up. Rosalind washed herself and pulled clothes onto a body that still felt unreal. All the time, she knew she was being watched.

The life of the commune made more sense now. Every day, all the others would gather round the maiden-creature and breathe matter into it. The rest of the time, they hardly spoke or gave attention to anything. Rosalind felt left out. What was expected of her was something different. She talked and acted for the maiden. She couldn't talk to it, but she talked to herself or Stephen, and the thing listened. Sometimes it followed her in the house, like a voiceless double. It mimicked her posture and the movements of her hands.

Rosalind could feel everything she did or said taking on a new intensity, like performance. She relived events from her childhood, making stories of them, weaving in lines from traditional songs that she hadn't realised she still knew. The blank-faced creature took in everything. It saw her and Stephen in bed together. It saw her panic on finding a nest of silverfish in the larder, then boil water to get rid of them, and then spill the water and scald herself badly. It saw her crying, swallowing painkillers, bleeding, coughing up phlegm from a cold on her chest. This went on for nearly a fortnight.

One morning, a few days into the new year, Rosalind walked out of the house. The sunlight dazzled her; she had to keep stopping until her head cleared. The upper windows of half-ruined buildings showed her the sky. From the doorway of the café where Sandra worked, a man whistled at her. "Get the message, love." She had a toothache. A yard full of silver-headed thistles was enclosed on three sides by blocks of flats, with washing hanging from the balconies. The harvest of seeds caught the light. A few hours later, when Rosalind was back in the house, she realized that she couldn't actually have seen that.

When Stephen saw she was ill, he told her: "You'd better leave." She ought to have known he wouldn't change. He spent more time close to the ghost-creature now, communing with it in a way she couldn't. She'd watched him kiss it, breathing substance into its blurred face. "It's not enough," he said. "You have to give yourself. You can't do it. It's not your fault." Rosalind realized that he wasn't concerned about her at all.

"What more do you want?" They were standing in the bedroom. Rosalind's face twisted with bitter emotions until it felt like a mask. Even her sense of failure was probably being used—and she didn't know for what. It was all hidden. Stephen looked out of the window, again. He was unshaven; it gave him the appearance of strength. Rosalind seized his arms and kissed him fiercely, trying to claim him. He turned away as though nauseated, and stared at the glass.

"Nothing in particular," he muttered. "You're not the first. And you won't be the fucking last."

Later that day, while Stephen was out of the house, Rosalind took out a half-full bottle of vodka that she kept among her clothes in a suitcase. She drank it all, mixed with water. A strange feeling of indifference grew in her. It felt like a snow child lodged in her abdomen. She collected together whatever tablets she could find—codeine, paracetamol, a dozen or so sleeping pills prescribed a long time back. She swallowed them all, sitting on the edge of the bath, watching the water run from the tap like a stream of pure light. It took more than an hour. Finally she went back into the bedroom, drew the curtains, and lay down on the bed.

She woke up in the night, and registered only that she was alone. Before dawn, she realized that she was going to be sick. She forced herself to stand up, but didn't have enough strength to walk. She leaned her head over the bare floorboards and tried to vomit. Only a few drops of clear fluid ran from her mouth. Between that night and the next, all she could do was be sick, or try to. Twice she managed to stagger to the bathroom and swallow a few mouthfuls of water, in order to bring it up later. She was still the only one who couldn't vomit ectoplasm. In between, she lay inert on the bed and felt the hard numbness shift inside her. In spite of the cold, she was drenched in sweat.

Some of the others watched her, without trying to help. Sandra came in with Alan, and said something to him that sounded like "No good to anyone." The pale creature hung around most of the time. She could feel it draining her, but it pretended to nurse her. It touched her throat with its hollow fingers, and stroked her hair, making gestures of sympathy. Close up, its vacant face was a mosaic, like a cracked window; everything human in it was broken up. Rosalind vomited on its arm, a yellowish bile that scarred it deeply. Or so she thought. There was nobody to share her point of view. Stephen was nowhere in sight. He was probably out looking for someone else. Self-help was all that remained to her.

A day later, she still hadn't eaten anything. But she'd gone on drinking water until eventually she kept it down. Her face in the bathroom mirror was jaundiced. It was probably liver damage, she realized. As soon as she could keep upright, Rosalind struggled from the house and began walking toward the city center. She could see the post office tower and clock from the roadway. It was getting dark. She watched the clouds moving overhead, a great open stretch of damaged tissue. The smoke of a factory chimney reflected the light from the city. All around her, buildings enclosed the view; but she felt as though she were on a hilltop. The chill of her freedom paralyzed her. What cried out in her mind, still, wasn't the atrocity half-realized in her or waiting to be fulfilled in others. It was the simple misery of knowing that the group had created something to unite them. And it had only left each of them feeling more alone.

AN INVASION OF ANGELS

by Nina Kiriki Hoffman

Born in Los Angeles on March 20, 1955, Nina Kiriki Hoffman grew up in southern California, whence she escaped to Idaho before becoming a Val Girl. For the past seven years or so she has lived in Eugene, Oregon, where she has been busy writing very many short stories for very many magazines and anthologies. Her versatility and audacious freshness of ideas have quickly gained her recognition in the fantasy/horror genre. With some authors I'm never really sure what they're on about; with Hoffman I know she's up to something, but I'm not quite sure what until she pounces.

Hoffman's first book, a collection of short stories entitled Legacy of Fire, *was published this past year, and she has recently sold a young adult novel,* Child of an Ancient City, *(written with Tad Williams) to Atheneum. "An Invasion of Angels" was written in a challenge she and Dean Wesley Smith have every holiday season: each author must write five stories in six days—this time writing around Christmas carol titles. For most of us, just writing Christmas cards is enough challenge.*

1. Bring a Torch, Jeanette Isabella

The morning of the celebration, her parents said she was too young to know, too young to help. "Stay home, Jeanie, and lock the door," said her mother, looking around the dark kitchen. Fire flickered in the fireplace, licking at the spit above it, scenting the room with the last sizzles from the meat they'd had for supper the night before. A cauldron hung from a hook above the flames. Bunched herbs dangled from the ceiling. "Keep the fire burning. Peel potatoes and scrub carrots. Cut up plenty of onions. Heat water, Jeanie. Daddy and I will bring home manna meat when the celebration's over."

Jeanie stood in the kitchen doorway and watched her parents walk away between the other low thatched houses. The evening air was chill. Her breath made thin clouds that melted before they reached the sky. In the distance she could hear the celebration in the town square, people hollering, or were they singing? Everyone else in Sheol must be there, dancing around the manna. She was not sure what the manna was, only that it was something to eat which had come from heaven.

Mama had kept her inside all day, ever since Ben Wright came in that morning, twisting his cloth cap between his hands as he stood just inside the kitchen door, saying, "Mr. Marshall, there's a thing down to the Coburn barn. It fell from the sky. They sent me to summon you to conference about it."

When Daddy came home for dinner, sometime after noon, he said they had passed a judgment on the thing; it was manna. Everybody was to celebrate the rest of the day and praise the Lord for what He provided. Daddy left again after dinner.

Presently the town got rowdier. Mama said they must be dipping into the Sunday punch. People danced past the house, calling. Mama closed the door and told Jeanie to stay away from the windows, but she smiled as she said it. "A manna," she said. "It was a manna day when I got you, Jeanie, a gift from the Lord. On a manna day, everybody's married to everybody else. That's why you got to stay inside, love. You're too young to be married."

Jeanie sighed, and shut and barred the door. She

peeled the potatoes and let them sit in water. She peeled and sliced the carrots and put them in to float with the potatoes, then cut onions into long crescents, not wiping away the tears because onion smell made her cry less than onion touch. How tired she was of being too young.

She dropped a wet cloth over the sliced onions, then fed the fire. She sat on the hearth and poked a stick into the flames until it caught fire, then played with it, teasing the flame up along it by pointing it at the floor, then flipping it up so that the flame tasted the stick but did not consume it. The red ember heart of the stick's fire ate its way down, leaving charred and blackened wood behind. Too young. Not too young to burn things.

Someone pounded on the door. "Jeanie!" yelled a man, his words slurred. "Little Jeanie, come out!"

She played with her flaming stick, glanced sideways at the barred door, and said nothing.

"Get away from there, Saul!" yelled her father. She heard thumps against the door, and the slap of flesh on flesh, then a whump. Must be Saul McManus. Did he want to be married to her because it was a manna day? He wouldn't be able to marry her if Daddy knocked him out.

"Jeanie," said her father, "you all right?"

If she didn't answer, would he break the door down?

"Jeanie?"

"I'm fine, Daddy," she said.

"You got the fire going?"

"Going great."

"Let me in."

She got up and unbarred the door.

Daddy's eyes were bloodshot, and he'd lost his belt; he held up his trousers with his hand. He had straw in his hair. "Jeanie, bring a torch," he said. She smelled Sunday spirits on his breath. "Bring a torch. We're roasting the manna meat down to the square, and everybody's fire has gone out, what with the celebration."

Jeanie fed up the fire so it would keep while they were gone. Sometimes everybody's fire went out, and then someone had to go to the fire lake and bring some back in a pot. It was a fierce job; the heat down on the lakeshore scorched your hair off. Jeanie would rather not have to go fetch fire.

She thrust a torch into the flames. When it caught, she followed her father out.

People lay like litter along the streets, huddling together, their clothes tangled and ripped. Some still moved. Jeanie watched a couple moving together and wondered what it felt like. Her father marched and sang ahead of her, oblivious to everything.

In the square, people danced. In the middle stood a white thing bound with ropes. It was tied to the stake they usually used in spring for the ribbon dances. It had the form of a robed, beardless man, save for the humped whitenesses at its shoulders. People had piled kindling and logs about its feet.

"I've brought Jeanie, she's brought fire," her father sang, and the people danced apart so she and her father could walk through.

Jeanie heard her mother scream, "Hiram! What are you—how could you—!" Jeanie looked toward the sound and saw her mother, bare to the waist, supporting her breasts with her hands, or maybe trying to cover them. Am I too young because my breasts aren't that big? Jeanie wondered.

"Set the fire, Jeanie," her father sang. A man came up behind her mother and put his arms around her, then leaned forward and kissed her ear. Mama struggled. Jeanie looked away, at the manna.

It had the most beautiful eyes she had ever seen. They were blue as sky. It stared down at her, no expression on its face, only a quiet gravity in its gaze. Its wingfeathers had been broken and hacked, the longer ones clipped. Dried blood clung to its white robe and stained its wings.

You are so beautiful and sad, Jeanie thought, and dipped the torch so it touched the kindling at the manna's feet.

2. What Child Is This?

Snow whispered against the roof of old Reenie's cabin. Wrapped in her patchwork quilt, Reenie rocked, paused to listen, rocked, paused to poke the fire. Snow hissed down the chimney, melting before it ever reached the ground. Sometimes she heard a falling noise, and thought: now the snow has built up on a branch and got too heavy for it, so the branch has dumped it. Nice to be warm and indoors on a night like this.

She was drowsing in her patchwork quilt when a new noise rose above the whisper of the snow. A wavering cry—or perhaps a thread of song? It came from outside.

She rocked a while longer. She glanced at the chair across the hearth from her and thought of Jacob. If he were alive he would have gone outside immediately to see what made that noise. He had been an old man with curiosity running through his veins, not a restful person to live with, always asking what's this or why's that. Constant questions wore a body down.

Reenie leaned back and closed her eyes, listening to the fire and the snow, hoping they'd talk her to sleep. But that little wail coming from out the door, it kept nagging at her, even through the warmth. At last she got up and put on her old red cloak, and stepped into her wooden shoes. Then she opened the door to the storm.

Such a white, quiet night. The snow so calm and dancy and thick she couldn't even see the fire lake in the valley below. The snow's clean scent had scrubbed away the sulfur smell of it. Reenie stood in the doorway a moment, thinking nights like this didn't come along often enough to suit her. Then she stepped out into the snow.

The little cry came from off to her left. She tracked her way through the snow and found, in a drift near where the cabin met the mountain, a wee winged babe. It wore no clothes, and its weak thrashings had stirred up the snow and half buried it. It reached its arms up to her and made its little cry.

She stood looking down at it, and felt something hot and hurting in the wound in her chest. She stopped and lifted the child in arms that had not forgotten a mother's clasp. It snuggled against her. Its wing brushed her hand. She had never felt anything so soft; not even the kiss of snow was so gentle.

Nothing had hurt her so much in a long time.

She stood and held the babe, feeling how her eyes were trying to make tears. She looked at her cabin, huddled up against the mountain, and thought of the little door inside that led to the ice cave. Jacob had built that door thick and well so the cold couldn't get into the cabin. They had gone into the ice cave often, when he was still alive, to look at the ice crystal formations. She had been back only twice since he died.

She carried the little child into the cabin and sat with it in the rocker for a little time. It no longer wailed, but spoke to her in words she did not understand. It plucked at the quilt and pointed, bright-eyed, at the braided rag rug on the floor. It watched the fire.

The wound in her chest ached.

At last she rose and opened the door to the ice cave. The light from the cabin came through enough for her to see Jacob and place the child in his frozen lap. It fluttered its wings and cried, reaching for her. She turned her back on it and looked at her heart, sitting on a stalagmite of ice. Yes, there was a little pool of water under it. That would never do. She mustn't ever let it thaw again. Nothing cut up a body's comfort so much as a feeling heart.

She ducked back into the cabin and closed the door, then tacked a blanket over it. Much better. She could no longer hear a sound from the babe.

She rocked and listened to the falling snow.

3. Do You Hear What I Hear?

Professor Caldwell didn't notice the snow when it first

started falling; he was staring at a spiral pattern on a rock, certain that if he contemplated it long enough and hard enough, some secret knowledge would uncurl in his mind and he would possess the Answer. Eventually he noticed he was leaning closer to the rock, almost with his nose to it, and still could not see the spiral clearly; it was only then that he realized snow had already drifted around his boots. He looked up and saw the sky dark with clouds and oncoming night. He cursed the loss of light. Then he realized his hands were nearly frozen.

As he creaked to his feet, he heard a new sound in the distance.

He walked down to the fire lake to thaw his hands. He had learned through experimentation that if one froze here, in Lethe country, one simply got colder and colder until some change in the weather brought enough warmth to uncrystallize the blood, and the consequent thawing was more painful than the freezing had been. It was one of a limited number of learning experiences he had had since he arrived. He had not yet found the courage to swim in the lake of fire, but if he ran out of other things to study, he might yet be reduced to that.

He held his hands toward the lake, warming them. Smoke and steam rose from the lake's burning, orange-yellow surface. It had a stench he found oddly pleasing: rotten eggs and singed hair. So definite, unlike other aspects of the environment. The storm was piling snow everywhere else, but around the lake a bubble of heat melted the snow from the air; drops fell hissing to the fire or turned to steam before they touched down.

There was that sound again. Was it an artifact of steam and snow? A wavering cry—what in this world would make a noise like that? Too pretty to be the scream of ice against rock, and nobody he had yet met here had that kind of voice.

In the rising waver of the lake's warmth, his hands tingled and burned. He decided he had experienced enough of that sensation the last time he had frozen, and turned his attention away from his discomfort. That cry. What could be making that cry? Now it was a steady ululation, coming from a clump of rocks over the snow line, toward his spiraled boulder. Really, it was an extraordinary sound, a pure, clean stream of—notes, yes, that was it; singing. He had been alone so much of late he had forgotten people could make a pleasant noise like that.

Curious, he rounded the rocks, searching out the singer.

She sat cross-legged on a rock, her hands open, palms up, on her knees, her pale wings folded against her back. She wore a white robe; her hair was pale, too, so that she almost blended into the tapestry of blizzard. With her face tilted up, she sang to the sky.

The professor noticed a strange tingling in his throat, a heat in the pit of his stomach, and a prickling near the top of his skull. She quieted and the sensations went away.

"Hello," he said.

Startled, she turned and looked down.

"Hello," he said again. "Please sing something else."

She spoke, foreign words. It sounded like a question. He observed that none of the strange effects he had experienced earlier repeated themselves, so the variable must have something to do with her singing voice.

"Sing," he said. He tried to sing a scale.

She sang the notes after him. His skull refused to prickle.

He opened his mouth and made circles with an index finger near it. "Sing," he said.

She sang. It almost sounded like words: "And the gory, the gory love a chord," she sang, a pure fall of notes that made the hair stand up on the back of his neck.

Definitely a phenomenon worth investigating. He gave her a smile and nodded to her to continue. If only he had a notebook; he could write down each sensation as it occurred, and if he had a watch, he could have timed the time it took each one to manifest. Would the symptoms vary from song to song? And would the songs affect others the way they did him?

But overriding these still very hypothetical questions, he felt a burning desire to investigate her vocal chords. He had explored a number of cadavers in the past. He liked to have things laid out in front of him, things he could get his hands on. Sociology and psychology were so nebulous. How did you ever know whether your subjects were lying? The data were subject to all sorts of interpretational errors. It wasn't that way with real physical evidence.

At his cave he had a collection of flints; he had spent some time flaking them into serviceable knives, exploring the properties of what he took to be some kind of volcanic glass.

The most intriguing question of all occurred to him: would she die? Things seldom did, here.

He smiled up at her and she smiled back, the glory of her voice mixing with the falling snow.

4. The Bells of Paradise I Heard Them Ring

Harry put a finger to the glass until a little round peephole melted through the ice. Sucking his finger to warm it, he leaned forward and looked out at the night. The snow had stopped and the moon was out. The stars looked like sun dots caught in crystal, and the snow lay sparkling like a graveyard of stars.

Down the hill toward town a column of smoke rose in the still air.

"Harry, come away from there," said his mother from her chair by the fireplace.

"But they're singing down in town. I wish I was there. They got a fire, too," he said.

"Harry," she said, and she came and touched his shoulder with her red hand, the one blood had stained. He flinched. She sighed.

"This is the first time since we got here I heard them being happy, Mama," he said.

"Oh, Harry." She hugged him from behind and kissed the top of his head. "I wish you never had to grow up."

"But Ma—" He turned his head so he could see a bit of her face. Didn't she know they had been here a long time and he hadn't grown at all?

But she was staring at the frost ferns on the windowpanes, and didn't hear him. She stroked his hair with her good hand. He stood quiet in the circle of her hug, thinking she was drawing lines of sadness on his head with her fingers, but not knowing how to tell her not to.

"I'm going to the bedroom now to sleep," she said. "Bar the door behind me." She kissed his cheek. "Oh, my dear, if you must go out, please don't go to the town. If you must go to the town, please don't go in among the people, just watch." A tear trickled down her cheek. "I love you so," she whispered. "You are my piece of heaven."

He stood wrapped in the queer quiet of the night and watched her go into the bedroom. When she blew out the bedside lamp, he closed the door, slid the bar across, and pegged it shut so her nightmares couldn't get out to hurt him. They rattled the door most nights, and shouted at him in his father's voice. In the morning his mother would be a mass of bruises.

She hated him talking to the people in town, even Jeanie, who was the youngest, just a couple years older than he thought he was. Except Jeanie was growing up. She had lived in the town by the lake of fire all her life, and couldn't remember any Befores the way Harry could. She asked questions. Sometimes Harry searched for answers he knew he had known once, but they slipped away from him.

Even so, he liked talking with Jeanie. She was somebody else, somebody besides Mama; Mama always thought about the same things, over and over, and tried not to talk about them.

After he bolted his mother's door, he bundled up in his coat, mittens, and cap, put on two pairs of socks and some hide boots, and strapped on the snowshoes he and his mother had made.

Outside, he stood and drew in frosty breaths of air. It tasted clean as toothpaste. Down in the valley, the lake burned and smoked beyond the town. He looked away, up the canyon to where the mountains crowded each other's shoulders like people packed into a bus. The moonlight lay on the snow like white scarves draped over pale overcoats.

Harry beat on his chest, wanting to yell like Tarzan and yet not wanting to wake his mother. He settled for a thin yodel that puffed from his mouth like a word balloon.

A strange sound answered him from up on the hillside. He thought of Christmas, and then his head hurt. He could feel things slipping away from him. He closed his eyes and clenched his fists and his teeth and concentrated on Christmas. Bells. Jingle bells. Or people singing, or both—?

He trudged up the hill, pushing snow back with each step. By the time he reached the little hollow behind the nest of boulders, he was hot in his clothes, and he could feel his cheeks tingling.

There they stood, three angels, tall and stern and white-robed, with wonderful, gorgeous wings. He wondered if they were boys or girls, and then he knelt before them, trying to remember from Bible class what one was supposed to say. It was all so misty and long ago, and it made his head hurt.

One angel took his hand and pulled him to his feet, and they all sang to him, their voices pure and clear as bells, ringing together like the most beautiful music he had ever heard. We have come for you, they sang. We offer you the chance to choose again. We offer you our hands and our wings. Come with us. Come home.

One took his other hand. He felt tears cooling on his cheeks. They flapped their wings and then they were rising, carrying Harry, the snow blowing in little spirals below them in the tiny wind of wingstrokes. Harry closed his eyes and let the earth go, taking with it the nightmares and the color of his mother's hand. Why had he ever thought the stars far away?

Then he was struggling, trying to pull free. He couldn't leave Mama alone back there. "No," he said, "no, please, put me back." She would wake up and he wouldn't be there to let her out of the bedroom. She would knock and call, knock and call, forever. Maybe she'd fall asleep again, never again seeing even the pale thin sunlight they had here. Her bedroom had no windows because her nightmares could go through windows. "Please, please," he said.

For a long time he thought they would ignore him. Finally they stopped their upward spiral and descended again.

"I have to stay here," he said.

One kissed his forehead. When he touched it later he felt a little hard lump under the skin.

The angels sang good-bye, good-bye, and flew up to the stars.

Harry walked back to the cabin and crept close to the hearth, listening to the banging and yelling of his mother's nightmares, trying to hear bells instead. "Come back," he whispered so softly that even he could not hear it.

5. Lo, How a Rose E'er Blooming

Hester woke with heat in her and knew the plague cycle was starting again. She edged away from Charles, afraid that he would sense her fever and throw her out into the snow while she was too weak to fight him. She curled up under the blanket and felt her armpits for buboes. Swelling heat pulsed against her fingertips, hard hot knobs under the skin. She moaned.

Charles stirred on the other side of the bed. Hester covered her mouth with her hand. Already she could feel the weakness invading her joints and knew that soon she would not be able to control anything—bowels, stomach, tears. She hugged herself and tried to think.

Surely it was Charles's turn to have the plague next. Sometimes it was chancy, though, and struck one of them thrice before afflicting the other, whether there was justice there or not. She tested the buboes again. Definitely present; she could feel more swelling in the place where her legs met.

Three or four days during which he would kick her and mistreat her, and all she could do was lie and suffer it. She knew he'd been thinking since the last time, planning some new torture without regard to the fact that once he used it on her she would inflict it on him the next time the plague struck him. They craved new things. Time stretched out ahead and behind, and the only marker they had was change.

She thought back to the bleak beginnings in London. The skies were dark with smoke from the fires of the burning dead. Poor Sarah, the last child they had left alive; when Hester came in that morning and found the ringed roses, the buboes, under Sarah's arms, she had wrapped the weakened child in a blanket, taken her to the nearest corpse bonfire, and thrown her, still moaning, into the flames. She had thought somehow that if one plague victim in the household were sacrificed alive to whatever evil demon was besetting the city, the rest of the household might be spared. Dreading the black, painted mark of plague on the front door, Hester told no one what she had done, insisting to Charles that Sarah had gone to her sister's in the country.

If only she had kept Sarah home. The child had screamed when the flames took her, and Hester felt horrible and wicked, but she couldn't bring herself to reach into that pile of burning pestilence and pull Sarah back.

Two days later Charles had carried her, still alive, to the same fire. She had not protested.

Here, on the other side of fire, they were together again.

She wiped tears off her face and tried to gather her thoughts. If she stayed here in the house as she had countless times before, he would hurt her, and then throw her out. If she left on her own, would she be spared the hurt? She knew there were others somewhere outside, though she had not spoken with them often. Between bouts of the plague she and Charles found themselves so drawn to each other they could hardly spare a moment to eat.

She rose, shivering, then found and donned her old dress. Fastening the buttons up the back was more than she could accomplish. She pulled Charles's coat on over the unbuttoned dress and ventured out.

The morning light hurt her eyes. She covered them with a hand and staggered on. The snow felt cool and soothing under her bare feet for a moment; then she seemed to be walking on fire.

The air was so still she could hear the faint crackles and hisses from the burning lake below. The hill's slope was treeless and gentle, and nudged her feet downward toward the lake. She turned away and stumbled up the hill. Somewhere above, there were trees. She was going to sicken and nearly die; she would like to be out of sight of everyone but God while she did so.

Then a hand touched hers; someone helped her up the slope. She peeked between her fingers and saw against the dazzling whiteness of the snow a dazzling whiteness of wings.

"Oh," she whispered, wondering if she were delirious. She had seen visions before.

A face turned back to look at her. For an instant she thought it was Sarah. But it was older, and its smile was more like a mother's.

"Oh," she whispered. She clutched her stomach, curled forward, and vomited.

When she had finished, the angel lifted her away from the steaming mess and carried her up the hill to the trees.

A little later some strength came back to her. "You must go away now," she said. "or I will infect you."

It leaned forward and stroked her hair away from her face.

"Roses," she said. "I'll give you the roses. Leave now, God willing."

It sat beside her in the snow as the flames consumed her again.

When she woke, she found red roses scattered about her in the snow, and footprints that led a little distance away and stopped.

6. Silent Night

"Eat up, Jeanette Isabella," said Mama. "That's the thing about manna meat: the Lord made it to last a day and no longer. If you don't eat it while you can, it gets wormy and bad and you have to throw it into the lake."

It was the best thing Jeanie had ever tasted, and yet it made her want to cry. She nibbled a bite off a bone. So light and tender, just a little salty, like tears washed with rainwater. She remembered how, when the flames had licked the ropes away, its crippled wings had lifted, once, stretched and flapped and then drooped again, and its hand had reached toward her, its eyes still on her. She couldn't watch, then, though everybody else had. She had turned away, wondering why she felt so strange, and why manna reminded her of little Harry.

She put the long, thin, hollow bone in her lap, wondering if it would go bad like the manna meat tomorrow. If it didn't, maybe she could make a flute from it.

Tonight, everybody was home feasting, no one singing in the streets. Her father stood at the door, gazing out at the town. He seemed shrunk inside himself, and he'd had a headache all day. Whenever Jeanie opened her mouth to ask a question, her mother shushed her.

But she was determined this time. "Mama," she said, "is manna always like that?"

"Not always. But sometimes. I heard tell of a manna that shape years ago, when Granny Lizzie was a youngster." Her eyes turned inwards. "There was one, or was it two? I think you had a great-aunt. I think Granny Lizzie had a little sister, and these manna came down, and one was a feast, but the other was wasted, Granny said; Sissy found it first, and run off with it, I do believe."

"Will the manna come again?"

"If you're lucky, in your lifetime. You might get some of the other kind. Little round bread thingies is how it usually goes."

Jeanie took a third helping. She felt full to bursting already, but if she had to wait a lifetime for more, she wanted as much as she could stand tonight.

THE SHARPS AND FLATS GUARANTEE

by C.S. Fuqua

Born April 2, 1956 in Andalusia, Alabama, C.S. Fuqua grew up in Pensacola, Florida, attending the University of West Florida and earning his B.A. there in 1979. Since then he has been living in Huntsville, Alabama with his wife and newborn daughter, Tegan. Yes, a Dr. Who fan. Fuqua's fiction, poetry and articles have appeared in some one hundred magazines, primarily in the small press. Last year saw publication of his book, Music Fell on Alabama, *a history of the Muscle Shoals music industry. As "The Sharps and Flats Guarantee" demonstrates, Fuqua knows the dark side of the blues.*

I started out this year vowing never to run another story written in present tense, or one about vampires, or one about a strange little shop. So much for New Year's resolutions.

The old lady in the cowhide-seat chair on the sidewalk rocked in time to Jelly Roll's "If Somebody Would Only Love Me," which blared from a speaker above the store entrance. I'd seen her ad in the Sunday paper a month or so before, listed in the personals just below my own: "Guitarist. Experienced. Blane Carter, 312-4116." I nodded good morning as I entered Sharps and Flats, the old lady's music store. The chair creaked as she rose to follow me in.

"Looking for something in particular?" she asked.

"Not really," I replied. Shelves bearing stacks of

sheet music, all original publishings, some dating back to Joplin, Morton, even Foster, lined the walls from floor to ceiling near the front. The woman rounded a glass case that doubled as a counter, lifted a hi-fi's needle, and the music stopped.

"So, you're a guitarist," she said. A speaker buzzed, popped. I must have looked confused because she grinned and nodded toward my chording hand. Of course, calluses on the fingertips, a guitarist's trademark.

A quaint little store, but out of my league, better suited to collectors. The only things I collected were bad debts, between a few gigs. Sharps and Flats was and remains a tiny building squashed between the old Evinrude dealership and a bar where the Shoreline Art Gallery once operated. Two blocks down, shrimpers dock their rigs at a pier where at least six people in the last year have ended their lives.

"How long you been playing?" the woman asked.

"Twenty years now." I'd played in a score of pop bands, a country band here and there, but I couldn't stay with those styles long. My thing's "new acoustic" music. I'd been busting my butt for what felt like for forever, and still I couldn't land a recording contract. The record companies called my work *too* different.

Resting against the case that housed several harmonicas, Jew's harps and a couple of mandolins, the old woman said, "I have some beautiful guitars." A mole above her left brow danced as she spoke. She pushed off the counter and seesawed toward the back, where several guitars hung on the wall. She reached for one, but couldn't quite bring it from its hanger. She stepped back and motioned for me to retrieve the instrument.

I examined it back and front, leaving fingerprints in the dust on the neck and body. I ran my fingers down the strings and over a fingerboard of immaculate inlay work. The body's sunburst finish glowed dully in the room's fluorescent light. The only thing the guitar lacked was a manufacturer's name on the head or inside the body. "What brand?"

"No brand," she said, waddling toward the front. I started after her, but paused when I thought I heard music from the wall. The corner speaker popped and the guitar work of Django Reinhardt began to play.

"What's the story behind this guitar?" I asked as I returned to the front.

"One of a kind. Back in the thirties, man named Johnson came in. Played the blues, but he needed money."

I figured she was trying to reel me in. "You don't mean Robert Johnson."

She nodded.

"Yeah, right. *The* Robert Johnson?" I examined the guitar more closely. "No way. Johnson couldn't have afforded this guitar. He played an old Decca."

"All I know is what I know." She waved a hand toward a corner where a stack of books rested under a large cobweb. "He sat right there and sang 'Hellhound on My Trail.' Wasn't too many days later, I heard he was dead." A smile lurked at the corners of her mouth. "Something about poison. Girlfriend maybe. Maybe not. One thing for sure, he could make a guitar cry his songs. Amazing, ain't it? Nobody really appreciates anything good till it's gone."

I nodded in agreement because I knew from experience. If I'd only swallowed my pride and played what the record companies wanted, I would've had no problem. And I would've had no self-respect. But sometimes the rejection got so bad I toyed with the idea of doing what they wanted, what I knew would sell, but then I'd get to thinking. Christ, it would've been the same as Da Vinci doing caricatures at a carnival.

The speakers popped as the old woman lifted the needle from the record. "Go ahead," she said, waving a hand. "Try it out."

I straddled a stool beside a nameless set of drums near the doorway and strummed the guitar, surprised to find it in good tuning, open G, an alternate Johnson regularly played in. My fingers began working the strings, stiffly at first, then easier, lighter, and the instrument resounded better than any I had played before. "Come on in My Kitchen" was the only song by Johnson I'd ever learned, and I found it working its way out of the guitar. I'd played the piece maybe five times in my life, but it sounded like it was part of my everyday repertoire.

The old lady laughed. "Even the guitar remembers. Robert played that song the day he sold it to me." She nodded appreciatively. "You pick real good, son."

I held the guitar out before me, examined its face again, then rose to put it away.

"You don't like it?" she said, the mole perched high.

I ran my thumb across the strings. "Sure, I like it. One of the best guitars I've ever played. Which means I can't afford it."

"How do you know? You haven't even asked the price."

I started toward the back. "I don't need to. If it really was Johnson's, it's out of my range. It should be in a museum." I placed the guitar on its hanger and started back toward the front. Something must have been wrong with her stereo because I was sure the corner speaker emitted a low resonance, similar to harmonics.

She brought a finger to her lips, tapping lightly, contemplating. Finally, she took a deep breath, patted the tight, gray curls of her hair, and leveled her gaze at me. "I'm an old woman. I don't have much need for money, even though you're probably right about its worth, but look how long I've had it here. And I'll tell you, I didn't give that much for it, no sir, next to nothing." She squinted an eye, and the mole sank into a roll of flesh. "What would you say to five hundred?"

"I'd say you're nuts. Either that, or it wasn't Johnson's."

All friendliness faded from her face. "I am not a liar. Robert put his life into that guitar."

"Sorry," I said softly. "I didn't mean to offend."

Her eyes probed mine, and her expression softened. "I'll tell you now, I wouldn't make this offer to anyone. But you've got talent. I think you're going places."

"Yeah, dives," I muttered.

"Five hundred, and it comes with a guarantee. If you don't like it, bring it back within six months. As long as it's in good condition, you'll get your money back, minus a ten percent service charge, of course."

Whether Johnson had ever owned the guitar or not, it *was* the best I'd ever put in my hands. Five hundred was a steal, period. I wrote the check.

Over the next few months, every time I picked up the guitar my playing improved, but it did nothing for my appeal to record companies. And the band that had hired me as a rhythm man told me to hit the road when I refused to switch from the light jazz music we played to heavy metal. "We're tired of eating beans, man."

After that, I worked as a single in a few clubs between Pensacola and Jackson, playing five sets a night, six nights a week for peanuts. I performed mostly my own music, but I also played a lot of other artists' work, everything from old time Jelly Roll-type jazz, to Chicago-style blues, to new age acoustic. And I'd learned more of Johnson's music to perform. With each Johnson song, people would actually shut up and listen, and, sometimes, they even gave me a standing ovation. It was though Johnson himself were playing.

I'd been working the Captain's Club, a dump on Airport Boulevard in Mobile, for about a month when the producer/owner of Southernways, a regional record label, decided to take a shot with me. In two weeks' time, I recorded thirty-three of my own instrumentals, direct to two-track digital, solo guitar, the way de Grassi does it. It felt great, let me tell you. Finally, a producer who'd take me all the way. Of course, he'd need cash to get me there, but I learned too late that all he had was pocket change. A week after I wrapped up recording the guy blew town, but at least I got the tapes.

Five months had passed since I bought the guitar, and I was in worse shape than ever. Twenty years of my life for nothing but a few digital master tapes and a guitar some crazy old hag claimed once belonged to the legendary Robert Johnson. What a crock. A person can only take so much. After he or she wastes a life chasing dreams, that person will probably sell out just to survive, produce what the record companies say the public wants. Yet another alternative exists.

As for me, I sold my equipment—amps, mikes, recorders—everything but Johnson's guitar. I decided to take it back to the old lady, let her sell it for what it's worth. Besides, money didn't mean a thing to me now. I packed it up, but by the time I got downtown, Sharps and Flats was closed. Next door, the bar was open, and from inside came the unmistakable sound of the band I'd last worked with. Glancing at the pier, which looked inviting in a gray, cold way, I locked Johnson's guitar in my car trunk and went into the bar for one last toast to myself.

For each song the band played, I downed a shot of Jack Daniels. After the set, Jim, the lead vocalist, came over, straddling the stool beside me. "Blane, my man. Never expected to see you where a band as *bad* as ours plays." He laughed. "Hey, somebody said you're getting out of the business."

I motioned for another shot.

Jim folded his hands on the bar and grinned. "Might be a good idea. For you, at least. Too damned concerned with that 'being true to yourself' stuff. Never will understand you gotta change the music from time to time just to eat, man. You ain't much for change are you? Not much for doing what you should, no matter who you drag down."

I drew a deep breath. Right then, in Jim, I could see everything I struggled against. I leaned back, curling my fingers into a fist beside the glass. "I prefer to make *music*." And I tried to punctuate that preference by slamming my fist into his grinning face, but he was quicker, pushing away from the bar as I swung. I missed by a foot. Then something cracked against my skull, and everything went black. I awoke in the parking lot, my forehead bleeding, my right eye swollen shut. A fitting beginning to a rightful end.

The following morning, the old lady was in her chair on the sidewalk, rocking in time to a cut off Miles Davis's *Seven Steps to Heaven*. She was on her feet by the time I reached the chair. Her eyes floated over my bruised face.

"Conversation with a friend," I offered.

She sighed deeply, glancing down at the case I carried. "Dissatisfied with the guitar?"

"No," I replied, but offered nothing more.

She searched my eyes briefly, then turned inside. She led me straight to the back wall, took the case from me, opened it and asked me to hang the guitar among the others.

"I was hoping things were getting better for you," she said.

"A regional company did record some of my songs, but it went belly up and the owner skipped. I got the tapes out of it, but no other company will even give them a good listen." I followed her up to the front and stared out the window toward the pier and the shrimp boats bobbing in the water. "Time comes when you have to face facts." I went over to the glass case. "After twenty years, I'm tired of it."

The stool creaked as she opened the cash register, but instead of cash for the guitar, she handed me a guitar pick. "A memento," she said.

A sliver of plastic pricked my thumb. I wiped a spot of blood on my pants. "My *Grammy*," I chuckled, feeling suddenly dizzy. I tried to hand the pick back to her, but the room abruptly tilted to one side. The pick clicked against the glass. The mole above her eye blurred into a large black hole, blotting out her face. My legs wobbled; my head slapped the concrete floor.

Her words came in clear whispers as her fingertips floated lightly over my chest. "You were planning something at the pier, weren't you?" Her voice resounded, rich and full. Light faded. "By itself, it would get you a small headline and a few paragraphs buried in section two of tomorrow's paper. For you, there must be more." Her words broke in soothing rhythms, in tones that reverberated like jazz. "They'll believe you jumped from the pier, just as you had planned, but they'll never find your body, and that will add to your mystique. In a few days, your tapes will arrive on the desk of a record producer who's heard of you. He'll listen, and he'll like what he hears. Your music will finally find a life of its own."

Her voice silenced. For a moment, all I could hear was her steady breathing, then came the sound of bones snapping as my skin hardened, my body curved, my neck stretched ever longer, and my skull flattened, narrowed. A few moments later, as the old woman lay me on the counter to string on the high E, the instruments on the back wall began to sing.

MEDUSA'S CHILD

by Kim Antieau

When asked for some biographical information, Kim Antieau responded with the curious information that she was born in a crossfire of hurricanes. However, painstaking research has since revealed that she is not Jumpin' Jack Flash, only slightly resembles Mick Jagger, and was actually born in Louisiana in March of 1955. Raised in Michigan, she now lives with her husband in White Salmon, Washington.

Of her latest exploits, Antieau writes: "My stories have appeared in a variety of mainstream, mystery, horror, and science fiction mags and anthos including F&SF, Asimov's, Pulphouse, Alfred Hitchcock's, Cross Currents, Final Shadows, Shadows 8 & 9, Twilight Zone Magazine, Space and Time, Time Travelers, Borderlands 2, *and* The Ultimate Werewolf. *I've got stories coming out in* MetaHorror, Weird Tales, *and* Pulphouse. *I've got a couple novels making the rounds and I'm plotting a new one,* The Jigsaw Woman.*"*

I found her on the steps of my apartment building. She was shivering, though the day was warm. Her light brown hair hung in strands about her face. Her cheekbones stretched her pale skin. I almost walked by her. I thought she was just another of the bag ladies who frequented my area. Then she looked up at me.

She had extraordinary eyes. They were black—two

black lightless pupils. I had to paint those eyes. I had to paint her.

I am not certain how I got her to come up to my apartment. I know I promised food. Whatever I said, she followed me into the building and to my apartment.

Once inside, I asked her her name. She did not answer. I told her to make herself at home while I started dinner. I had spaghetti sauce from the day before, so I put it on the stove and started water to boil for noodles.

She stood in the middle of my living room which doubled as my studio because of the huge picture windows. I had several paintings on easels and two leaned against the wall. She walked over to them and touched the edges of each one with the tips of her fingers. She did it almost reverently.

"An artist," she whispered.

"Yes," I said. I glanced at her. Although her body was bent and her face lined, I guessed she was not even thirty years old.

She turned and looked at me with those huge black eyes.

"An artist," she said again.

I wondered then if I had latched on to some very strange person. She could utter only two words: *An artist.* Maybe she had been in love with a painter once and he had killed himself because she left him—or something equally as dramatic.

She came and stood close to me while I cooked and watched me stir sauce and break noodles into the boiling water. Once she reached out tentatively and touched my arm with one finger. Poor girl, I thought, she hasn't eaten in days and she's grateful to me.

"Leila," she said.

At first I did not know what she was saying, and then I realized she was answering my first question.

"I'm Matthew McClean. Matthew means 'Gift of God,' " I said, as I pulled two plates from the cupboard. "I was the sixth child after five girls. You can see why they thought I was a godsend." I laughed. She did not even smile.

"Leila means dark as night."

That was all she said. No story behind it. Was she born on a stormy night? Was her grandmother's name Leila? She's not much of a conversationalist, I thought, but that was all right. I hated chatterbox models.

I told her to sit down and we ate our first meal together. Neither of us said much. I was curious about her, but I did not want to pry and scare her away. I was getting more and more excited about the prospect of painting her: the mysterious woman lost in strands of greasy hair and ragged clothes.

She was more animated by the end of the meal. Color returned to her cheeks. She pushed her hair behind her ears, and I saw she was not unattractive. When she had finished her meal (she didn't eat much), she looked over at me. She smiled and said, "Well, Matthew, you want to paint me, don't you?"

I nodded.

"What will I get in return?" she asked.

I impulsively looked toward the door, wondering where the cowering waif was who had walked into the room a mere hour ago.

"I can pay you my standard rate for models."

She shook her head. "I don't want money. I need other things." She gazed at me. "How long have you been an artist?"

I was a little annoyed by her tone. First I had practically scraped her off my steps and put food into her starving body and now she was asking for my qualifications.

"I have been an artist all of my life," I said. "I have been commercially successful the last five." I was proud of that. Pretty good for only being thirty years old.

She nodded. "Young," she said. She sat quietly for a moment, looking around the room, and then she rested her fingers lightly on my arm. The hair on my arms stood up, as if drawn to her fingertips. Her touch was cool and pleasant.

"I want to stay here."

"Here? Don't you have a place to stay?"

"No."

Normally I would have tossed her out then and there. Several women had wanted to move in with me at different times and I had always said no, except once, and that had been a terrible mistake. I hardly painted at all until she moved out.

"Please, Matthew, I won't be any trouble. Just for a while, until you finish painting me." Suddenly she was the waif again.

I smiled and said, "Okay."

I made a sketch of her that night. She sat on my couch with her hands folded demurely in her lap. The sun was setting. The walls of the room turned gold and red. The gold touched Leila's head. For a moment her hair was flaxen, Rapunzel reincarnate. And then the red tinged her skin and she was like some fiery goddess, her hair gold snakes snapping at dust particles in the air.

The next morning I found her padding around the kitchen in a pair of my jeans and a T-shirt.

"I lifted them while you slept," she said. "I took a shower and washed my clothes. I'm baking an omelet for us."

She appeared taller than she had the night before, probably because she had bathed, eaten, and had a good night's sleep. My sofa bed was more comfortable than my own bed. Her eyes were bright and her cheeks rosy. She looked like a well-scrubbed college kid.

"Thanks," I said. "I am hungry."

I sat at the table and rubbed my eyes sleepily. What had possessed me to let this woman stay with me? I glanced up at her as she put the omelet in front of me. It's those damn eyes, I reminded myself.

She was a good model. She sat very still and looked off into some place within herself. The natural light from the overhead windows flattered her. Work went slowly. It was hard to capture the quality in her that had first attracted me. I could not get the eyes. They were too black. On canvas, they looked like huge holes in her face: she looked like a zombie, or as if she did not have a soul, something queer like that.

"What do you do when you aren't hanging around apartment buildings?" I asked while we ate lunch.

"I do things."

She continued eating, apparently not interested in answering my questions. I glanced out the window. Clouds had covered the sun and it looked like a summer storm was approaching.

"There goes the day's painting," I said.

"That's all right," she said. "We can spend the day getting to know each other."

I was surprised she wanted to talk, but when she got up and went to the couch, I followed and sat beside her. I began talking about myself. She held my hand loosely in hers and listened while I told her about my life, my crowded but happy childhood filled with dreams of becoming a famous artist, my time spent traveling before college, my successful years as an artist. For some reason I poured out my life to her as if it were some kind of liquid she could drink. It frightened me a little, letting someone know so much about me. She probed me for details—gently squeezing my hand when I was not sure what I wanted to say. As the storm washed against the windows, Leila seemed to grow more beautiful. Her voice became stronger, more assured. She was no longer the trembling bag lady I had met yesterday. I was amazed at the difference and chalked it up to my company and good food.

We talked the afternoon away (or rather I talked; she mostly listened). When we got hungry, she suggested a pizza. We ran outside into the rain, laughing and splashing in puddles as we made our way to the neighborhood pizza joint. I forgot she was a bit strange, forgot she was a hobo, and realized I had found a new friend: someone who liked to listen. My artist friends were not big on listening; they liked to talk and talk, mostly about their own work. Leila wanted to know more about me and I loved it. I sat with her in the pizza place, sipping a malt and pushing strings of cheese into my mouth, and I wondered why I had not found someone like her before.

When we got back to my apartment, Leila stood in the middle of the living room and began undressing. I sat on the couch and watched her. My stomach tingled. Soon she stood before me naked. She was beautiful. How could I have thought she was ugly? She came to me and I put my arms around her and pulled her toward me. My clothes slipped away and we were side by side on the couch.

"Imagine anything you like," she whispered. "I can be anyone or anything you want. Let yourself go."

For that moment, Leila was all I wanted. Her movements were gentle at first and then she was astride me, pushing herself down hard on me. She bent to bite my chest. She kissed my ear, her tongue darting in and out. "Imagine," she whispered, and she loomed up before me, her golden hair clinging to her breasts like hundreds of tiny fingers.

The next day I tried the portrait again. The work was frustratingly poor. I finally threw my paintbrushes down in a mock fit and cried, "You are impossible to paint!"

She laughed and put her arms around me and kissed the top of my head.

"Why don't you try something else?" she suggested.

"You don't want me to finish your portrait because you think I'll make you leave," I said, turning around to hug her.

"I hope you won't make me leave," she said quietly. I glanced up at her. She was staring at something I could not see, somewhere in her mind, and it made me uncomfortable. I knew so little about her.

In the days and weeks to follow I came to love Leila with an intensity I had never known. We did everything together. I wanted her with me all of the time. Nights we made love and then sat up for hours, talking about my current project. During the day, I often looked up from a difficult piece to see Leila dancing around the living room, swirling her skirts like some exotic dancer.

I learned little about her past. Sometimes she gazed out the window toward the heart of the city. She looked frightened. Her eyes paled, as if the life were slipping from them. When I went to her, she clung to me, seeming to draw life from my presence.

"What's out there?" I asked her.

"Nothing," she answered, turning to me. "All those people who don't know or care about me."

We stayed to ourselves most of the time. Leila wanted to meet my friends, but I always found an excuse not to call anyone. I liked having her all to myself.

A few weeks after I first met Leila, I went into a painting slump. And then Leila began to wane. That is the only word I can use. As my paintings grew worse, she changed. I urged her to go out while I tried to paint, but she would not. She stayed on the couch, sometimes biting her fingernails, sometimes looking out the window. When I asked her what was wrong, she just shook her head.

One day she said, "Leave me alone, Matthew. It's you, don't you understand? You've changed." She went to the bedroom and closed the door.

I stared at her unfinished portrait and wondered what I could have done. What was happening to us—to her? She had been such a vivacious person. Now she was withering away.

I stopped dreaming.

Leila and I grew further apart. Though we still slept together, she spent most nights hugging her side of the bed and would not let me near her. Those were the worst times. I felt so alone. Other nights she turned and made love to me furiously. No longer the golden goddess. A fury. Or a gorgon. Medusa's child.

Things worsened, and I was afraid she would leave me. I still loved her. I sat down and tried to figure out why. We never talked; she only listened. I never learned anything new from her. She was beautiful. Or was she? Had she ever stood tall? Was her hair golden? Had she danced for me?

"I need to meet new people," she told me one afternoon. "I feel like a prisoner here."

I sat at my easel turning one of my dark blobs of paint into a spider. Tracing a line here. Putting meat on it there.

"All right," I said. "We'll have a party Sunday."

She chewed her fingernails. How tired she looked. Was it really my fault? Was I somehow draining her of energy?

For the party, Leila wore a black floor-length V-neck gown. I had bought it for her weeks earlier. I remembered the pleasure I had gotten seeing it on her then—and later off her. The silk had clung to her body, moving as she moved. Now the black dress hung unattractively on her, barely touching her skin anywhere.

Poets, artists, writers, and dilettantes filled the apartment. Ice hit the sides of glasses and twirled madly in baths of gin, vodka or rum. I passed around hors d'oeuvres, shrugging when anyone asked how the work went.

Leila was everywhere. Touching. Listening. The color returned to her face. She was animated, laughing, touching, listening.

Something was not right.

"I've met her before." A fellow artist, Pete Dobson, was tapping my arm.

"Really?" I turned to him.

"She looks a bit different, but it's her."

Leila was striding to another group. Tall and lithesome. Her golden hair shone and caught the light . . .

"Do you remember Franc de Winter?" Pete was talking to me again.

"Yeah, I think so. Isn't he in California?"

"He was." He sipped his drink and watched Leila. Her fingers lightly stroked the bare skin in the V of her dress.

"Leila used to live with him," Pete said. "Saw her at a party there. I'm pretty sure it was her."

Her eyes were dark holes, bright with life.

"What happened to him?" I asked.

"Don't you remember? He stopped working. Artist's block or something. She sort of disappeared right before he died—he killed himself."

Everything stopped. The people. The smoke. Time. For a split second, only Leila and I were in the room. She turned those horrible eyes on me and she knew I knew.

The terror and repulsion was with me all evening. I felt as if I were sinking into a quagmire and no one would help me out. I drank too much; someone gave me a pill and I swallowed it. Somehow I got through the evening. I kept wondering how she could have done it. She pretended to love me and had taken away all that made me me.

Leila was putting her things together before the last guest left. In fact, one man sat in my living room. A poet I barely knew.

"Where are you going?" I demanded.

"With Henry." Henry? The poet.

"So you can do to him what you did to me?"

She stared at me. I turned away. I could not look at those eyes.

"What have I done to you?" she asked. I was silent. She shrugged. Her indifference infuriated me. I wanted to smash my fists into her eyes.

She shut the suitcase and clicked the locks. 'I'm leaving."

I grabbed the suitcase—it was mine, after all—and hurled it against the wall.

"Are you all right, Leila?" A voice came from the other room.

Didn't the little twit know she would ruin him? I charged into the living room. Before the man had a chance to react I had him up against a wall. I was not prone to violence, but Leila had bled me, and I was not going to let her off easily.

"Get out of here, you creep," I said.

"Leila?" he asked, his voice suddenly very high.

"It's all right, Henry," Leila said as she came out of the bedroom. "I'll catch up with you later."

The door slammed. She looked at me. "This is silly, Matthew."

There was no emotion in her voice. She had used me; now it was time to let me go. Suddenly I felt tired, worn. How long can a person live without dreams?

"Will I ever get it back?" I asked. "Or will I end up like Franc de Winter?"

"Get what back?" she asked. "Who's Franc de Winter?" She went to the window and looked out.

"You just take, don't you?" I said. "You find people like me and you drain them of their imagination, their creativity."

She laughed harshly. "Is that what you want to believe? First I was your muse and then I became some kind of monster sucking away your life? Believe what you want! When you took me into your apartment that first night you were going to paint me, make a masterpiece, use *me*, and then send me away with a cheese sandwich, weren't you? Woman does not live on bread alone." She laughed again. The sound was horrible.

"You disgust me," I said.

"I wasn't always this way," she said. "There was a time when I could take care of myself. You artists and your pomposity. You think you are the best dreamers? The most creative? My first love was an artist, too. I was a child. All he did was take from me, cage me with his love, keep me to himself. I had to do something to save myself. I learned to please him." She turned and stared at me. "I gave you what you wanted, didn't I? And when you couldn't paint anymore, you blamed me."

She looked back at the city.

"I lived the longest with an old Mexican woman. Five years," she said. "She could build an entire world around a worm hole."

"And you took that from her, didn't you?"

She shook her head. "No, Matthew, she gave herself to me freely."

She went back into the bedroom and returned with the suitcase.

"You can't leave, Leila." Maybe she could give it back to me; I didn't know for sure, but I could not let her go.

She sighed. "You will tire of this, Matthew. There is nothing left between us."

She tried to leave several times, but I threw her back. The hours turned into days. I locked her in the bedroom at night and only let her out after I slept. I spent the days pleading with her to give back what she had taken.

"I can't live without dreams, without my art," I told her.

"I don't care," she said.

I was without reason, I believe, during those days. I did not let her eat very much. I wandered around my apartment looking at my painting. I thought of Franc de Winter, I thought of the Leila I had loved. Everything was crumbling around me. The woman in the apartment was not the Leila I had known. With each hour she grew more sullen and ugly and nervous.

"I'm begging you! Please let me go," she said. Her eyes were dead, her hair straggly, her mouth cruel. "I'm dying." She stared out the window.

"I don't care," I said.

I realized then why the city frightened her. All those mindless people going to their mindless jobs. They were so frightened, so dazed; many of them thought of how to get home at night and little else. They had no imagination. Leila would die in that city.

"If I could help you paint again I would," she said on the fifth day, "but I can't."

On the tenth day I was tired and I believed her. She had emptied my soul and no humanity remained. I took her out of the building and led her into the heart of the city. She did not have the energy to struggle; she let herself be pulled along.

We walked down the stairway and into the subway station where hundreds of people waited to board the morning trains. I pushed Leila into the crowd. The people paid no attention to us. They stood on the gray floor in their gray suits waiting for the train.

Leila stumbled and almost fell into a man reading the paper. He sighed and moved out of her way. She touched his arm and peered into his eyes. "Help me," she whispered. "This man is crazy." She veered from him and into another person. I stood apart from them. Leila's face crinkled in pain again as a woman pulled her arm away. She bumped into one person after another. They ignored her or pulled away. Lines of pain ran down Leila's face and into her body. The emptiness of the place was devouring her. She began sobbing. "Someone help me, please," I heard her cry. She touched another person and he pushed her. She fell against the wall and crumbled to the concrete floor. Her head bobbed. Her mouth slackened. Saliva dribbled over her lip and down her chin. Her eyes were black stones. People kept a neat distance from her, either pretending she did not exist, or else not caring.

I did not care either. Not anymore. She had taken that from me. Foul air rushed around me as the train approached.

I climbed stairs as the train pulled in. I heard people shuffle to get aboard, heard the doors swish closed. I stepped out onto the streets and walked toward home.

My dreams returned. Rather I should say: I dream now. Just one dream. I close my eyes and sleep comes and with it Leila. The dream is always the same. Leila sits on the cold concrete floor of the subway, lifeless, people walking around her. Saliva drips from her mouth, slowly at first, and then more rapidly, and suddenly the clear liquid is red, it is blood, and the blood pours from her mouth until the whole subway station is filled and though I am on the steps, the blood follows me, envelops me, and finally fills my lungs and drowns me.

When I awaken from this nightmare, alone in the dark, I am terrified for a few moments, wondering if I could have been wrong. And then I close my eyes and dream again.

WALL OF MASKS

by t. Winter-Damon

t. Winter-Damon lurks in Tucson, Arizona, and from his lair he has been corrupting the small press for some years now with his demented and depraved poems—more than 200 at last count. Not content with these crimes, Winter-Damon also writes short fiction (as the following story might indicate) and has written a novel in collaboration with Randy Chandler, Duet for the Devil, *which is currently stalking a publisher. Winter-Damon promises that it is the first of a trilogy,* The Books of the Beast. *His latest slim volumes of verse include* Dedicated to Darkness *and* l'Heure d' Hallucinations.

Winter-Damon takes second place only to fellow gonzo, Wayne Allen Sallee, in weirdness of manuscript submission inclusions. While Sallee stuffs in weird cartoons and photos of his various surgeries, Winter-Damon favors Chinese fortune cookie fortunes, grotesque finger puppets, and xerox copies of stories by other authors he thinks might be of interest for The Year's Best Horror Stories. *No, Virginia, that's not what they teach you in creative writing classes.*

As an erstwhile student of anthropology, my interest early on was captivated by the subject of ritual masks. I suppose that this fascination could perhaps be traced back to my childhood, into those most impressionable and formative years. The pages of *National Geo-*

graphic opened worlds of strange and mysterious lands, and the exotic and bizarre customs of their peoples lured my imagination. I had caught the "scent of the tradewinds," and like so many before (and after) me, my youthful mind was hooked by the burning need to see these faroff places for myself—to taste, to smell, to hear, to touch, to experience rare and elusive dreams of jungles, bazaars and temples, to travel with caravans through ancient paths of wonder and mirage. Add to this crucible a head filled with a wild jumble of faerie tales and fables (read to my brother and me, at first by our father, a professor with a natural talent as a storyteller and orator, later from a bookshelf crammed with *The Jungle Book, Faerie Tales from Many Lands, A Thousand and One Arabian Nights*, ad infinitum . . .), as well as such pulp classics as *The Shadow, The Phantom, Tarzan and the Jewels of Opar, Batman, Hawkman, The Flash, Green Arrow,* and *Iron Man* . . . Then, as a catalyst, salt this already potent formula with a bent for the delightful *frisson* of Halloween and the garish masque of jack-o-lantern-lit personas. *Voila!* (or should I say "SHAZAM!") and *The Mark of Zorro* had forever carved its dark signature upon my developing psyche. Every shadow infused with secret life. Every mask tempting with its promise of alter egos and assumed adventure. An equation that could not help but lead with inevitable predictability to

My fascination for realms of the mind, of dream and nightmare, their chronicling and their expression in the tangible in art and artiface. (Witness my previously-mentioned interests, along with an almost obsessive delight in the hellish paintings of Bosch and Brueghel, the masklike Cubist portraits of Picasso, as well as the fugitive images of beauty, evoking the Janus' faces of terror and laughter—the skillfully-applied warpaint of the Amerindian and the grease-paint of the carnival clown). These, along with my native intelligence and proficiency in learning, could only serve to place me in alienation from, if not direct confrontation with, my more plodding and physical peers. Classmates dubbed me an "egghead." Teachers and counselors alike deemed me as "introverted." The neighborhood bullies forced me to run a gauntlet of petty sadism, bloody noses and black eyes, as I played out the role of scapegoat for their own insecurities and arrested feelings of self-worth. Girls termed me a "dork" or "nerd," unworthy of their at-best-fickle affections. Instead, I became the mere object of their derision, their tauntings, and assumed the role of jester, pitifully striving to gain some slight measure of control through courting their laughter rather than merely suffering it (and showed the world my own foolish, grinning mask of hidden pain . . .).

I excelled in my schooling, particularly in the humanities; yet, in my own personal relationships, in the development and exploration of my own humanity, after two failed marriages and a bitter string of pitiful affairs, I had (to quote Woody Allen, probably inaccurately . . .) "failed at life."

But even as my personal relationships flickered by in twitching exaggerations of shared emotion, darkly, painfully humorous (like silent movie stereotypes in frenetic, puppetlike mimicries of life, larger-than-life, yet existing in two dimensions only), even as each new reel spasmed through its predictable routines and faded into black, the one constant that remained was my ever-growing collection of masks.

I used them as accents, as conversation pieces, as fetishes of my acquisitive lust for ever rarer, ever more bizarre *objets-fixes*.

Scattered pieces of my collection decorated each room of my habitation. Office. Bedrooms. Kitchen. Dining Room. Study. Den. And bathrooms. Each piece was carefully selected to correspond with the inherent functions, the essence of each room. The entrance hallway was lined with masks of warding and initiation. There were masks of leadership and power. Mardi Gras masks and antique dominos and harlequins that had been the playthings of debauched French aristocrats. Masks associated with rituals of agricultural fertility and harvesting. Museum-quality replicas of Dionysian masks of ancient Greece, and the Bacchanalian masks of Imperial Rome. Theatrical masks from a variety of cultural milieu. Exquisitely-crafted replicas of Egytian mummy masks, electroplated with the authentic sheen of precious gold. Masks of purification, and masks of disease prevention: measle masks from China, cholera masks from Burma, and a representative selection of the nineteen *rākasa* of Sri Lanka.

But the heart of my collection was the wall of masks that lined my living room, a delightful nightmare realm of light and shadow, arranged with that transcendent precision of form and implied relationship that only the truly obsessed, their focus keened to a visionary pointedness beyond the merely human, can ever hope to muster. The lighting of the room, as well, was a study in perfection. A custom-designed track-lighting system with polished chrome, spherical heads (fitted with servo-linked, rotating color filters, and rheostated calibration through a full spectrum of output from the subtlest whispers of color to a dramatic blaze of neon-brash primaries), self-swiveling through a three-hundred-and-sixty-degree arc, was wired into my stereo and P.C., making it programable or manually controlable, as my mood dictated, from the solace of my contour recliner: state-of-the-art indulgence.

I was an habitue of antique dealers, locally, and on both coasts, benefitting as I did from the urgencies of the import trade that made frequent business trips a foregone necessity.

The mail-order trade benefitted also from the acquisitive hunger that possessed me. I had long since tapped into the sometimes-legitimate and oftentimes-clandestine network of *sources* that could pander to my fevered questings. And through the Publishers Central Bureau and its like, I matched my masks with ethnic and mood musics in a comprehensive library of tapes, to evoke a total environment sympathetic to the primal experiencing of each treasured piece: anthropomorphic (human-featured) and theriomorphic (animal-featured) alike.

Well-known to the anthropologist, but quite possibly unknown to the casually-interested layman, is the role of animism central to the creation of the ritual mask: spirit power dwells within all matter, organic and inorganic alike; therefore, the mask will harbor the spirit power of whatever matter was used in its making. Similarly, the tools used by the craftsman in its conception. Precise rituals of protection must be followed in its creation, the mask itself possessing greater and greater spirit power in its own right as it takes form. Specific taboos serve to dictate the making and handling of the mask object, and, of course, its eventual use as a thing of power. Vital forces are awakened and contained in its creation, and only the most stringent adherence to the prescribed rituals can ensure against the intolerant dangers involved in the manipulation of spirit power. In these precepts the primitive and superstitious believe with a truly religious fervor. But, to the rational and scientific mind, such delusions are seen for what they are—culturally enforced hysteria . . .

And my own rational and scientific mind was my surest amulet, warding me from the sometimes-potent powers of suggestion. . . .

So night-after-night I reclined in the controlled darkness of my sactum sanctorum, savoring the sounds and visions that modern technology and primitive beliefs could manifest for my enjoyment, setting free my subconscious to indulge in a cinema-of-the-mind, limited only by the variety of my meditative objects and the strength of my imagination to touch upon their essence and to explore the paths of vicariously perceived experience where they might lead. . . .

Also documented by both the anthropologist and psychologist is the somewhat unusual association between the mask and its wearer. As the mask alters the physical appearance (to himself and to the world) of the wearer, there is a definite and measurable loss of his previous identity and he in turn assumes the persona of the mask. By donning the mask, the wearer may undergo an actual psychic change, his ego submerging itself, trancelike, into the depths of archetypical, collective unconscious, releasing the alter ego of the mask, the spirit character which is "summoned." Usually, the wearer does retain control, serving as a partner in skillfully creating the ritual persona with the assistance of the object of spirit power, the mask. Through his conscious actions, he brings life to the inanimate through his gestures, his movement, the reflected light dancing in his own eyes through the hollow eye-holes of the mask. However, this control is often tenuous at best, and the possibility of the wearer becoming psychologically attached to the created persona often becomes, in fact, the reality, as the wearer loses his own identity and becomes an automaton, without will, driven by the urgings of the dominant ego of the mask-persona, the *creator* subserviant to the dictates of the *created*.

But I felt my rational mind to be totally in control as I toyed with whatever mask might strike my fancy. A true connoisseur, as I knew myself to be, devises many nuances of personal ritual, thereby intensifying and prolonging the desired experience so as to savor it most fully. Sometimes I would first select a mask, lie back in the relaxing semi-darkness and run my fingers across the surface, in the manner of a blind man, relishing the tactile stimulation that each carefully sculpted curve and angle afforded my day-weary fingers. The lighting and the music selected would be carefully chosen, serving, again, to heighten the total experience. I would, after sufficient fondling of the ritual object, place it across my own features, and let my imagination flow as the persona of the mask suggested. Finally, I would stand, and, almost casually, wander into the brighter-lit corridor of my entrance hall. There I would stare into the large and elaborately framed antique mirror, delighting in the *outré* image that the worn mask created—a delicious *frisson* would for an instant seize me, perhaps hearkening back to that garish masque of jack-o-lantern-lit personas, or to some older and far darker moment of ritual.

At other times, I would let myself select some tape of ethnic music or natural phenomena (wind and surf, rainfall, or the like . . .) through sheer random choice (as some Dada mindgame), then let the music control the play of light and shadow, the subtleties or splashes of color conjured by the key and tonal variations, thrilling at the shadowlife imbued into each individual mask-face as the light played upon first one and then another in my collection, my Wall of Masks . . .

Barrellike, cylindrical masks of leather, *kachinas*, of the Hopi and Zuni tribes, with noses of corncob and plumes or horns, and bristling tufts of hair. Cornhusk masks of the Seneca, woven like basket faces. Carved, grimacing masks of the Iroquois' False Face Society, with trailing horsehair wigs, and bits of metal set about the eyes to glisten grotesquely in firelight. The *menpo* or mask-helmets of the Samurai. Representative pieces of all five basic Nō masks of the Japanese theater: old persons, gods, goddesses, devils, and goblins; red, black and white (I could not hope to own each of the one-hundred-and-twenty-five named varieties, but was ever in search of another piece to add to my collection). *Tupeng* from Java, of wood, cloth, metal, and horsehair. And the terror masks of the Dukduk, immense constructs of sacking and feather tufts and skirts of leaves, standing almost five feet in many cases (I owned but one, but had collected photos and miniatures of quite a number). These, and many more, hung from my gallery of strange and occult objects of spirit power.

Then, on a business trip to San Francisco, in an out-of-the-way dealer in antiquities (quite deliberately sub rosa, for its stock-in-trade was, in most cases, of most dubious origin and procurement), I discovered a *find* of unequaled rarity. At first glance, it appeared nothing more than a hood of black leather—one of those tawdry sexual appliances of the kinko set, certainly nothing out of the ordinary in this American version of Sodom or Babylon. But, despite myself, I found that it held the most peculiar *fascination* for me. There was, perhaps, a tangible aura of *age* about it, and *something more* . . . a sensation of spirit power stronger than any I had ever sensed, raising a delighted prickle of gooseflesh as I at last reached out to touch it.

It seemed a thing of titillating *evil*. The satin-gloss of its midnight-black leather, the still-supple texture, cool and buttery to the touch, spoke of loving care taken in its preservation. It was *old*. Of that there could be no question. Its scent was musty with uncounted years, and the leather scent was mingled with the ancient sweat of fear and pain (I could sense it as the hunter winds the hunted's terror). A small, verdigrised plate of brass within the collar bore the initials "D-A-F" in rococo script.

Upon questioning, the proprietor ("panderer" might have been a good deal more correct) advised me that he could provide documents that linked it undeniably to the estate of the late Aleister Crowley, Satanist extraordinaire, drug fiend and debauchee-with-a-vengeance. It was reputedly a favored appliance at his *darker* ceremonies, in particular, those rituals of flagellation that are every bit as much a part of the Satanic orgy as they are a part of the devotional rites of the Jesuit penitent extremists, the Penitentes, and similar contemporary brotherhoods in Latin America, or the primitive ceremonies of initiation, purification and fertility. And there were rumored details of a genesis that spoke of far older, more wicked days-of-infamy of which this very mask had been a vital part.

That the use of the mask in such depraved ceremonies was, in essence, a perversion of the shamanistic vision-quest was verifiable through an extensive body of scientific research and empirical data alike. The potent synergism of combined sensory deprivation and intense physical pain (often with the added element of ingestion of mind-altering substances) formed a reductive agency capable of stripping away the rational, conscious levels of experience to grant access to the nightmare gulfs of the darkest subconscious: an altered state capable of unleashing the primal energies of the id (to use the psychological jargon), or the demonic (in the terminology of the metaphysical).

No wonder that the mask radiated an aura of tangible evil.

It was invested with the spirit power of untold journeyings and tools of shaping . . .

The proprietor suggested much yet said little. As befitted a panderer, he was a master of innuendo, relying on calculated shifts in modulation and pacing, along with subtleties of body language, to excite my own already-stimulated interest, touching chords of resonance in my imagination through keying the flow of his dialog off perceived touch-points in my responses.

My purchase was carefully wrapped and parceled, my check drafted and verified, and the door closed shut behind me (and, yes, now, in retrospect, I certainly imagine locked and designated dually, "CLOSED," "CERRADO") before I fully realized what had transpired. . . .

There was an overwhelming sensation of IRREALITY. As if, were I to turn, the building and all its contents would have simply *vanished*.

But (as though the impulses of the irrational now mutinied and held the helm that my critical faculties had previously controlled), I could not force myself to look—

Like some superstitious savage, I could no longer will even this fleeting, voluntary response.

An image of the biblical Lot (and his wife) flashed through my mind, the implied contrasts in our respective dilemmas afforded me one of those intense *frissons* of rare and visionary insight.

I stood on the downslope of a narrow, seedy sidestreet, no doubt the haunt of derelicts and deviates, carrying a brown-paper-wrapped package for which I had just paid *a sum of several thousand dollars*. The scene seemed a despondent study in Payne's Gray—the sprawling squalor of the Victorian and Neo-Victorian, pierced willy-nilly by the phallic upthrusts of rearing skyscrapers, fell away to The Bay and The

Bridge, the far shore hidden by a veil of fog. All seemed some fevered passage from Oscar Wilde or Baudelaire.

Despite my pervading sense of confusion, I had maintained sufficient presence-of-mind to seek out the nearest UPS depot, where I paid for Blue-Label service to my self-addressed destination, heavily insured—although I must admit to sudden feelings of anxiety when the moment came to hand my prized package over into a *stranger's* care.

(In retrospect, this may sound quite cool and assured on my own part; however, the occurrence itself was truly a nightmare of wandering drizzling, unfamiliar alleys, of telephone call-boxes eyed by vicious-looking derelicts while I felt the goldfish-in-its-bowl surrounded by monstrous images of hungry cats, of whirling taxi-rides through a veritable maze of rain-swept, traffic-crazy streets. . . .).

I can only imagine what embarrassed explanations I should have been forced to make, what reproving stares I should have faced, in the *inquisition* that would surely have ensued had I attempted to carry my acquisition on board my homeward airline flight and triggered their metal detectors through the presence of that engraved plate of brass—

(*If only it had! If only I had failed to be so cautious! If only I had never entered that accursed shop! Upon such slender threads of circumstance our futures ever lie. . . .*)

My business in 'Frisco had already been concluded. I had a 7:14 flight out scheduled for the evening.

During my homeward journey to Tucson, one odd incongruity (among so many) in my recent experience kept playing and replaying through my half-drowsing consciousness: the physical appearance of the shop's proprietor had held much of that awkward (not careless) sloppiness that so often is a hallmark of the blind. Mr. R. (my caution tells me that this ellipsis of his proper name is dictated by the circumstances) most certainly was sighted. His suit coat and trousers were matched and neatly pressed, as was his shirt with its crisply folded, button-down collar. His tie was of a fashionable cut and color, knotted with great precision. No, it was his face, the haphazard stubble on his chin and cheeks, several noticable razor-cuts, a crust of snot protruding slightly from one nostril, something about the tousled look of his hair. And a certain *vacancy* in his stare. Why this should bother me so I could not account for. But I couldn't keep his features from my mind.

My package was delivered late the next afternoon. I had begged off returning to work, with feigned illness, so that I would be at home to receive my acquisition when the UPS truck arrived. I found myself possessed by an uncustomary, extreme nervousness and irritability all day prior to its arrival. Every passing car or truck drew me to the window, peering out with expectation, waiting for that awaited dark brown van.

I drank far too much tequila in the interim.

So it was with hearty buzz that I at last carefully tore open the brown paper wrapping of my parcel. Perhaps that had much to do with my susceptibility to the influence that bizarre object exerted, most surely, upon my reason. That it was only a thing of leather was as if to say that the Liberty Bell is but a thing of metal, or the Shroud of Turin is but a piece of cloth. This mask of leather that I lifted so reverently from its corrugated cardboard shipping box was, without doubt, a sacred artifact of immense spirit power—a manifestation of pure, seductive evil.

I examined it carefully, noting the workmanship, the excellent condition of the leather and the stitching, verifying the "D-A-F" initials on the brass plate within. The apparent age of the mask, along with the rococo script and its rather peculiar hyphenization, had begun a train of thought that caused my spine to tingle and my skin to bristle with gooseflesh, as it always had when watching such classics of the macabre as *Nosferatu, The Cabinet of Dr. Caligari* and *Un*

Chien andalou. Some spark of intuition seemed to lead me on to a discovery, but I was as yet unsure. My fingers explored the smooth, coolly clinging surface of the leather's curves and folds.

Fortunately, it was already Thursday, so my wait for a bout of serious researching was less than a full twenty-four hours away. But time seemed to crawl painfully, like some crippled animal, through a long night filled with recurring, but unremembered, fever dreams.

I awoke the next morning to the rasping jangle of my alarm clock, feeling singularly unrested, the pillow and sheets sodden with sour sweat and the telltale, rotting-protein-and-ammonia scent and stains of other nocturnal emissions.

(*What dreams of tormented lust had troubled me throughout the night I could only hazard to fathom. . . .*)

I brushed my teeth and gums with abnormal savagery, striving to erase the soiled and bitter taste of too much liquor and too much dreaming from my mouth, and in the process made my mouth a raw and bloody mess.

My testicles felt bruised and swollen. And when I stood to drain my bladder, the crust of stale semen on my penis filled me with the nausea of shame and disgust.

I showered with a ritualistic fervor, turning the harsh spray of water to near-scalding, lathering myself profusely, as if this act of purification would absolve me of the sensation of *uncleanness*. . . .

That day required my last reserves of will to somehow endure. I skipped lunch, as I felt as if were I to break the routine I could not bear to return at all. Perhaps it was the self-chastising martyrdom of the suffering from hunger pangs and the euphoric dizzyness brought on by vacillating blood-sugar levels that saw me through this eight-hour-plus eternity.

I grabbed a junk food "fix" at the nearest Burger Box: a couple of *Bacon Cheez-Burgers*—their paper wrappers dripping grease—an *X-tra* large bag of fries and a *Chok'lat Thik Malt*. (Usually I'd have opted for a stop at Feig's Deli or The Good Earth or maybe Old Peking, but by dinner time the craving for Fast Eat was like a mandrill riding my shoulders, sinking his fangs into my back brain . . .).

The evening was spent at the public library, referencing and cross-referencing a wildly free-associated range of subjects from "adept" and "Azazel" to "yoni" and "zebub." Riding the jagged rush of a sucrose-and-sodium high, my mind reeled with the informational overload that I was striving to absorb. The brunt of my researches centered upon Crowley himself, the Theosophical Society, the Isis-Urania Temple of the Golden Dawn (later, "the Hermetic Order of—"), the internal power struggle that pitted W.B. Yeats, the actress Florence Farr and the majority of the Temple's members versus Crowley and Samuel Mathers, Crowley's subsequent break in of the London headquarters, the Rites of Eleusis, Crowley's delusion that he was the magus Eliphas Lévi reincarnated, *The Book of the Law* (and his catch-phrase, "Do as you will"), Crowley's founding of the British branch of the Order of the Temple of the Orient, his experiments with Tantric techniques, and his association with Victor Neuberg (involving sex magic and homosexual sado-masochism), his string of mistresses (each refered to as the "Scarlet Woman"), and, of course, his earlier (tragic) marriage to Rose Kelly, and his addictions to heroin and cocaine.

As if I needed any further facts to bridge my presumed connection with those initials "D-A-F," I seemingly stumbled upon a rather obscure poem, "Beyond this Shaman's Mask of Leather," by an anonymous author. Therein I discovered these quite *visionary* references: ". . . *crimson drapes it is madeleine-laure & rose keller. they giggle girlishly & each blows a pouting kiss. (rose keller tricked-out in nunnish habit stands behind the young girl's pale & sloping shoulder & gently caresses the lilac-scented flesh).*" and the refrain "*advance the winch./tighten those straining cords about the slender wrists./savor the hand of glory if it's offered!*" (*INKBLOT*, Winter 1986, Oakland, CA).

There could be no coincidence in the allusions, let alone my "accidental" discovery of the poem itself—there was, indeed, a thread of the occult that tied each element unerringly together:

"Scarlet Woman"/"crimson" and "tricked-out"

"Rose Kelly"/"Rose Keller"

The intimations of homosexuality and sex magic

The implications within its context of Satanic ritual—"nunnish habit," "behind . . . shoulder" ("Get thee behind me, Satan!"), and "hand of glory" (the Hand of Glory is, alternately, a charm made of the root of the mandrake, or the severed hand of a hanged murderer, dried and pickled or smoked over a fire of juniper: the latter, if a candle made from the fat of a hanged malefactor was lit and carried in its grasp, was believed to render all to whom it was presented motionless as the dead themselves; hence, the term "thief's candle" was also used to describe it . . .)

The link of sado-masochism

Even the place of purchase, "San Francisco," and that of publication, "Oakland," could hardly be laid to chance

But, above all else, the mention of "madeleine-laure" proved the link to the initials "D-A-F": from my readings I knew her to be none other than the daughter of Donatien-Alphonse-Francois, Comte De Sade . . .

Despite my state of nervous exhaustion, which earlier had bordered upon total collapse, sleep taunted with its promise of soothing oblivion but merely spilled across my jangled senses momentarily to evade me again and again, like the ebb/flow/ebb of slowly lapping night-tide, leaving me in the swirling wash of jumbled images, the pounding of my pulse and the soaking dampness of my sweat-drenched sheets . . .

My tormented nerves shrieked for solace and the muscles of my back and shoulders seemed knotted twists of aching pain. I tossed fitfully upon the mattress, seeking some position that might bring me the elusive promise of comfort, but I felt trapped upon some rack of torture. And, from the dark pools of childhood memory, I was reminded of the Grimm's tale of "The Princess and the Pea"—

Among the thought-flotsam bobbing to the surface of this tide of dream and wakefulness, the title of the poem, "Beyond this Shaman's Mask of Leather," washed up onto the haunted, moonlit beach of my perception and then once more was dragged into subconscious depths. But another phrase was tangled with it, as they rolled and fluttered in the ebb/flow-currents, the subtitle of the *INKBLOT* publication, "*PINK INK SAYS GIVE UP THE GHOST . . .*"

And snatches of song from my college days kept dragging at my consciousness. The ghostly wail of the harmonica and the nasal rasp of Dylan biting each syllable from *Desolation Row* and spitting out their bitter thought-stream: "*Dr. Filth, he keeps his world/ Inside of a leather cup . . .*" Endless-looping from *Just Like Tom Thumb's Blues: "I started out on burgundy/ But soon hit the harder stuff . . .*" intermingled with "*And picking up Angel who/Just arrived here from the coast/Who looked so fine at first/But left looking just like a ghost . . .*" From the eerie *Ballad of a Thin Man: "Now you see this one-eyed midget/Shouting the word 'NOW' . . .*" and "*Because something is happening here/But you don't know what it is/Do you, Mister Jones*?" And somewhere from the litter-and-graffiti-strewn darkness of his grave at Père Lachaise, Jim of the Doors, perhaps in some special Hell of debauched Parisian poets chants: "*BREAK ON THROUGH TO THE OTHER SIDE . . .*"

My nightmares writhe with soft and tender flesh, whips and black leather, and the wailing of the damned . . .

A lancet of pain-bright desert sunlight sliced through the closely clinging shroud of sleep, piercing some minute fold or flaw of my drapes to raise me from my soiled and twisted sheets.

The clock in the niche of my headboard read "11:31."

My head pounded with a pulse of pain.

Again, I felt the uncleanness of shame. Even more savagely than on the preceding morning I raked the toothbrush through my evil-tasting mouth, then scoured my body with a bristle brush and foaming lather, scalding my flesh red with the penitence of showering.

I spat out blood into the swirling vortex of the drain, perversely pleased with the contrition of self-injury. For some untold reason, a favored quote from Ducasse, my Philosophy prof in college, flooded back to me with singular intensity: *"Coincidence is nonexistent: there are only threads in a greater tapestry that we cannot, except in the rarest moments of vision, ever hope to see . . ."*

With sudden vividness, an essay that I had skimmed in the *INKBLOT* recalled itself to mind—Charles Herrick's "An Analysis of Jim Morrison, The Prince of Darkness," hit me with the profoundness of its revelation . . .

The day was spent in intensive research, ferreting out all the information I could find regarding the infamous De Sade. My skull throbbed with a savage headache that defied banishment, despite the Bufferin and Darvon (left over from a tennis injury several months back) that I quaffed in too-frequent and immoderate doses, washed down with gulps of ice-cold Coca Cola from the vending machine nearby the University's library. I ate nothing, as my stomach felt bruised and queasy, and I was loathe to lose the time from my fevered studies into this life of unequaled degradation and perversity, whose fascination held me like a moth circling about an open flame . . .

From among the titillating details of De Sade's sordid life, one detail, above all else, tugged at my imagination: that this man (or fiend, depending on one's viewpoint) of towering and dominating ego should have ordered that upon his death his remains be scattered, and all portraits or sculptures of his countenance be destroyed or defaced. In his words, "*the traces of my grave (shall) disappear from the face of the earth, as I flatter myself that my memory will be effaced from the minds of men.*" In a world where untold suffering is caused by the desire of the individual to see that those who follow shall remember them, only the infinite perversity of will could bring upon himself this bizarre curse of utter anonymity . . .

When, at last, the doors of the library were closed at 6:00 p.m., I bundled my notebook crammed with hasty scribblings under my arm, and wandered back to my parked car, the concrete and asphalt still quivering with heat-induced mirages, puddles of glistening wetness slithering away at my approach, in the yet blistering retreat of the westering sun.

I swung by the University Square outlet of ZIP'S RECORDS & TAPES to purchase some vintage Morrison. I bought *The Doors* and *Strange Days* in tape, and, out of sheer indulgence, the record of *Strange Days* (for the bizarre erotic imagery of its cover illo—*it seemed to speak to the darkest oubliette of my subconscious, the place where screams forever echoed* . . .). And, at the urge of secret whisperings, I sought among the "V's," and selected a copy of *The Velvet Underground and Nico* . . .

I locked my package safely in the trunk, then cut north to Speedway, hung a left, and headed west toward the Miracle Mile. The horizon burned red as blood, shading slowly to violet.

It was only dusk, and the night pulse of The Strip had yet to throb to sin-ready wakefulness. I took a room at the NO-TEL MOTEL, one of those kwik-hump specialists touting WATERBEDS and XXX-VIDEO in every room. I settled in to waste a couple hours, and tuned in, surprisingly, to the classic porn-fest, Marilyn Chambers' *Behind the Green Door*. The flick was already part way through, but its erotic circus of depravity soon roused me to erection. I was unable to control my private urgings, and soon found it necessary to scrub my hands and shower. By the time I returned to the bedroom, *The Story of O* was just beginning. It was the perfect orchestration for my current jaded turn-of-mind, the definitive exercise in bondage and domination . . .

When I cruised out into the neon-jittering Strip of Sleaze, I was live-wired for some kinko action, seeking what diversions might come my way in the flow of this Poor Man's Neo-Babylon . . .

For the first time since my college days, I scored two dime-bags of pot, and a foxy little teenage hook, like a gene-splice between Debbie Harry, Madonna and Cindi—state-of-the-art punk-kink fembod jailbait. I asked her if she had a friend in need of cash, and flashed a roll of fifties. . . .

The other girl looked nearly like her clone, or perhaps her even-younger sister. I commissioned them for an all-nighter.

In the warren of my room, both were soon stripped of their chains and leather. I flipped on the TV for a bit of background warmup, and found myself and my little foxes embroiled in the opening credits of an S&M flick named, appropriately, *Beyond De Sade* . . .

In the frenzy of my stimulation, I abandoned all pretense at safe-sex guidelines. . . .

I think the grass we smoked was "laced," perhaps with Dust, as the room dissolved in a blur of ever-increasing savagery and violence.

I found myself playing their chords of pain, twisting and biting and tormenting. . . .

The girls were pros despite their age, but neither had bargained for such brutal treatment. During the early hours of the morning, the younger girl, Mindy, escaped (quite naked), and returned with the pistol-armed manager and threats of calling the police. I paid all three off for their silence, and quickly fled into the night, driving as cautiously as necessity and my drugged haze permitted.

My state of agitation made it impossible to sleep, so I put on the tapes I'd purchased, and lay back in the comforting confines of my recliner, fondling and examining the leather mask, and letting my psyche sync with the music.

Velvet Underground's Lou Reed snaked out the lyrics of stoned sex-and-drug seduction, phasing to the shouting acid-chants of Morrison.

I pulled on the mask, tugging it carefully down across my features, into place. My breath echoed in the muffled silence, filling my ears with inner white noise, hissing from the mouth-slit of the voluptuously clinging leather. . . .

My mind swarmed with a montage of incredibly bizarre perversities, and I relieved my imaginings again and again. . . .

At last, I staggered from my seat, seeking the entrance hallway through memory, the way a blind man would.

I stood where my careful paces told me that my mirror hung.

Slowly, I stripped off the leather headgear, and stared into the smooth and featureless face of a mannequin. . . .

The curse of the Marquis fulfilled.

The domination of his will asserted.

MOVING OUT

by Nicholas Royle

Born in Manchester on March 20, 1963, Nicholas Royle now lives in London. One of England's fastest rising stars in the horror genre, he has now sold more than fifty stories to magazines and anthologies, including recent sales to Interzone, Sepulchre House, In Dreams, Narrow Houses, *and* Dark Voices 4. *Three novels are with his agent, and Royle has started work on a fourth,* Dark in the Daytime, *which he says: "should be less difficult to categorize—and therefore easier to sell—than the others. It will be grim and frightening." He has also recently edited the small press anthology,* Darklands, *whose stories have been placed in several year's-best anthologies (including this one), and Royle is planning a follow-up,* Darklands 2.

I don't know what she told her friends about her reasons for moving out, but I wasn't convinced it was just because of the new job. It was based on the east coast, seventy miles away. She could hardly commute, could she? her look seemed to say.

But did she really have to shift *all* her stuff and *buy* a flat rather than rent somewhere?

I thought we'd got on OK in my flat; it seemed to work fine. There was no indication that she tired of my frequent games and traps, which were never anything more than elaborate jokes.

Sometimes, for fun, I used to try and frighten her;

tense my muscles and affix an expression to my face, then move slowly toward her. She'd return the stare as long as she could, then fear crept suddenly into her eyes and I had to laugh to break the spell. "Did I really frighten you?" "Yes," she said, hurt. "I'm sorry." I showed concern and concealed my pleasure. It was only a game.

She took everything. Her collection of masks left a very empty wall in the bedroom, stubbled with nails. The bathroom shelf was suddenly made bare; forgotten tubs of moisturizing cream and rolled-up flattened tubes of toothpaste, even these things were taken. I saw her cast a mournful eye over my tailor's dummy.

"When I get my own place," she had once said, "will you give me this?"

She often asked. I didn't know why it was so important to her; she could have picked one up in any junk shop. I saw her from the kitchen one day, when she hadn't heard me come in from outside. She was kneeling at the mannequin's castors and clinging to its waist. Crying her eyes out.

I still didn't understand its significance.

She moved on a Saturday. I went along to help. Her new job came with a car, an estate, which was good because she would never have squeezed everything into my Mini.

I was ignored when I offered to drive. I knew what she'd say if she bothered to answer: I wasn't insured because we weren't married.

She didn't even give me a chance to climb in next to her, before moving swiftly away from the curb, spinning her wheels through gutterfuls of litter.

I looked at the features of the Mini as I approached it. The radiator grille—the car's mouth—had been buckled for a couple of weeks, and one of the eyes had a smashed lens. I had to wrench the door open. The engine wheezed into life and I moved off. The front offside wheel scraped against the wheel arch, but a bald tire was a small sacrifice. I'd said I'd help her move, and help her I would, with or without her cooperation.

I had my work cut out keeping up with her. She darted and surged, switching lanes in her haste like there was no one else on the road. I had to rely on steady progress, the weight of the boxes in the back of her car and the re-tuning I'd had done two months earlier.

Her block of flats had a lift. If there hadn't been so many heavy boxes and bags to carry, she would have climbed the stairs, despite her flat being on the sixth floor. She had always hated lifts.

It wasn't just the discomfort of being crammed into what was basically a large tin, with a number of strangers; nor was it the embarrassment of awkward silences and accidentally crossed stares. Lifts terrified her.

Which offered me endless opportunities whenever we went anywhere and had to use a lift.

I only had to stand there, glaze my eyes over and turn slowly toward her, and she would panic.

"No, Nick! No!"

She once bolted out of a lift in a multi-story carpark and ran straight into an old Vauxhall. She might have got away with a few bruises, had the car been stationary.

Some months later, one afternoon when she had gone out for a walk to help build up her strength, I rigged up a dummy out of some of my clothes, which I found in the wardrobe, and had it hanging in a noose from the kitchen doorway by the time she got back.

The relapse set her back about three months.

I regretted doing it but as I explained, it was only a joke.

It always puzzled me why she liked masks when she was so easily frightened by faces.

"A mask is only a mask," she said. "It's not ambiguous. There's nothing behind it." But in order to frighten her, I always had to start off by masking my features.

"There's nothing but wall behind my masks," she'd explained.

"Why do you like them so much?" I demanded.

"People used to believe that traumatic events that had not yet taken place could send back echoes from the future," she explained. "These echoes would sometimes register in masks."

"Like a satellite dish?" I quipped.

She gave me a black look.

"Why don't they show up in faces?" I asked.

"Because we block them. A mask can't. That's why you scare me when you fix your face like a mask. Sometimes the echoes are like the real thing."

I stared at her now from the corner of the lift in her new home, but she looked no more distressed than she had when I'd snatched glances in her mirror during the drive up. Now it was her turn to wear a mask, the mask of tragedy. Yes, it would hurt, but she had to make the break. That kind of thing. Stony-faced resolve, with just the occasional glimpse of what looked like terror animating her glass eyes. She only had to say, if she didn't want me there.

But not a word was uttered. In fact, I couldn't recall the last time she had addressed me at all. I was blurring reality and imagination, not sure afterward if she had said something or if I had imagined it from the look on her face.

The flat was on two floors. Not bad for the price and with a sweeping view of the sea front and port. At night the lights on the promenade would be pretty.

The staircase leading to the upper rooms was situated in the middle of the flat between the kitchen and the living room. You could walk right around the enclosed staircase, through the kitchen, the hallway and the living room. Actually under the stairs there was a cupboard, at its tallest about as tall as me.

I was able to follow her around from room to room and remain unseen. I tailed her just close enough to let her know I was there. She stopped and looked round, eyes flashing with anger and fear, but I was always just out of sight.

Later, after a light meal, I tried to talk to her. As if *I'd* done anything to upset *her*. "What's wrong?" I asked her.

She didn't feel like talking.

She slumped in a chair in front of the French windows. The curtains were closed, which meant she couldn't see the view. I pulled them back for her. It was dark now. The lights *were* pretty.

But with a snort she'd jumped up and quit the room as soon as I opened the curtain.

Anyone can take a hint, but it's somehow nicer to sit down and talk things out.

She clung to the edge of the sink, her face white as enamel. "I'll make a drink," I suggested.

Thrusting out an arm she opened the fridge door and bent down to get the milk out. She started when she saw the car keys next to the butter. I'd put them there just after we'd arrived.

"What's the matter?" I pleaded.

I'd often hidden her things in the fridge at my flat, as a joke; her reaction never more than a laugh or a groan.

She slammed the fridge door, ignoring me, and ran upstairs where she shut herself in her bedroom.

I took the keys out of the fridge and put them quietly down on the table, then sat down and thought about what might happen next. The simplest would be for me just to go. Would that be seen as giving in or a dignified withdrawal? Two of her Malaysian leather masks gazed unresponsively down at me from the wall above the portable television.

I became aware of a murmur of conversation through the ceiling. I stood up and craned my neck. Although the actual words were indistinguishable, I could tell it was her voice, and unanswered.

I walked quietly down the hall to the telephone extension. Hoping she wouldn't hear the click, I lifted the receiver to my ear.

". . . Mini was his."

I frowned. What were they talking about?

". . . but the things that are happening here, I'm terrified. I feel like I'm going mad or something. I keep hearing this terrible squealing."

I dropped the phone and rubbed my forehead, which was prickling with perspiration.

I couldn't decide what was the best thing to do, given her state of mind. But since my presence was obviously not helping, I decided to call it a day.

Closing the front door quietly behind me, I stepped into early morning darkness and thick fog. The car was some minutes' walk away. The plastic-covered seat was cold and sweating, the windscreen obscured inside and out. I proceeded, hunched over the wheel, the choke full out, wiping the condensation away with tissues and the fog with protesting wipers. The headlamps pushed into the fog, illuminating nothing but clouds of billowing moisture. The full beam was less help.

More by chance than navigation I found the dual carriageway and caught up with a set of red lights, which, when I narrowed the gap to eighteen inches, I could see belonged to a large container lorry.

In order to continue to enjoy the false security of the lorry's slipstream, I was obliged to accelerate to sixty miles per hour. I could scarcely credit the drivers who from time to time overtook me in the outside lane. My own knees had liquified in the fear that I would fail to register the lorry's brake lights, should they come on.

Because of the unshrinking blanket of fog, I never saw the sign warning of roads merging and so remained ignorant of the danger until six lanes of traffic suddenly tried to squeeze into three.

Given the appalling visibility and the speed the influx of traffic was traveling at (coming from the west, where the fog would be thinner), there were bound to be some casualties.

A USAF jeep shunted me into the lorry I'd been sheltering behind, and an Audi overtaking on the outside caught my wing.

Then, dimly, I began to understand what she had meant about the echoes. Sometimes, she had said, the echoes are like the real thing.

I only stayed long enough to pick up the tailor's dummy.

It would function as a present and as a surprise. Hopefully, she would have calmed down overnight and was probably already indulging herself in contrition.

Driving back up with the dummy lying silently on the back seat, I saw its bulk whenever I checked the rear-view mirror. Was it not too silent and bland? It needed a mask.

Also in the mirror I saw the mask I would give it.

The car coughed and clanked, but somehow made it.

She was out, at work, as I'd anticipated.

I went to the cupboard under the stairs. Three boxes sat in a corner and a couple of coats hung on hooks. The dummy, with its mask, was the same height as me.

Patiently I awaited the end of the working day.

I heard the key in the front door, the shuffle of letters, the tap of an executive briefcase on kitchen linoleum.

Footsteps. A yawn. More steps.

She pulled open the door.

A tremor went through her body; she stepped back; her mouth fell open but any sound was choked in her throat.

All apologies, I slid forward toward her, castors squealing.

"No, Nick! No!" she managed to scream.

BETTER WAYS IN A WET ALLEY

by Barb Hendee

Barb Hendee is yet another newcomer to The Year's Best Horror Stories, *although I suppose she might claim prior infiltration on the strength of having been an editor for the small press magazine that first published C.S. Fuqua's story from last year's volume, "Walking After Midnight." Born in Everett, Washington in 1963, Hendee now lives in Moscow, Idaho with her husband, J.C., and ten-year-old daughter, Jaclyn. She and her husband are co-editors of* Figment, Tales From the Imagination, *for which they receive about seventy submissions a week. Her fiction has appeared in a number of the leading small press publications. Hendee says that she "loves gourmet coffee and makes a habit of collecting homeless, pregnant, unwed cats, and friends with really sick senses of humor." That last should pertain to half the writers in this book.*

The cardboard finally soaked all the way through and one large, wet drip landed on top of my head. Pulling my damp skirt tighter around my legs, I tried to think of somewhere else to sleep but came up blank. I didn't have enough money to buy a coke at the pool hall, and last week I had slipped out of Mr. Leon's all night coffee shop without paying my bill. Usually no one cared if you curled up in a corner at the pool hall or Mr. Leon's as long as you had a little money to spend.

But I was broke and no john in his right mind would come out in a rainstorm if he didn't have to, not even if he were dying for a blow job. God only knew what shit this rain was bringing down. Sometimes it was just water, but sometimes it burned your skin or made you choke. Better not to take a chance if you already had some place with a roof.

My box started falling apart and my back teeth clicked together over and over again. I couldn't stop them. I was cold. Not icy cold like you feel in the snow, but a deep cold like even my bones were wet.

What am I gonna do? Think.

I shoved my hand into my pocket, and it closed over a scrap of paper. I pulled it out and uncrinkled it.

RoseWood Motel. Clean Rooms. Hourly rates.

At the bottom was scribbled in pencil.

"I've got it for a week. 555-3941.

Cheers, Torrie"

I stared at it for a few minutes while rain blurred the lead. I'd forgotten Torrie had a room this week. If he had a room in this storm, though, he'd probably be working. If I called in the middle of things I could fuck up his trick's mood and ruin any chance for extra money.

But then the top of my box collapsed over my back.

Holding my jacket up like an umbrella, I decided to make a dash for Arnie's market. He hated most of us, but sometimes he'd let me use the phone.

His fat, store-keeper's face scowled when I fell in the front door dripping all over his chipped linoleum.

"What the hell do you want?"

"I'm stuck outside, Arnie. I need to use the phone."

"This ain't fucking GTE. Go to the corner booth."

"I ain't got a quarter."

This was a game he always played—pretending that it was some great financial drain for me to make a local call. But no matter what he said, he was okay on the inside. Once, when some john broke my wrist and Torrie had done a bad job setting it, Arnie gave me some extra-strength *Tylenol*, took me down to the free clinic and stayed with me until some nurse called my name. He never mentioned it afterward and neither did I.

"Please, Arnie. Torrie's got a room this week, and I need to call him."

When his scowl deepened and he didn't answer, I cried, "For Chrissakes! It's *raining*."

"Oh, use the goddamn phone then," he snapped. "But this is the last time, Baby. I don't want to see you again unless you're shopping."

"Thanks," I sniffed and dialed. God, I hated this shit, but if you're desperate enough you'll play anyone's games. At least he didn't want to get laid.

Torrie answered on the second ring.

"Yeah."

"It's me," I whispered. "Are you alone?"

"Hi, Baby." He sounded glad, and I felt my shoulders ease. I hadn't fucked anything up. "You stuck outside?" he asked.

"Uh-huh. You got a vacant spot?"

"Yeah, it's dead. I've even got some cold Chinese food left. Room #5."

"Okay. I'll be there in a little while. Thanks, Torrie."

I hung the phone up slowly and watched the angry, black rain punish Arnie's front-store windows. Then I pulled my jacket tight over my head again and made a run for the *RoseWood* motel—room #5.

The line about clean rooms was bullshit. There were dead coach roaches in the air vents and yellowed paint peeling off the walls. But tonight it looked like heaven.

Torrie started peeling my clothes off the minute he pulled me inside. My skin didn't burn and I was breathing all right, but I like the attention. It was nice to relax and let somebody else worry about things for a few minutes.

"Get in the shower," he ordered.

Water from the city's plumbing system was clean,

or least that's what they told us. We all wanted to believe it, so we did.

The hot, steamy water felt good. I washed my hair and rubbed it half dry with a towel, then put on one of Torrie's t-shirts. By the time I stepped back out to where he was lying on the old motel bed watching *Hogan's Heroes*, my body felt warm and happy.

"This place is great," I smiled. "How long have you been here?"

"A week." He almost smiled back at me and then jumped off the bed. "Come'ere, Baby."

A little electric burner was plugged into the wall socket sporting a small pot of boiling water. Torrie pulled a jar of instant coffee out of his pack and fixed me a cup. Then he reached for two red-inked boxes of Chinese food on the nightstand.

"I ate all the almond fried chicken, but there's still rice and chow mein left."

I didn't know what to say. We'd always sort of stuck together in hard times. But this was different. He was making me coffee and giving me his food. I couldn't remember being warm, and dry, and full all at the same time.

"Thanks," was all I managed to get out.

He nodded and climbed back up on the bed so I could eat. I watched for a few minutes. He looked good clean. Torrie was sixteen—a year older than me—he had short, white-blond hair and a thin, baby face that made him look younger.

My food tasted great. I stopped chewing long enough to ask. "Where'd you get the money for all this."

"I followed some blue collar leaving the bank on payday and killed him over on 6th and Washington. It's pretty dark there."

I nodded. Torrie was thin but tough. The general concensus of the street voted him "most likely to grow up."

I finished eating and bounced up on the bed beside him. "A TV set." I grinned. "Your very own TV set and we can watch whatever we want. Are there any movies on later?"

This time he did smile and reached for the guide. "I don't know. I'll look."

I felt so good I could barely stand it. All this and I hadn't had to do anything.

Torrie rested the guide in his lap and looked at me. "I'm glad you called. I kinda hoped you would."

That threw me. "You did. Why?"

He shrugged with a funny expression. "I don't know. I've been thinking about you a lot lately. I even took the subway to the outskirts last week and applied for a job at a steel factory."

I sat straight up. "You did?" No one I knew had ever done that. "What did they say?"

He twisted the guide with right hand. "Nothing. They looked at me like I was dirt—like I was a kid. You have to be eighteen and have an address—references and shit like that." His eyes wandered farther away. "Tonight's the last night I paid for this room. God, I hope it stops raining."

"Haven't you made any money while you've had this room? They always pay me more if we don't do it in the alley."

"Yeah, some. But I didn't try too hard. I'm so sick of that shit it's getting to the point where I'd just rather cut'em."

"No! You can't pick off too many or the rest will get scared. Then we'll all starve."

He nodded impatiently. "I know that! Why do you think I went to the steel factory? I thought maybe I could get us out of here."

I stared at him. God, he was in a weird mood tonight. "Us?"

"Yeah, us." He flipped the TV switch to off. "I'm tired, Baby. Let's just get some sleep."

"Okay." I was a little disappointed 'cause I hadn't seen a movie in months. It's funny how people think. Two hours ago I would have been happy with a dry box, and now I was bummed because Torrie turned the TV off.

I put out the lights, curled my back into his chest, and closed my eyes, enjoying his warmth. Then an odd thing happened. He softly touched my stomach with the flat of his hand and moved it up my side. For a minute I thought he was just trying to get comfortable, but then he pushed himself harder against me and kissed the top of my head.

I wasn't scared. I mean . . . I didn't mind. I'd probably rather have Torrie touch me than anyone. It wasn't that. It's just that we'd been sleeping together on and off for years to keep warm. One time we got snowed into a warehouse—with only half a roof—for two days and he'd kept us both alive by starting a fire in a barrel, taking his shirt off and wrapping a ratty blanket around us to insulate our body heat. We'd slept in alleys, boxes, doorways, the pool hall, Mr. Leon's coffee shop and once we even set up housekeeping in an abandoned box car next to the tracks on the East side, but Torrie had only been thirteen then and an over-sized bum threw us out. We'd grown up together. We were friends or as near to it as we could be.

I rolled over in his arms and looked up at his face. "What's wrong?"

"I don't know," he whispered. His voice was shaking. "I was just trying to pretend like this place was ours. Like we could hang onto it and come home every day. Like the blue collars and people you see in movies. We'd eat dinner together at night and you belonged to me."

Poor Torrie. Maybe they were right. Maybe he would live to grow up.

I didn't know what to say, so I buried my face in the crook of his neck. He pulled me back gently and pushed his tongue into my mouth. I'd never gotten anybody off who wasn't telling me what to do, so I just laid there and kissed him back. It was soft and strange—his mouth I mean. What a weird night. He was touching me all over and it felt good. In a few minutes I didn't even care that he'd turned off the TV.

* * *

Somehow, afterward, I thought that our unusual night together would make him happy, but it didn't. When I woke up, he was on the phone talking to the manager.

"I'll have the money by nine o'clock tonight. Just don't give the room away."

"Torrie, what are you doing?"

He hung up and looked at me. He seemed scared, almost panicked. "We need to keep the room. I want us to stay here."

"How much more money do you need?"

"About $60.00 if we want it another week, but don't worry. I'll get it."

"Yeah, okay. I can help too. I look a lot better after that shower, and it stopped raining. They'll be people on the streets tonight."

"No!" he snapped. "I told you I'd get it. You just stay with me."

I didn't like him yelling at me, and I didn't understand what was wrong with him. "All right," I said, staring at the blanket. "*Mr. Pancake* should have taken out the garbage by now. You want to see if we find some breakfast?"

"No. Just get dressed and we'll go buy some rolls or something at the store."

He was really starting to worry me. Hadn't he just got done saying that he needed all of his money to pay for the motel room.

"At the store?"

"Yeah," he said tiredly. "Just come on."

It was dark by seven that night, and by eight Torrie was acting like a psycho. We were haunting alleys, and I knew he was going to kill somebody. Like I said, he was tough and there were times in the past when his killing somebody had done somebody else a lot of good. Like last year when Packard's gang beat up old Charlie Brown.

There was this sweet old one-handed man who lived in a tiny apartment on Fourth Street. I don't know what had happened to his hand, but the government sent him a small check every month. He was the only person I knew that the government had ever helped. Anyway, he was always nice to us, and Torrie called him Charlie Brown. One day when we were just kids, we got bored and started tearing the stamps off all the letters that we found in the garbage. We made our own white-paged book and started a stamp collection. When old Charlie Brown heard about it, he made a point of saving any brightly-colored or special looking stamps and giving them to Torrie. After that, Torrie said that he was one of us and we should help look out for him. Then last year Packard's gang waited for him on the first day of the month when his check came and beat him up pretty bad with a bicycle chain. His face never did heal all the way.

Torrie was so mad that he broke into a hardware store, cut off a long strand of barbed wire, caught Packard's second lieutenant alone, and hung him from a broken street light with a note pinned to his chest that read:

> "Don't touch that old man again.
> P.S. You won't ever find me and
> you won't see me coming."

Nobody ever bothered Charlie again, and the scabs in Packard's gang deserved to die anyway, so Torrie had done a good thing.

But tonight he was scaring the hell out of me. We'd been getting along just fine with no place to live for years.

"Come on, Torrie. Just forget it. Let's go down to the pool hall and see what we can scrounge up."

"No. I told the manager I'd have his money by nine o'clock." He leaned up against the front of an old burned out tavern. "You stand over there out of sight and wait. Something'll turn up."

You mean someone.

So I waited, staring at my old Mickey Mouse watch. Torrie let about six people go by without a word.

Then at ten minutes to nine, a big man in a business suit came toward us. I got nervous right away. The only business suits who came down here were looking for shit they couldn't get uptown. I always stayed away from them.

He stopped when he saw Torrie. His face was close-shaven and hard.

"I seem to be lost. Could you show me the way out?"

Torrie nodded. "I can show things you've never seen."

The guy's eyes glowed. "Where?"

I watched the side of Torrie's pale, white face as he stepped back into the alley. "Right here."

Then I lost sight of both of them while I listened to harsh breathing sounds that I'd heard a billion times before. I was scared. In fact, I was seriously thinking about taking off when the breathing changed to a gasping scream and a curse.

"Jesus Christ!"

I jumped toward the shout until I could see them through the darkness. The suit's throat was bleeding, but not deep enough. He had Torrie pinned up against the wall, and I got there just in time to watch him ram a knife through my friend's thin chest. It was Torrie's knife.

The guy stepped back, breathing hard, and seemed terrified. I heard somebody screaming and then stopped when I realized it was me. He grabbed his throat. Dark fluid squeezed out between his fingers, and he bolted past me. I never saw him again.

"Torrie?"

There was a hole in his chest the size of my fist, and his head was laying at an unnatural angle. His eyes were closed.

I ran out of the alley as fast I could and headed straight to Arnie's. I was hysterical by the time I rushed through his door and didn't give a shit what he thought.

"Arnie, call an ambulance! Torrie got cut real bad," I sobbed. "I can't even tell if he's breathing."

Arnie stared at me for a long time with an odd, ashen face. Then he calmly picked up the phone and put it under the counter.

"What are you doing!" I wanted to tear his face off. "No games tonight. Gimme the goddamn phone!"

"No, Baby. No games tonight," he whispered. "Let your friend die. It's a better way for him. It's a better way for all of you. None of you really have lives anyway."

Fuck him. I bolted back out onto the street, but couldn't help hearing him call, "A better way," after me.

There was a pay phone two blocks North. I hit the "O" button and an operator came on the line. Forcing myself to breathe, I told her that I needed an ambulance and exactly where Torrie was. Then I hurried back to him.

Kneeling down, I noticed the ground was wet. Some of last night's rain had been trickling out of the gutter pipes and soaked the ground. Torrie was lying in filthy rain and his own blood with no one to care but me.

I pulled his head into my lap. "It's all right. They're coming."

He wasn't breathing, and part of me, way in the back of my head knew it. But I thought that doctors could do things beyond my understanding and once they'd gotten here, somehow Torrie could get fixed.

But thirty minutes later two paramedics pulled up without even a siren blaring. One of them got out sucking on a Tootsie pop. They both looked nervous about having to come down here.

The first one glanced down at Torrie. "Too late for this one. Jesus, look at that hole."

"So what's the verdict?" his partner called as he pulled out a stretcher.

"No way. Dead puppy."

I couldn't believe it and whispered. "Where are you taking him?"

"Down to the hospital." He couldn't make it to the center of his Tootsie Pop and bit down. "We've got to have a doc pronounce him D.O.A."

While they struggled with the stretcher, I slipped out from under Torrie's head and moved away down the alley.

"Hey, where'd that girl go? We don't got nothing for the report."

I jumped to the top of a wooden fence and as I climbed over, I wondered where they would bury him.

We all met at Mr. Leon's the next day for his funeral. Word travels fast here. We were an odd collection of people. Joe and Marlin were a couple of loner kids that Torrie helped look out for, there were a few bums who called him friend, Charlie Brown of course, and rumpled Mistress May who believed in God.

We all came to talk about what Torrie had been to us and to say good-bye in our own way.

"Once, when I passed out in the snow, he put me in a dry spot and brought me hot coffee," one old bum said, sniffing.

"Amen," said Mistress May.

"After they hurt me, he strung up one of them Packard boys up with barbed wire. He wouldn't say it, but I knowed it was him," said Charlie Brown.

"Amen."

I stopped listening and couldn't get Arnie's words out of my mind.

A better way for him.

What the hell what that supposed to mean? Maybe I already knew. Maybe I just don't want to face it.

"At least he's not cold anymore," I whispered, "or hungry, or blowing off some blue collar in a wet alley."

"Amen."

But then the sight of his open chest flashed by me and Arnie's calm, almost triumphant face. Maybe that was their plan—just ignore us long enough and we'll all die out. Maybe they did figure that was the better way.

"Bullshit."

Everyone stopped talking

"What's bullshit, Baby?" Charlie Brown asked.

"What I just said about Torrie not being cold or hungry."

"Why is it bullshit?"

They all looked at me expectantly, like they expected the mysteries of the universe to come pouring out of my mouth.

But I turned my gaze away and stared out at the street. "Because anything's better than being dead."

"Amen."

CLOSE TO THE EARTH

by Gregory Nicoll

Barb Hendee sent me a photo of herself, looking rather pensive. Gregory Nicoll sent me a photo of himself, looking decidedly morose, sitting in front of his beloved Volkswagen Rabbit pickup truck after it went head-to-head with a six-point whitetail buck. I've decided to keep a scrapbook.

Born in Concord, New Hampshire on April 22, 1958, Gregory Nicoll was raised on various army bases before settling down in Georgia in 1967. Using Joe Bob Briggs as his role model, he has emerged as a Southern horror writer with a fondness for splatter films (redneckpunk?). Recently he has sold stories to the anthologies, Chilled to the Bone, Cold Shocks, Freak Show, Still Dead, *and* Confederacy of the Dead. *He has also dabbled in movie work, providing publicity and uncredited additional dialogue for the 1989 horror film,* Blood Salvage. *Presently he is polishing the manuscript of his first novel. Nicoll writes that he "loves dark beer, hot chili, Volkswagens, and the smell of diesel in the morning." Fellow VW lovers should send flowers to Nick's Body Shop, Tucker, Georgia.*

The early evening cold sliced at Tacker's neck like a frozen knifeblade. Cursing the imperfect manufacturing which kept his Oldsmobile's windowglass from fitting precisely into the doorframe, Tacker groped for the controls on the car's heater. They were already set on maximum.

God, it's cold, he thought. *A Georgia boy can't take too much more of this.*

Billboards hyping small hotels loomed invitingly along the roadside, promising shelter, comfort, and warmth at budget prices.

SLEEP CHEAP.

HEATED POOL.

FREE BREAKFAST.

MOVIES.

SPEND A NIGHT, NOT A FORTUNE.

The signs gleamed in the twilight and then whisked past like shooting stars. Tacker kept driving

Another hour, he thought. *At least another coupla hours. Gotta make it as far as Harrisburg tonight.*

He reached up with his curling, nearly numb fingers and tried to pull the zipper of his much-too-thin cotton jacket up higher. His fingers couldn't close on the metal tab tightly enough to pull it. *Must be 20 degrees out there. A Georgia boy just can't take this. . . .*

The radio in the dashboard sprayed snowy static. He'd already lost the only good North Carolina station over an hour ago, its dim signal breaking up in explosive crackles as Tacker drove out of range.

Antenna's probably broken, he grumbled.

He kept the radio switched on—the static had a soft sound, a small comfort to him in the unfriendly evening chill.

The car smelled of cold plastic and frosted vinyl. The once-inviting aroma of coffee was gone now, another victim of the freezing air slipping through the cracks in the Oldsmobile's door. A tiny reservoir of the muddy brown liquid still splashed around the bottom of the jumbo styrofoam cup he'd bought three hours ago at the truck stop, where he'd topped off the fuel tank with a few gallons of overpriced diesel, grabbed the coffee for his head and a couple of Eskimo pies for his stomach, charging the whole mess on the company's credit card. It was against policy to buy food with one of XCCD's fuel cards, but Tacker was past the point of caring about policy.

It's "policy" that we site inspectors get a company car with a heater that works and an antenna in one piece, he reasoned. *Anybody fusses, I'll tell 'em to cuss out the joes down in motor pool. Lousy maintenance. Probably the fuse or something. . . .*

His personal disgust with company policy was mixed with professional annoyance. Heavy on his mind was the spill at the new site east of Memphis. Heavier on his mind was the "spill" that had leaked around Evelyn's birth control device six months ago, an accident of a far more personal nature. The long, lonely quiet drive had given him plenty of time to worry about both, and he was hungry for a distraction.

Preferably a warm distraction, he mused.

Another sign loomed in the graying twilight.

MARYSWOOD DINER—COFFEE, EATS, BREAKFAST ANYTIME.

Coffee. I should stop and get s'more coffee, he thought. *Maryswood . . . How far's that?*

He fumbled with the auto club map of Virginia, its thin rectangular pages fanning out from the tiny binder ring like dead white fingers on the car seat.

Four miles. No problem.

Yeah—a little coffee—that's what I need. Maybe make a quick call home to Evelyn. Hope she's got something else to talk about besides the usual complaints. . . .

Then maybe find me a waitress or a cashier who still knows how to really warm up a man. . . .

As Tacker drove on, the clouds overhead converged to blot out what remained of the daylight. Yet the ground on either side of the highway retained a strange luster. It was several minutes before Tacker realized what he was seeing.

Snow! Must've snowed here recently. Well, I'll be. . . .

The minor novelty of a snowfall—Tacker had only seen enough snow to cover the ground a half dozen times in all his 39 years—was mitigated by the agonizing extra degrees which the temperature fell as the Oldsmobile crawled nearer to Maryswood. Tacker shivered. He eyed the dirty, patchy snow—mixed in the muddy soil like grits and gravy—with a combination of wonder and helplessness.

Despite the fall of night, no lights burned in the windows or parking lots of the scattered warehouses and smaller buildings Tacker saw from the highway. The rolling fields, where corn and tobacco plants would grow in warmer seasons, now lay dark. Unlit farmhouses rose like lonely tombstones in the middle of the empty, lifeless acres.

The diner's probably closed too, he thought. Still, it's worth a chance. . . .

Sure hope the coffee's hot. . . .

Tacker could recall stopping in Maryswood before, but couldn't recall when. *Sometime last year . . . maybe the year before. . . .*

The exit loomed on the roadside up ahead. Just beyond the big, green metal sign put up by the highway department was a smaller one, made of cracked boards painted blue. Faded orange letters spelled out:

WELCOME TO MARYSWOOD.

Below the town's name was a row of small symbols—a bale of cotton, a peanut, a tobacco leaf, an ear of corn—and a tiny inscription in gold.

Tacker glimpsed it briefly as he drove down the ramp:

A COMMUNITY CLOSE TO THE EARTH.

Locating the Maryswood diner was relatively easy—it was the only building at the small, rural crossroads with its lights still burning. The hardware store, the International Harvester dealership, the dry goods shop, and a few others nestled beside them seemed to be closed for the night. The gas station on the south corner looked like it had been shut down much longer, if the shockingly low price-per-gallon displayed on its rusting sign was any indication. Tacker swung the Oldsmobile into the diner's empty seven-car parking lot and switched off the engine. The big diesel shook with a death rattle and went silent.

Wind whistled, then howled, outside the car.

Tacker sighed as he slumped back in his seat. For the first time it occurred to him that perhaps the diner was closed, too—that its lights had been left on by mistake. After all, there were no other cars in its lot. He surveyed the building carefully through the mist of his own condensing breath.

It was a classic '50s diner—a long streetcar-shaped building of bare, gleaming metal with wide windows from end to end. A single amber lamp lit the metal-railed rampway leading up to the door, and blue-green light glowed from inside. Tacker noticed that a powerful spotlight had been mounted on a pole behind the diner, illuminating a huge open lot out back. *Must be for the employees' parking,* he mused, *or maybe to light the way to the dumpster.*

Tacker sighed. *With all those lights on, somebody's got to be on duty inside the place. . . .*

Clenching his teeth to brace against the chill, Tacker pushed open the Oldsmobile's door and climbed out. His toes went numb before his shoes even touched the icy pavement. It was all he could do to shove the car door closed and stagger up to the frosted glass entrance door to the diner. He fell against the restaurant's metal door handle and, with a tremendous rush of relief, felt it swing inward on its hinges. An instant later he stood inside, sweet warm air soothing around him as a heavy blanket. He took a deep breath of it.

Tacker was alone in the place.

The turquoise-colored pads of its counter stools stood uniformly empty, menus and napkin holders arranged in neat rows on the gleaming surfaces. The air smelled faintly of eggs and bacon. A coffee pot steamed on a warming station near the cash register.

"Hello?" he called out. "Is anybody there?"

There was no answer.

Tacker took a tentative step forward, then climbed onto a padded stool near the cash register and began to defrost his curled fingers over the steam rising from the coffee pot beside it. The earthy, dark-roasted fragrance was bracing. He looked around hopefully for a mug but didn't see one anywhere. He remembered the styrofoam cup still propped up in the Oldsmobile and considered going back for it.

Maybe after I've warmed up a bit more, he thought, looking out at the car through the diner's windows.

"Can I get ya something?" asked a voice from behind him.

Tacker whirled around on his stool.

"Coffee, mister?"

She was relatively young—about 29 or 30, Tacker figured—with wide, dull gray eyes darkened by circles from lack of sleep and edged by slight wrinkles. Her hair was long and straight, frizzed with split ends, and badly in need of a comb and cut. She wore a tan fur collared bomber jacket, hanging open to reveal a creased blue uniform blouse with *Marie* stitched on it in red letters over the right breast pocket. A thin trail of slush—part mud, part melting snow—on the tile floor behind her suggested she'd recently been outside. Tacker tried not to stare too intently at her, yet since reaching puberty he had developed the habit of evaluating each new female as a potential sex partner. *Give her some rest and a trim, and I bet she'd clean up nice.*

"Coffee," he said, diverting his eyes to the pot. "Yeah—some coffee would really hit the spot right now. Bring it on."

She reached beneath the counter and produced a white ceramic mug with the casual grace of a stage magician. "You want cream or sugar with that?" she asked as she poured.

"Black'll be fine," Tacker answered. He accepted the steaming mug gratefully. As he hefted it from her grasp, he noticed something odd about her left hand—but caught only a quick glimpse. *Did she have five . . . or more?* He sipped the coffee. It was good. And *hot*.

The woman shrugged off her jacket and hung it on a peg near a small doorway marked "EMPLOYEES ONLY." She quickly slipped a cooking mitt over her left hand.

"Cold out there," Tacker observed.

She nodded. "I was out back checking on something. Didn't hear you come in. Sorry. Been waiting long?"

"No, not at all."

"That's good. You want some food?" Tacker looked up at a row of small posters displayed overhead. Laboriously hand-lettered with felt tip marker on sheets of pastel paper, they advertised various special dinner combos and breakfast platters. He chose one at random. "I'll have the two-eggs-with-corn-fritters, please."

She hung her head as though ashamed. "Our corn crop was bad again this year," she said, speaking almost in a whisper. She looked up purposefully at him, forcing her eyes to meet his. "I should be able to find a few good eggs, though. Would you mind waffles or pancakes instead of corn fritters?"

He smiled, sipped his coffee—its warmth was nectar of the gods to his frozen body—and hunched his shoulders. "Waffles'll do fine. Long as they're hot."

She nodded and turned her back to him, removing a carton of eggs and a container of waffle mix from a tiny refrigerator on the cooking console. She began to pour the waffle mix into a large electric waffle iron.

Tacker took another revitalizing sip of the coffee, feeling its warmth spread through his system, breathing its earthy aroma. He watched the woman working, admiring the curve of her fanny as she bent over the stove. "Local corn crop went bad, hunh?" he said, just to make conversation.

She moved her head in response—Tacker couldn't tell exactly if it was a nod.

"Don't you ever bring corn in from other places?" he asked.

She closed the waffle iron and turned a switch. A tiny red light came on. "Sometimes we do," she answered quietly, "if we have to. But the folks in these parts usually take a lot of pride in using our own. We're close to the earth here. Take only what God sees fit to let grow in our own soil. Don't usually bring much in from other parts."

"I see," said Tacker. He finished his coffee in one final, searing swallow. He smiled. "Another cup of that brown joe might let me see even clearer."

She turned, glanced down at his empty mug, and distractedly refilled it.

"Thanks," said Tacker. "It's *good* coffee." He sipped it again.

"It's Colombian," she muttered unpleasantly, turning back to the cooking console. "The coffee's one thing we *always* have to get from someplace else." She moved the egg tray under the warming lamp and began to examine the eggs. Picking one up with her mitt-covered left hand, she prodded it and turned it over, studying the egg with the professional attention of a diamond cutter.

Tacker was fascinated. *What's she doing*? he wondered. He tried to remember what she'd said when he first placed his order. *Something about being able to find a few good eggs. . . .*

Finally she cracked the egg on the griddle. It hissed like a viper as it oozed across the searing hot metal surface, its gooey translucence slowly clouding to a chalky white.

The sweet, delicious aroma of sizzling egg—sunny-side up, of course—made Tacker's mouth water. His stomach growled with impatience. It occurred to him that he hadn't told her his name. "My name's Tacker," he offered. "Jim Tacker."

The woman glanced back at him and smiled briefly as she reached for a second egg. "Call me Marie," she answered. She cracked the egg and spread it, hissing across the griddle.

As Tacker admired her smile—*No sir,* he thought, *I definitely wouldn't kick her outa bed*—he sensed that something was suddenly, terribly wrong.

It started with the smell—a thick, pungent stink that seemed to come from everywhere at once, as though the air itself had gone instantly sour. Then came a fierce crackling, as if a string of firecrackers had been tossed on the sizzling griddle. At last there was smoke—an eerie blend of dark colors which swirled menacingly from the cooking surface like a tiny tornado.

Tacker nearly dropped his coffee mug. "What the—?!"

"It's okay," she said loudly, to be heard over the crackling. "I know what to do with it."

The second egg was arching up in its center as foul smoke sprayed from its edges. It looked like a little snowhill, as though a miniature snowman were struggling to stand up on the cooking surface.

Marie quickly rolled a small metal cart over to the cooking console. In its center was a large metal bucket half filled with some dark, oily liquid. Beside it lay what looked like a set of fireplace tools—poker, tongs, and a small, long-handled shovel.

Tacker was on his feet backing slowly toward the door, his coffee cup abandoned on the counter. *Christ Almighty,* he thought, *what the screaming hell is going on here?!*

Marie had the little shovel in one hand, the tongs in the other. She scooped the shovel blade under the pulsating, amorphous white glob and clamped the tongs around it. The thing quivered, changing shape as she hoisted it off the griddle, and Marie struggled to control it. Finally she swiveled in place and dropped the writhing, smoldering thing into the bucket. It dissolved in a cloud of gray vapor as soon as it hit the solution sloshing inside.

Tacker stood frozen in place, watching the final wisps of smoke drift from the bucket. Marie also watched purposefully, the long-handled tools still clenched tightly in her fists. She did not move.

With a surprisingly cheerful metallic *ding*, the waffle iron announced its contents were fully cooked. The little sound reverberated like a rifle shot through the otherwise silent restaurant.

The bell snapped Marie from her trance. She set the tools down on the cart and peeked over the rim of the bucket.

Tacker took a step backward toward the exit. His bare hands wrapped around the frosty cold door handle, stinging at the touch. He pushed and the door opened slightly. Piercing, freezing cold air rushed in, attacking his bare neck.

"Everything's all right," Marie called. "The acid ate it right up. You can come back now."

Tacker let the door swing closed. He didn't want to go back—but neither did he want to face the winter weather outside without a hot meal first.

Oh, yeah, he remembered, *and I didn't call Evelyn yet. . . .* He eyed the payphone with a tiny pang of guilt.

Marie opened the waffle iron and busied herself brushing butter across the waffle, sprinkling cinnamon on it, and preparing the plate for her customer with casual dedication, as though the alarming incident with the weird white glob had never taken place.

The warm, inviting aroma of the toasty waffle—and the one good egg still hissing on the griddle—drew Tacker back to his seat at the counter. He watched Marie expertly fit the egg onto a plate, then select another and examine it carefully as she prepared it. She ignored him, avoiding his gaze and saying nothing until his meal platter was fully prepared. Within minutes it was set before him, steam rising from two perfect sunnyside up eggs, a pat of butter melting slowly into an inch-thick brown waffle. There was even a garnish of parsley and a side dish of toast cut into perfect triangles.

Tacker accepted the plate happily and began to eat, but found he couldn't keep his mind off the scene Marie had made with the peculiar egg. He devoured the waffle and the toast, washing it down with more hot coffee, but couldn't bring himself to touch the eggs.

They watched him from the plate, two bulging yellow eyes.

Marie refilled his cup and began to prepare a fresh pot. "Can't blame ya for passing on those eggs," she said as she poured water into the coffeemaker. "Guess I owe ya some sort of explanation."

Tacker sipped at his coffee and pushed the plate away.

The eggs continued to watch him.

He covered them with his napkin.

Marie switched the coffee maker on. It gurgled like a drowning man. She walked a few steps away and looked out the window, her back turned to Tacker.

"So tell me," Tacker said quietly, "what's going on around here?"

Marie continued to stare out the frosted glass. "It started back in the 1950s," she answered, her voice weak and nervous, "but nobody really noticed it until about twelve, maybe fifteen years later. Took that long to put all the pieces together."

"Pieces?"

She nodded. "Stories in the news about Love Canal, Three Mile Island—places like that—were what finally convinced *everybody*. Some of us, though, got wise to it all a whole lot earlier."

Tacker swallowed hard. "You mean, uh, radiation?"

"That's part of it. The chemical waste was the main thing. Ever heard of XCCD?"

Tacker set down his cup. "Sure. Xavier Commercial Chemical Development. Big Company. Everybody's heard of it. But you know, I think some of those news stories are a little far-fetched. I've been around chemicals all my life and *I've* never had a problem."

The napkin had soaked into the eggs on his platter. The two yellow eyes stared through their paper blindfold.

"Well, I guess you're one of the lucky ones, then," Marie continued. "XCCD's got one of those processing plants a short ways up the interstate from here. Lots of folks from around these parts got jobs in it when it first opened back in '55, though most just ignored it. Maryswood's been a farming community for hundreds of years. We're close to the earth here."

"So you've told me," Tacker responded, trying to avoid looking at the eggs, to ignore their unblinking stare.

"It was almost 1960 before the first babies were born *different*," said Marie. "Most of 'em died still-born or else they came premature and didn't last long. But some lived all right, even though they were different." She stroked her left hand, still completely covered by the cooking mitten. "I came along in '63 myself."

Tacker looked down at his coffee mug. It was empty. "When did it start affecting your crops?"

"Slowly," she said. "It was even slower getting to the livestock. It always got the people first."

She turned to face him, leaning on the cool, smooth surface of the counter. "When I was growing up, there was a tanker truck that always came from the XCCD plant twice a week. It rumbled up and down the dirt roads of our neighborhood, pouring something thick and purple from a spout in its back end. Supposed to keep the dust down, they told us. Filled up the gutter on one side of the road, then the other. We kids used to ride behind the truck, splashing in the stuff, yelling like wild Indians. Later, when we went home, it was our mothers' turn to yell—we tracked it into the house all the time. It was all over our shoes."

She paused, thinking. "I remember Pokey Johnson, the little girl next door, sitting on the curb all covered over in the stuff and laughing, laughing, laughing. We had so much *fun* with it—it looked like runny grape marmalade and stuck to things even better than the paste we used in art class in school. Sure did keep the dust down, too, just like they said it would."

Tacker smiled weakly. He fidgeted with the empty cup, turning it in circles on the counter as though it were the gear in a machine.

"Pokey died when she was 22," said Marie. "They told us it was cancer." She looked at her right hand, stroking it slowly through the concealing kitchen mitten as she spoke. "She didn't have a chance . . . all messed up inside. Children don't ever stand much of a chance in Maryswood. I know it for a fact. None of us born since the early '60s have been altogether right. Even my . . . my son."

Tacker cleared his throat. "Ahh, you have a little boy, hunh? My wife's expecting our first in the Spring. What's your boy's name?"

Marie ignored the question. "I don't know who the father was," she continued quietly. "Coupla years ago I was drinking a lot. "Don't remember a lot from those days. I—I was *with* a lot of men. You know, strangers passing through. Maybe even you."

The coffee gurgled in Tacker's gut. He shuffled slightly on his stool and glanced back at the cash register, wanting very much to get back on the road. Marie had begun to look a bit familiar to him, but he could not quite be sure. *There've been so many. . . .*

"Come take a look," she said. "He's out back."

"Oh, that's okay—I need to get going again." Tacker eased himself off the bar stool and stood up. He reached for his wallet. "How much do I owe you?"

She looked at him pleadingly, her eyes wide—almost desperate. The purplish semicircles under their sockets seemed to darken. Marie seemed a fantastic figure, at once pathetic and menacing. "Please," she said. "He's right out back. Come see him."

She gestured at the small door marked "EMPLOYEES ONLY."

Tacker took a deep breath. *Guess she's bound and determined to make me look at this kid of hers,* he thought. *Oh, hell, I'd better do it just to pacify her.* He feigned a smile. "Okay, sure."

He glanced one last time at the two eggs under the napkin. A thin line of moisture had seeped through on one side, creating the illusion of a tear running from one of the yellow eyes.

He followed Marie through the restricted door, passing into a strange, dimly lit storage room where stacks of wooden crates and pallets of cardboard boxes rose like crooked towers. A skull and crossbones leered from a gray metal canister near the back door. The chilly room smelled of flour, sawdust, and corrosive chemicals. Marie put her fur-collared jacket back on and zipped it up tightly. She left the oven mit on her hand.

Out behind the diner, the huge spotlight lit an eerie circle of dirty, snowy ground.

Tacker shuddered as the night chill attacked his joints and muscles through his thin cotton windbreaker. His breath puffed out in cones of frost. He crossed his arms, tucking his bare hands into the pits.

"There," said Marie.

Tacker squinted. He didn't see anything at all resembling a child—just a black, cold wall of night, with a filthy carpet of earth spread in front of it. "Where?" he asked, shivering. "I don't see him."

Marie pointed solemnly to the east. *"There."*

He saw it now—a simple wooden stake pounded into the snowy dirt, a tiny pyramid of accumulated snowfall crowning its flat upper surface. There was a band of fluorescent orange ribbon tied around it. The loose end of the ribbon fluttered in the icy breeze, gesturing weakly.

Tacker looked at Marie, who stared hypnotically in the direction of the stake. "Is that where he's buried?" Tacker asked.

"There," she answered. "There he is right now."

Tacker glanced back just in time to see something small and brown begin to quiver in the ground near the stake.

A tiny head emerged from the nearly frozen muck. Thick fur grew on one side of it, and a black, toadlike eye peered from the other. The thing whined feebly once through its single nostril, then burrowed its way back down below.

"He likes it best here," Marie said quietly, her breath thick and white as smoke in the air. "He's close to the earth."

The dark empty highway spread before him, a tunnel through the night.

Tacker's freezing fingers clutched the steering wheel painfully as he drove. *Just a few more miles,* he thought. *Just a few more and then I'll stop. Sleep. Rest. . . .*

He had a lot to think about; and tonight, he knew,

he would suffer from troubling dreams—dreams of the child he had seen, and another child he might see three months from now when Evelyn gave birth.

When the sun returned the next day, he would meet as scheduled at the main plant with the XCCD Board. They would have much to discuss; and, Tacker told himself grimly, he might lose his job before the meeting ended. Probably so.

He drove on, thinking. Wondering. Fearing.

Through many lonely nights, out on the road, Tacker had awakened in unfamiliar motel rooms with his arms around equally unfamiliar women and wondered to himself that the world could be such a dark, cold place. But tonight it had never seemed darker.

Or colder.

CHURCHES OF DESIRE

by Philip Nutman

Philip Nutman is English, although he is now with Tundra Publishing Ltd. and living in Massachusetts. A late-bloomer, he has rapidly been making a name for himself in the horror genre. Since his first appearance in these pages last year with "Full Throttle," Nutman has been busier than ever, although he's written less short fiction as he's been involved with a number of comic book projects. The stories he has recently sold are "Blackpool Rock," a semi-sequel to "Full Throttle," for the forthcoming Paul Sammon edited Elvis anthology, "Kafka's Kiss" for Ellen Datlow's collection of erotic horror fiction, and "Boilsucker" for Iniquities. *Earlier this year he finished* Sympathy for a Devil, *his second novel, and he is now at work on a third. As a journalist he continues to cover horror movies for* Fangoria *and to pen celebrity profiles for* Gallery.

"Churches of Desire" reads a bit like Thomas Mann's "Death in Venice" penned by William Burroughs.

"What the twentieth century needed was eroticism; what it got was pornography . . ."

—Henry Miller

Meredith shivered in his brown leather jacket as he stood before the porno cinema. The wind was rising, the streets devoid of life, yet his body shook not from the chill factor but from a deep, sudden sense of dread. After hours walking the Eternal City's empty thoroughfares in search of a fellow soul with whom he could share a moment of sexual warmth, his journey ended here.

It was once said all roads lead to Rome; all the Roman roads he had traveled in his nocturnal hunt for release seemed to lead here. And as he stood before the building profound desperation pulsed through his tired, alcohol-soaked body. Just looking at the place made him feel sick.

The facade of the Passion Pussycat cinema was an affront to good taste. Green and purple neon mixed to create an emetic spill of light that washed over the marquee to luridly shower the pavement. Its curved front was segmented by electric signs depicting nubile sixties-style go-go dancers with cat ears and tiny tails. There was no indication of what was screening inside.

A newspaper scuttled against his legs making him jump, then performed a dervish dance to the gutter. He ran his hands over the week's growth of stubble that covered his face to massage his tired eyes. He guessed the program would consist of typical Scandinavian, German, and American hetero hardcore, par for the course and boring. But whatever was playing there would at least be some buggery to keep him entertained, although he hoped if there were German movies unspooling, the footage would not be as extreme as one he'd caught in a Parisian theater.

The loop had started mundanely with a domestic scenario involving a couple, the man going to take a bath. The scene soon turned into a laughable watersports sequence when the woman rinsed his hair with her urine after he had shampooed it, but this was succeeded by an anal scene with a surgical device that had been clinical in its presentation, almost abstract in its relentless close-up, and even to Meredith's jaded sensibilities, offensive.

He stood hesitantly like a schoolboy on a first date, the promise of a sexual encounter almost unreal after the endless hours he had obsessed over the subject. Yet it was more than nervousness; a primal instinct made his balls contract painfully to the point of groaning. Still, there was no turning back. Not now. Not after the day's hollow promises had faded as breath to the wind. All Rome had to offer was vague hopes of financial gain and a cold, dirty room at the *pensione*. That thought in mind, he walked up the steps to the door and opened it.

. . . and the world of concrete and glass, stone and slate, garbage, and dog shit disappeared, broken by a surging synaptic fracture . . . and what lay before him was in one instant an apocalyptic flash of total destruction, an unrelenting holocaust, a subliminal flash frame instantly replaced by the stronger all-encompassing vision of a Void: black, unforgiving.

He turned from the doorway to vomit his dinner of spaghetti carbonara, several glasses of mediocre *frascati*, on the grime-encrusted steps. He stumbled with a second heave, grabbing the incongruously fake Doric columns of the facade for support, easing himself into a sitting position a few feet away from the puddle of bile. He looked up the street in an attempt to clear his rolling vision. In the distance were two faint figures, one tall and painfully thin, the other short and squat. With the final wave of surreal nausea he wouldn't have been surprised if they turned out to be the Walrus and the Carpenter. A coughing fit disrupted his eyeline, his mind rolling vertiginously, and a distant voice questioned how he had come to this, reached such a state of dissolution.

He knew the answer.

As the telephone rang for the seventh time a sense of hopelessness descended on Meredith like a carrion bird swooping to a corpse in an arid landscape.

Come on! Answer the damn phone!

The tension in his stomach tightened another notch. Since arriving in Rome two days ago he'd been feeling a sense of trepidation so strong he could almost smell it, an aroma that churned his gut and diminished his appetite. Thinking of stomach ulcers, he clutched the call box receiver so tightly his arm trembled, jarring loose a length of ash from his cigarette. His mouth was dry and he badly wanted to take a pull from the bottle of Johnnie Walker in his bag.

The tone buzzed for the eleventh time and he hung up, running a hand through his thick, black hair, pushing back the stray strands from his forehead, then threw the cigarette to the floor. On the opposite side of Via Paisello trees moved with the early evening breeze. It was 5:45 P.M. He would try Masullo one more time. After he took a quick pull from the bottle.

Where the hell was the producer, or his secretary for that matter? There was no reason why she should be ignoring the phone; he'd called each day at the same time in a frustrating attempt to get Masullo to fix a time for the proposed interview, already rescheduled four times in the past week. With the way things were going, it looked like *Film Comment* wasn't going to get the definitive story of Italian exploitation movies. This was Masullo's chance to gain some mainstream respectability, which, for a producer of over thirty cheap horror movies and soft-core skin flicks, was hard to come by, and Meredith couldn't understand why he was being given the runaround. Still, the producer of such bad-taste gems as *Emanuel and the Satanists, The Sex Crimes of Doctor Crespi,* and pseudo-documentaries like *Savage Africa*, complete with scenes of clitoral circumcision, probably didn't care about anything other than money. Sex, maybe, but Meredith could relate to both areas.

A sharp knock on the glass of the booth cracked him from his reverie. A large woman in a sickly green raincoat was rapid-firing unintelligible Italian through the glass that kept the chill of the Roman night at bay. Her face was a sour rictus, the corners downturned over cheeks the color of dough, like a bloated tragedy mask, and the coat fabric taut over the huge breasts.

Meredith vacated the booth as the woman pushed past him into the cubicle.

"Fuck you," he said with a smile. *On second thought, don't.*

The woman was truly gross. A dried shitty substance stained the back of her coat and legs, and her black hair hung in greasy rat's tails.

As far as he could make out, all Italian women belonged to one of two groups: over twenty-five and overweight, like the whores at the hotel, or under that age and curvaceous. He'd seen one Dachau-thin woman in, he surmised, her late thirties, a walking skeleton who served in the cafe near the station. But she had to be the least attractive woman he had ever laid eyes on, a woman who seemed thinner each time he saw her. Still, the opposite sex wasn't on his list of priorities.

He lit another cigarette while the woman dialed. The brown stain disgusted him. Rome was potentially the dirtiest city he had ever visited, the buildings heavily blackened from the cancer of carbon monoxide. And as soon as he stepped off the airport bus he'd trodden in a sizable turd—human, not animal. *Great.* Dirty. Smelly. Winos in the gutters near the *pensione*, rubbish spilling from the bins by the Villa Borghese. Shit in the Tiber. Meredith had had enough.

He had, however, much more to worry about than shit and magazine articles. More to the point were screenplays and movie deals. If Masullo would agree to read one or two of Meredith's novels he felt certain they could get a deal going. *Film Comment* would have to make do with what he sent them. At least he'd interviewed Dario Argento, Joe D'Amato, and Ruggero Deodato. But he had a lot riding on the idea of selling Masullo the rights to at least *Blood Stunt*, if not *A Killing for Christmas.* Throwaway thrillers deserved to be made into movies by hack producers, and Meredith was under no illusions about art: all he wanted was money. And soon. If he could get Masullo hooked he could be out of debt for the first time in seven years.

A grunting noise made him look up. The green blob vacated the phone booth, bustling past with a florish of body odor. Meredith belched in response as he fished in his pocket for a *getone* and re-entered the cubicle.

The phone buzzed against his right ear.

One . . . two . . . three . . . four . . .

Jesus! Answer the bloody thing!

. . . six . . . seven . . .

A click.

"Pronto?" said a woman's voice.

"Zebrafilm?"

"Yes."

"This is Bruce Meredith. I'm calling again about the interview with Signore Masullo."

"I have bad news, Signore Meredith. Signore Masullo asks me to apologize for not being able to see you this evening, as was suggested. He has to go to Milan for a meeting. But he can see you at 10:30 A.M. Monday."

"What? Oh, I have to return to London this weekend. Is there any chan—"

"In that case, Signore Meredith," the voice interjected, "I'm sorry. Signore Masullo has been very busy. Perhaps you will be in Rome again soon?"

Meredith threw down his cigarette. "No, that's out of the question. The magazine deadline is in two weeks. Would it be possible to see him this weekend—say Saturday?"

Please say yes!

"No, Signore Meredith. That's out of the question. Thank you."

The line went dead.

Bitch!

Monday! Damn Masullo. Damn Rome. Damn the whole shitty country.

He stepped from the booth and stood awhile, worrying his bottom lip before fumbling in his shoulder bag for the bottle. He took a large pull, the Scotch hitting instantly, burning his gut in a fiery rush. Without further thought he began to walk.

A light breeze rustled the trees, which whispered their secrets in return. What could he do? He couldn't really afford to come here in the first place and had only managed to do so by conning his sister out of five hundred quid under the pretense of repairing his car, conveniently neglecting to tell her he'd sold it. He couldn't cancel the return flight, as he didn't have enough to purchase another ticket. If he'd thought the situation through before coming he could have anticipated delays, made provisions for an alternative course of action, but as usual he had done everything in a rush. It was too much to think about, the decision requiring a ruthlessly objective look at his position, so he did the usual; procrastinated for several minutes while he paced up and down, neither thinking or acting, lit another cigarette. He looked vacantly at the trees, the pavement, the walls. He would decide tomorrow. He needed to rest, relax. And that meant one thing: sex. Yes, a night of fucking would burn out the cloud of depression that was already filling his system like ink in water. If he could get laid he'd awaken refreshed in the morning, be able to take the situation in hand. Sex always provided peace of mind.

He turned into Via Piciano, moving along the northeastern edge of the Villa Borghese. Each step he took, however, increased his sense of steadily deepening depression. His mind performed cartwheels. Images from the past appeared in a montage of disillusionment: Vanessa stating she'd need the money back by early November as it was for Christmas; Michael crying after a violent argument; Alison, his agent, informing him he had to cut back on the sex scenes, especially the rape of the pregnant woman in *Dead Dogs and Englishmen*, because every publisher she showed it to found the book gratuitous; Wilmott, his bank manager, turning down his request for a loan; Michael leaving, bags hurriedly packed, tension charging the smoky air of the flat.

"You selfish, self-pitying bastard!" his lover threw at him as he gathered his things in the hallway. "I'll be back for the rest of my stuff."

Meredith was silent, a contrite expression on his face, a bottle of Scotch still in his hand. Michael was so angry they had come to blows over the damn thing.

Embarrassed, he tried to hide it behind him but Michael saw him.

"Put the bloody bottle down! Stop pissing your life away."

"Sorry," he mumbled.

Michael fiddled with the straps of his baggage as Meredith watched him, not sure what to say or do.

"I'm sorry," he said again.

No response.

Michael looked up, tears in his eyes.

"You're always sorry afterward. But words aren't enough. When you drink you're like a little kid—*and that's all the bloody time.*"

Meredith looked at the carpet.

"This is it. *Over. Dead.* You killed it."

And with that, Michael was gone, the door slamming like a gunshot in the heavy air.

Although he'd felt a tremendous sense of relief after the last of Michael's things had gone, the first few nights without him to hold had been an empty, cold time. But there were always other bodies to be found, and since the split his sex life had been a calm sea dotted with occasional faces floating like driftwood through a perpetual twilight. It was easier that way. But the immediate problem was how to find someone in this godforsaken place. The local cruising scene, if one existed, was nowhere to be found and the only form of night time sexuality he'd seen was transvestism, which held no appeal. The only possible place he could think of was the Spanish Steps.

While passing them the previous night he had been surprised by the number of people spread out on the impressive monument and the relaxed atmosphere. Couples entwined passionately, all but copulating, locked into their own romantic universes. Cigarette smoke drifted on the breeze, mingling with the sweeter aroma of hash as a guitarist had strummed old songs. The Steps were a short walk away and would be a good starting point. Failing that, the main railway station would almost certainly provide what he was looking for.

He'd gone but a few yards and had turned into Via Veneto when he came across the first gaggle of transvestites he'd seen that night. One, a blonde wearing an awful wig, tried to waylay him but he continued without stopping, scowling. When he reached Piazza Barberini he paused to scan the headlines of English newspapers on sale at a cramped news cabin. Try as he might to focus on the front pages of *The Sun* and *The Star*, his attention was drawn to the cheap colors of the hardcore magazines on sale.

Teenage Lolitas promised all girls under sixteen with text in English, German, and Italian. Who, he mused, cared about text? He'd always smiled at the French slang for such publications—books to be read with one hand. But what he found most interesting was the plethora of *fumetti*, pocket-sized, crude, explicit comics filled with a staple diet of black magic, murder, sadomasochism, rape, and mutilation. There were dozens of titles ranging from entrail-eating zombie stories to tales of futuristic sex and violence and more mundane tales of adultery and wife swapping. Nothing was left to the imagination, atrocities bursting forth on each page like rotten foliage. He'd found one in his room at the *pensione*. After skimming thirty pages of semi-literate dialog he could not translate his eyes had widened at a sudden explosion of brutal sex and degredation—close-ups of fellatio, sodomy, and a young man having his skull smashed open after orgasm by the husband of the woman he'd just serviced. Somehow, he felt these popular comics told him more about the Italian cultural psyche than he wished to know, a world view consisting of naked lust and commonplace violence. But this, after all, was the country that had made throwing people to wild animals the main form of entertainment. He laughed aloud as a black vision eclipsed all else; so this is what it all comes down to—two thousand years of civilization and it's the same as it ever was. This is where it ends.

A soberly suited businessman examining *S & M Sextacula* looked intently at him over his glasses and Meredith walked away with the bitter laugh still on his lips.

As if submitting to the dark reality was his only means of finding hope, he felt a strange sense of correctness in his situation and he suddenly saw it all for the killing joke it was, a long, hollow laugh in the face of nothingness. He continued to chuckle to himself until he came to the junction, his attention shifting to the pleasing smells coming from a restaurant on the corner. His stomach growled in appreciation. He entered without further thought, drawing the aromas from the kitchen deep into his lungs.

Like the previous night the Spanish Steps were littered with people. Small groups and couples. The lone guitarist, now surrounded by a small crowd. Here and there were boys on their own or in twos or threes. At the bottom he turned left under the pretense of looking at the Keats house, allowing his gaze to wander in the hope of making eye contact.

Directly in front of him two teenagers spoke softly, the taller of the two nodding toward a pair of giggling girls seated a few feet above them. To Meredith's left, near the bottom, sat a lone handsome youth dressed in brogues, tapered trousers, and a red pullover. The writer walked toward him.

"*Buona sera,*" Meredith said as he sat beside him. The boy—no older than seventeen, he judged—nodded.

"Do you speak English?" The boy nodded. "Perhaps you can help me," he continued slowly. "This is my first time in Rome. Can you recommend a good nightclub?" The boy did not turn to face him for several seconds, then looked in his direction. Above them the guitarist started murdering "Ticket to Ride."

"There are some." He spoke softly, trying to enunciate correctly.

"Something to suit a man my age," he said, holding eye contact with the boy longer than was polite. He lit a cigarette.

"There is a place. Not a nightclub."

Meredith waited for him to continue but the boy was not forthcoming.

"Would you show me where? Is it far?"

The boy remained silent, then: "Pardon, I have to meet my girl," he said crisply, standing. "I have to go."

The boy began to trot toward the fountain at the base of the Steps. A blonde girl was heading in his direction. She smiled, waved, opened her arms. The boy ran to her. They embraced. Meredith watched them walk away arm in arm.

"Bitch," he muttered under his breath. The boy was nice-looking and had a good mouth. "I bet you're going to suck his little dick until it's as dry as a twig," he added before a coughing spasm cut off his words. He ground out the cigarette.

It was nine o'clock.

The entrance hall of Stazione Termini was largely deserted as Meredith entered the doors opposite the huge clock that hung above the electronic information board. It was 9:27, the display informed him mutely. His feet had started to hurt. It looked like coming here was a bad decision. There was no one around except a Gypsy woman with a small child in her arms and a comatose wino sprawled beside the photobooth near track seven. The woman saw him and started in his direction.

As he turned to go, the woman grabbed hold of his left arm, pulling frantically at his jacket. Like other cities the world over, Rome had its underclass. New York had its legion of homeless, London its alcoholics, Paris its migrant work force of Moroccans. Rome, however, was infested with Gypsies such as this wretch clutching at his clothes, beseeching him for money in whatever dialect she spoke.

He jerked away. She continued to claw at him undeterred.

"Get off!"

She paused for a beat, then continued her litany of despair, and his temper erupted.

"Fuck off!" He pushed her away. She stumbled, nearly dropping the child.

With a screech she flew at him, pounding his back with her free arm, her tone now abusive. The child started to cry loudly. Meredith strode toward the nearest exit, but she was persistent and the blows continued to rain down on his back.

He stopped suddenly, stepped to the right, and turned, slapping away her hand, glaring at her, his eyes enflamed with rage.

"I said *get the fuck off me*, you diseased cunt!"

Like a slap his words silenced the woman for an instant, then she started to coo as she placed her arms protectively around the child, a calm expression of total hatred directed at him. The child was silenced by its mother's soft sounds and she turned, moving away at a measured pace. He watched her go, unnerved by the sudden outburst. Then the Gypsy stopped, turned again to face him. He took a step back as if pushed by the force of her expression, an expression that went beyond loathing, beyond hate. But there was something there he could not read. A glimmer of fear was apparent, and . . . revulsion? She began to babble, then spat two words at him.

"Il morto."

Even with his limited command of Italian he understood.

Dead man.

She spat at her feet, then ran toward the nearest exit, the words hanging in the air.

Dead man.

The frozen moment was broken by a coughing fit that swept up from his gut to constrict his throat, his heart shuddering in response, legs rubbery as gravity increased its pull, making him stumble to the nearest wall for support, the hundred yards elongating as his sense of space expanded, rolled, a wave of nausea hitting his system in a huge spasm. He closed his eyes to halt the roller coaster motion and took a deep breath, counting slowly to ten. He opened them, coughed, and tried to focus, blinking rapidly.

Go. Get out of Rome, his instincts screamed, *return to London.* To familiar territory. But he would be lonely there, too. Lonely. Lost. As he always had been.

No. No, he would find a kindred spirit to ease the emptiness with, someone with whom he could forget his troubles, albeit temporarily. There was one other place he could try; the porno cinema near the *pensione.* There he was certain he would find what he was looking for; there among the other lost souls would be a fellow spirit in search of release, of fulfillment.

He forced himself to smile, smile and regain his former optimism. His consciousness pirouetted with the slapstick grace of a clown. It worked. A ray of optimistic sunlight penetrated the storm clouds of depression that approached, breaking the darkness up into jagged shards as he pulled the bottle from his bag, and his internal horizon lightened further as he took a deep pull, coughing as the Scotch caught at the back of his throat. He needed to sit down. The cafe where the Dachau woman served was opposite, its light an island in the darkness pushing against the glass wall of the exit. He lurched away on shaky legs. He had to keep it together. One step at a time. He negotiated the revolving door and made it over the tram tracks to the cafe without falling flat on his face.

The bar that dominated the room was long and thin like the woman who served behind it. She stood looking down at the wood, a ghost of a time not so long past, her thinness painful to observe. The Dachau woman. What, he questioned, had caused her to resemble a victim of the Final Solution? She was white as a sheet, her cheeks deprived of the faintest hint of pink, her eyes the color of bruised mushrooms. If she heard him enter she did not acknowledge his presence. Neither did the three locals huddled around a TV set in the far corner, their attention consumed by *Magnum P.I.*

The woman—surely she was thinner than the previous day, but no, that wasn't possible—continued to look at the counter as Meredith ordered an espresso in his halting command of the language. As she turned to the coffee machine he noticed the spinal defect which pushed her head forward, explaining her limited movements. She handed him a steaming cup of black liquid with a trembling hand as he slapped down his money and shuffled to the nearest seat, turning his back so he wouldn't have to look at her funereal visage.

Meredith continued to tremble on the steps of the cinema, his stomach raw from its expulsion. The figures were closer now and he could see it was the Dachau woman and the fattest of the bar's occupants. The man was absently rubbing his crotch as he escorted the emaciated woman, though as they drew nearer Meredith realized the man was not holding her by the arm but caressing her arse. The thought of those two in a sweaty sexual embrace did nothing for his nausea. Yet it had been the atmosphere in the bar—or rather the invasion of the whores—that had finalized his resolve to come here. He looked up. The couple stopped by a dimly lit doorway and entered.

Doors. Opening and closing.

They seemed to punctuate every aspect of his life.

A sudden cold draught and explosion of noise from behind pulled Meredith from his thoughts as two of the whores who plied their trade outside the *pensione* entered the cafe. They cheerfully stepped to the counter, laughing and joking in a torrent of sound and broad gestures. One lifted her ample bosom to the other and broke into a loud cackle, the other echoing her movements, then joining her friend's laughter with a deep chuckle.

Each night these women had fractured his sleep with their nonstop chatter and bargaining outside his window. The Three Weird Sisters: Miss Piggy, the Vacuum Cleaner—because her mouth, a perfect, puckered circle, reminded him of the line "nothing sucks like an Electrolux" from a blatantly sexual advertisement for domestic appliances—and Mother Mary, as he'd dubbed them. They stood on the corner by the *pensione* for over twelve hours at a stretch, gossiping, joking, smoking, spitting, and scratching their fat arses.

The first night he had not been able to sleep before three A.M. with the noise coming from the street. Initially the wailed hymns of the drunks stumbling from the bar down the street, then from the endless chattering of the whores. Periodically a car had drawn up and he'd heard doors opening, then slamming shut, each vehicle pulling away fast only to return a while later as the cycle of copulation continued throughout

Miss Piggy made a masturbatory motion to the Vacuum Cleaner, who laughed again, then whispered to her companion, who giggled in reply, pointing at Meredith. The Vacuum Cleaner blew him a kiss, then returned to her conversation. The Dachau woman was pouring two shots of rum without request, obviously a ritual for the whores, who toasted each other, swallowed as one, threw their money down, and departed as they had arrived: loudly.

Although his feet still ached, his legs were regaining their strength and he felt restless, the appearance of the whores once again bringing thoughts of sex to the fore. He started to luxuriate in a sense of inevitability and, as if lured by an invisible Ariadne's Thread of lust cast by the streetwalkers, stood from the table and departed the lifeless cafe.

So here he was, tired, queasy, and shaken. But the thought of returning to the grim confines of the *pensione* stirred his resolve. He'd check the place out. What he'd felt a few moments ago was the culmination of days of heavy drinking and a poor diet. No wonder his stomach had rebelled.

He stood.

And entered.

A dry, dusty smell hit his nose, the smell of a place not inhabited by man but rodents. The interior was red, tidy and functional though, not an abandoned place. The only decoration was two wilting potted palms standing sentinel on either side of the doors he assumed led to the screening room beyond. Inside the ticket booth sat an overweight, middle-aged man with black hair slicked back in an attempt to cover his large bald patch. His complexion was sallow, waxen under the spotlights illuminating the booth. Meredith placed a 20,000 lira note on the counter. The cashier continued to concentrate on his cuticles. By one pillar to the right lounged a swarthy youth with a sneer, his body language aggressive, his jeans taut over muscular thighs as he reclined, his rough trade gaze passing through Meredith's flesh as if he could see into his soul. He knew then he had come to the right place.

Click.

He turned to face the cashier. A ticket protruded from the metal counter like a small pink tongue. He took it and his change, stepping to the left of the booth to enter the inner sanctum.

For an instant blindness caressed his eyes, total, eternal. Then some distance in front a scrambled rainbow of light jumped and he made out a fuzzy rectangle of video-generated imagery with the sound of muted voices. He stood against the rear wall, mentally counting to ten as his eyes grew accustomed to the darkness. The light from the enlarged video image cast meager illumination on the aisles before him. A nigrescent sea of seats dotted with heads bobbing in the blackness like buoys came into focus. Here and there tiny beacons of cigarettes, clusters and constellations of red points, produced trails of smoke that hovered like ground fog above the body of men that composed the congregation in this church of desire. The majority of heads were separated by empty seats, the fractured symmetry of which was disrupted by occasional groups of twos and threes. But these couplings were in the minority. This was the refuge of the lonely, the lost, not a place for comradeship, yet paradoxically a vessel for communion with the flesh.

Meredith strategically took a seat in the back row

to survey the audience. On screen a girl with hair the color of rotting wheat swallowed a penis.

Reverential silence blanketed the cinema. Not even the sound of bodies repositioning themselves interfered with the litany of lust coming from the screen. He lit a cigarette.

Behind the miasma of tobacco smoke lay the unmistakable musk of dust and damp. Yet there was more, and his nose wrinkled in reaction. There was a slight excremental aroma; this appeared to sweeten until a rich trace of hash rolled past his face; then this, too, changed, making him think of rotting orchids. This persisted for a while, then faded. One moment the atmosphere appeared damp, the next chalk dry. Suffocating. Then from somewhere in the auditorium came the unmistakable copper tang of blood. That, too, retreated. As he inhaled the cigarette the conflicting smells made his mind spin and he ground out the Marlboro as he tried to stifle another coughing fit.

The girl continues to deep throat the long, thin phallus. Suddenly it twitches spastically and a dribble of sperm leaks from the girl's lips as she continues to eat it, then two jets of semen shoot from her nose.

The image jumped, faltered, faded. There was no discernible movement in the audience and the house lights remained off. On screen a rectangle of dots and wave patterns writhed, reminding him of the opening to *The Outer Limits*, but no Control Voice sounded from the speakers, no new picture took the previous one's place for what seemed minutes. Finally, a smeared visual flicked onto the screen. Music with too much treble tinkled along in accompaniment.

On the left side of the auditorium a figure rose to use the exit, the movement prompting Meredith to try contact with a fellow lost soul. Sticking to the row he was in, he picked his way along to the other end where a man of similar age sat. Meredith selected the seat next to him, opening his legs so his right knee brushed the other's left thigh, yet the man remained immobile, even when Meredith let his hand fall to his crotch as he watched out of the corners of his eyes. The man continued to stare dispassionately at the screen.

A white Rolls Royce cruises an Alpine road. Inside sits a big man sipping champagne, a woman on either side of him. One is a short blonde with her hair up in a bun, giggling as she drinks and caresses her naked breasts.

Meredith turned to his neighbor, smiled, and held his gaze. The man ignored him.

Lost in your own little fantasy, aren't you? Probably about the blonde and what you'd like to do to her. What a waste.

The girl pours champagne over her breasts. The other woman—a brunette—leans over the man to lick at the liquid, the blonde's nipples erecting.

Meredith stood, walked back along the row of seats to cross the aisle. Three rows in front sat another man. Balding, overweight.

No, too old.

The man, the blonde, and the brunette enter a large room. In the center a group of nine people surround a young woman laid out on a table, silk cushions holding her off hard wood. She has a phallus in her mouth. Another thrusts in and out of her vagina. The crowd kiss, masturbate, caress each other in slow abandon until they perceive the presence of the man. The orgy pauses. The crowd clears and the woman on the table turns over to present her backside to the man who opens his robe in return, his large penis ready to enter her. She begins fellating the phallus of a skinny youth as the man sodomizes her. The group then couple in abandon.

Meredith paused to watch the film, smiling to himself at the excess on screen, before letting his eyes wander.

To his right, in the middle block, lounged a boy in his early twenties. Meredith homed in on him.

On screen the woman groans as the skinny youth ejaculates on her face. The man does likewise, his semen covering her back in a torrent. The group re-

spond in a frenzy, the other men baptizing the woman in a monsoon of ejaculate.

He sat next to the boy, spread his legs to brush his thigh. The boy turned. Meredith looked him in the eye while fumbling for his lighter.

"Pardon," he said.

The boy nodded slowly, then provided a light.

In the sulfurous flash of the flame Meredith knew he was the one. The boy had a perfect complexion: olive-skinned, a light corona of stubble adhering to the fine, neoclassical lines of the face, the hair jet black, magnificently sculpted over the scalp. His eyes, Meredith saw in the instant of the flame, were brown, an unusual shade between gold and bronze. His lips were full, rich, ruby.

Meredith felt the heat in his groin explode through his system, causing him to look away, shocked by the fallout from the chemical charge that passed between them. The boy continued to hold his gaze.

On screen the image skipped as a new film replaced the previous one and Meredith was glad of the distraction.

A close-up of a mouth, open wide.

The camera pulls back to reveal a man, naked except for a leather harness, strapped to a chair. A tall dominatrix, her black hair matching her cat suit, masked, nails his scrotum to a piece of wood. In the background two old men bugger a child.

A boy or a girl? Meredith could not be sure.

Next to the pederasts is a woman, her feet and hands chained to the wall, her body systematically invaded with sexual devices wielded by a woman of indeterminate age.

A title slowly superimposes itself over the tableau: Crucified By His Cock.

Meredith chuckled at the pretension, then dared to look back at the boy, who was still gazing intently at him, a trace of a smile on those inviting lips.

On screen the masochist screams.

Behind the intensity of the boy's expression lay a deadness that, had he been more aware and less drunk on the sexual pulse pounding through his body, he would have noticed, but the charge between them was so strong his judgment was impaired. He'd been through enough encounters to see the danger signals but his instinctual warning was lost in the riptide of deep desire. All he perceived was the object of his passion.

The boy stood, squeezed Meredith's knee, moved toward the exit sign.

He was halfway across the auditorium before Meredith gathered his wits to follow. He dropped the cigarette and walked after him, nearly tripping in his eagerness to do so.

The boy went through the left exit. Gathering his composure, he followed.

The exit doors led to a narrow corridor. To the right was a bar with a few patrons. Meredith didn't take any notice, as the boy was heading in the opposite direction. Meredith moved quickly. He could not lose him. Not now.

Curving to the left, the corridor paralleled the auditorium. Both walls and carpet were deep red. Small orange spotlights cast pools of tangerine on the floor. Every fifteen feet a palm that had seen better days resided in a red pot.

The boy stopped and turned, smiling with satisfaction as he spied the writer was in pursuit.

Meredith stopped dead. Something was not right. The adrenalated pursuit had cleared out his system, the warning signs flashing.

No.

Dread gripped him, desire and fear in conflict.

He stumbled as he turned, heading back in the direction he'd come.

Meredith ran, the sense of threat increasing with every step. As he rounded the curve, approaching the bar area, his heart fluttered, a steel band tightening around his chest. He collided with the wall, clutching at his torso.

Oh God, I'm having a heart attack.

Then he was filled with a vision of the boy's eyes. Inviting, placid, offering peace. He gasped.

The image persisted as his breath came in tight gasps. Then he sensed a presence behind him, felt a hand on his shoulder transferring a sense of emotion unlike any other. He turned, falling into the boy's arms. Their tongues automatically entwined and he stroked the boy's crotch, which felt full and heavy. After a moment the boy pulled away, yet it was not a rebuff. He smiled, squeezing Meredith's crotch in return, began to unbutton his jeans, turning to face the wall.

Finally, he was in.

Moving gently, Meredith pulled the boy toward him, devoting his attention to the hymn of his thrusts. From the auditorium came a faint sound of applause mixed with screams.

The boy's heat excited him further and he knew he could not last long. Tension in his groin rose like water filling a lock and the threshold was breached far quicker than he expected. Then, behind the bodily heat came a numbing coldness, a chill so sharp it cut into his cerebral cortex, disrupting the wave pattern of lust instinct for a split second that expanded into eternity. He opened his eyes and panicked.

Before him was the Void. Total, unforgiving, relentless. To ejaculate into such a place struck him with primal terror, the horror of the Void absolute. Surely, to give an offering to such a place would not be enough; he would be consumed without a trace. If he had sought the darkness before he had done so in error. Now he wanted no part of it.

Then it was gone.

Meredith withdrew as his cock jerked spastically, spitting his seed onto the humus lining the palm's pot. He grunted. The boy stood still. For an instant the image of the void returned, then was gone as quickly as it had arisen. He felt suddenly sick, as if a cold ethereal hand grasped his scrotum, passing through the skin to penetrate his bowels. The boy turned to face him.

The smile was still on those ruby lips, but the light that had resided in his eyes was gone.

Meredith, dazed, was pushed gently to his knees: the boy's erection appeared in front of his sweat-washed eyes. He opened his mouth. The offering stretched him to the limit. His eyes shut, the boy pushed into his throat, slapping him as he did so to force open his eyes.

"Look at me," the boy said, his voice only a fraction above a whisper. "This is my body, this is my blood. Drink in remembrance of me."

He withdrew, spraying the writer.

The world went white.

Meredith lay there for an uncertain time. Were minutes seconds, or the other way around? He had no idea, no sense of proportion. Eventually he wiped the residue from his face, pulled himself upright, and moved toward the bar area, the sensation of a frozen hand performing a five-finger exercise in his guts. Sweat crowned his brow.

Three people were at the bar. The woman behind the counter ignored him as she carefully wiped a glass. She was familiar. Where had he seen her? Her hair was the color of rotting wheat, but he couldn't find the jigsaw piece to complete the picture. Two men were in front, one seated on a high stool. He turned to Meredith as the writer stumbled past at a snail-like pace. He, too, was familiar, causing further confusion in Meredith's unfocused mind. As he inched by he noticed the man's fly was open, his penis hanging off the stool rim, puncture marks in the phallus manifested as stigmata. Where had he seen him?

(Screams)

Nails through flesh . . .

Thinking clearly required too much effort. Despite throwing up before entering the cinema he still felt drunk; the alcohol still in his system had him cornered, was ready to lay him out in the third round.

He shuffled into the street. The two thousand yards to the *pensione* took an eternity to cover.

Of course, the Three Weird Sisters were outside the impoverished Spanish-style hotel, its edges crumbling with age, the walls tattooed with a patina of carbon. Miss Piggy laughed at him as he careened by with the precision of a seasoned drunk. He tried to snarl "fuck you," but it came out as "fug tu," his speech slurring with every step. He'd never felt so tired.

As he came through the entrance of the *pensione*, the concierge looked up for an instant, then resumed watching the TV set behind the counter. The Englishman's condition was nothing new; the old man had seen it many times. Nothing mattered to him anymore, hadn't since the passing of his wife, yet he flinched when the guest kicked open the door to his room, realizing the fool had collapsed onto the creaking bed and wasn't going to close it. He forced himself from the comfort of his armchair to trot down the hallway, pulling the door closed without looking in on the prone figure of *il morto*. He'd watched the process take place before—once had been enough—and if it took place behind closed doors, even if they were his own, he could convince himself it didn't exist. The world was changing in strange ways and denial was his only defense. But the sex zombies, the emotionally dead, posed no threat to him. They stuck to their own kind, their bodies rotting as they performed their dance of empty desire. The old concierge grunted to himself, fully aware of his own mortality; he was not long for this world and wanted to live out his last few days as peacefully as possible. Let them inherit the earth.

Several minutes later he heard the bed creak through the thin wall. It would be the last noise to come from the room for some time.

Inside, despite the unbearable weight of exhaustion pushing down upon him, Meredith managed to raise himself from the mattress to discard his clothes and crawl between the dirty sheets.

* * *

It had begun.

The road lay before him, bright in the sexual flush of a newly aroused sun; a future of limited possibilities, restricted variations of the sex act, for their bodies were not strong. A barren future, predictable, life-negating, not life-affirming, sterile in its simplicity. Yet what faced Meredith did not appall. He welcomed it with open arms and mouth, and it in return welcomed him. Not with arms but with a multitude of genitalia and orifices: big ones, small ones, every taste, color, texture. A pornucopia of organs transformed from the frustated parameters of the human state to that of a new flesh. Flesh, nerve endings, and blood that now coursed with a life—and death—of their own; a transmutational entity so powerful the host would atrophy within months.

In truth the transformation had begun long ago. A summation of desires misaligned, of emotions discarded, left to fracture in the cold expanse of a life misdirected.

Meredith lay between the dream and the desire, comfortable between the sheets of change. Somewhere in his cortex memories skipped like daguerreotypes, flickered, jerked, then faded. Fragmented scenes from his childhood, soft-edged with an innocence long lost, revolving one last time. He frowned, then smiled serenely in his sleep of the damned as the dream took shape, wiping the screen of the old, tired images, replacing them with visions of the future. The future inside his body.

Time would be short, but what a time. The fact there would be no laughter, no light, no love didn't matter anymore. If indeed they had once truly mattered, they seemed now nothing more than trivial concerns, of little consequence to the wider scheme of death within life. That was all behind him. It was easier this way, lack of choice soothing in its streamlined shape. And in the dream a line from a song crept unbidden to provide a momentary soundtrack: Don't dream it, be it.

He slept on, safe in the knowledge his Sisters outside were spreading their gospel to the heathens. All over the world it would eventually be the same: one Church, one Body, one Belief.

The Church would welcome fresh converts that night and there would be new films to watch, new stories to tell, Meredith's amongst them. In the name of the Father and the Son the congregation would sing silent praises to the Gods of Flesh and Fluids.

He slept like a newborn baby, his shallow breath rising and falling in a psalm to the rhythm of the deathly desire.

CARVEN OF ONYX

by Ron Weighell

Born November 22, 1950, Ron Weighell lives in Portsmouth, where he is a carpenter by trade. I've read his stories in the British small press with interest over the past few years, and I was pleased to find recent appearances in Richard Dalby's excellent anthologies. Weighell has written several fine pastiches firmly in the manner of M. R. James which nonetheless displayed flashes of his own vision. A chapbook collection of his stories, An Empty House, *was published recently, and soon to appear is* The White Road, *a novella in the tradition of Arthur Machen. In addition, Weighell writes that he is "currently working on a novel set in an alternative Britain where not Christianity and Rationalism, but Gnostic magic, Hermetic philosophy and Fortean phenomena are the norm."*

"Carven of Onyx" starts out like a leisurely Jamesian version of The Name of the Rose. *However, it isn't.*

Given clement weather, an obedient donkey or any kind of horse, the journey from Malmswell Abbey to the Priory in Longlenn could be accomplished easily in a day. The two monks had left Malmswell before dawn, but had walked their donkeys for much of the way, paused by the river in Charnwood Forest for a meal of crusty bread, cheese and home-brewed ale, and only ridden the last few miles of open moorland;

so light was already fading on the low hills of Longlenn by the time they reached the Priory. Their first sight was of the spire aglow in the mellow rays of sunset. The dying light picked out the windows of the church with points of flame and a bell was tolling for vespers.

But for a deer in the forest and an unkindness of ravens over the moor, they had seen no living thing all day. Any passing stranger would have seen two men in the black habit of the Benedictine Order and given them little thought, save perhaps for the observation that the older of the two men was an individual of some bearing, slim but wiry of build, with a long, neatly bearded face that gave little away. The tight, pursed lips and lean jaw, the narrowed, searching eyes, these might have suggested a man given to keeping his own counsel. What they could not have suggested was the actual rank of this humble monk, which suited the Abbot of Malmswell. The highways were full of brigands who would not stick at murder or ransom, and the prelate of a great religious house was reckoned a wealthy and influential prize. By traveling in so humble a fashion to Longlenn, where he acted as confessor to the Priory's forty nuns, he could dispense with pomp and protection yet remain safe from molestation. Longlenn Priory, like all the Benedictine nunneries, lay under the overall rule of the abbey, and the nearest was Malmswell. On the Abbot, then, fell the responsibility for the general running of the house. Whether the fields and forests were forbidding with chill, penetrating rain, transformed beyond recognition by a blanket of snow, or withered under the intolerable heat of high summer, he would travel at the appointed times to hear in confidence the small sins and misgivings of the Longlenn sisters.

And Heaven knew those sins were small enough to make him wonder within himself whether the work was worth the journey, for little that was disruptive to the harmony of godly living occurred there. Longlenn was not a closed order, but its isolated position naturally made it as insular and tranquil as one.

Insular and tranquil were not descriptions that could be applied to Malmswell. The Abbey stood by a great market town, and ministered to the spiritual and medical needs of a large community. For that reason, the Abbot insisted on his quiet, disguised journeys, and jealously guarded them as holy retirements in a life burdened by great responsibilities.

Longlenn had lain deserted for many years before the Order had bestowed it as the foundation for an order of nuns. The shell of the building, much dilapidated, had been allowed to degenerate still further under a succession of old and conservative prelates. The appointment of Sister Clare as Prioress had brought about a transformation, for with an enviable will she had set about rebuilding the Priory, a not unimpressive task when one considered the comparative poverty of nunneries in general. The nuns could not labor as monks—or were not generally expected to do so—and did not attract large gifts as did the monkish foundations. The Prioress had, nevertheless, instigated some extreme, though admirable, changes, encouraging the nuns to labor in the fields—by example, it had to be said—and closing the school, which had struggled to force basic lessons into a handful of children from the outlying farms for no appreciable financial return. Instead she had concentrated the efforts of the sisters on needlework and soon established a reputation for the production of the finest embroidered copes and altar cloths in the country. The ailing funds of the Priory had been steadily replenished, and in time grew great enough to allow extensive renovation of the building. Having once engaged the nearest craftsmen to repair the gutters and install a proper drainage system, the Prioress had retained them to undertake an ambitious series of extensions to the original shell, raising a finely appointed infirmary, a small guest house and new reredorter. The nuns themselves had undertaken the basic labor to avoid the expense of unskilled help.

And lately it seemed, unceasing in her determination to make Longlenn the finest religious house in the county, Sister Clare had employed a roughmason and ordered the demolition of the curious semi-circular transepts of the church in order to construct orthodox oblong structures which would produce a more fitting cruciform groundplan. No doubt, when that had been accomplished there would be some other task.

The Abbot and the novice were admitted into the cloister in time to see a group of black-habited nuns pass along the lines of carved stone pillars in the direction of the church. The Prioress herself was among them. As she saw the visitors, her full, ruddy face drew into a warm smile which the Abbot returned.

"I'm afraid we dallied on the way, Sister Clare. After so hard a winter the lure of the sunshine proved too strong."

The Prioress nodded. "It has been a beautiful day, Father. The new guest house is ready, so we can accommodate you properly at last."

"Yes, I could see as we arrived that you have not been idle! Unless I am mistaken the sun is setting on new tiles; for the first time since the Priory was built, I should think."

The Prioress flushed with a forgivable pride. "*Labore est honore*, Father. The work is progressing. I hope you can look around before you leave."

"Of course, of course. We should be interested to see what you have done in our absence, shouldn't we, Sebastian?" The young novice stammered his agreement.

At the corner of the cloister, the Prioress opened a door and led them up a flight of winding stairs. A narrow corridor gave off into several small rooms, the first of which had been prepared for the novice. At the second door, she paused, and motioned for the Abbot to precede her. He found himself in a finely proportioned room that still smelt of planed wood and fresh plaster. The windows faced west, affording a glimpse of low hills, and a crest of trees, standing out sharply against a broad band of purple sky. Higher, the afterglow was fading gradually, into the subtle green of old copper.

The room had a narrow cot, above which the wall was decorated with a painted design of trees and flowers, encircling the Divine Lamb on a field of green.

"Quite charming!" exclaimed the Abbot.

"Sister Catherine," said the Prioress with a smile. "She has quite a remarkable talent."

"Indeed she has. You seem to produce an unending supply of delicate skills and hard physical endeavour here. I confess I could not see my brothers at Malmswell, dedicated and worthy as they are, producing such diverse talents."

"But they would not have to, Father! Malmswell is already a beautiful building in good repair. Longlenn lay deserted for many years before we came here."

"And yet," continued the Abbot, pressing the point, "you are the first prioress in fourteen years to undertake any restoration work."

The persistence of his praise threw the Prioress into a momentary confusion which she covered by saying brusquely, "Well, there is still much to be done."

At Longlenn two periods of rest were observed. At two in the morning the day began with matins and lauds, when the morning praises were sung. After a second period of sleep came that time of the day given over to religious duties, and it was then, at the chapter which followed mass, that the Abbott heard the confessions of the nuns. Later in the day, after dinner, came a period of recreation, during which the nuns would walk or play at ball in the garden on the north side of the church. It was then that the Abbot would compete with the Prioress at chess, a game at which she excelled. And as he moved the heavy pieces patiently on his way to customary defeat, the monk would discuss any problems raised during the chapter. On this occasion, the subject was Sister Catherine, a youngster who had but lately completed her noviciate.

"Has she shown any indiscipline with regard to her work?" he asked.

The Prioress looked distressed. "No. In fact, she has always been such a good, hardworking child. And you have seen her work on the wall of the guest house. Her behavior has always been exemplary."

The Abbot nodded. "It was for this reason that I showed leniency. But I would talk to her if I were you. She complains of disturbed sleep, bad dreams. We will always come up against this kind of problem in novices, but this girl has passed that period and should have come to terms with our life, or left us! I hope that there has been no mistake in admitting this child to our Order."

As he said these last words, the Abbot stared pointedly at the Prioress.

"I am sure there has been no mistake, Father. She is devoted, I'm sure."

"Her heart is not in question; it is her soul that concerns me. Is her soul troubled? Talk to her, Sister Clare."

When such exchanges were necessary, one or the other of them could generally be relied upon to turn the conversation to lighter things, and on this occasion the Prioress raised the subject of Malmswell's massive library, which she knew to be a source of pride to the Abbot.

He, in his turn, took the opportunity to mention with enthusiasm a certain volume residing in the more modest bookroom of Longlenn. The inevitable question was asked.

"Would it trouble you to let me look at the commonplace book again, Sister Clare?"

He knew well enough what her answer would be. A slow smile spread over the nun's plump face.

"We could stop off at the cloister press on our way to look at the renovations, if you still wish to see them."

The press, which lay in the eastern cloister, was too small to be called a room and too large to be called a cupboard. The walls were lined with rough deal planks on which stood a modest collection of books. There were the usual histories, a few standard ecclesiastical works, lives of the saints and the records of Longlenn through the previous fourteen years, written in the diverse hands of the succeeding prioresses. In this unlikely setting fate had placed a rare jewel, as rare as any that could be found among the priceless works at Malmswell.

Soon, the Abbot was opening the cover of carved ivory with trembling fingers, turning the exquisitely illumined pages with the gentlest of touches, feeling again the mingled sense of awe and exhilaration that a fine work of art never failed to produce in him.

Ironically, the volume belonged to that group of works called commonplace books, though a more uncommon book would have been difficult to imagine. On its parchment pages some monkish scribe had copied fragments of borrowed books: poetry and chronicles of war; bestiaries with their quaint amalgam of real and mythical animals; tales of strange explorations, of fabulous beasts and devils, cosmological diagrams. There was a page from an astrological manuscript showing a man with the signs of the zodiac on his body; an illustration from an early fourteenth-century French Bible *moralisée*, showing scenes from Revelations; allegorical figures of the daughter of Babylon, and Satan's dominion over the world in which the left leg, about to sever the right, was the dragon of death. The borders of every page were decorated with traceries of gold and fine images of beasts and devils. Raising his eyes at last, from a scene of the damned in Hell, the Abbot asked, "Have you given any more thought to our offer, Sister Clare?"

The nun flushed and shook her head. "I'm sorry, Father. The first Prioress of Staverdale wished it to come to Longlenn and remain in the keeping of the sisters. We only brought it here on that understanding."

The Abbot nodded ruefully. "If, for any reason, you change your mind, I would gladly purchase the book for Malmswell library."

A bell sounded nearby. Replacing the book, the Prioress locked up the press and said, "Well, we will see. And now, Father, would you care to look at our work on the church?"

The Abbot, gamely concealing his disappointment, suffered himself to be led toward the eastern corner of the cloister, where the assembled nuns were distributing shovels and woven baskets. As she approached, the Prioress chanted *"Eamus Ad Opus Manuum,"* and led the way through the slype to the cemetery.

No stone memorials marked the graves there; simple wooden crosses had been raised over those who had died during the recent tenancy of the nuns. Of those who had worshiped at Longlenn before them, no trace remained, save for hummocks scarcely distinguishable from the grassy field itself. The sun was shining strongly, but a stiff breeze had sprung up; new-fledged clouds drifted lazily overhead, casting patches of chilly shadow upon the land.

Passing the chapterhouse, they came to what had until recently been the northern transept. All that remained was a heap of stone and a gaping hole in the church wall, covered by canvas. A mason struggling with the heaps of stone paused to greet the nuns. Without ceremony, the women set to, shifting the rubble aside in their woven baskets. Some began to dig between pegged lines, preparing the way for the new foundations.

As the Abbot stood watching, the Prioress suddenly drew him away to a space near the chapterhouse wall, where a single block of stone, some three feet high and a good fourteen inches in both width and depth, remained.

Placing her hands upon its discolored surface, she said, "This is something of a puzzle to us, Father. I know you have studied widely all forms of worship, godly and otherwise."

The Abbot frowned. "We should know our enemy, Sister Clare."

"Of course," she agreed quickly. "I meant that you might help to explain the mystery. When we broke down what we thought was the only wall on this side of the transept, we came upon this space, concealed between the chapterhouse and the transept wall. The stone, as you can see, stands inside this space."

On scanning the ground the Abbot saw that there were, indeed, two lines of foundations. The concealed space between them formed a shallow crescent of some twenty feet from tip to tip.

"A place of concealment in case of persecution?" he ventured.

"But the stone, Father. See the top of it. This is surely tallow from a candle, though it has become quite blackened with age. It must have been an altar of some kind."

On examining the stone, the Abbot noticed that a section some nine inches square had been removed from one side, leaving a neatly carved recess. The missing section lay on the ground close by.

"There are words carved on this," he said, brushing the block with his hand.

"*Hinc—Hinc lucem* something *sacra.* Ah, there I have it! *Hinc lucem et pocula sacra.* 'From this source we draw light and draughts of sacred learning.' Yes, it was clearly an altar!"

"Sister Catherine found the stone was loose and removed it," offered the Prioress.

"And there was nothing inside?"

"Yes, an old silver chalice, quite tarnished."

"I would like very much to see it."

The Prioress called to one of the nuns and sent her back to the cloister where the chalice had been temporarily placed.

"You see why I described it as a mystery?"

This brought a smile to the Abbot's lips. Clasping his hands thoughtfully before him, he turned to her.

"Not necessarily. The building may have been constructed around the altar because it was a place of particular sanctity, a shrine of some kind. Croxbury still has the original altar from a wattle church that once stood on the site. Longlenn, I think, does stand on the foundations of an older church, I seem to remember."

The Prioress looked greatly relieved to hear this.

"You think there is some such explanation? I had thought . . . well, no matter. Ah, here is the chalice, Father."

The Abbot took it carefully and turned the tarnished stem in his hands. So discolored and worn was the surface of the chalice that he could only distinguish with great difficulty the designs embossed upon it. On the stem itself, there was a rod entwined with serpents. A row of bestial faces ran around the rim.

"It is very old," commented the Abbot. "These twelve faces might well represent the disciples, though clumsily drawn. The snakes below them on the stem—well, perhaps the serpent over which we must all triumph."

"It has an evil look about it to me," ventured the Prioress.

"If it will put your mind at rest, Sister Clare, I will personally consult the histories at Malmswell and find who worshiped here before."

"Would you, Father? I would be most grateful."

"Very well, then. But do not worry in the meantime. I feel sure the altar was put to quite innocent use."

So said the Abbot, though he found much to contemplate on his ride back to Malmswell the following day. The skies had grown overcast, and the wind bitterly cold, but considerations deeper than the inclemency of the sudden "Blackthorn Winter" prompted him to forgo his customary rest beside the river in Charnwood Forest. The Abbot wished to be among books, for he knew the tallow stains upon the hidden altar were not black by age but by design, and saw more in the symbolism of the chalice than he had disclosed. Although at pains to allay the fears of the Prioress, he could guess the purpose for which they had been fashioned.

About the Priory of Longlenn there had long been something of a conspiracy of silence more damning than words. The last Benedictine Order of monks to worship there had been disbanded with indecent haste, and the general feeling seemed to be that the affair was best left to the healing hand of forgetfulness. But in blotting out the past, had the Order guessed just how far those Longlenn monks had wandered from their chosen path?

Furthermore, the discovery of the stone altar had thrown some light on another mystery, the confession of the young nun, Catherine. That once pious and gentle child had fallen prey to thoughts for which she herself could hardly find words. And in her fitful, nightmare-ridden slumbers, a feeling of growing enmity toward the Prioress had taken root. This last was the most striking of her confessions, for the impressionable young nun had previously held Sister Clare in a position dangerously close to that of a beloved saint. That Sister Catherine should have been the one to discover the hole in the altar was a remarkable coincidence, and the possible significance was not lost on the Abbot. Had the removal of the stone released some disruptive spirit? That some influence was at work upon the young nun, he could not doubt. There was frightful power in the old worships; that the Abbot had learned in his scholarly investigations of the pagan mysteries.

At Malmswell he had access to information he sought, for at his command the rarest books and scrolls in that wealthy abbey had been rescued from the damp limbo of the cloister presses and housed in a room designated the library.

Large and lofty it was, with rough, enduring beams above and a floor of good stone flags below, and what little natural light entered fell faintly through flamboyant traceries of stained glass. Once there, he lost no time in drawing his high-backed chair of oak up to a great lectern, fashioned in a fearsome representation of the Beast of the Apocalypse. The volume supported on its carven back was huge and bound in tan leather. Around him were ranged Bibles, histories, monkish manuscripts and more—much more—for he had amassed a vast number of works on paganism and the black arts, driven by a desire to familiarize himself with all the tricks, temptations and illusory rewards to which the enemy of Christ might resort.

Thus, he could reach out and lay a hand upon *The Mysteries of Iamblichus* or the lewd and bawdy *Transformations of Lucius Apuleius of Madaura* or upon Euripides' rhythmical evocation of orgiastic rites *The Bacchae*.

In scolls and hand-decorated folios lay fragments of alchemical works; the vivid, convoluted Latin of Ripley's *Cantilena* and the *Medulla Alchimae*: Jabir's *The Book of Furnaces* and the *Splendor Solis*, exquisitely worked on vellum and reputedly owned by Solomon Trimosin himself. Beside these could be found tomes on the art of magic and on demonology: Khalid's *The Book of Amulets*, the *Malleus Maleficarum* of Sprenger and Kramer, as well as Antonio Stampsa's *Fuga Satanae*. On a smaller reading desk behind him lay Sinistrari's *Daemonialitate; et Incubis et Succubis*.

The volume on the lectern though was somewhat more prosaic: Sterner's *History of the Religious Orders*, from which he pieced together something of the full story of Longlenn.

The existing priory had been raised on the site of a Templar monastery; so much he had surmised. But he soon found that the circular church in which the Templars worshiped had been suffered to stand, retained as the central tower of the new, so that the swelling curve of its walls formed quaint semicircular transepts on either side of the new church. The Abbot was unable to ascertain on whose instructions such a plan had been adopted, but a more effective way of retaining, while concealing, the older worship could hardly have been found. Had the old Baphometic altar been knowingly concealed behind an innocence of new stone, or had the brothers gradually succumbed to the influence of some horrible *genius loci* and raised their own stone to the Dark One? There was no way of knowing, but what little he had learned convinced the Abbot that the altar had been raised for ungodly purposes, and that the chalice at least was a Templar relic. The source of their "light and learning" was clear. The voice of the Abbot broke the silence in a tone of irony and reflection.

"Hinc Lucem et Pocula Sacra!"

The long halls and corridors of Longlenn grew ever more cold and forbidding; the cloisters where the nuns walked and studied were immersed in gray light. Howling winds invaded the church through the canvas-covered gap in the north wall to ripple and dim the candle flames at mass. And with every rush of disturbed shadow, every howl of wind, the glowering wooden eagle that supported the brass-bound weight of the antiphoner seemed to stir its wings and cry.

Among the less hardy sisters it was a time to don again the thick woolen undergarments and fur-lined boots of winter, so recently discarded in hopeful anticipation of the sun. The night vigils in the great unshielding spaces of the church were once more cruelly cold.

Work on the reconstruction continued unabated. The mysterious altar was demolished and the first of the new, square transepts begun. And not before time, for it seemed that discord had entered with the searching spring winds. Or was it rather that the pace of work was telling on the tempers of the house? With every passing day the Prioress had been forced to deal with a growing number of minor contentions until discipline was threatened, and the rod, so long abandoned at Longlenn, was reintroduced at her command.

Amid this flurry of argument and recrimination Sister Catherine grew daily more pale and withdrawn. The Prioress, prompted as much by her own concern as any order from the Abbot, summoned Catherine to her room. The child would not admit to any conflict of faith and when she broke down wretchedly and asked what she had done wrong, the Prioress found herself at a loss to answer, for Catherine had been exemplary in the execution of the duties and denied with tears the least suggestion of personal unrest. So the Prioress could do no more than ask the girl to come to her in need, and then dismiss her. What, she reflected, has the poor child done wrong?

Into the dark, unheated dormitory, into her small cell with its hard cot and simple desk, the pale, unconnected Catherine retired and knelt wretchedly before the cross as though to pray; but in a moment she was shifting her weight from knee to knee, casting glances about her. It seemed that her devotions were so easily disrupted of late; the flimsy thread of attention broken by the creaking of a joist, the call of an owl outside in the pine tree: even by the muttering of a sister in a cell close by. She picked up her Bible and opened at a chapter of Isaiah, at certain verses which had recently done much to soothe her fears. She read quickly under her breath, her pale gray eyes flitting across the page. "Oh thou afflicted, tossed with tempest, and not comforted, behold I will lay thy stones with fair colors, and lay thy foundations with sapphires. And I will make thy windows of agate, and thy gates of carbuncles, and all thy borders of pleasant stones."

Thrusting the Bible aside, she drew from her habit a glazed tube of fire-hardened clay sealed with a stopper of black wax. And there she remained, clutching the tube, her eyes unfocused and afraid.

"I meant no deceit, Reverend Mother. I meant to tell you about this when I found it, but all thought of it disappeared from my mind; I found myself showing you the chalice as though it were the only thing inside the old altar. And then later I saw the light of the sunset like blood upon the lancet window, and the long pointed shape made me think of it again. I was afraid you would punish me for keeping it a secret. If I tell you now . . . The rod is cruel, Reverend Mother."

As she whispered this, her hands were working at the stopper, reopening old cracks around the waxen seal. She emptied on to her upturned palm a piece of stone of a profound black, with faint concentric ripples of lemon-gray. Heavy and cold lay the stone against her flesh, the quaint design engraved upon its surface partly masked by encrusted smears of some yellow substance. Absentmindedly, she rubbed the stain under her thumb, until the whole design was clear. Like a lightning flash, she thought; a lightning flash entangled in its descent with strange letters and many-pointed stars. A peculiar design indeed, but one she found soothing to look upon. When visited by pain or weakness or by anger, a moment's concentration on the stone was somehow comforting. It was as if her troubles could be poured into it, leaving her lethargic but soothed. She had poured much of herself, the turbid depths of her emotions, into it, and felt a growing gratification in return. Of late it had occurred to her—with what secret thrill of horror—that the act was like a prayer; it comforted and unburdened like a prayer. That thought itself was surely blasphemous, and yet, was the finding of comfort in a stone, the only comfort in an otherwise hard and lonely life, really a sin? Had not the Lord, according to his prophet Isaiah, promised to those "not comforted" stones with fair colors; offered foundations and borders of pleasant stones as a refuge? And this to *release* one from terror, to establish the tempest-tossed in righteousness! If she had come to need the stone, come to long for her times of communion with it, what then? The Lord provided; but one corner of her confused mind kept crying "Which Lord?"

Seeking further to unravel the mystery of Longlenn, the Abbot turned to a work on the heresies of the Knights Templar and discovered there, amid the familiar accusations, agonized confessions and heartless lists of "sundry entertainments" provided for the overworked torturers, certain admissions of practices peculiar enough to nonplus even their avid enemies. Though some among the knights had broken down and admitted to the "Worshippe of Baphomet" and to various "obscene observances" before an idol, there was one among their number who, while stoically denying the trampling of the cross, told how the brothers had "resorted privily to horridde incantation, an bye so doing raised an Elementarie to which ende they had employed certain attentionnes to a stone moste strangelie fashioned." The stone to which these strange attentions were paid had been "given them bye the deville-worshippers of Saladin's armies."

The demon, or "elementarie," in question had originally become entrapped within the stone and could be released by a method which the Knight refused resolutely to divulge, even under the most atrocious suffering imaginable. Neither would he divulge the whereabouts of the stone, claiming that the "Elementarie was more holie than our own Baphomet, being of no element known among men, neither of the earthe nor aire, nor of the fires nor waters of this worlde," for the stone had, according to its previous heathen worshipers, "come from the stars."

There he had it then! Surely this was the cause of the unholy influence to which the Longlenn monks had exposed themselves, unknowingly or otherwise. There they had gathered to narrow their communal will to a common devotion with so dire a result that the foundation had been dissolved and their place of worship left untenanted through years of silence, doubtless until the natural elements had swept away the odor of corruption. But the Abbot suspected from his studies that what has once been raised cannot be so easily put down. Brooding there among his books, the learned monk began to ponder on the young nun Catherine. Had she been entirely honest when recounting the contents of the hidden altar?

At that moment, the young nun was lying on the hard cot in a corner of her cell, gazing blankly into the darkness. Though her period of rest had lasted only an hour, it seemed that she had lain for days uncounted, lost in the sleepless vacuity of exhaustion. Her surroundings—her very identity—had slipped away, and something else was filling the dangerous void. She saw before her eyes the stone with its carved design, stretching above and beyond her like a great wall. The yellow smear, deposited so many centuries away in time, was gone. Why was she so irresistibly drawn to that strange design, so obsessed by it that it had become more familiar to her than the lines upon her own palm? More dear to her than the cross? She had become one with the stone, and knew within herself the true significance of the deeply incised lines upon it. They formed a kind of gateway; slots in the wall of Hell, and through them something had begun to seep. At first, an invasion indistinct and brief, it had grown strong and insistent, moving upon her ceaselessly, like a clutch of tattered darkness, locked to her flesh. Her struggles were tamed easily by rustling congeries of greasy tendrils that seemed to drain her resistance. She moaned and her mouth was at once smothered by a searching feeler as soft and noisome as mildewed cloth.

And then she knew only the grip of many limbs; so many hard, insistent surfaces that sought to penetrate and rub until despite herself, she moved with the evil rhythm of it, while the very breath was drawn from her body and the weight upon her grew.

At the tolling of the matins bell, the Prioress paused at each cell in turn, stirring the sleeper with a knock, a shake or a whispered word. Soon, small groups of nuns were shuffling along the draughty corridors by lantern light, emerging into the cold blast of the cloisters.

Having counted them into church, she paused briefly before following, to look up at the sky over the cloister garth. The clouds had passed, and the night was spattered with stars. Inside, she found the dark vault of the chancel starred too, with many tiny flames, for a candle burned beside the place of every novice who had yet to learn the psalmody.

From her place, Sister Catherine watched the service in a daze. All seemed to shift before her eyes as she glanced around the chancel. Behind the altar stood a massive reredos in the form of a triptych in oils, the central panel of which depicted the crucifixion. In the tremulous light of the candles she could see the pale, twisted body of Christ upon the cross, the noble head sagging to one side in pain, and below, the Virgin kneeling, hands clasped in despair. To gaze upon this image while the echoed chanting of the sisters swelled and eddied all about her had become the most precious of feelings, but now her hand was slipping deep into the pocket of her habit, searching out the source of an altogether stronger emotion. As her fingers closed upon the stone, she felt at once the intrusive presence darkening the air about her. Before the altar the Prioress and her obedientaries moved like shadows.

For one second Catherine surrendered to the blissful agony erupting in her, and the church, the chanting voices, the beautiful triptych were lost. Then a part of her rebelled, she struggled through the thick, black tide, her eyes instinctively seeking the living image of her faith, as though even the painted Savior held the power to close the gate that she had opened. But the central panel too had darkened, and the figure raised there on the cross was neither noble nor benign. The head lolling upon its sinewy shoulders was horned, dark with fur, disfigured by a leering tusked snout in which she saw grotesquely blended suggestions of a pig, an ass, an owl. A phallus, rigid as a rod, rose from the shaggy haunches. There were claws, prehensile claws, upon its threshing lower limbs and they were throttling the voluptuous, naked Virgin with her own flowing hair.

The Prioress rose to take her place in the pulpit. The *Te Deum* rolled away into silence and for one second of reverent expectation there was only the sound of canvas whipping in the wind. Then a high-pitched scream rang back from the vaulted ceiling. Amid waves of hushed whispers and turning heads, Sister Catherine was writhing. A hand reached out to support her, and the screams turned into hysterical laughter. In no time the Sub-Prioress was at her side and with the aid of another nun the girl was ushered swiftly away to the infirmary. But the echoes of that insane laughter rang through the minds of all those gathered in the chancel. Knowing this, the Prioress mounted to the pulpit swiftly and opened the Bible as though nothing had occurred. Her voice, strong and determined, drew their attention sharply back.

"Thou shalt not be afraid for the terror by night;
Nor for the arrow that flieth by day;
Nor for the pestilence that walketh in darkness."

For all her outward calm, the Prioress was shaken by the incident. As soon as her duties were discharged she made her way to the infirmary at the south-east corner of the Priory, and found Catherine in a fever, her brow afire and running with sweat. Dismissing the Infirmarian, the Prioress sat down beside the bed, and taking up a dampened cloth, pressed it upon the young nun's face. Leaning close, she caught the words mumbled through immobile lips.

". . . windows of Agates . . . stones of fair colors . . . I meant no wrong . . . only some . . . comfort . . ."

Turning her head toward the Prioress, Catherine opened her eyes with a look of relief.

"Help me please . . . keep it away . . ."

She closed her eyes again and the head fell back.

"It is so cold here . . ."

She began to writhe, kicking her blanket to the floor. Retrieving it the Prioress made to spread it once more over the girl, and found to her amazement that there was a second blanket gathered in a heap upon her breast. Reaching to straighten it, she felt it move under her fingers. Like a great black stain it was spreading outward, growing, it seemed, from the prostrate body itself. One arm of darkness reached out to smother the objecting mouth and the mass began to move rhythmically upon the body of the reclining nun.

For all her numbed horror, the Prioress retained the presence of mind to draw from her pocket a phial of holy water, whispering a prayer hoarsely as she did so. No sooner had the first word been uttered than the thing paused in its unholy movements, drew up sharply and took on the tint of trodden slush. A faint smell of leaf-mold wafted across the room. Catherine squirmed again. One half-stifled moan broke from her and she fell quite still.

Tearing at the lid of her phial with trembling fingers, the Prioress emptied it out across the body and its ghastly burden. For the space of one long-drawn breath nothing moved within the room. The frantic praying apart, there was silence. Catherine—the pale, dead Catherine—and the mound of evil on her were like the painted image of a nightmare. Then the thing rose up from its anchorage on the dead loins, drawing its soft and malleable bulk into a tall, swaying column. A sluggish succession of protruberances rippled up its surface like so many flattened faces pressed against a flimsy veil, gathered half way up into one shifting lump and merged deliberately into an idiotic, distorted semblance of the dead nun's face. The Prioress stepped backward, holding out the small cross of her rosary before her; the thing shifted off the bed and followed. There was a horrible fascination in the face, the gray rippling semblance of a face, so like and yet so unspeakably unlike Catherine. The Prioress watched spellbound as the thick, gray lips began to mumble soundlessly, then broke into a slack, toothless smile. Dragging open the door she fled into the dark corridor.

Ushered gaping into the great room of stained glass and books, the roughmason Robert handed over a folded parchment to the Abbot and stood awestruck as the grim prelate broke the seal and read, with barely controlled emotion, the pleas which it contained.

"Father, Sister Catherine died yesterday, and I have reason to believe that the opening of the concealed altar played its part. Mercifully, the other sisters have mistaken certain marks upon the body as a sign of disease only, and, may the Lord forgive me, I have not attempted to disabuse them. There is a curious stone involved, clearly fashioned for some talismanic purposes. Father, you know the methods of our Church where such practices are even suspected. My thoughts turn in desperation to you, with your deep knowledge of the Dark Arts. May I plead for your privy assistance in this matter? Had the journey to

Malmswell been possible without attracting speculation this petition would have been delivered from my own lips, but alas this is not possible. Robert, the roughmason, into whose hands I entrusted this note, can be depended upon and has sworn silence."

So, his surmise had proved correct. How wise the Prioress had been to seek his assistance privily. Turning gravely to the mason, the Abbot asked, "Do you know what is in this letter, Robert?"

The young man shook his head emphatically. "No, Father. I was only told to give it to you, and you alone."

The Abbot smiled. "Very well, then. It is enough, I think, to say that it is a matter of some urgency; a matter in which I will require your help."

The mason fairly swelled with pride. "I will do what I can, Father."

"This is what I want you to do, Robert. Leave at once, and take the Charnwood road. Not far from here there is a knoll with a dead oak . . ."

"I know it, Father."

"Good. Wait for me there but take pains to ensure that you are not seen. You will not fail me, Robert?"

The mason shook his head eagerly.

"Very well, you may go—and remember—wait at the oak."

When he was once more alone, the Abbot sat before the carved lectern, considering the sudden turn of events. So, it was all true! The Templars had found a stone of power in the East. Taking down Khabir's *The Book of Amulets* he began to read.

It was the Abbot's duty to hear the petitions of the monks early in the evening, so little could be done before then. Afterward, while the brothers took themselves back to the recreation room, he returned once more to the library, where he remained until the stroke of seven, when the bell rang for compline. By eight the brothers had retired and the Abbey was at rest.

At such an hour the cloisters would be locked, but,

being in possession of a second key, the Abbot passed unseen into the blustery darkness.

There was a ceaseless rushing in the black spaces above, trees whipping loudly in a near gale, and when the tumbling clouds broke briefly overhead, the moon showed like a yellow talon raking at the sky. Without attempting to open the stables, he looked once at the ravaged clouds, slipped his wrist into the leather thong of a heavy walking staff and set off on foot toward Charnwood.

The night services were over, the church lay empty, and Sister Joan, the Sacrist, had only to replace the Book of Collects in the cloister aumbry to complete her duties. Alone in the echoing blackness, she felt no fear. With Sister Catherine dead and the Prioress stricken down by the same strange fever there was talk of devils and possession but Sister Joan was in complete accord with the Sub-Prioress, who had lost no time in quelling such ridiculous rumors. That talk of devils should find purchase in certain minds, however, was little wonder to the Sacrist. If the Sub-Prioress but knew what Sister Joan could tell; if she could see what Sister Joan now carried in her pocket, then her worst fears would be realized, and her hand would fall more ruthlessly on any who displayed the slightest sign of superstition. Perhaps, thought Joan, it was as well that on finding the heathen talisman upon the person of the poor Prioress I slipped it thoughtlessly into my pocket and forgot it. There was enough ill feeling in the Priory of late, Heaven knew. Had the curious stone—evidence as it assuredly was of an unbecoming idolatry—come to light, why the very name of the Prioress would have fallen into shame. And Sister Clare had done so much! No, it would not happen.

Thinking this, she slipped out through the cloister door with her awkward burden of lantern and heavy book. The wind was hissing fiercely through the covered ways, brushing like a great serpent by her legs, tugging the folds of her habit. Drawing upon the heavy studded panels of the aumbry door, she replaced the Book of Collects and locked up.

And with that duty done, she loitered a while at the edge of the pillared way, drinking in the restful outline of the slumbering Priory against a wild turmoil of moonlit cloud. She would hold her peace concerning the stone. Perhaps it was just a harmless fancy on the part of the Prioress. How cold and heavy it was though, and smooth under the fingertips.

As her thoughts ran on, she glanced across the grassy garth and discerned a figure waiting at the confluence of the southern and western walkways. Her curiosity aroused by this—for she would hardly expect anyone to walk there at such an hour—she called and received no response. Approaching, she noted that the build and bearing of the figure matched those of the Prioress, and yet poor Clare was ill in the infirmary! The thought of a sudden recovery cheered Sister Joan, but just as quickly she was visited by another, less pleasant thought. Had the poor woman wandered away, delirious, through the sleeping Priory?

She called again. The other did not respond. The posture suggested reveries too deep to be penetrated by any human call. At closer quarters, where the small circle of light from the lantern fell, the dark fabric of the habit glistened as though wringing wet. The lantern was lifted and the circle of light fell upon the face.

There was, undeniably, a certain resemblance to the Prioress in those waxy, embryonic features, but the skin of the head was only partially opaque, and flushed rhythmically with a swirl of blood-coloured tendrils moving just beneath the surface. The pale face turned magenta, and like a soft bag stretched from within by a rummaging hand, distorted, expanded, the features twisting as the whole head swelled outward and burst in a rush of soft tendrils. Sister Joan felt the unclean grip upon her and screamed, dropping the lantern. The tendrils fastened on the face and neck of the fainting nun, clung and spread while the vaguely human outline of the thing fell in, billowing and swelling; the habit-black camouflage turned livid green. Anchored upon the fallen body, the tendrils contracted and fattened as the thing began to reel itself in.

The weeks had passed quickly enough at Malmswell, for the Abbot had received a consignment of books bequeathed by a wealthy patron, and the cataloguing and arrangement consumed much time. He could have been excused for feeling somewhat frustrated when the time came to make his customary visit to Longlenn, but he dropped his task patiently and set off without complaint. Certain of his obedientaries had urged him to travel with a proper escort, for the body of a young man, battered beyond recognition, had been found beside an oak on the Charnwood road, and there was concern for the Abbot's safety. But his mind once made up could not be altered, and he refused an escort, taking only the young novice.

The day was fine and warm, a foretaste of what was to be a glorious summer, but the Abbot insisted, no doubt with their safety in mind, that they forgo their period of rest beside the river and press on to reach Longlenn by early afternoon. And that they did, arriving hot and tired but in good spirits. The Abbot had been exceptionally talkative all day, telling the novice of his own early days in the Order, and encouraging him, not altogether successfully, to talk of his own experiences. The poor youth had been too overawed by such sudden familiarity to say much.

From without, Longlenn appeared peaceful; the sun poured warmly down upon the sprawling complex of old and recent stone. They knocked for some while without reply and were at length forced to break open the door. At once they came upon a corpse lying spreadeagled in the cloister. The smell was sufficient to tell them that it had lain undisturbed for several weeks.

The Abbot at once pushed the novice out into the open, shouting into his stricken face, "Go back to Malmswell. Tell them something has happened here!"

"But I was told to stay with you at all times, Father—"

"I will be all right, my son. Go! I will follow just as soon as I have discovered what has happened here."

Eventually, the novice was cajoled on to his donkey and driven off toward the hills, complaining bitterly, far from convinced of the Abbot's safety. The prelate watched him out of sight before walking to his own donkey and drawing from the saddle pouch a piece of white linen and a brightly painted amulet on a chain. The cloth he tied across his nose and mouth, the chain he draped around his neck with a peculiar gesture of his right hand. Only then did he return to the cloister and begin what he guessed would be a long and unpleasant search.

The body in the cloister, though disfigured by decay, was by no means the longest dead. Certain corpses in the dormitory and the infirmary were quite putrescent. The air was fetid with the smell of them, but the abbot unflinchingly searched every one.

A year or so before, the Prioress had built a tiny chapel of the Virgin beside the church, and to it she had returned, touchingly, in death. A makeshift bier draped in black stood there with burnt-out candles at the corners. The Abbot paused there a moment, looking on the lean gargoyle that lay upon the bier, unable to equate it with the plump, smiling Prioress. It was a shame. There had been a spark in Sister Clare. He had at times thought that they were two of a kind. It was a waste of a mind of high calibre, but unavoidable. There would be no more victories at chess now, he thought, as he searched the corpse.

When at last he came upon the onyx stone, it was clasped tightly in the hand of a novice sprawled upon a bed in the second guest room. The garments of the corpse were in disarray, the body and face covered with livid marks, and a yellow stain like pus discolored the flesh. Slipping the stone into a leather pouch at his belt, the Abbot made a repetition of the strange sign, and returned to the cloister.

With the aid of a shovel from the tool locker, he

forced the press door and took up the precious ivory book. Sacrificing the protection of his mask to wrap it in clean linen, he turned to go when the glint of silver caught his eye, and he saw, with a little smile of irony, the silver chalice. One of the nuns—perhaps the unfortunate Catherine herself—had polished it, revealing clearly the raised circlet of horned heads around the rim, and a deeply embossed rod entwined with serpents and crowned with wings along the stem. This he placed, along with the ivory book, in his saddle pouch. Almost as an afterthought he took off the amulet from the book of Khabir and threw it with them. It had not been necessary after all. From the strange marks upon the corpses, he concluded that the stone had been protected by a curse of pestilence. Given enough time, it had worked itself out.

So he had the stone, the book, the chalice; and no suspicion would fall upon him. After all, what had he done? They had all come to him by *not* doing what the Prioress had asked him to do; quite literally by not doing anything.

There was undoubtedly an atmosphere, other than the obvious physical one, about the place, enough to make any man's spine crawl; but that was to be expected. Powers had been invoked here. If any magic remained in the curious stone he would control it quite satisfactorily at Malmswell. The old sorcerers could call them "Elementaries" and give them human qualities, but the Abbot was an educated man, and he could control "powers" easily enough. It was the application of the will in the correct quarter, merely.

The sun was touching the low western hills as he mounted. A long ride and a night in the open lay before him, but he saw no reason to tempt providence and remain at Longlenn once the sun had set.

Striking upward through the high windows, a single ray from the setting sun spread a sanguine glory across the vaultings of the church. Shadows deepened and drew in down the long aisles. And from the area of the northern transept, where the canvas flapped fitfully, an unearthly shape emerged, drifting like a half-filled sail against the intricate darkness of the rood screen. It paused, spiraling in the space below the central tower. Opaque now, with the look of substantial weight, it was fabulously rich with changing color. As it spun, delicate red filaments trailed about it; wispy films of lace-like membrane gathered and spread upon its underside. With what unguessable sense did it discover the intruding presence moving around among the used-up husks in some far corner of the building? As the tide by the moon, it was drawn by this new satellite of flesh and blood, its movements apparently involuntary, slow and inevitable; the tide by the moon.

The intruder forced a door, rummaged among the objects within, and it was but five paces from him, separated only by thin panels of the cloister door. It waited, moving ceaselessly within its self-defined borders like some column of uneasy liquid. The man different. There was about him some veil of protection which could not be penetrated.

Unknowing, the man walked the covered way, and it was following, just out of sight, dark and elusive among the shadowy pillars. He made as though to mount, paused to throw off some portion of himself, and the shield was gone.

As he rode toward the hills, the thing gathered itself lazily by the gate, sank to the ground and shifted smoothly through many shapes; suggestions of horns, humps and wings rose and fell on the body; beaks, snouts, featureless globes and human features passed in succession over the slowly forming head. A fleeting semblance of the Prioress, her face contorted in fear and loathing came and went, and then a thin secretive face—or something sufficiently like one—solidified above a body in which the pulsing waves of color grew dim and darkened, until it seemed that a tall monk wrapped in hanging folds of black cloth stood there. Then, the required form achieved, the thing moved off into the gathering dusk.

Its pace was leisurely; perhaps a little faster than a trotting donkey.